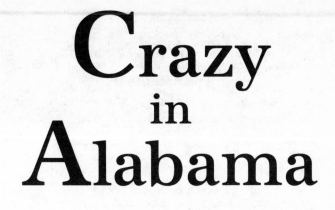

Crazy
in
Alabama

Mark Childress

VIKING

VIKING

Published by the Penguin Group
Penguin Books Ltd, 27 Wrights Lane, London W8 5TZ, England
Penguin Books USA Inc., 375 Hudson Street, New York, New York 10014, USA
Penguin Books Australia Ltd, Ringwood, Victoria, Australia
Penguin Books Canada Ltd, 10 Alcorn Avenue, Toronto, Ontario, Canada M4V 3B2
Penguin Books (NZ) Ltd, 182–190 Wairau Road, Auckland 10, New Zealand

Penguin Books Ltd, Registered Offices: Harmondsworth, Middlesex, England

First published in the USA by G. P. Putnam's Sons 1993
First published in Great Britain by Viking 1993
1 3 5 7 9 10 8 6 4 2

Printed in England by Clays Ltd, St Ives plc

A CIP catalogue record for this book is
available from the British Library

ISBN 0–670–85122–1
Trade paperback 0–670–85123–X

For Mark Daniel Chastain,
who liked the idea

Alice began to feel very uneasy: to be sure, she had not as yet had any dispute with the Queen, but she knew that it might happen any minute, "and then," thought she, "what would become of me? They're dreadfully fond of beheading people here: the great wonder is, that there's any one left alive!"

—Lewis Carroll, *Alice's Adventures in Wonderland*, 1865

The Negro has many pent-up resentments and latent frustrations. He has to get them out. So let him march sometime; let him have his prayer pilgrimages to the city hall; understand why he must have sit-ins and freedom rides. If his repressed emotions do not come out in these nonviolent ways, they will come out in ominous expressions of violence. This is not a threat; it is a fact of history.

—Martin Luther King, Jr., Letter from a Birmingham Jail, 1963

Peter Joseph

San Francisco, 1993

I am out here in California waiting for the walls to come tumbling down. We have had omens. Ten years of plague. Seven years of drought. Firestorms. Mudslides. Floods. Pestilence. Riots. Tremors. Visions of the Virgin.

The millennium is bearing down on us fast. Nobody knows if 1999 will bring the end of everything, or the beginning of something else.

I kick back in my junior-one-bedroom apartment and look out at the shimmering night-lights of Telegraph Hill and the East Bay. I wonder how it will look when it all falls down.

Remember Jimmy Stewart's house in *Vertigo*, where he takes Kim Novak to dry out after he's fished her out of San Francisco Bay? I live up the hill from that house. They've painted it slate-blue and the shrubs have grown up. Otherwise it looks the same.

I sit by the window in my rocking chair, where I can see Jimmy Stewart's house and my TV at the same time. I freeze the laserdisc on the wide shot of the house: Cool blond Kim Novak strides to her car, forsaking Jimmy on the front porch.

I compare the scene as it is now, in real life, to the forty-year-old view through Hitchcock's camera. I drink bourbon and sit for hours, studying the subtle differences.

Everyone else is worried about the future. I have this thing about the past.

One night I was running Kim on a continuous slow-motion loop from Jimmy's front door to her green sedan and back again, when the telephone rang.

A quavery voice said "Peejoe?"

Nobody calls me Peejoe anymore. "Aunt Lucille?"

"God, it sure takes me back, just to hear you," she said.

"Me too, Aunt Lucille." I hadn't heard her voice in years, except on late-night reruns. I glanced up at my face on the cover of that old *Life* magazine, framed and hanging on the wall, and suddenly I was back in the deepest summer of my life, the summer of 1965, when everybody went crazy in Alabama.

1

Peejoe

Pigeon Creek, Alabama, 1965

My grandmother used an old embalming fluid bottle at the ironing board. She said the rocket-shaped tip put out just the right amount of water for sprinkling clothes.

I loved to be in Meemaw's room while she ironed, that big friendly room with a four-poster bed and framed pictures of Jesus and George Wallace and Grandpa Joe Wiley. Meemaw didn't mind my climbing up in her bed with my red-stained feet. I loved the hiss and suck of the steam iron, the moist rising fragrance of starch when the iron's hot face met the fabric. I loved the mysteries of the ritual: wet the clothes to wash them, dry them in the sun, wet them with the sprinkler bottle, dry them with the iron—a ceaseless baptism of dresses and white cotton shirts.

Meemaw hummed "O, My Papa" while I sprawled among her pillows, sketching floor plans for the funeral home I dreamed of building one day.

"Looka here, Meemaw, look at this one." I clambered down from the bed. "See, this is the front door where people come in, and here's the casket parlor, and these are the laying-out rooms."

She pointed the bottle at a corner of my sketch. "What's this part with the cow?"

I rolled my eyes. "That's not a cow, it's a dog. That's the kennel."

"The kennel?"

"So people can bring their dogs to funerals."

"You've thought of most everything," Meemaw said. "What's this squiggly-looking thing out back?"

"A swimming pool."

"Well now what would they need with a swimming pool?" She

11

smoothed a white shirt on the ironing board. "Folks coming to a funeral, seems like swimming would be about the last thing on their minds."

"It's not for *them*," I explained. "It's for me. I'm gonna be living upstairs. On my day off, I can go swimming."

"Oh. Well. That makes sense," she said. "Will you let me stay up there with you, Peejoe?"

"Sure. You can have the room over the casket parlor, see? It's the nicest one."

"You're an angel," she said.

Funerals run in our family.

My grandfather, Joe Wiley Bullis, was a gravedigger. One day he was standing at the back edge of a funeral, trying not to laugh at some wisecrack another gravedigger had made, when a grief-crazed mourner grabbed his shovel away and hit him in the head with it. That put an end to the joke, and to Grandpa Joe Wiley.

He left Meemaw with three sons and one daughter.

The daughter, my Aunt Lucille, dreamed of becoming a Hollywood movie star but wound up instead in Cornelia, Alabama, with six children and a husband who didn't understand her.

All three of her brothers went into the funeral business. Uncle Franklin was a traveling casket salesman. Uncle Dove ran a funeral home in the town of Industry. The baby of the family was my father, John Lewis Bullis, who introduced the concept of Perpetual Care to south Alabama. He set up memorial parks from Andalusia to Wolf Bay. He and Mama were driving home from a cemetery convention in Mobile when Daddy fell asleep at the wheel and ran up under a log truck, making orphans of my brother Wiley and me.

Wiley was five when they died. I was three. I have only the haziest soft-lap recollection of Mama, and none at all of our daddy. Wiley said he was a big man who smelled of beer and Lucky Strikes, and slapped his knees when he told a joke. Wiley said Mama was pretty and sweet with the loudest sneeze you ever heard, but he didn't remember much more than that.

After the accident Meemaw took us in. I know now she couldn't afford us. Apparently Daddy felt he was too young for life insurance and left us without a nickel. Uncle Dove did the embalming himself, and the plots at Shady Acres Memorial Park were free, of course, since Daddy had been responsible for carving the place out of piney woods. Uncle Franklin got the caskets at cost. Preacher Lambert donated his sermon.

Meemaw sold off five acres at the back of her property to buy a fine marble headstone. When it was over she was left with us two little boys and a falling-down house on two hundred ninety-five acres of scrub pine. She started taking in ironing from the other white ladies of Pigeon Creek. That's how I remember her, humming, and sighing, and ironing.

"Listen, Sweet Pea," she said, "when Lucille comes with your cousins, I think maybe you ought not show 'em your little drawings, all right?"

"Howcome?"

Meemaw bore down on the shirtsleeve. "Well, now, it hasn't even been a year since their Grandma Vinson passed away. It might bring back a sad memory. Not everybody thinks about funerals the way you do."

I was twelve years old that summer. I knew everything about everything. "You mean they're crybabies," I said.

"No, not exactly. . . . You don't want to make 'em feel bad, do you?"

"I don't know why they should feel bad." I toyed with the fringe on the chenille bedspread. "So what if their grandmother's dead. My mama and daddy are both dead but I don't go around crying about it."

Meemaw blinked and pushed a strand of silver hair from her eyes. "That's 'cause you don't remember," she said.

Wiley's .22 went *crack* in the woods.

"Meemaw, what do you think happens to you when you die?"

She whipped the shirt off the ironing board and nudged a wire hanger into the sleeves. "Why don't you go out and shoot some with Wiley."

"I hate that gun."

"Well go on out anyway." Her voice was hoarse. "Beautiful a day as this is, and you in here messin' around with old me."

"I wish I could stay with you every single minute, Meemaw."

She fixed me with one of her Lordy-lord looks. "If wishes were niggers, we'd all have slaves," she said. "Now go on. I'll ring the bell when they come."

I climbed down from the bed and sulked out into the afternoon. Adolf bounded up to lick my hand and bat me with his big eager tail. Adolf was Meemaw's albino German shepherd, named after the only German whose name she could remember. I pushed him away—"Go on, you nigger."

That word tasted dangerous on my tongue. Meemaw never said it when there was a nigger around; then she called them "colored people." Whenever one of them came to cut grass or rake leaves or move a chifforobe for her, she was sweet and friendly as if they were anybody. But if they asked for a drink of water, she always offered them the same chipped red Liberty National coffee mug from the high shelf at the back of a kitchen cabinet.

Meemaw must have imagined fantastic diseases lurking on the rim of the mug, left by the Negroes who'd drunk from it. Maybe she thought it would turn you Negro to drink after one of them. I pulled the mug down one day and was peering into it when Wiley came wandering through.

"What are you doing with that nigger cup?" he said.

I said "nothing" and put it back in its place. But that cup held a special fascination for me. I wanted to drink from it. I wanted to taste the difference.

Adolf frolicked at my knees. I crouched through the barbed wire and started down the ravine where we dumped our garbage.

Meemaw was right, this was a beautiful day. Already May, but not hot yet—a murmurous breeze, wild azaleas and fresh green leaves in abundance. The bugs made a rhythmical *zizz, zizz* in the weeds. There was nothing to do, all the time in the world to do it. Adolf sniffed and peed on everything.

A rifleshot cracked in the distance.

"Hey, it's me! Don't shoot!" I picked my way through the blackberry thorns, peering ahead to where the trees opened out. A chorus of bluejays hollered from the high branches. "Hey Wiley, where are you?"

I came into the clearing. On a fallen log near the great mound of garbage, Wiley had arranged a line of Nehi soda bottles for execution. Fragments of glass glittered like jewels in the sand.

A voice startled me from above—"I could kill you right now."

My knees went swimmy. Wiley was wedged in the crook of a tree directly over my head, with the mouth of his rifle pointed directly at me.

Adolf ran to the foot of the oak, barking up a big noise.

My brain said to run but my legs were frozen by the sight of that round little hole where the bullet would come out to kill me. "Quit that!" I said. "Put it down!"

Wiley adjusted his aim. "You'd make a lousy Green Beret, Peejoe. You sounded like a herd of cattle coming through the woods."

"You quit pointing that thing or I'm telling!"

It was my only weapon against him, the threat to *tell*, and Wiley knew very well I would use it in a minute. After the big long lecture Meemaw gave him along with the rifle, we both knew she would skin him alive if I told about this.

He lowered the barrel, slung the rifle over his shoulder, and dropped to the ground. "Let's take out the bullet and play Green Beret," he said. "I can kill you and then you can kill me."

"I like the other guns better," I said, meaning the cut-out plywood guns Uncle Dove had made for us when we were little. Mine had PEEJOE inscribed in Magic Marker on the stock.

"You wouldn't be scared if you'd go on and shoot it," said Wiley. He pushed Adolf's nose out of his crotch and thrust the rifle at me. "You're just a scared little chicken."

Wiley was my faithful best friend, yet he took a peculiar delight in torturing me. We were so different it seemed impossible that we were brothers. He was tall and thin, gangly arms and legs, tangled black hair and fierce stone-green eyes; he was handsome and square-chinned like Daddy, in the photograph. He loved fishing and shooting off guns. He was always running or jumping or batting squishy high fly balls with rotten peaches in the orchard.

I wanted nothing more than to be just like Wiley, but way down deep I was Peter Joseph, irrevocably. I was Peejoe. I was round-faced, blue-eyed and blond, easily sunburned, clumsy, a bit pudgy. Could not catch a ball if it landed in my hands. Terrified of guns. I had hated hunting ever since I'd seen *Bambi,* and I detested fishing—the terrible moment when my prayers were ignored and a fish actually bit my hook and I had to touch the poor squirming thing.

"Come on. You can do it." Wiley offered the .22. "Go on up closer and see if you can hit the bottle on the end."

I looked all around the dump for some distraction or inspiration. Flies swam happily in the smelly air. "I know. Let's tie up junebugs."

He looked at me a long minute. "That's boring."

"No it ain't." I stuck out my chin and planted my hands on my hips to show him he might as well go along with me, I was not going to touch that rifle if he stood there for a million years.

At last he said "oh, all right" with a superior air. "Let's find some string."

We went over to the garbage mountain and began poking through with sticks, holding our noses, gagging, laughing at our own disgust. Wiley found a usable Bama mayonnaise jar. I came up with four filthy lengths of twine.

We set out through the buzz and hum of a summer day, searching the branches and weeds at our feet, listening for that peculiar click-rattle— "Hey! Over here!"—following the sound down to a clump of cow-grass, a hard shiny bug nestled in like a tiny bottle-brown Volkswagen. Careful now—junebugs were not fast, but they possessed mysterious powers of evasion.

It took Wiley and me the most part of an hour to catch four of them, and then we discovered the first two had expired because we forgot to punch air holes in the jar lid.

"Damn it to hell!" Wiley liked to curse out of Meemaw's earshot. "I'm sick of looking. Let's just make do with these two."

He unscrewed the jar lid and slipped in his hand, trapping the larger of the surviving bugs. Gripping its glossy shell between his thumb and first finger, he made a loop in the end of the string and began trying to snare the tiny gesticulating hind leg. It took him three passes to snag it and close the tiny noose. "You ready?"

I held tight to the other end of the string. "Ready."

Wiley opened his hand. The bug lifted away, buzzing furiously—then it snapped the slack from the line at the edge of its new universe.

I jerked the string. The bug tugged and danced, zipping every which way, hopelessly trapped.

"Don't yank too hard, Peejoe, you'll pull off his leg."

"Don't tell me how to do it." I turned a circle with my arms out. The junebug was my prisoner, my little captive helicopter, my razzing, indignant living yo-yo.

Wiley knelt in the weeds to tie up a bug for himself. In a moment we had two live ones leading us back through the woods to the garbage ravine. Adolf whined and ran circles around us.

The junebugs never quit trying to outwit the string. They would let it go limp as if they were just on the edge of surrender, then strike suddenly down and to one side but Oh, Ho! We were their gods! We held the strings! We made them dance! They would dance for an hour or two and then conveniently die of exhaustion about the time we got bored with them.

I was in charge of the funerals. I made caskets out of Jell-O boxes lined with toilet paper. I dug holes in red clay with a rusty trowel, placed the boxes, spoke a few solemn words, tossed the first handful of dirt.

"I'm gonna call mine Ratface," said Wiley. "What's yours?"

"I don't know." My bug vibrated the string. "Maybe—Steve or something."

"Steve?" Wiley stared. "That's the stupidest thing I ever heard. A bug named Steve."

"I haven't decided yet," I said, thinking *what's wrong with Steve? It's a nice, modern-sounding name. I wish my name was Steve.*

Wiley's bug landed on his knee and began crawling down. "That's your last mistake, Ratface," he said. Plucking the bug from his jeans, he carried it to the fallen log and tied its string to the neck of a Nehi bottle. The bug strained against its tether.

Wiley picked up his rifle.

I moved out of the line of fire. "What are you doing?"

He thumbed the barrel at the junebug. "Moving target."

Adolf waggled up to the log, wrinkle-nosed, snapping his teeth at the bug. Wiley shouted "Go home! Go *home!*" and made threatening jabs with an imaginary stick until Adolf slunk off.

"Don't, Wiley. You'll mess it up. We won't get to bury it."

"I'm shootin' mine," he said. "You can bury yours."

"But burying it is the fun part!" To me it seemed the smallest decency to let a bug die struggling at the end of a string, and give it a proper funeral.

To me, but not to Wiley. Or maybe he was feeling cruel that afternoon. He raised the rifle. He set his tongue between his teeth and squinted down the barrel.

He fired.

The junebug had reached a state of such perfect panic that a bullet whizzing by made no difference at all.

"Jesus Christ." Wiley reloaded.

I covered my ears. "Stop! It ain't fair!"

"Life ain't fair," said Wiley. He fired again and missed. "Besides, he ain't all that easy to hit. Hold still, Ratface!"

My junebug quivered the string in my hand, as in sympathy.

Wiley fumbled for bullets. "Take yours down there and tie him up, Peejoe."

"He's mine. You ain't shooting at him."

"You're such a baby," he said.

"You're just mad 'cause you can't hit it."

"Oh yeah?" Wiley raised the rifle to his shoulder and fired. The bug exploded, a liquid brown pouf! The string draped itself over the log.

Wiley's mouth dropped open.

I tried to look unimpressed, although to this day that remains the single most spectacular unaimed shot I have ever seen.

"Guess we can bury the string," I said.

"I *got* it!" He stuck his thumb in his belt, all in awe of himself. "Go on, Peejoe, go tie yours up. Let's see if I can do it again."

The bell began clanging away up the hill, Meemaw calling us home.

I wound the string around my wrist. "Too late. Last one there is a rotten old pig."

"Wait," he said, "I can't run with the twenty-two."

"Too bad!" I took off with my bug in my hand.

Adolf chased my heels. I ran all the way.

I pitied that poor bug, wiped out without warning, without a chance in the world. Even a lowly junebug has a right to a better end than that. I imagined a junebug widow in a pillbox hat. A tiny junebug toddler raising his hand in a solemn salute. I had a vision of the junebug's soul rising to heaven, freed from the cares of earth.

I stopped running. I opened my hand. The dazed bug sat on my palm, awaiting the next part of its fate.

I bent my head and bit into the string, an inch from the knot. Faintly I tasted spaghetti sauce. I gnawed until the string broke.

The bug scuttled forward, testing its freedom. Then it unsnapped its wings lifted up flew away and did not come back.

Wiley beat his way through the bushes, huffing and blowing. "Look," he said. "Aunt Lucille."

2

Peejoe

Pigeon Creek

Sure enough that was Lucille's white Galaxie sedan abandoned under the pecan tree, doors flung open, kids scattered all through the yard. Aunt Lucille and Uncle Chester had six of them, ranging from one year to thirteen, all named for Hollywood movie stars. The Vinsons didn't just come for a visit, they descended like a plague: swarming, hollering, squealing, swinging on our rope, climbing in our treehouse, rolling our hoop down the sand lane with sticks. Aunt Lucille sat in the porch swing with Meemaw, ignoring the uproar.

Wiley looked glum. "She brought every last one of 'em."

"Just once you'd think she could leave Sandra home," I said. Sandra was our least favorite Vinson. She put on all kinds of airs because we were orphans. Right now she was lolling about in our treehouse as if she owned it.

Meemaw spotted us and waved us in.

Lucille squinted over her cat-eyed sunglasses. "Hey boys," she said, "come here and give us some sugar!" I went for a squeeze and a hug and a smack in the air near my cheek; lipstick was important to Aunt Lucille. "Hello Wiley, been shootin' your gun?"

"Yes ma'am."

"You be careful with that. I had to take Cary's gun away from him. He was shooting Louise Simmons's cats." Lucille wore a dozen jangly bracelets on each wrist, a pale-green sweater draped over her shoulders, tight blouse with big yellow polka dots, white clamdigger shorts that showed off her long tanned legs. Blue smoke curled up from her cigarette. She seemed nervous, worked up about something.

"Wiley's careful with his gun," Meemaw said, "ain't you, Wiley."

19

"Yes ma'am." His eyes dared me to contradict him.

I said nothing. I let him owe me one.

The Vinson cousins were too busy playing with our stuff to pay any attention to us. Wiley went off to put up the rifle. I stretched out in the white iron lawn-glider to listen to Lucille and Meemaw.

"I'm so excited I can hardly stand it," Lucille was saying. "This is my big break, Mama. I just know it."

Meemaw shook her head. "I hope you know what you're doing." Meemaw worried more about Lucille than anything on her list. She said Lucille was peculiar and liable to do anything at any time. Her head was full of Hollywood dreams. She was always getting her "big break"— when she landed the part of Maria in the Cornelia Baptist production of "The Sound of Music," and when the *Montgomery Advertiser* ran a picture of her in an Easter hat with the caption "One of the Beauties of Spring."

Lucille didn't want to be a mother, or the wife of Chester Vinson. She wanted to be a Hollywood star.

I was quite sure she was beautiful enough. She had big sparkly swimming-pool blue eyes, a wide, glamorous mouth, and lanky blond hair that flowed over one side of her face, like Veronica Lake. You couldn't see the tiny wrinkles at her eyes until you were right up next to her.

"Harry says this is the chance of a lifetime," she was saying. "I've got the money to go. Chester's not going to get in my way this time. Marlon Vinson, if you pull her hair one more time I'm coming over there to slap you."

I flipped over in the glider to watch Marlon stalking little Judy through Meemaw's okra patch.

"Harry thinks I might be perfect for it," Lucille went on. "He says my accent is perfect. Don't you see I've got to try? It's national television. It's the kind of break some girls wait their whole lives for."

"That's just real nice, Lucille," said Meemaw, "only you're not a girl anymore. And anyway, who is this man calling you? You don't even know him."

"His name is Harry Hall. He's in the big time, Mama, he's a talent agent, he lives in Hollywood. Can you believe he saw my picture and went to all that trouble to find me and call me, person to person?"

I couldn't contain myself. "Are you gonna be on TV, Aunt Lucille?"

"I don't know, honey, I might," she said. "All I know is I've got a chance at a big audition for a network show."

"Wow, that's really neat! Which one?"

"I'm not supposed to tell," Lucille said, but immediately she couldn't help herself: "'The Beverly Hillbillies.'"

"Wow. That is *neato*." Everybody loved that show. Personally I considered Elly May Clampett the loveliest girl in the world.

"Peejoe watches that show," Meemaw said. "That's the one where they ride in a T-Model Ford."

Lucille looked at Meemaw as if she was ignorant. "It's one of the most popular programs on television, thank you," she said. "I play Jethro's old girlfriend from back home. I come to Beverly Hills to try and get him to marry me. If I get the part. I can't count my chickens yet. Oh, Jesus Christ, I hope I get it." Lucille rooted around in her purse for another cigarette. She lit it, took three puffs, and stabbed it out.

Sandra slipped into the swing beside Meemaw. "Hey, Peejoe."

I mumbled hello.

"Mommy's going to be on TV," Sandra said.

Meemaw stroked her hair. "Yes I know, sweetie, she was just telling us." Sandra was Meemaw's grandchild, too, she deserved a hug and a love-pat as much as I did—but I couldn't stand the sight of Meemaw loving on anybody but me.

"On 'The Beverly Hillbillies,'" said Sandra.

"*If* I get the part," her mother snapped. "Don't jinx it."

"What does Chester have to say about all this?" said Meemaw.

"He's not saying much. He is not saying much about it." Lucille shook her head. Her smile was grim. "Chester never believed in me, Mama. He shot down my dreams, one by one."

"I want to go to Hollywood, too," said Sandra. Poor Sandra got none of Aunt Lucille's looks. You could see right up her nose with those big horsey nostrils. She was always trying to get Wiley and me into kissing games, which might not have been so bad if it hadn't been for that nose.

"Sandra, go stop your sister from killing herself."

We all turned to see white-headed Marilyn tottering headlong through a daffodil bed, on a dead run for the road. Sandra took off in pursuit.

I scrunched down, invisible.

"Chester just never understood how much it meant to me," Lucille said. I heard the scritch! of her Zippo. "Do you know what he said when Harry Hall called, Mama? When I got probably the most important phone call of my whole *life*?" She sucked in a lungful of smoke. "He said, 'Kiss my ass, Lucille. You're not going anywhere.'"

"Lucille! In front of Peejoe . . ."

"That's what I said! Cary and Sandra standing three feet away, they heard him all right! I said Chester, you son of a bitch, now you listen to me. I *have* kissed your ass. I have been stuck in this house, raising your damn kids for thirteen years, cooking and slaving for you while my life slides right down the drain! Now I got a chance to get a little something for myself. And you are *not* gonna stop me."

"You did not say that," Meemaw said.

"I'll bet you a gillion dollars." Lucille smiled. "I said it and then he hit me. And I hit him back."

"Oh, you didn't. Lucille, never ever hit a man. I have told you. That's just an invitation."

Lucille smiled, leaking smoke through her nose. "Chester's not going to hit me again."

"Lucille . . ." Meemaw sounded strange.

Lucille pulled her feet up in the swing and began picking at her little toe. "For God's sake, it's national TV! Doesn't anybody understand how important this is?"

A little spider dropped onto her shoulder. Meemaw reached out to brush it away. "Honey, of course I do. It's something you been dreaming about a long time. You know I always said you were too pretty for your own good."

"He said I was crazy," Lucille said. "He said I was crazy."

"Lucille . . ."

"He said I couldn't go. He said he'd never give me a divorce, never." The cigarette trembled in her fingers.

"Lucille . . ."

"Mama, I killed him."

"Oh Lucille, you did not. That's not funny. Don't say that."

"I did."

"You did not. You shut up that mess."

"Night before last, after I put the kids down."

"Stop it!" Meemaw came out of the swing. "This is not a thing to make one of your sick jokes about!"

"Mama." Lucille smiled. "You don't believe me, do you. You don't think I could do it."

"No I don't," said Meemaw.

"Good for you. You just keep on like that."

I could not keep quiet. "Did you really kill him, Aunt Lucille?"

"You bet I did, honey. It was better than he deserved."

"Now, I want you to stop this!" Meemaw's face flushed all red. "You must be crazy!"

Lucille pulled down her sunglasses and peered at us. "Maybe I am," she said. "But I'm alive, and Chester's dead. And I'm going to Hollywood. And he *never* thought it would turn out like *that*."

"You scare me when you talk this way, Lucille. Half the time I think you're serious."

Lucille said "I just need a little help from you."

Meemaw's feet stopped moving the swing. "What kind of help?"

"I need you to keep the kids," Lucille said, in a rush. "While I'm in California. Three or four weeks at the very, very most. I know it's a lot to ask, Mama, but they'll be really good, I made them swear."

"You don't mean you're leaving them here. Today." The startled look on Meemaw's face told me everything: Aunt Lucille was off on one of her famous wild tears, and now our home would be overrun by Vinsons.

"I've got to, Mama. The audition is next week. It takes forty-eight hours from New Orleans on the train. Farley, if you can't share that thing, I'm going to take it away and neither one of you will get to play with it."

Farley loosened his grip. The kitten took off yowling like its fur was on fire.

Meemaw said, "Lucille, honey, you know I would take them if I could. But I can't. I just can't. I'm getting old, you don't realize. Peejoe and Wiley and me, we fill up this house pretty good."

"Mama, now listen to me." Lucille was not smiling now. Her eyes hidden by bottle-green lenses, she pulled the thin sweater around her. "I killed Chester, I really did. Do you understand me? I am not kidding you. I killed him and now I am going to Hollywood, thank you very much. I'm asking you to watch after my children. I have never asked you for anything."

Meemaw shook her head. "I think you need a doctor."

I didn't know what to think. Lucille looked completely serious, to me, and more than a little pleased with herself.

Wiley wandered up just then. He flopped on my feet to make me holler but I pulled them in, gave him plenty of room. "Aunt Lucille says she killed Uncle Chester," I told him.

"Oh yeah?" Wiley grinned at her. "What for?"

"It's a long story." She shrugged. "He said no when he should have said yes."

"Lucille, there ain't one thing funny about this and I'm not going to hear another word, now, do you hear me?" Meemaw lurched out of the swing, shaking her head. "I am going inside. Crazy talk."

"Wait, Mama, don't go." Lucille jumped to her feet. "I'll show you." She went to the white Galaxie and rummaged around in the trunk.

Meemaw stopped, hands pressed together.

Lucille came up with a translucent green plastic lettuce keeper. There was something dark inside. She carried it to Meemaw.

"Isn't that nice," Meemaw said. "Tupperware."

Lucille put her thumb on the green plastic tab. "This is Chester."

"Oh my God, Lucille." Meemaw's voice curdled. "You really are sick."

Lucille popped the seal on the lettuce keeper, lifted the lid. Inside was something tangled, greasy—it was hair.

"I had to make sure he was dead," she said.

She grasped the hair with her fingers, and lifted the dripping head of Uncle Chester from its plastic container. His eyes were staring at me.

3

Peejoe

Pigeon Creek

The worst part was the look on the children's faces when they realized what their mother was holding in her hand. It looked like the head of a doll or a statue, horribly made up like their father—except for the hair, which was too very real.

They ran screaming from the yard.

I thought *this is some joke.* I don't know whether I breathed. Wiley stood beside me, stone white—I thought he might shatter and crumble and pour to the floor in a heap. I knew I would not shatter because I was concentrating on holding Wiley together with my eyes.

Meemaw began asking questions in a calm voice, distracting Lucille while she circled in closer and closer.

"How did you do it, Lucille?"

"With the electric carving knife. Can you believe I finally found a use for that thing? It never would cut a turkey." She turned Chester's head this way and that.

"You did it yourself?"

"The kids were asleep." A light flickered in her eyes. "It was awful, Mama . . ."

"But why, honey? Why?"

"Oh, I don't know, what do you want me to say? Killing him just wasn't enough. He didn't suffer enough."

Meemaw pressed her hands against Uncle Chester's ears as if she didn't want him to hear. She took the head from Lucille and lowered it into the bowl and snapped the lid on.

Around front I heard somebody puking.

"Lucille, go sit in the swing," Meemaw said.

Lucille did as she was told.

Wiley glanced at me. My face must have jarred something loose inside him. He bolted. He ran for the woods.

Meemaw carried the Tupperware lettuce keeper to the car and placed it on the back seat.

The worst part: Lucille was so calm. She sat in the swing with that strange little smile on her face.

Meemaw said "Peejoe, you stay there with her" and hurried inside. In a moment her telephone voice carried into the yard.

Mixed with the horror I felt a spreading unspeakable thrill, burning cold, like the numbness you feel when you put your foot in a tub of scalding water. Lucille was my aunt, she had rocked me and sung to me. She was so casual it made me want to laugh but I knew she was crazy and Lord it was real, it was real. Those grainy spatters in the sand were real blood. Uncle Chester's blood.

The worst part was being alone with her while Meemaw talked on the phone. I stared at the Galaxie's shiny hubcaps to keep from seeing her face. She spoke in a low, composed voice, telling a kind of bedtime story. She told how Chester came home from the hardware every day with the same sulky face, the same grunt for hello, he always collapsed in his chair and read the paper, ate dinner, watched TV, drank a cup of coffee with the ten o'clock news . . .

She put three heaping tablespoons of D-Con in his coffee. She tried to disguise the taste with milk and sugar. Chester took one sip and said it was the worst cup of coffee he'd ever tasted. Lucille offered to throw it away and make fresh, but he said, "No, you're always trying to waste my damn money," and drank it on down.

In thirty seconds he was foaming at the mouth.

He sputtered and lunged at her, got his hands around her throat. She managed to break free. He staggered and fell. He hit the floor so hard she knew the thud must have awakened the children. He didn't move.

She ran up the hall to their rooms. She found them still sleeping, by some miracle. She returned to find Chester sprawled on the floor, his eyes staring at nothing. She sat with him a long time, she said. He wasn't breathing. She didn't believe it could be that easy.

She rolled him up in the rug and slid him down the hall, out the front door, all by herself across the yard to the toolshed. It was raining. She slipped in the mud, strained her back trying to heave him in through the door of the shed.

When she unrolled him from the rug his eyes were still staring but she didn't believe it could be that easy.

Alone with him in the toolshed, she began to imagine he was still alive, just pretending to be dead. That would be just like Chester. She looked at the side of his neck, thinking *what kind of blade would it take? Would you have to strike one heavy blow, or could you do it by sawing?*

That's when she remembered the Sunbeam electric knife, with its vibrating serrated blades. She fetched it from the kitchen, plugged it in, and went to work.

"It was hard," she told me. "Harder than you would think."

I shuddered all over. If she could do that to Uncle Chester, what might she do to me? My neck tingled where the blade would bite in.

"There I was cleaning up his mess again," she said.

I wanted to run for the woods, run try and find Wiley, and Wiley would know what to do. I knew I could not sit there much longer with that glazed expression on my face.

A breeze passed through the yard, east to west. There was no sign of the Vinsons, her children. I imagined they would run and keep going and never come back.

Lucille said, "Peejoe, I had to do it. You've only got one life, you know? You can't sit around waiting for your next life. Not if it's something you've just got to do. Do you understand?"

"I don't know." My words came out breathless. "I always kind of liked Uncle Chester."

"You didn't really know him," she said.

Just then Meemaw opened the back door, her face gray as ashes. She steadied herself on the railing, came across the yard to lean on the swing.

"Lucille, I talked to Dove. He's on his way." A terrible tremor beneath the calm surface of her voice. "Some people are going to come out from town to help us."

Lucille said, "You didn't call the police."

"Well, now, honey, I did call the sheriff, I sure did. Dove told me to. He says the sheriff can help us."

"I wish you had asked me." Lucille got up from the swing. "I thought I could stay and visit awhile. Now I've got to go."

"Dove said sooner is better than later. They won't put you in jail, Lucille. They'll just ask you some questions. You tell them it was self-defense."

Lucille laughed—a sound like glass breaking. "Mama, don't be silly.

You don't cut off somebody's head in self-defense. They'll put me in the electric chair."

"Now don't say that, don't think that way. You were troubled. You didn't know what you were doing."

"I hid the rest of him," Lucille said. "I could have gone to California and gotten the part before anybody ever found out, and then it wouldn't matter. Because I would have done it and I would be happy. All I asked for was one lousy bit of help from you."

"Lucille. You shouldn't have showed that to the children."

"I know, I know." She sighed, tangling her fingers in her hair. "I don't know what's wrong with me." Her face crumpled. Behind the sunglasses she was crying. "I've got to go, Mama. I might not be seeing you."

Meemaw clung to her, but Lucille slipped her grasp and ran to the car.

"Honey, where are you going?" Meemaw hurried after her.

Lucille jumped in, started the engine.

"Lucille, wait!"

"You tell her, Peejoe, tell her why I did it. I have to go. They are not going to catch me." She flipped down the sun-visor and took off with a roar, flinging sand, fishtailing onto the road.

Meemaw wrapped me up in her arms.

The sound of the car dwindled to a distant singing of tires, and then Aunt Lucille was gone.

"What did she tell you, Peejoe?"

"She said she only had one life. She can't wait for the next one."

"It's terrible, Sweet Pea, I'm so sorry. I hated to leave you like that, but I had to call Dove."

"It's okay."

"The sheriff will be here any minute," she said. "I guess I should have tried to keep her from going."

"Maybe she'll get away," I said.

"Maybe." Meemaw's face looked old, suddenly old and destroyed. "Peejoe, go see if you can find your cousins. Bring them back to the house."

Suddenly I was afraid—of Lucille, who was gone. "I want to stay here with you."

"Go on," she said. "Make them come back. I need you to do that. You're the only one here."

.   .   .

I wandered and called and kept calling but I never found any of them.

Hours later Judy crept out from under the front porch with Marilyn, who said she'd had a bad dream. The others straggled back to the house one by one all afternoon. Sandra wandered in without a word, went to Meemaw's bed, buried herself under quilts. Cary stumbled in after dark, covered with scratches and brambles, and then Marlon, who couldn't stop crying.

Farley stayed gone.

The deputy sheriff came with his siren screaming. That was a powerful sound out in Pigeon Creek, where we never heard anything louder than a gunshot. That brought folks to their porches for miles around. Before long there came a procession of fieldhands and kids and old ladies hastening up the road to see what was up.

The deputy called me over in the glare of his revolving light to give a description of Lucille's car, since Meemaw knew nothing except that it was white. I told him it was a Ford, a Galaxie 500.

I didn't tell him I had memorized the license plate, Alabama 9-10878, while Lucille poured her story into my ear. "I think it had an eight in it," I said.

He let me go.

The neighbors crowded at the fence, gawking, pointing, consulting. The deputy told Meemaw that if the death took place in Cotton County it was not his jurisdiction—he looked disappointed—but he headed out after Lucille anyway.

I huddled behind the trellis of Confederate jasmine. The look in Uncle Chester's eyes was burning a hole in my mind. His mouth hung open. His eyes looked surprised. I could not summon up a picture of how he looked before he was dead.

Wiley came out of the woods then. He came up to me and said "hey," and looked at his feet.

I said "Where have you been?"

"I climbed a tree. Where's Lucille?"

"Gone." I wrapped my arms tight around my knees. "Meemaw called Uncle Dove."

"They'll catch her," Wiley said.

I shook my head. "I hope she gets away."

"Uncle Dove is coming," said Wiley. "He'll know what to do."

4

Peejoe

Pigeon Creek

Wiley and some neighbor men found Farley three miles from the house, huddled beside a gravestone at the Spring Hill A.M.E. Church. They brought him home wrapped in blankets. He didn't even see me standing there. His eyes were round black windows, wide open. He looked as if his soul had been sucked out of him through the holes in his eyes.

Nightbirds stirred in the trees. I sat on the porch steps, waiting for Dove. I heard them moving around inside, the little ones crying, Meemaw trying to calm them. I couldn't sleep and I didn't know how to act in there. I saw Uncle Chester's head twisting in Aunt Lucille's hand. He was watching me.

The sound of a car, far away on the road, and then a patch of brightening in the trees. I jumped from the steps. Powerful headlights swept over the yard, leading a long cloud-white Cadillac Eldorado hearse into the sand lane on a cushion of quiet.

"Uncle Dove!" I ran to meet him.

"Peter Joseph! Come here to me!" He climbed from the car and swallowed me up with his hug. "You all right, boy?" He held me at arm's length in the headlights. "Where's Baby Sister?"

"She's gone. She got away."

"Damn. I was afraid of that. That makes it worse." He switched off the lights and led me toward the house. Dove was a big man with big shoulders, a rolling belly straining the buttons of his shirt. His size made him gentle. He had vivid blue eyes (like my eyes, like Aunt Lucille's eyes), a skeptical mouth. His nose was big and cakey, shot through with fine blue veins. His hairline had retreated since the last time I saw him. He

30

smelled of Hai Karate and bourbon and some indefinable chemical odor the Hai Karate could not quite overcome.

"Let's go in," he said.

"I want to stay here."

"Aw come on, Peter Joseph, the skeeters'll eat you alive. Here. Here's something for you." He dug down among his keys and came out with a quarter. Uncle Dove would give you a quarter on the least excuse. It was one of many things I loved about him.

"It's gross in there," I said. "They're crying and stuff."

Dove placed his hands on my shoulders. "Oh, boy. It's a scary old world, ain't it, Peter Joseph," he said. "You saw something you ought not to've seen. That was mean of Baby Sister, to show that to you. I don't know what's the matter with her."

"Meemaw says she's crazy."

"I believe she's right." Uncle Dove squeezed me up under his chin. "I never knew *how* crazy. Did she take Chester with her?"

"Just his head. She hid the rest of him somewhere."

"Well damn, that was thoughtful," said Dove. "She never did give a minute's thought to anybody but herself. I guess that means I'm going to Cornelia. You want to go with me?"

I didn't know what to say. Nobody ever asked me to go anywhere.

"You could help me out," he said. "You and Wiley. Where is he?"

"In bed."

"Well go get him up. You boys are coming with me."

He led me to the kitchen where Meemaw sat with the children. Cary had cried so much he looked like he had the flu. Meemaw started crying, too, the moment she saw Dove. He folded her up in his arms, bent his head to murmur in her ear.

I hated when grown people cried. It felt like the world was flying apart, the sky ripping loose from the horizon.

I found Wiley in the front parlor, knotted up on a pallet on the floor. I tugged his shoulder. "Uncle Dove's here. He wants us to go with him."

He rolled over, rubbing sleep from his eyes. "Go where?"

"Cornelia."

"What for?"

"To find the rest of Uncle Chester."

Wiley said, "I guess I wasn't dreaming, huh."

"Nope."

Uncle Dove came in with a big blue pasteboard suitcase, one of

Meemaw's, plastered over with SEE ROCK CITY stickers. "How you doing, son," he said, reaching out to smooth Wiley's cowlick.

"How long are we gonna be gone, Uncle Dove?"

He opened the suitcase. "I don't know. Your grandma's got her hands full with Lucille's kids. I think y'all might come to Industry for a while." The town was pronounced *in-DUST-ree,* emphasis on the *dust.* "That is, if it's all right with you."

Wiley looked at me. "Well I reckon we can't stick around here."

I said nothing. Dove peered at me a long time, as if his big sad eyes saw right through to the place where Chester was watching me.

He patted my shoulder. "We'll have a big time, Peter Joseph. You'll be all right."

I gathered my underwear in silence. The prospect of going off with Dove in that fine shiny hearse filled me with anticipation and dread. I was headed off for a brand-new life before I had the first inkling my old life was over.

I had never been away from Meemaw overnight except one New Year's Eve when I got overexcited playing dodgeball with the Vinsons, and accepted Aunt Lucille's invitation to spend a night in Cornelia. I was fine until bedtime, then I turned suddenly homesick and hysterical. Lucille had to drive me all the way back to Meemaw's, eighty miles in the middle of the night.

I wouldn't be going alone this time. Wiley would be with me.

All my possessions fit neatly in the left half of the suitcase: school shirts and pants, clip-on Sunday necktie, T-shirts, pajamas, jeans, Batman pin, lucky rock.

"We're coming back, aren't we, Wiley?"

"How should I know?" Wiley took down his track-and-field ribbon, his certificate of perfect fourth-grade attendance, the photograph of Mama and Daddy.

I stood over the suitcase, studying that picture. I knew it by heart. It was their honeymoon in Panama City. They are happy and young, arm in arm, wearing loud-print beach clothes. Behind them a palm tree stirs in the breeze, a flat ocean stretches into infinity. Mama strikes a movie-star pose with her wide-brimmed straw hat and shapely legs, a big brassy smile like Aunt Lucille's. In the photograph her lipstick is black; I could only imagine that red in real life. Daddy is laughing at something she said.

Wiley folded a sweatshirt over them. Meemaw came in, dry-eyed but pale. "I know you boys will have a good time with Dove."

I said "Meemaw, I want to stay here. I can help you."

"I need you to go, Sweet Pea." She bit her lip, and turned to rearrange our things in the suitcase. "You know this will always be your home. It's just too much for me right now. You stay with Dove awhile, then you'll come back."

"But I don't want to go."

"Shut up, Peejoe," said Wiley. "Don't be a baby."

I turned on him. "*I* didn't hide in a tree."

Meemaw folded my Sunday shirt. "Baby, it's not forever. This whole thing is bound to work out, somehow. Lucille didn't mean to do what she did. She's just—Lord, I don't know. She's mixed up."

"Howcome the stupid Vinsons get to stay here and we have to go?"

"Peejoe. Keep your voice down." Meemaw moved to shut the door. "I'm ashamed of you. This isn't their fault. Right now they need me worse than you do."

I flung myself facefirst on the bed. For the first time, I felt like an Orphan with a capital O. I counted for nothing. I belonged to nobody. My only parents were in that photograph under Wiley's sweatshirt. My dead parents loved me but to the rest of the world I was an inconvenience, an extra mouth to feed.

Meemaw rubbed my shoulder blade with her thumb. "It's nice down in Industry. It's a whole different place. Come on, now, Sweet Pea, don't be contrary. This has been a bad day."

I buried my face in her side. I tried not to cry.

Uncle Dove came in to snap up the suitcase. "Mama, I'll call you soon as I know something. Boys, let's us go."

And that's when I had to let go of Meemaw, give Wiley his turn. I stood to one side with my useless hands in my pockets.

I loved Uncle Dove, but it wasn't the same. I had always thought Meemaw would take care of me, and now I saw that was foolish. Every stick of furniture, every porcelain hen and pincushion cried *Look! Remember, Peejoe! This is your home!* but I didn't have time to say goodbye to everything.

Uncle Dove hoisted the suitcase. We followed him out through the kitchen. I brought the plywood play-guns. Wiley carried the sack Meemaw had loaded up with fried chicken, biscuits, bananas, and milk.

Adolf followed us out to the hearse, whining. He always wanted to go for a ride.

"You boys mind your Aunt Earlene," said Meemaw. "Wiley, make Peejoe brush his teeth."

"He doesn't have to make me," I said.

"Well then make yourself."

Wiley said, "Uncle Dove, you got a new car!"

"You know we Bullises always travel in style." The dome light illuminated a plushy blue interior, woodgrained dashboard, and the latest gadgets. In back a gleaming copper-colored casket reclined on a castered steel carriage. Uncle Dove wedged our suitcase in beside it. "It's brand new, a 'sixty-five Caddy. Y'all get in."

"It's beautiful, Dove." Meemaw touched the upholstery. "You must be doing good business."

"Fair," he said. "Listen now, if Baby Sister calls, you tell her to stay where she is. I'll come get her."

I slid to the middle of the seat. I had never been anywhere *near* a car this fine. A limousine for dead people. "Uncle Dove, is that somebody dead in the back?"

"No, that one's empty just yet."

Meemaw stood in darkness, stroking Adolf behind his ears. She seemed older than the great old oak tree behind her. Her shoulders sagged. I snapped a picture with the camera in my mind.

"Now Dove, don't drive too fast."

"Don't worry, Mama. You need to try and sleep."

"I am way behind on my ironing," she said.

Dove drove a circle around the tree and headed for the road. Meemaw waved with both hands. Wiley and I stuck our arms out the window and waved until she disappeared in the darkness.

Dove rolled up the window with his button. We sank into the plush-velvet seats.

Wiley touched a six-sided plunger knob on the dash.

"That's the siren," Dove said.

"What's it for?"

"I'm the county coroner, you know, and sometimes we fill in if the ambulance gets too busy."

"Turn it on!" Wiley said. "Can I turn it on?"

"Let's get far enough away so your grandma won't hear it."

"What does it mean, county corner?" I said.

"Cor-oh-ner," he explained, "means it's my job to go out and issue a death certificate on everybody who dies in Cotton County."

He fished in his pocket for a cigarette and switched on the radio. Herman's Hermits sang in their strange accents, *Meeses Brown you've got a lovely daw-ta . . .*

I examined the casket, shivering at the idea that someone would ever put me in a box like that. It would be so dark in there. Think how terrible if they made a mistake and you woke up in there, still alive.

"You sure Lucille didn't say where she might have put him?"

"She said he was heavy," I told him. "She probably couldn't carry him very far by herself."

"We'll find him." Dove drove with two fingers on the wheel. The speedometer needle climbed past seventy. The hearse flashed over dark curving hills, through the piney woods, a hint of sunrise off to the left.

Wiley sat up on the seat. "Now, Uncle Dove?"

"Let 'er rip."

Wiley pulled out the plunger. A throaty purr rose from under the hood, growing louder, rising into a high liquid scream, rising, falling.

Dove reached under his seat and came up with a cherry-red police light. He licked the suction cup on the bottom, stuck it to the dashboard, and plugged the cord in the cigarette-lighter socket.

"Okay, Peter Joseph," he shouted over the racket, "let 'em know we're coming."

I hit the switch. The light blazed to life. A brilliant red beam pierced the car and the night beyond the car. We raced through the hour before dawn.

5

Lucille

On the Road

Lucille never meant to show Chester's head to her mother. She felt terrible about the children. She didn't even know they were watching until they ran screaming from the yard. She lost her place. That had been happening a lot lately, Lucille lost her place in things. This smooth grayish mood came down over her, just lowered around her like a dense fog. She couldn't see anything, she walked around in her body inside the fog. When the mood lifted up, things were further along than before and sometimes Lucille had done something. Afterward her mind was clear as the air after a crackling thunderstorm, not a cloud in there, not a speck of dust, just clean pure washed air and an idea or two.

After these spells Lucille had some ideas that would curl most people's hair, but they seemed like good ideas at the time.

She didn't exactly know why she brought Chester's head to her mother's. It seemed like the thing to do. Something told her not to leave the two pieces of Chester too close together. She remembered the scene in *Fantasia* when Mickey Mouse chops the wicked broom into splinters, and the splinters turn into hundreds more wicked brooms. She feared Chester might pull some trick like that.

You wouldn't have thought a man's entire head would fit into a Tupperware container designed to hold a head of lettuce, but Chester had a small head for a man his size. The lid snapped right on with its patented press-and-lock seal. She burped it so he would stay fresh.

She didn't realize her mother had returned the container to the Galaxie until the sun was rising, thirty miles north of Mobile, and she happened to glance in the back seat.

"Oh, my God. Hello, Chester."

Chester said nothing.

Lucille liked that.

She lit a Salem and breathed the car full of smoke. Every inch of Alabama sliding under her wheels was another inch closer to freedom. Once she got across the state line she would change her name and begin a new life. She would miss her children but now she had Chester's head to keep her company.

Poor Mama. It was bad to drop that load on her and run. But she would do the children more good than Lucille, any day. Lucille's heart was never in it.

She stopped for gas in a town called Axis. The pump boy made googly eyes at her as he filled the tank. He was not worth looking at twice, but she had the craziest notion to take him in the back there, in the shed among his daddy's lawn mowers and greasy tools, pull down his britches and crawl all over him.

She had never done any such thing. But this was her new life. Her old life was behind her. She sauntered past the boy with her Samsonite cosmetic case. "You be sure and wash that windshield, you hear?"

"Yes ma'am." His Adam's apple bobbed up his throat. His eyes walked all over Lucille.

She went around to the toilet. All while she sat there she hoped the boy would summon up some courage. She peed, all breathless, her heart racing like a schoolgirl's, randy and ready and looking. She changed out of the clamdiggers into a sexy print dress, deep purple on red, a flaring Mexican skirt. She retouched her makeup in the light from the lone dangling bulb. Did she look old to the boy? Did he know he could have her? Did he have any idea that she was a murderess?

When she went out, the boy had finished pumping her gas. His head was stuck up under another lady's radiator. He didn't even glance at Lucille when she handed over the money.

She flushed red. Anyone looking at her that moment would say *that woman is guilty,* and they would be right.

She got in her car and scratched out of there in a hurry.

She trembled at the thought of what she'd almost done, what she had wanted to do.

As the miles passed, a slow smile crept over her face. She *could* have done it if she'd wanted to. Maybe next time she would.

"He was homely, Chester," she said. "If he hadn't been so homely I might have done it."

Chester sat in perfect silence on the back seat. Lucille remembered how his moods used to darken the car whenever they went anywhere. He had a terrible sense of direction, couldn't find his way out of a paper bag. He always got lost and then angry, and blamed it on Lucille. Then the kids whined, explosions and conflict and tears. None of that this morning. Lucille knew exactly where she was going: south and west, to New Orleans, to a long silver train which would carry her across the country to Hollywood, and her destiny.

Some people are born to be wives and mothers. Lucille was not one of these. She figured this out at the movies when she was a little girl. She saw Margaret O'Brien prancing around with Judy Garland in *Meet Me in St. Louis* and a voice whispered in her ear: *You can do that.* Her whole life since that moment was one long dream of the movies, with herself in all the starring roles.

Only Chester got in her way. She didn't even remember a time when she loved him. She married him to get away from home, that was the truth. She cooked his pork chops and raised his children, six children dear Lord and Lucille wasn't even thirty-four—but all the time she was teaching herself how to dance, sing, walk, smile, dress nice, wear the right makeup. She was reading *Silver Screen* and *Hollywood Confidential*, and building up her bosom with a Mark Eden exerciser. Chester never encouraged her, not once. When the man from the Industry *Progress* wrote that her performance as Maria Von Trapp had a "vivid glow," Chester smirked and said "he makes you sound like a light bulb." Right then she made up her mind to kill him.

It took her a while but she did it. Now she was on her way to Hollywood.

She had been making lists of new names for weeks. She was thinking along the lines of Lana Loveman, Lauren Rainier, Lucille D'Evereaux, Linda Marcelle. She liked the Frenchy sound of D'Evereaux and Marcelle . . . Lucille Marcelle? No. Lana Marcelle—sounded like a girdle. She wanted something exotic, yet simple. Like: Grace Kelly. Kim Novak. Marilyn Monroe. Now there was a perfect name. If there hadn't been a Marilyn Monroe, Lucille was sure she would have thought that name up for herself.

Marilyn: Evelyn: Carolyn. Carolyn. Not bad. Carolyn what? Carolyn Monroe. Carolyn: Adams. Jefferson. Washington. Lucille pored back through American history. Franklin. Madison. Webster. Clay. Carolyn Clay.

Lucille glanced at her eyes in the mirror. "Hello there," she whispered aloud. "I'm Carolyn Clay."

It rolled off the tongue. It sounded serious but sexy, sophisticated, with a beat you could dance to. It sounded famous.

Carolyn Clay in "That Girl from Alabama." Our guest star this week, Carolyn Clay. Ladies and gentlemen please welcome to the stage the lovely, the talented . . . Miss! Carolyn Clay.

"Carolyn Clay," she repeated. "You like that, Chester?"

She took his silence for approval.

Just then a sign flashed by, the Confederate flag and some words and a white magnolia blossom.

"Hello," Lucille said. "My name is Carolyn Clay. Welcome to Mississippi, the Magnolia State."

Mississippi looked just like Alabama, but Lucille felt the weight of eternity lifting up off her shoulders. The perfect name had appeared by magic at the moment she crossed the border into her new life. That was a sign. Her luck was changing.

6

Peejoe

Cornelia, Alabama

We found a window unlocked in back. Dove boosted me through on his knee. I wiggled over a radiator and dropped to the floor. I recognized the boys' room: unmade bunk beds, unfinished model airplanes, a litter of pajamas and toys. The time I got so homesick, it started in this room—a dreadful unease, a disturbing intuition that I did not belong here. Now, smelling the sour-milk smell in the air, I felt that sensation again.

"Go on," Dove said through the window, "go open the door."

The floor creaked under my shoe. Everything looked normal, a little messier than Meemaw's house, but nothing like murder.

Then I noticed a stain on the living-room rug, and bent over to examine it—a dark stain in the shape of Louisiana.

Wiley rattled the door.

I let him in. "Where did Dove go?"

"Out to the toolshed." The screen door slammed behind him.

I led him to the stain. He knelt down to touch it. "It could be blood, I can't tell. Here, taste."

"Gross!" I jerked back from his hand.

He laughed. "Just think, Peejoe, he could be anywhere in here. He could be right in yonder. Let's go find him."

"I think we ought to wait for Dove," I said, but Wiley wandered on to the kitchen and I followed to keep from being alone.

The remains of breakfast cluttered the table—half-eaten doughnuts, spoons in cereal bowls—as if the Vinsons had gotten up in the middle of their Frosted Flakes and fled the house. I imagined Lucille hurrying them through breakfast, hurry hurry come on, knowing what she had done, knowing what she had in that Tupperware bowl.

40

"It's too quiet in here," I said.

"Look. Chester's cigarettes." Wiley pointed to a pack of Pall Malls on the coffee table. "You can tell something happened in here. The air smells dead."

At the sound of footsteps we grabbed each other, scared little boys—then Wiley grinned feebly and let go. "We're in here, Uncle Dove."

Dove came in mopping his face with a handkerchief. He clumped all over the house, checking in every room.

"Did you see anything?" Wiley said.

"She did it in the shed, all right. She tried to clean it up, but . . . shooee." He shook his head.

"Can we go see?" said Wiley.

"Forget about it, I don't want you out there." Dove wiped his mouth on his hand. "There's two drag marks, one going and one coming. He's got to be in here somewhere." He went to the refrigerator, flung it open as if *surprise!* took a wax carton of orange juice from the top shelf, and drank from the unfolded lip. "You want some, boys?"

A dead man's orange juice? We shook our heads.

"Peejoe, did she say when she killed him?"

"Monday. After the ten o'clock news."

"Two days." Dove shut the Frigidaire. "We ought to be able to smell him by now."

I must have turned green. Dove said I could wait in the car, but Wiley was acting so collected that I had to stay. I stayed close behind Dove.

Wiley volunteered to climb up on Dove's shoulders into the attic—a desperate attempt to show courage, I thought, after his performance at Meemaw's the day before. I know this much: *I* wouldn't have gone up there.

He poked around in the dark for long minutes with a flashlight. At last he angled down from the hole, giddy with relief. "Nothing there."

"Wait a minute," said Dove. "She had his head in Tupperware, right? She wanted him to keep."

"Yeah . . ."

"Come on." Dove charged down the hall, moving as fast as I'd ever seen him. He ducked through a narrow door and clattered down the basement stairs, trailing us behind him.

He jerked the chain. The lightbulb swung crazy shadows over collected junk and dead houseplants, moving boxes, washing machine and deep freeze, bicycles, cedar chests, broken-down toys. Dove stilled the swinging light with one hand. He went to the ancient Frost Queen chest freezer and flung it open.

A cloud of vapor boiled up. Frozen foods glistened and smoked in the harsh light.

Dove began hurling things over his shoulder—chickens, hams, cans of Minute Maid, turkey pot pies. A Cornish hen struck Wiley's toe. He hopped and shouted.

Dove gave a grunt and stopped throwing things. "Oh, Baby Sister. What have you done."

I crept to his side. A frozen hand reached up between bags of mixed vegetables, the fingers rigid but delicately posed, as if reaching out to pick a flower.

A chill seized me.

Dove put the heel of his hand on my head and gently pushed me back. "In the hearse there's a black vinyl bag, a body bag with a zipper. Run bring that to me. Wiley, go with him."

Our shadows did a wild dance up the stairs. We beat a path to the kitchen and outside, where the sun was warm.

I took a lungful of wide-open air. "She froze him."

"Can you believe it? Like a Popsicle." Wiley sank to the grass, toppled over backwards, and rolled on his side, a credible imitation of death.

I rubbed my freezing hands on my pants. "You know, I can't even remember what he looked like. It's scary. I can't put the two pieces together."

Wiley got up on his haunches. "He liked TV. Remember he used to watch the 'Wide World of Sports'?"

"I can't remember."

Wiley said, "I wonder why she took his head."

"Maybe she wanted to prove it to Meemaw."

"There's other ways to prove it," said Wiley, and after all he was right.

I found the body bag wedged under the casket carriage.

We went back in the house and downstairs to the sound of frozen foods striking the concrete floor.

Dove glanced over his shoulder. "Give me that."

I stepped up with the bag. I couldn't help seeing into the whorling mist of the deep freeze. Uncle Chester reclined in the floor of the box with one hand reaching out, the other tucked under his arm. Where his head should be was the stump of his neck, glassy and marbled like a frozen roast.

Wiley touched my arm. I yelped.

"Sorry." He edged past me for a better look.

Dove's eyeglasses fogged. "See if you can grab around his legs."

Wiley and I got up under his knees. Dove took his arms. We wrestled Chester out of that box. He was hard as stone and extremely heavy, wedged against the freezer wall. His clothes cracked and shed ice crystals where we touched him. He felt like a thing that had never been alive.

I pretended I was not doing this.

Chester's shoe snagged on the lip of the freezer. "Whoa, come this way," Dove warned.

The load shifted. I sank to one knee, lost my grip. Wiley staggered. "Look out!"

Uncle Chester slid out of our hands and came down with a weighty *chink!* like a block of granite. I thought he would shatter, but he sat in one piece on the floor, steaming, as if we had lifted him from a hot bath.

Dove shook out the body bag along his length. He opened the zipper around the rim and began tucking the bag around Chester like a blanket. It took some maneuvering to get it all the way around him and zipped shut over his outstretched hand.

"We'll never get him in that casket," Dove said. "It'll be tomorrow before he starts to thaw. It looks like we're going to need some help."

We followed him upstairs to the phone. He called his friend John Doggett, the sheriff in Industry, the county seat, twenty miles south.

The sheriff covered those twenty miles in twelve minutes, followed shortly by three carloads of deputies. They fanned out all over the yard, drawing a crowd of onlookers to Uncle Chester's chain-link fence.

"There's no need for all this hullabaloo, John," said Dove. We stood behind them on the porch, surveying the yard full of red-blinking black-and-white cars. "There's nobody here to arrest. It's just one body and I needed a hand getting this casket out of my hearse."

"We'll need to call out an APB," said Sheriff Doggett. "That is one dangerous woman."

"Come on, John, for God's sake, this is a domestic dispute. I told you she did it. It's open and shut."

The sheriff rested his hand on Dove's shoulder—a compact, powerful man with a glinting badge and a swaggering belly that he carried before him like a battering ram. His wavy brown hair and the dimple in his chin reminded me of Kirk Douglas. "There ain't a lot of action around here. I got to give these boys a piece of this. This is something special. I been on this job twenty years and this is my first decapitation."

Four deputies unloaded the coffin into Chester's garage; Dove would come back for it later. Other deputies carried the casket dolly into the house, provoking a buzz from the spectators at the fence.

"This is some serious mess." Sheriff Doggett held out a clipboard. "Listen, Dove, I'm on your side. I'm sure she had her reasons. She'll get a fair hearing. They'll probably send her up to Bryce's when it's all said and done."

Bryce Hospital was the looney bin in Tuscaloosa. The meanest teachers in school said if you misbehaved too much they would sign a paper and send you to Bryce.

Dove scribbled his name and returned the clipboard. "John, you and me go back a long way. You got to look out for my family here."

Sheriff Doggett lowered his voice. "If you know where she's gone, you might want to tell me. I can make sure we bring her in safe."

"I don't know, I have no idea." Dove waved his arm. "All I know is it ain't doing nobody one bit of good to have a circus out here."

"Folks like to see their sheriff keepin' busy, election's coming up in the fall." For the first time, the sheriff appeared to notice Wiley and me standing behind him. "Which one is the boy she talked to?"

"This is Peter Joseph." Dove reached to mess with my hair. "Shake hands with Sheriff Doggett."

His grip was momentary. His eyes passed right over me. "He's a witness to her confession," he said. "I want him where I can talk to him."

"He'll be with me," Dove said.

"Heads up!" A shout from inside. I scrambled out of the way. The deputies wheeled Chester through the door on the dolly, like a piece of black-plastic sculpture.

Wiley and I climbed in the front seat of the hearse. The men loaded Chester in back, clanking, shoving, snapping straps. The rear gate slammed shut.

The three of us spent an uncomfortable long moment alone.

Dove got in. "Let's get the hell out of here." He pressed a button to raise the glass panel between front and back. He cranked up a blast of cool air, then the radio, Righteous Brothers soaring harmonies in front of a big glassy echoing chorus, *wo-ho that lovin' feelin'* . . .

I sat between Wiley and Dove. We eased out of the yard. The fence people gawked at us. It felt good to roll out of there.

Uncle Dove touched death every day. Now I had touched it, and Wiley had touched it. We were members of the death club. We tried to forget Chester in the back of the car. We sang along with the radio and tried to forget him completely.

7

Peejoe

Industry, Alabama

At the center of every county seat in Alabama you will find the courthouse, a stately old building, a monument to the durability of justice. Every courthouse is surrounded by a square: stores and trees and a gray stone Confederate statue; a flagpole with the Stars and Stripes flapping above (but just slightly above) the red-X-on-white flag of Alabama; old men propped against cars and on stoops, spitting, trading speculations on the weather. On that day in May when we coasted into the square in Industry, the stores were doing healthy business, the white folks looked happy, the colored folks were largely invisible, and the dogs had enough sense to lie down in the shade.

The old men on park benches straightened as we glided by in the hearse. They took off their hats and covered their hearts. I felt sorry for them; before long they would all be Uncle Dove's customers.

All the way from Cornelia I had witnessed the powerful effect of the hearse on other travelers. They averted their eyes. They backed off, or passed and sped up to get away from us.

Industry had a movie theater and a Dairy Dog, a cottonseed mill, a Purina feed store, a John Deere dealer and a used-car lot and a couple of cafés, but not much in the way of industry. Dove explained that the town's name had been dreamed up during the Depression by some merchants who thought it might attract a factory or two, but so far it hadn't worked.

I peered out at the sleepy green town. "What was it called before?"

"Snubbville," he said. "So I guess it was an improvement, anyway. Here's our new swimming pool." He pointed out a park in a green shady valley, down the hill from the Dairy Dog. A white concrete-block building stood beside a rectangle of unearthly blue water, with a diving board and gleaming chrome ladders.

I had seen swimming pools in magazines and on TV; the Beverly Hillbillies had their "cee-ment pond." Whenever Wiley and I swam in the spring behind Meemaw's I pretended to be swimming in a real pool just like this. "Can we go, Uncle Dove?"

"Soon as it's open. They just filled it with water. I don't think anybody's even swum in it yet." He turned up a hill, onto Lee Street. "You boys hadn't been here since we bought out the competition, have you?"

"No sir," said Wiley. "Meemaw says you got a big place now."

We came out on a rise overlooking the town.

"Look at that," I breathed.

It was plainly built to be the finest house for miles around—an enormous decrepit mansion sprawling at the head of a great weedy lawn, a rambly pile of clapboard and columns that once had been white, before time and the weather went to work on it. Whatever great money had built it had long since disappeared, and the house had been permitted to run way on down: flaking paint, missing shingles. Twelve columns marched across the front, supporting a wide sagging second-floor gallery. In the yard, a hand-painted sign: CROAKER-MOSELEY FUNERAL HOME.

Dove stopped at the foot of the driveway to give us time to admire it. "What do you think?"

I couldn't believe it. "This is where you live?"

He beamed. "You like it?"

"It's *huge.*" All my notions of funeral homes sprang from one brief visit to Dove's former place of business, a squared-off brick building on the poor side of Industry. My sketches and floor plans were glorified versions of that place. I'd never imagined such a majestic ruin.

"I told you we had plenty of room," he said. "Now I realize it needs a coat of paint, but it's still quite some old place, ain't it?"

"It's the biggest house I've ever seen," Wiley said. "It's a mansion!"

"Well, it used to be, anyway. Been a funeral home for thirty years." We drove up the long driveway to a black asphalt courtyard in back. An older-model black Lincoln hearse stood under a flat-roofed carport. "Moseley bought out Mr. Croaker."

Dove honked the horn.

A metal door rolled back in the hand of an old colored man with gray hair like steel wool. A big grin opened up on his face. His name was Milton. He had worked for Uncle Dove a long time. I had never seen him wear anything but that dark-blue workshirt and pants.

"Walsuh, look here," he crowed, "didn't know you was bringing us company, Mist' Dove! Look here at these fine young men, how y'all gettin' along."

"Hey, Milton." Wiley shook his old hand.

"Y'all just shootin' up like corn," he said. "I wouldn't hardly know you."

Dove came around the hearse. "Milton, that's Chester Vinson in the back. We need to get him inside."

"You don't mean—now hold on a minute, Mist' Dove, you don't mean Mister Chester?"

"I do. He met with an accident."

"Aw no. All them younguns of his—how many'd he have?"

"He had six. You get a gurney out here. I'll take these boys in and come help you."

"Mm, *mm*. And he was a young man, too. 'Scuse me, suh, but how Miss Lucille, how she doin'?"

"Holding up," Dove said. "Come on, boys."

We followed him into a gleaming linoleum hallway. The rear wing of the house was severe and empty as a hospital corridor. Dove stopped before a gray door. "There's one rule in this house," he said. "Are you listening? You don't ever, *ever*, open this door. Do you understand me?"

We said *yessir*.

Of course that made me want to open the door. I wondered what on earth could be so awful in there, after I had seen both parts of Chester.

"This back wing is the mortuary," Dove said, moving on. "The parlors and the casket display rooms are in front. We live upstairs."

The front of the house was a hundred years older, stale air and uneven plank floors, worn brown rugs. A grandfather clock counted the moments with its sluggish tick, tick. Massive dark furniture loomed in a succession of parlors, arched doorways framed with musty velvet curtains. In the front hall a double staircase led up to the second floor.

I glimpsed a roomful of caskets, artfully arranged under spotlights.

Dove started up the stairs. "Come on, Peter Joseph. You'll have plenty of time to look around."

A wall of Sheetrock blocked off the second-floor landing. Dove opened a door. Cool air flowed out.

"Wow," Wiley said, "air conditioning."

We stepped in. The second floor of the house had been remodeled into a modern, self-contained apartment, the walls removed to make a huge living room with high ceilings, an open kitchen, two rooms off the back.

Window units churned out refrigerated air. The room was enlivened by Aunt Earlene's futuristic furniture: a blue-velvet overstuffed sofa with pink pillows, matching armchairs, white sheepskin rug, a kidney-shaped Jetsons coffee table inlaid with pink-and-blue boomerangs, an expensive color console TV, a wrought-iron stand holding a huge aquarium with water and bubbles but no fish.

I heard water splashing in a bathroom. Uncle Dove tossed his jacket on the sofa. "Earlene, you here?"

"This is great," Wiley said. "You'd never even know you were in an old house."

"You boys'll sleep on the third floor," Dove said. "No air conditioning, but you got all the room in the world up there."

"You mean there's more?" I couldn't believe it. This house went on and on.

"Twenty-four rooms, I think. Count 'em and let me know. We'll put you a box fan up there, you'll be fine. Milton will bring up your stuff. Earlene, where are you?"

"It's about time you got back." She breezed in from the bathroom wearing a satiny crimson robe with a feather collar. "Hello, boys. Dove, do you have a clean shirt to wear tonight?"

Dove looked blank. "What's tonight? I forgot."

"Oh you didn't forget, baby, it's the first decent cocktail party we've been invited to in over a year. The McGuires, remember?"

"The McGuires."

"I was afraid you were going to stand me up. What took you so long?" Earlene was a handsome, big-boned woman with a mouth that turned down at the corners, and a certain resemblance to Lady Bird Johnson, except her hair was a brassy red. At the moment it was wound tight around bristly curlers. I had forgotten Earlene's abrupt manner, and her loud, emphatic voice, like a truck horn. She always spoke to us exactly as if we were adults, and we were expected to act that way too; no mushy hellos or kissy stuff.

"We had to come through Cornelia," Dove said, "and then there was all this mess with John Doggett, who suddenly decided to play big-city sheriff, don't ask me why."

Earlene drew water into a coffeepot. "What's the trouble?"

Dove shrugged. "No trouble. Except Baby Sister is running around God knows where, wanted for murder."

"Did she really poison him and cut off his head?"

"That's what she said."

Earlene ladled coffee from the Maxwell House bag. "I don't know, Dove, if you ever pushed me too far I might do you the same way." She waved the measuring spoon at him, and laughed. "Don't mind me, boys, I always carry on this way. There's peanut butter and Ritz crackers if you're hungry. Mabel's around somewhere. Dove, you better hurry up and get in the shower."

Wiley said "Is it okay if we watch TV?"

"Go ahead," said Earlene. "We only get two channels, so I hope you like what's on."

Wiley and I flopped down on the sheepskin and switched on the TV. Industry was so far from everywhere that our only choices were "Romper Room" from Pensacola or an old "Rifleman" out of Mobile. I wondered why Dove and Earlene had such a fine TV set for such a lousy signal.

Dove said "Earlene, I got to tend some business with Milton."

"Well, get on with it. We're due there at six-thirty." She patted her curlers and headed for her room.

Dove rolled his eyes, and went out.

Wiley rubbed his palms on the sheepskin, and got up. "Two lousy channels."

I followed him into the humid air of the old house. A narrow staircase led up to the third floor. The moment I topped those stairs I knew this was our special place, this vast attic room under the sloping roof at the way very top of the house. The air had a rich smell, like old books. The room stretched sixty feet, end to end; it was empty except for a pile of boxes and abandoned curtains, folding chairs, two Army cots with thin mattresses. The floor was smooth as dusted ice.

Wiley opened a grimy dormer window, and south Alabama spread out before us, green and rolling into the distance—rivers, clouds, houses, barns, the town, endless miles of trees.

"If the ceiling was a little higher you could shoot baskets up here." Wiley took three steps sideways, dribbling an invisible ball.

I slid like a skater on the soles of my shoes. "Come on. Let's go look at the caskets."

We thundered downstairs. After the spacious air of the attic, the first floor was a lesson in gloom, lit by electric candles with red flamelike bulbs set in wall sconces. Concealed speakers let out faint organ music, so soft you couldn't make out a tune—just a spooky tweedling, way at the back of your ears.

I stepped around a curtain into the casket room to find our cousin Mabel perched on a barstool between two open coffins.

I backed up a step, colliding with Wiley.

She heard us but she kept her eyes closed, her hands floating out in front of her. She looked spooky. Her hair was brilliantly red like Earlene's, only Mabel's was long and frizzy, a burning bush of red hair. Her pale skin made it seem even redder. The spotlights cast stark shadows on her face.

Nine caskets sat around on movable dollies, nine empty coffins propped open. The satin linings looked cushy and inviting, like comfortable beds.

"Hey, Mabel," said Wiley. "Whatcha doing?"

"Don't say anything." Her hands began to tremble. "You're upsetting them. They don't know why you're here."

"Ho-kay . . ."

The quaking in her hands grew violent, uncontrollable, then the hands reached out for me. I backed away. She seized my arms and pulled me in. Her eyes flew open. "Hey, Peejoe!"

"Huh—hey, Mabel! What's the matter with you?"

She grinned. "God, you both look bigger!" Mabel was fifteen. There had always been a breath of mystery in the air around her. We used to play hide-and-go-seek when we were little, and we never could find Mabel. She would just vanish into thin air, gone, goodbye. When we finally gave up and trudged back to home base she would always be sitting there waiting for us.

"Who are you talking to, Mabel?"

"The people."

"What people?"

"This house is full of people. Mother says I'm neurotic. I'm glad you're here."

Wiley inspected the caskets, fingering the frills on a lace pillow. "This is mighty fancy stuff just to go in a hole in the ground," he said. "How much does one of these things cost, anyhow?"

"There's one in the back that costs two thousand dollars," she said. "Solid bronze."

Wiley whistled his appreciation.

Aunt Earlene sounded her horn on the stairs: "Mabel!"

"Down here, Mother."

"We're off now. The McGuires' number is on the refrigerator." Earlene stuck her head around the velvet curtain. She was all dolled up in a red party dress, her hair frozen in a gravity-defying bouffant by a thick application of hair spray. "Try not to call unless it's an emergency, okay?"

"Have a good time, Mother."

Earlene walked away down the hall. "Dove? Baby, are you ready?"

Mabel answered my silent question. "She gets all beside herself about these social things," she said. "She worries about all these stupid women, what they think about her, who gets invited where." She closed her eyes. "Listen, Peejoe. Can you hear that?"

Wiley was busy examining a splendid pewter-metal casket with a tufted turquoise satin lining. "I wonder what it feels like to lay down in one of these things," he said, moving a folding chair beside the casket. He sat down and began to unlace his shoes.

"Uncle Chester's dead, isn't he?" Mabel said. "Aunt Lucille killed him."

"That's right."

She covered her eyes. "I wonder what made her do it."

"She wanted to go to Hollywood. Chester didn't want her to go."

"Is that where she is now?"

"I guess. On her way."

"The people are unhappy," she said. "It must be Chester. He won't speak to them."

"He doesn't have a head," I said.

She blinked at me dreamily. "They want you to take him away. They don't like him. They don't want him in the house."

"Aunt Lucille didn't like him either." That was Wiley, behind us. He was stretched out full-length in the coffin, hands folded over his chest.

I wandered over to examine the silky upholstery, the pillow under his head. "How does it feel in there?"

"Kind of hard," he said. "Not near as comfortable as it looks."

"I guess it doesn't matter when you're dead. Is it scary?"

"It's kind of peaceful. I could almost take a nap." He shut his eyes. "Listen, Peejoe! They're talking to me! I can hear them, woo-ooooooo. . . . They're saying Mabel's gone crazy, Mabel's gone crazy." He grinned, and opened one eye to wink it at me.

Mabel got up from the barstool. "They don't like *you* at all, Wiley. They don't want to talk to you."

"Whoo, I'm so concerned. Peejoe, look at me, look how I'm shaking." He sat up in the coffin. "Give me a hand out of here."

"Peejoe's much more mature than you," she said.

Wiley hopped to the floor. "Mabel, you're weird. I'm going outside. Come on, Peejoe." He stooped to put on his shoes.

Mabel's game was giving me pleasurable goose bumps. "I might stay here awhile," I said.

Wiley gave me his move-your-butt look.

I felt my mouth opening up, saying, "Mabel, I think I want to go out now."

"Go on, then. I don't care."

I followed Wiley outside. Evening was falling all over the lawn.

"Race you to the road," he said.

"But you always beat me," I whined, to distract him—then without warning I took off running, a sneaky head start. It was the only way I ever had a chance in a race against Wiley. The tall weeds concealed ruts and fire-ant hills, but I gained a good lead on him and held it the whole way down the yard. I heard him at my elbow, laughing, pumping to pass me.

His foot snagged mine and we tumbled in the grass all botched up together, rolling over and over, catching weeds in our teeth. We laughed and pounded the earth.

I flopped on my stomach. "Wiley, do you believe in ghosts?"

"What, Mabel? She's fifteen. Girls that age act like that." At fourteen, he was an expert.

"But I felt something in there. I did."

"What did you, get a little hard-on? Mabel's too old for you."

I felt my face redden. "Don't be gross."

"She's kind of skinny. Not exactly my type. Watch out, Peejoe, she's our cousin."

"You think she's play-acting?"

"Listen, there's one thing you'll find out about girls. They are weird, and when they grow up they turn into women."

I looked out across the valley. Wiley could shrug it off, but I knew Mabel was right, there were spirits walking around in that house, spirits and other lingering presences. Uncle Chester standing without saying anything. Aunt Lucille somewhere out in the twinkling distance. Meemaw a hundred miles away, might as well have been a million. Was she looking out her window this moment, thinking of me? I wanted to go home, but I wasn't a little boy. I couldn't cry my way back to her now.

8

Lucille

On the Road

L ucille detested bridges. She held her breath whenever she had to drive across one. As long as she held her breath she knew the bridge would not disintegrate and topple her into the water, car and all. South Mississippi was one terrifying bridge after another, swamps, creeks, and bays interrupted by an occasional patch of dry land. By the time Lucille made it to Louisiana, her back was sweaty and stuck to the seat.

She came out on a bluff at Mandeville, on the north shore of Lake Pontchartrain. A bridge stretched for miles and miles away from this shore, straighter than any line ever drawn by the hand of God.

Lucille pulled the Galaxie to the shoulder to collect her nerves.

The lake was so wide she could not see the far shore. The bridge just kept going and going forever, tailing off in the morning haze.

She fished the map from the glove compartment. Of course she had seen this bridge on the map but she had simply not allowed herself to think about it. Now the truth stretched before her, two lanes, thirty miles long, across a lake as vast as the Gulf of Mexico.

The highway around the lake looked about two hundred miles out of the way. The Southern Crescent left New Orleans for Los Angeles at three-seventeen. Lucille's watch said noon.

She scolded herself: If she wanted to be a star, she would have to do many things more difficult than driving across a bridge. This was only one simple test. Look at everything she'd done so far that she never thought she could do.

She summoned up her courage and drove to the tollbooth. She paid fifty cents for the privilege of driving onto the Huey P. Long Memorial

Causeway—a mighty substantial name for such a skinny bridge. Trucks whipped by at breathtaking speeds.

Lucille clutched the wheel. "Chester, I wish you could see me. Your wife is being so brave."

She locked her eyes on the road. She smelled the salt air but told herself those were green cotton fields stretching out flat and wide on both sides, not water. She switched off the radio to improve her concentration. Talking helped.

"I wish things hadn't turned out this way," she said, "but you know you were always impossible to live with."

At the fifteen-mile marker, the bridge rose way up in the air, soaring up, up . . . Lucille gritted her teeth and drove over the top. She gave thanks for a glimpse of the south shore, a green horizon way in the distance. It faded again as the roadway sank to lake level.

A trucker roared around blasting his indignation, spitting rocks at her windshield.

The last miles crawled by. Lucille stared at the double yellow line and told Chester whatever came into her head. "We never went anywhere our whole lives," she said. "Remember the time we went to Rock City? All the way up there, those signs on the barns saying 'See Rock City, See Seven States,' and when we got there it was raining so hard we couldn't even see across the parking lot. Oh, you got so mad, Jesus God, I thought you would kill us all. Did we even spend the night? No. You turned around and drove us straight home. You wouldn't even let the man put the bumper sticker on the car when you knew the only reason to go to Rock City is to get the damn bumper sticker. You were *always* such a son of a bitch."

After an eternity, the shore came rushing up to meet the road. Lucille had never been so glad to see a shopping center and a bunch of gas stations. She would have stopped to kiss the ground, but there wasn't time.

She was almost done with driving. In the immediate future, all bridges would be the responsibility of the Southern Pacific railroad, and once Lucille got to California and became a star she would hire a chauffeur to take her everywhere.

New Orleans's outskirts were nothing special, motels and used-car lots and billboards: VISIT WORLD FAMOUS MONTELEONE HOTEL, ROYAL ST. HEART OF HISTORIC VIEUX CARRE. DO YOU DRINK JAX BEER?

She planned to abandon the Galaxie on a side street near the station, but first she wanted to buy her ticket and decide what to do about Chester.

She hadn't meant to bring him in the first place, then she thought she'd left him at Mama's. But Chester was not so easy to lose.

She hadn't opened the Tupperware since Mama's house. Probably it would be wiser not to, as long as the press-and-lock seal did its job.

She couldn't very well carry Chester in a lettuce keeper on a train across the country, but leaving him in the car to be discovered by any passing stranger was unthinkable. She might as well have left his body in the toolshed, instead of taking all that trouble to get him into the Frost Queen.

Now that Chester was dead Lucille felt some tiny respect for his head. She had even begun to enjoy his company, in an odd way. She couldn't just stuff him in some garbage can and ride off into the sunset.

She wished she'd thought of all this in the middle of that thirty-mile bridge (though she'd never have worked up the nerve to stop). Now the city was thickening in, big oaks shading the streets, graceful old houses dripping with wisteria. There was no convenient place to dispose of him.

Lucille coasted up to a clutch of Negro children playing kickball on the sidewalk. "Any of you know how to get to the train station?"

"I do," said a boy about ten, very black, in a ragged shirt and cut-off trousers. "I tell you for a dime."

"My word," said Lucille. "Where I come from, colored children don't talk so sassy." She had no time to waste. She found a dime in the crack of the seat and held it up between her fingers. "Now tell me."

"Down yonder three blocks," the boy said, "and turn thisaway. Then you go three mo' blocks, and turn thataway. Just keep going. The station down there."

He reached out for his dime, but he wasn't quick enough. Lucille mashed the pedal to the floor. The Galaxie leaped ahead, tires squealing. The boy jumped back to keep from getting his toes run over.

Lucille laughed at her cleverness for three blocks, turned left, chuckled for three more blocks, turned right. Pretty soon she wasn't laughing. She was lost in a weedy neighborhood of cramped houses, narrow streets running at angles.

Finally she asked a fat woman in front of a liquor store. The woman said "Honey, you ain't even close. Now go back down that way, that's Esplanade . . ."

Lucille thanked her and headed down a tiny street, barely wide enough for the Galaxie. This was New Orleans from the pictures, rowhouses crowded together with lacy cast-iron balconies. When Lucille got to be a star, her dream house would have iron railings just like that, and a leafy green courtyard down a brick walkway.

"Take a look, Chester. Old New Or-leens."

Royal Street spilled out into Canal, a bustling wide boulevard lined with hotels and department stores, glitzy lights flickering in time to the traffic.

Lucille spotted a name she recognized from the fashion pages: Maison Blanche. She had an idea, and halfway across Canal Street she decided that Maison Blanche would be just the place for it. She executed a wildly illegal U-turn against traffic.

Tires howled. Lucille pantomimed "sorry, sorry" and held up her hand across six lanes until she got the Galaxie headed uptown toward the Maison Blanche, trailing a chorus of taxi horns.

She pulled into a big open space at the curb, checked her lipstick, stepped out.

A fire hydrant glared at her.

She wouldn't want any policeman looking in the car and wondering what was in that Tupperware, but there was no time to find a legal parking place. She took the lettuce keeper from the back seat and tucked it under her arm. It felt warm from the sun. "Come on, Chester, we're going shopping."

The hubbub of the street gave way to a civilized sound, the clink and hum of an expensive department store. Lucille breathed the rich mix of perfumes. A polite lady in Misses' Sportswear directed her up the escalator.

She found the hat department past a display of elegant mink coats. They were lovely, and the wad of bills was eating a hole in Lucille's purse: three thousand four hundred dollars in hundreds and fifties, the entire Chester Vinson nest egg, nestled in alongside Chester's blunt-nosed .45 automatic rat-shooting pistol.

Ah, well. Lucille would have no use for a mink coat anyway. It was always sunny and warm in Hollywood.

A silver-haired saleswoman approached with a professional smile.

"Hello," Lucille said, "I am Carolyn Clay. I'm looking for a hat."

"Good afternoon, Miss Clay, my name's Dorothy. Won't you come this way?"

Lucille felt a little thrill: Miss Clay! "I want something big and flouncy," she said. "Do you remember the hat Audrey Hepburn wore, in that movie about Tiffany's?" She realized the woman was staring at the Tupperware container. She set it down on a counter. "My lunch."

"I see. Well, now, let me think, big flouncy hat. We have several . . ."

Lucille rejected the first three—too fussy, all ribbons and trim. She wanted something simple and attractive that would conceal her face, and more important, she wanted a nice big hatbox. Quickly she settled on a wide, wide straw hat, like something Mata Hari's grandmother might wear. Forty dollars. She was all set to put her money down. "What kind of box does it come in?"

"Oh, there's no box," the saleswoman said. "I can put it in a nice shopping bag for you."

"I don't want it if it doesn't come in a box."

"I'm sorry, we only offer hatboxes for our couture lines."

"Well show me those, then."

"I don't think we'd have anything for you in couture." Dorothy's nose went up. Her smile was wearing thin. "Of course, you're welcome to come back and look."

"Or else you could just sell me this hat," Lucille said, "and a box to go with it."

"That's against store policy. Sorry . . ."

She was not at all sorry. She was a big-city bitch who thought she was better than anybody. Lucille had a mind to tell her so, but also she had a train to catch and she badly needed a hatbox for Chester.

She picked him up and stalked after Dorothy into the velvet-curtained couture parlor. Among the furs and cashmere sweaters were six hats on ebony mannequin heads. Most of them were old-lady hats, or too extreme, but one was a simple, broad-brimmed velvet number, rich black with an elegant sprig of gold at the brow.

"That's the latest Chanel," said Dorothy.

Lucille set Chester on a table and adjusted the hat on her head. A spotlight defined three views of her in the mirror; rich velvet, a glint of gold, her face in shadow. It wasn't Audrey Hepburn, it was . . . Ingrid Bergman as a spy, about to step on a train with her forbidden lover and a secret formula.

She ran a finger around the brim. "How much?"

"Four hundred fifty dollars."

"I'll take it. And I want a really nice box." Lucille savored the surprise on the woman's face. Four hundred fifty dollars was four and a half months' house payment, in her old life. But this was her new life. She slit open the envelope with her thumbnail, counted out five one-hundred-dollar bills, furled them in her fingers.

Dorothy returned with an elegant octagonal box of glossy white cardboard, fancied up with black ribbons. Lucille handed over the money.

She lifted the lid and wedged the Tupperware down into the tissue paper. A snug fit. She put the lid back on and tied up the ribbons.

"It's a lovely hat." Dorothy handed over her change and receipt. "You have wonderful taste."

There was nothing like a handful of money to make somebody sing a new tune. Lucille lifted the box by its ribbons. "See you later."

"Thank you. And do come again."

Lucille had never felt so sophisticated as she did walking through that store, click-click-click on her high heels, sweeping people out of her path with her fabulous hat.

She stepped into the street. She saw a cop with his foot propped on the Galaxie's rear bumper, a tow truck backing into position.

She took two steps in that direction, her mouth open to protest, when something cried *No! Don't!* and saved her. She veered away, pulled down the hat, hurried off.

Halfway down the next block, she sidled up to a jewelry store and fished a cigarette from her purse. Her hands trembled the match. She took a drag and blew out the smoke, staring at the gaudy zirconium rings in the window. At last she dared a glance up the street.

The Galaxie's wide nose was tilted into the air on a tow-cable. The cop climbed aboard his motorcycle, and leaned his weight onto the kick-starter.

Lucille's luggage was in that car, all her clothes, makeup, and shoes . . . what else? Registration papers with Chester's name on them. She'd meant to clean out the glove compartment.

Too late.

The tow truck pulled off from the curb. Lucille stood by the jewelry-store window, following the Galaxie with her eyes all the way up Canal Street until it was gone.

Her instinct had saved her. Now her instinct told her to get on that train, get the hell out of town before she got caught. She would sightsee in New Orleans some other time. Already the news of her crime might have traveled here from Alabama.

She spotted a Yellow Cab cruising toward her, and stepped off the curb directly into its path.

The cab squealed to a stop, smoking tires. "What the hell, lady!"

Lucille leaned in. "Can you take me to the train station?"

"Get in before you get killed," said the driver. "What's the matter with you? Are you blind or just crazy?"

She slammed the door. "I'm in a hurry. I don't want to miss my train."

The driver pulled away, shaking his head. It was not a bad-looking head, in Lucille's opinion. Early thirties, maybe thirty-five. A big chiseled chunk of a guy, really, to be driving a cab in New Orleans. His arm on the back seat was so muscled and ripe with blond fur that she wanted to sink in her teeth.

In the mirror he noticed her looking. His jaw moved in a little circle, chewing his gum. "Where you headed?"

"California." She smoothed her skirt. "I'm an actress. I'm going to be on television."

The cab bounded into a district of solemn office buildings. "Are you a star? Should I know your name?"

Lucille smiled at his eyes in the mirror. "I hope you will one day. It's Carolyn Clay."

"What show are you on?"

"'The Beverly Hillbillies.'"

"Oh, my wife and I see that," he said. "She'll be real excited when I tell her."

Lucille spotted the gold band on his finger. "Your wife," she said. "Isn't that sweet. She's a lucky woman."

He grinned. "Nice of you to say that."

Lucille toyed with the hatbox ribbons. If she weren't in such a hurry, she would tell this man to turn off his meter and take her someplace and do all the things to her that he never did to his wife. She imagined hiking her skirt in the back seat and doing it right there with her bare feet pressed against the window.

The first time she and Chester ever did it was in a car, an old broken-down Dodge. It was never exciting again, never once.

Come on, she said silently to the back of his neck. Come get on this train and do it to me all the way to Hollywood.

Oh goodness. The excitement of the big city was getting to her. There was no gray fog of confusion now. This notion was coming out of a clear blue sky.

The driver said, "I guess you make a lot of money at something like that."

"The money's not important," she said. "I do it for the love of performing."

The driver swung into a traffic circle and turned at the sign for UNION PASSENGER TERMINAL. Instead of the big marble train-palace Lucille had imagined, this low-slung modern building looked like the headquarters of an insurance company. Only the masses of taxis and red-coated porters with hand trucks testified that anybody was going anywhere.

"No luggage?" the driver said.

"I travel light." Lucille handed him a five-dollar bill. "Keep the change."

"Thank you, ma'am." It was not her imagination, there was something warm and regretful in his eyes. "I'll keep an eye out for you on TV."

Lucille thought what the hell, I'll never see him again. She puckered her lips and blew a kiss from the end of her fingers. "So long, honey." She stepped out into the sunshine with the hatbox.

He grinned at her all the way to the door.

A porter swept it open. Lucille hesitated. Two black-and-white police cars sat among the taxis at the curb.

She tugged down the hat and hurried in.

The terminal was brightly fluorescent and modern. Her heart speeded up. Suppose those cops were looking for her? She had spilled it all out to Mama and Peejoe—her plan, New Orleans, the train. Suppose the local police had arranged a stakeout? This hat was no real disguise. If the cops had a picture of Lucille, she was about to walk right into their hands bearing Chester's head in a hatbox.

Lucille steeled herself. She had no choice. Her car was gone. The audition was a week from Tuesday. She had to risk it.

She walked to the ticket window. "One ticket, one way to Los Angeles, please."

A bespectacled man said "Name?"

"Carolyn Clay," she said. "C-L-A-Y." She let her eyes drift around the big room.

There they were—two cops in blue, standing just inside the tunnel that led to the tracks.

"One way, ninety-four dollars."

"How much does it cost for a sleeper?"

"Lemme see if there's one available." He disappeared.

Lucille toyed with her hat. The cops seemed nonchalant, arms folded, talking, but they were keeping an eye on the passing stream of travelers.

"Yes ma'am, there's one sleeper left, that would be two hundred eleven dollars one way to Los Angeles. You want to take it?"

"Yes. I'll pay cash." Lucille fumbled with her purse. Her gaze traveled back across the room.

One of the cops stopped a young blond woman, and asked a question.

Lucille's heart bounded up in her chest.

Think on your feet, now, think like a secret agent in a sticky situation. Move calmly. Attract no attention.

"Hold that for me. I need to make a phone call." She marched across the shiny floor to a row of telephone booths, stepped into the one on the end.

She picked up the phone, pretended to drop in a dime. She had a clear view of the cop smiling, chatting up the blond girl.

Another blonde came along then, a young thing of nineteen or twenty, dragging a heavy steamer trunk across the floor. The second cop motioned her aside. He made her open the trunk, and poked around inside before waving her on.

An old man walked by, and two matronly brunettes with suitcases. The cops barely gave them a glance.

Now why would two cops hang around the train station on a Friday afternoon, picking young blond women out of a crowd?

Maybe they just liked blondes.

Unlikely.

"Okay, see you, thank you very much," Lucille said to the dial tone, and hung up. She gathered her hatbox and purse, stepped from the booth and walked out of the station without a glance at the ticket window.

Possibly she was being silly. Those cops could be looking for anyone, they could be picking up dates for tonight. She didn't know what to think. She had never been a wanted woman before.

Instinct told her to flee, find some other way, don't chance it, don't let them ask you any questions.

She checked the line of taxis; her muscled dream driver wasn't in any of them. She got in with a swarthy Greek-looking man in his fifties and said, "Take me to the French Quarter."

Neither of them said another word until the driver told her the fare and let her out at the corner of Canal and Bourbon. Now that was a famous street, Bourbon Street, famous for sin. The name had a full-blown sour mash Jack Daniel's taste on the tongue. Lucille fashioned the ribbons on the hatbox into a handle, and set out in her heels down the uneven sidewalk.

The sight of two Negro boys tap-dancing for pennies made her conscious of her aching feet. She looked for some quiet place where she might have a drink and get her thoughts herded up together, try to figure out what on earth to do next. She was not much of a drinker but she truly could use a belt of something right now.

Shrill trumpets echoed down the street, bars and striptease parlors clamoring for attention. Barkers shouted unspeakable things in the doorways. Semi-naked women posed in bleary posters. "Come on in, little lady, I'll buy you a drink." The Famous Door looked respectable enough, but a Dixieland band was thumping away so loud Lucille couldn't hear herself think.

She wandered on down the street until she spotted an ancient Creole cottage on the brink of collapse, with ragged gaps where plaster had fallen away to reveal the old bricks. A sign announced JEAN LAFITTE'S BLACKSMITH SHOP.

Inside looked cool and dark. The sound of a piano floated through the open window.

Lucille went in. A very old woman hunched over a battered piano in the corner, rippling out "Just in Time" with gnarled fingers. She looked old enough to have played here since the place opened.

A rough-looking bartender in a crimson Hawaiian shirt stood washing glasses at the horseshoe-shaped bar. Half a dozen people sat around at little tables drinking beer, reading newspapers in the slats of light falling through the shutters. No one glanced up.

Lucille took a seat at the bar, placed the box on the stool beside her. At the end of the bar two paunchy conventioneers in knit shirts laughed boisterously. "The wrong end of the stick!" the man in the green shirt kept repeating, and every time he said it his friend busted up laughing all over again. "The wrong end of the stick!"

Lucille studied the backs of their necks, thinking how some men truly deserve to have their heads cut off.

The bartender noticed her eyeing the men, and came over. "What do you want?"

"A drink of some kind." Lucille drew her compact from her purse. "What's a real New Orleans kind of drink?"

"Herbsaint," the man said. "Or a Sazerac, or a Hurricane."

Lucille didn't recognize any of those, but she did not want to appear unworldly, so she ordered a Tom Collins.

The little bent-over woman finished her song, and paused while everyone patted hands politely. Then she launched into "What's New, Pussycat" with surprising gusto, thumping away and making funny little cat-meows on the high keys.

The bartender plunked a tall red drink on a napkin, dropped in a slice of orange and a cherry, and slid it across the bar. "Two-fifty. You're not a local girl, are you?"

Lucille blotted her lipstick on a napkin. "Just passing through."

The bartender regarded her with a cool gaze. "That drink is two-fifty."

She gave him a five and told him to keep the change.

That only served to make him suspicious. "The lady throws her money around," he said. "Listen, I don't mean any offense, but you know you can't work in here."

The conventioneers stumbled over another punch line and exploded in laughter.

"I beg your pardon?" said Lucille.

"We don't allow working girls." He planted his hands on his hips. "This ain't that kind of place. Get my drift?"

"I'm not looking for a job. I'm an actress."

"Yeah, right, and I'm Fred Astaire." He produced her five-dollar bill and flopped it out on the counter. "You take your money, drink your drink, and take off."

All at once Lucille realized what was in his filthy mind. "Oh my goodness," she said, "you think I'm—you think I'm a—why, you *bastard!*" Without thinking she picked up the Tom Collins and flung it all over his shirt.

His face flushed. He started around the bar.

"What's New, Pussycat?" ended abruptly.

Lucille opened her purse and pulled out Chester's pistol. "Don't you come one step closer."

"Whoa, lady, hold on!" The bartender stopped where he was and held up his dripping hands. "No harm done!"

Lucille flicked the grip safety with her thumb. "How dare you," she sputtered, "how dare you insult me. What do I look like to you? This hat cost four hundred and fifty dollars!"

"Listen," he stammered, "it was a simple misunder—"

She squeezed the trigger. The gun exploded. The piano lid fell with a *whanng!*

People scrambled under tables.

Smoke and commotion, but no blood. Lucille had shot a hole in the floor between his feet. Now she brought the gun up on a direct line with his manhood. The astounded bartender covered himself with his hands.

Lucille said, "Do you have a car?"

"Yeah, sure, right outside. Nice new Caddy. I'll take you anywhere you want to go. Only—"

"Give me the keys." She held out the pistol. "I have seven more bullets."

He dug in his pocket with a sorrowful look, as if he were about to betray his best friend. "Just don't shoot anymore."

Lucille's ears sang from the explosion. Nudging the air with the gun, she snatched the keyring from his hand. The gun made her powerful. "Get down on the floor."

"Jesus, man, what did you put in her drink?" said the conventioneer behind the ice machine.

The bartender dropped to his knees. "Don't take my *car*," he pleaded.

"All the way down! Put your head on the floor." Lucille was amazed at herself. She hadn't planned this but here she was doing it, and by God she was good at it, too. Moving on instinct. Her natural acting ability coming through. One little bang and she had them all cowering in terror.

The cash drawer stood open. *What the hell.* Lucille leaned over to yank a half-inch of twenties from under the metal tongue. She grabbed her hatbox and her purse and backed to the door, waving the gun.

"Listen, buster," she said, "you ought to learn the difference between a whore and a lady."

She took three steps to the curb, tossed the gun and the hatbox through the open window of the shiny maroon Coupe de Ville, and jumped in. The key fit. The engine roared to life. Lucille slammed it in Drive and shrieked off down the street. She made a clean getaway.

9

Peejoe

Industry

I t took Chester two days to thaw out enough so that Dove could perform the autopsy required by law. By that time it was plain that Lucille was not coming back with his head, so Dove decided to embalm and bury the rest of Chester as quietly as possible. "I guess we could have an open casket," he said with a weary smile. "If we opened just the bottom half."

He enlisted Wiley and Mabel and me to go along as mourners. Earlene had a United Daughters of the Confederacy meeting, and anyway, she said, it would be hypocritical of her to go. "I'm not saying Chester deserved what he got," she said, "but I'm not going to stand over him boo-hooing, either."

We put on our best clothes and piled into the white hearse. Wiley rode in back with Uncle Chester's casket and three pots of orange chrysanthemums. I sat in front beside Mabel, pale and ladylike in her black high-necked dress.

We drove to Meadow Acres Memorial Park, one of the cemeteries established by our daddy before he died. "I remember when this was just a cow pasture," said Dove.

To me it still looked like a cow pasture, with a plaster Jesus and a few scrawny crepe myrtles and a trailer park just past the fence. Bronze markers were laid flat in the grass instead of headstones, for easier mowing.

Besides Milton, who'd come early to supervise the backhoe, nine people had showed up to mark Chester's passing—colleagues from Johnson's Hardware, assorted ladies of the Cornelia Baptist condolence committee. They clucked and fussed over Wiley and me, saying how brave we were. After they found out we weren't Chester's children they ignored us.

I went to peer into the grave. The backhoe had sheared clean walls in the clay and left teeth marks on the floor. It was dark down there. A shiver ran its finger up my back.

Dove introduced Wiley and me to Preacher Nathan, a wrinkled old man in a long frock coat, squinting through thick spectacles like Mister Magoo.

For some reason, my name got stuck in the preacher's mind. Midway through his funeral oration he began saying "Peter" when he meant to say "Chester." He was burying me! "We should not fear for the soul of Peter, for he was a good man . . ." He kept on like that right through the benediction. Nobody made a move to correct him. Blood rushed to my face. Dove squeezed my shoulder as if to say *never mind, I know you're alive.*

I looked at all the people praying with their eyes closed, their faces all pious and silly and vulnerable. Wiley wasn't praying, either. He was watching me with a tight little grimace, trying not to laugh.

I stuck out my tongue.

Dove bopped me with the heel of his hand.

"Amen," said the preacher, releasing us all.

"Pretty funny, Peejoe," said Wiley.

Mabel said, "I didn't think it was funny. It gives me the willies."

"Aw, it didn't bother him," Wiley said, "did it, Peejoe."

I shook my head no, but it felt awfully strange to hear my own last rites spoken aloud.

Milton pressed a button. The hydraulic lift whirred and jerked. Uncle Chester descended into the earth.

Everyone started back to their cars. I stayed to watch the coffin settle in the floor of the hole. The backhoe operator cranked his engine, and filled in the dirt over Chester.

Sheriff Doggett was waiting for us at the funeral home. "They've recovered her car," he said. "New Orleans police picked it up Friday, routine parking violation."

Dove winced. "The head?"

"Nope. A couple of suitcases. Lots of shoes."

"That's her, then. Any word from the train station?"

"Nothing. They've had a lookout on every train since Friday. I been kindly surprised, those fellows are real damn cooperative down there, for a bunch of Catholics."

Dove turned to us. "Y'all go in and change your clothes."

"Not him." The sheriff pointed to me. "I want to talk to him."

"Mabel, Wiley, run on."

They peered at me curiously and went inside.

"Listen, son." The sheriff crouched down. "When your Aunt Lucille talked to you that day, did she happen to say how she killed him?"

"No, sir," I lied.

"Did she say what she did with the, you know, the knife or whatever she used to cut off his head?"

"No sir."

"Did she say anybody's name, anybody at all she was planning to see in California?"

I remembered the name Harry Hall just fine but I kept it dangling right there in my head where the sheriff could not get at it. "No, sir, I don't remember." I didn't want to tell him anything. I wanted Aunt Lucille to get away.

"She mention any reason she might be going out to California?"

"She wanted to be in the movies."

"The movies?"

"She's always had this daydream about it," Dove explained. "She's been in a lot of these local kind of things, you know, church plays."

"Son, did she mention any place at all, any movie or the name of a company?"

"I don't think so," I said, picturing Elly May Clampett at the cement pond with her critters.

"Did she have a gun, any kind of weapon?"

"I didn't see one."

The sheriff turned to Dove. "A white female fitting her description pulled a forty-five automatic on a bartender in the French Quarter yesterday and stole his car."

"Oh that's ridiculous," Dove said. "Baby Sister wouldn't do that."

"Waaal, I believe she did. They found a box of forty-five cartridges in her car. We're operating under the assumption she is armed and dangerous," said Doggett. "We'll bring her in. I think you better do what you can to help us."

"What do you want me to do?"

"She's bound to call you. She'll see the story in the papers, she'll want to know what we're doing to find her. Just say whatever it takes to bring her back in. I don't care what you say." He climbed in his car, rolled down the window. "I'll give you ten to one she's gone from New Orleans. Bet she spotted our little stakeout and got scared. I'll call you if I hear anything. You do the same."

"Thanks for coming to tell me, John."

The sheriff nodded and backed down the drive.

Dove put his hand on my shoulder. "You know, Peter Joseph . . . anything Baby Sister might have told you, you can tell me. I wouldn't necessarily have to tell the sheriff."

"His name is Harry Hall," I blurted. "The man she was going to see. Can they put me in prison for lying?"

"Not unless you're under oath," Dove said. "Anything else?"

His calm washed over me. I wanted to tell him everything. I knew he would look after me. "I don't want them to catch her, Uncle Dove. I don't want her to sit in the electric chair. I mean, it's terrible what she did, but it won't make it any better if they kill her too, will it?"

"I don't expect they'll kill her," Dove said. "Tell you the truth, I don't expect they'll catch her."

"You don't?"

"Peter Joseph, you forget. I grew up with Lucille. I know her. She's a clever girl, had to be, to survive in the house with all us boys. She never got anything unless she went and took it for herself."

"Do you think she really stole a car?"

"Absolutely, I wouldn't put it past her," said Dove. "If Baby Sister needed a car she would get one, and nothing could stop her. I tell you something else. I bet she's having a great time off by herself, no kids . . . I bet she's living it up. Hope she is. Because if they do happen to catch her, that's where the fun stops."

"Sweet Pea, is that you? How you getting along down there? Are you being nice for Earlene?"

"Yes ma'am."

I had never spoken to Meemaw on the telephone, never been far enough away for that. She sounded elderly and unfamiliar over the wire. "Dove said the funeral went all right. I wish I could have been there with you, honey."

I told her all about the preacher's mistake, Sheriff Doggett and his questions.

"They've been out here asking me, too," she said. "Remember, Peejoe, you don't have to tell them any more than they ask you. Use your head. Lucille was defending herself."

"Meemaw, when can we come home?"

"I don't know, sweetie. It's hard here right now. These poor babies . . ." Her voice trailed off. "Peejoe, put Dove back on now."

He took the phone. "Yeah, Mama. Mm-hmm. Well, I know, but I can't tell him how to run his—what? I know, but he's also a witness. I know, I know. I keep thinking she'll call. I'm sure she's all right . . ."

I wandered out of the kitchen, pondering what Meemaw had said. *You don't have to tell them* . . . Suddenly, Lucille's little bedtime story in Meemaw's side yard seemed very important. She had confided in me and nobody else, while Meemaw was inside calling Dove. Only I heard her tell how she had killed Chester, and why.

I wandered downstairs. The clock ticked. Faint organ music tweedled along its continuous loop. A solid *thwack!*—outside, Wiley's bat meeting the ball. Bluejays racked the air with their cries.

Lie. Make up a story. Meemaw would never say that, but I heard it in her voice. She wanted Lucille to escape, just like I did.

Chester was dead. We couldn't help him. Lucille had done this terrible thing, but she was our family, and that was more important now. It was our job to save her.

I peered around the velvet curtain. Mabel sat in the casket room, talking to herself.

"I cannot believe she buried me in this dress," she said. "I hated this dress. She knew I hated it, I never wore it, not once. It makes me look fat. She was just waiting for me to die so she could humiliate me this way."

Her voice shaded into someone else, someone deeper. "I know," she said. "They buried me in a nightgown. Can you imagine? A nightgown. As if I didn't have the good sense to get dressed."

My neck hairs prickled up. I peeked again to make sure no one else was in there.

Her eyes drifted open dreamily. "Oh hey, Peejoe. Did you hear them?"

"I heard you," I said. "Who are you talking to?"

She smiled. "That's Mrs. Morton and Mrs. Stubbs. Mrs. Stubbs is the one with the kitten."

"Have you ever seen 'em?"

"They're real shy," Mabel said. "They don't like to show themselves."

10

Peejoe

Industry

I suppose Earlene's cooking would not have seemed so bad if I hadn't eaten at Meemaw's table all my life. Earlene had a thing for modern convenience foods. If it didn't come in a can, or frozen, or in a box with directions, she wasn't interested. We ate Pop-Tarts in the morning, Chef Boyardee ravioli at noon, Tater Tots and Mrs. Paul's fish sticks at night. Earlene didn't care whether we ate it or not. Once she'd heated it up and slapped it out there, she considered she had done her part. Usually Dove dined alone at the table while the rest of us sprawled in front of the TV with plates in our laps.

This was Wiley's definition of good eating. Also Wiley had a sweet tooth and all of Earlene's meals turned out sweet one way or another, even the frozen French fries, even the Campbell's alphabet soup. I pined for Meemaw's black-eyed peas and cornbread and fried chicken and the fat slices of tomato from her garden. Wiley said I was stupid, that was country food.

I admit the TV dinners fascinated me: two salty pieces of chicken with bones so soft you could eat through them, chewy nuggets of yellow corn, a triangle of mashed potatoes like buttered air, and a brown-colored apple thing in the corner that always tasted salty from the potatoes.

Walter Cronkite was telling about the astronauts floating in a giant water tank to practice being weightless. They looked happy as dolphins doing spins, blowing bubbles, fooling around. I pretended I was an astronaut eating my TV dinner in orbit around the earth. I cleaned out each aluminum compartment with my finger before moving on to the next.

The telephone rang.

Earlene answered: "Hello? Oh, hold on, he's right here." She covered the mouthpiece. "Don't talk too long, Dove, I'm expecting a call from Myrtle Yelverton about the Azalea Club luncheon."

Dove wiped his fingers, and took the phone. "Yello, this Dove Bullis. Oh hey, J.D. How you?" His face grew serious. "Oh, I'm sorry to hear that, I sure am, she was a fine lady. When did it—uh huh. No kidding. Well, don't do a thing, I'll be there in fifteen minutes. All right. Goodbye." He hung up. "J.D. Eldridge's mother."

"Aw no," said Earlene. "What happened?"

"She fell off a ladder and hit her head. They said she was out in the yard trying to pick peaches."

"At this time of year?"

"Mm-hmm. And it was a pine tree." He rinsed his hands under the tap. "Poor lady's been out of her mind now for nearly a year. They found her three weeks ago sitting in the chicken coop without a stitch of clothes. I guess it's a blessing she finally passed. You boys want to go?"

I jumped up: "Sure!" Dove had been out on several coroner calls in the nights since we arrived in Industry, but this was the first time he'd asked us along.

Wiley made a noncommittal noise and stretched flatter on the sheepskin rug.

The phone rang again.

"Come on, Wiley, go with us."

"I bet it's nothing but a bunch of folks weepin' and wailin'," said Wiley. "I've seen enough of that for a while. I'd rather stay here and watch TV."

"Sure, Myrtle, she's right here," Dove said. "Hang on a minute." He buttoned his collar and reached for his necktie. "Peter Joseph, run tell Milton to get ready for Miz Eldridge. I'll be down in a minute, meet you at the car."

"Y'all throw your plates in the garbage before you go." Earlene uncovered the phone. "Myrtle! How are you, darling?"

Milton lived in a small room under the stairs, between the laying-out parlors and the casket display room. I knocked softly.

His slippers made a scuffing sound. He opened the door a few inches, releasing the aroma of frying pork. "Why hello, boy!" He grinned as if I was the best surprise he'd had all day. His open workshirt revealed the sag of his chest, a shine of sweat in his silvery chest-hair. Patty sausages sizzled behind him on a hotplate.

"Hey, Milton. Your supper smells good."

"Want to come in and have some?"

"No thanks, we had TV dinners. Listen, some lady died and Uncle Dove says you're supposed to get ready for her."

"I sho will. Is she here now?"

"We're going to get her."

"Well, I reckon that gives me time to eat," he said. "Thank you kindly, young son."

"See you, Milton." I skipped down the hall, through the mortuary, out to the white hearse.

Now I would see what being a funeral director was all about. I would be very quiet and pay close attention and maybe Dove would let me help.

I climbed in. "Aren't we taking a casket?"

"No, we'll bring her on back, this is what we call a removal." He steered down the drive. "You got to embalm 'em before you put 'em in a nice casket like J.D. Eldridge is going to buy."

"How do you know he is?"

"Because I'm gonna sell it to him. His daddy worked for the railroad, so his mama's got a good policy all paid for. And J.D.'s not a poor man. He can kick in a little something extra to make it nice. He's always been partial to his mama."

"You know all that just from talking on the phone?"

"It's my business to know everybody in town," said Dove. "You got to know how old their folks are, how much insurance they carry. You can't make people die any faster than they do, so you got to maximize the funeral dollar."

We drove through the darkened town square, out the Old Goshen Road. You can't make people die any faster than they do . . . it was something, to think I could improve Dove's business by knocking off a few old folks around town. The idea fired my imagination: a funeral director's best friend is the murderer, the reckless driver, the freak accident, the stray bullet, the incurable germ. Also it was exciting to do a job nobody else wanted. It was all very well for people to turn their heads and pretend that death didn't happen, but when it did, they called Dove to come take care of the details. And he brought me along to help.

"Can you teach me?"

"Teach you what, son?"

"How to be a funeral director. That's what I'm gonna be when I grow up."

"Oh, Peter Joseph, I hope not." He ran his hand through his thinning hair. "You gotta be a rocket scientist or a great composer or something.

You've got the smarts for it, you'n Wiley both. You can be anything in this world."

I had never considered the possibility that Dove was not completely happy in the funeral business. "What's wrong with your job? Don't you like it?"

"It's not so bad. The work is steady, you're pretty much your own boss. You got to like being around dead people, though. It really gets to some guys."

"Not me, I'm brave. I already helped you with Uncle Chester, remember?"

"You sure did. I was proud of you." He dug down in his pocket and came up with a quarter. "Here. Buy yourself a Co-Cola at the pool tomorrow."

"Thanks." I tucked it away. "I heard Mabel talking to her ghosts again this morning."

"I wouldn't pay too much attention. Mabel's got some wild ideas," he said. "Okay now, this is it."

Lights blazed from every window of the Eldridges' brick ranch-style house. The yard was jammed with cars. Two men waited under a porch light.

"Keep in mind, the lady ain't been dead but an hour or two," Dove said. "The family's liable to be upset. Don't say anything, try to keep your face ordinary. Just stay right behind me and keep still."

"Can I help?"

He smiled. "You're keeping me company, that's a big help right there. This gets kind of lonesome sometimes."

A toppled stepladder and a straw basket lay at the foot of a pine tree, just beyond the front stoop. Dove backed the hearse to the steps, and climbed out. "Hello, J.D."

I got out behind him, trying to blend with the shadows.

The taller man came down two steps to shake Dove's hand. "I can't believe it, Dove." His voice was unsteady. "Mama's *gone*. . . ."

Dove patted his shoulder. "I know, J.D., it's a terrible time. We're here to help. Peter Joseph, climb in and unsnap the snaps on those front wheels, would you?"

I did as he said, thankful to get out from under the awful blankness in that man's eyes. I freed the stretcher, walked it out of the hearse on my knees.

Mr. Eldridge took my end from me. The second man held the door. The living room was crowded with Eldridges young and old, standing around watching TV, leaned against the stone fireplace, sprawled on the L-shaped Naugahyde sofa. When we came in everyone glanced up from "Hootenanny." Their faces were closed, uneasy.

I hurried after Dove.

Mrs. Eldridge lay under a white sheet on a four-poster bed. Dove cranked the stretcher to mattress height, and leaned over.

"Don't hurt her!"

"Don't worry, J.D." Gently Dove turned back the sheet.

The only light came from one dim lamp on an antique dresser. The dead woman's hair was a stark white shock standing straight up, mouth gaping open, cheeks sunken, eyes staring. She looked like some horrible movie monster, laughing or screaming.

Dove closed her eyes with two fingers, and brought her jaw together. His touch was so tender—he paused a moment to smooth her hair. Her mouth dropped open again.

"It won't stay shut," Mr. Eldridge said.

Wiley would be sorry when I told him what he'd missed.

"All right now, J.D., I'm going to lift under her shoulders, and I want you to take her feet. We'll just ease her onto the stretcher, bring the sheet with us. Ready? Peter Joseph, hold it still. One, two—"

They lifted her onto the gurney. Dove drew the sheet over her face. "Anybody see her fall?"

"No. We just found her out there."

"Doesn't look like she hit her head. She must have had a heart attack or a stroke maybe. I'm sure she never knew."

"Oh, Mama . . ." Mr. Eldridge's voice thickened. "Oh Jesus, I've prayed for this day, and now—God, I didn't know it would be like this." He sank to a chair, buried his face in his hands.

Enthusiastic TV applause floated in. A telephone rang.

"J.D., we'll take her on out now." Dove's voice was colorless, almost impersonal. I sensed him backing off to give the man room. "Why don't you come on to the house later and we'll see about the arrangements. Come about ten, or else call me." He cranked down the stretcher and motioned me to the other end.

Everyone looked up again when we rolled Mrs. Eldridge through. A lady in curlers called from the kitchen—"Mr. Bullis? Telephone."

"Thank you, ma'am, I'll be right there." Dove backed through the door. The man who'd been waiting with Mr. Eldridge helped us lift the stretcher into the hearse, but we could have done it ourselves. The old lady was weightless.

"Peter Joseph, fasten her down and wait for me."

I locked the stretcher one wheel at a time. I felt like a bigshot performing this duty while that man watched me from the porch. I closed the tailgate, returned his respectful nod, and went to the front seat to wait.

Dove came back in a minute. "We've got to make a stop on the way home. A colored boy died in Dog Junction. I've got to fill out the certificate."

He drove a mile toward town and turned off on a rutted dirt lane. The headlight beams bounced in the trees. I glanced back to make sure Mrs. Eldridge was still on her stretcher.

"You did good back there, son. You got good nerves."

A cat skittered across the road, showing weird jewels instead of eyes. We drove past the city dump into Dog Junction, the poorest of the Negro settlements scattered around Industry. Through the windows of the shacks you could see people living by the light of one bulb. We jounced along until Dove had to slow up for a commotion in his headlights. People crowded the street in front of one house. An old black hearse stood in the yard beneath a flickering streetlight.

We glided to a stop. A woman burst from the crowd and threw herself across the hood of our car, shrieking, pounding with her hands.

Two men came to drag her away.

Dove let out a breath through his teeth. "I should warn you, colored folks can get kindly emotional. You gonna be all right?"

"I think so."

"You can stay in the car."

"I want to help you."

The keening got louder when Dove opened the door, three or four women in the yard, more inside. Men stood around murmuring; their consolations dwindled away in thin air. Everyone fell back to clear out a path for us. Some of the children wailed with their mothers. Others stood stock-still staring with frightened wide eyes, as if Dove and I were agents of the devil.

A large woman on her knees blocked the door to the back room, letting out great whoops, pounding the floor with the flat of her hand.

"This is Mattie, his mama," a man said behind me.

Dove made a move to go around her. The woman staggered to her feet, slapping both hands at him. "Naw naw naw naw, don't take my baby, oh don't take him, oh naw . . ."

Dove stood with his arms up, accepting her blows. "I've just come to see about him. I'm not gonna take him." He caught her wrists, holding her off in an awkward kind of dance. I wanted to run for the car, to get out of this smell of anguish and sweat. I had never imagined grief could be such a spectacle.

Skillfully Dove handed Mattie over to a young woman, and we slipped through the door to the back room.

One lightbulb hung on a chain, attached with a long string to the dresser so that someone groping in the dark could find it. On the wall, a pair of framed photographs: John F. Kennedy and Martin Luther King.

The dead boy lay on a cast-iron bed, naked from the waist up. I thought he was just a boy but I could not be sure; his head and face were a glistening mess of bruises and wounds. Blood from his right ear pooled on the pillow and dripped down the side of the mattress. His arm flopped out at an unnatural angle, like a doll's broken arm. My stomach flopped over. I looked away.

Dove said, "Jesus H. Christ."

A deep preacherly voice from the shadows: "Good evening, Mr. Bullis." The man who stepped forward was much smaller than his orotund voice: dapper and anxious, with close-cropped fuzzy hair, bowtie and glasses and a prim moustache. Who was that comic on TV? Wally Cox. If Wally Cox was thirty years older, and a Negro, he would look something like this.

A boy stood behind him in the shadows, a dark lean boy with stunned eyes, strong bones in his face.

"Evening, Nehemiah," said Dove. "What happened here?"

"This is David Jackson," he said. "And that's his brother Taylor back there."

In the shadows the gaunt boy flinched, and looked at his shoes. The whites of his eyes were yellow. Blood on his shirt.

"They dumped David off the back of a pickup truck. He was already dead when Taylor found him."

"Who did it?"

"The same ones," said Nehemiah. "The sheriff's buddies. You know who they are."

Dove said "Was he in some kind of trouble?"

"He had done some work with the voter registration."

"Mm-hmm." Dove bent over the bed, touching the boy in his delicate, tentative way. He turned the body with his hands, pressing here and there, exploring with his fingers. "Say his name's David?"

"David Jackson. He's my sister's oldest son." I could see the man struggling to maintain his reserve.

Dove let out a long sigh. "God, Nehemiah, I'm sorry, I didn't know he was kin to you. Did you call the sheriff?"

"He said to call you. Said it wasn't his department." The little man shook out a white sheet, snapped it in the air. It settled over the body like a deflating balloon.

"What do you want me to write here?" said Dove.

"Well sir, I don't want to cause any trouble—"

"And neither do I. I'm going to write this as gross head trauma, multiple skull fractures probably resulting from a fall from a vehicle. Pending further investigation. Does that set all right with you?"

"That hardly tells the whole story, Mr. Bullis, do you think?" Nehemiah's eyes flashed. He tugged at his collar with a finger. "You and I have had this conversation before. Is this just going to keep happening?"

I heard Dove's pen scribbling, gales of weeping from the front room. Dark stains grew on the sheet.

"You know I've got nothing to do with enforcing the law, Nehemiah. I'm here to sign off on cause of death and that's it."

The little man drew himself up. "Perhaps you could use some more descriptive phrase, then. Perhaps 'lynching.'"

Taylor Jackson looked up from his shoes.

"You don't know that," Dove said. "Neither do I. That's up to the sheriff." Dove signed the certificate, and tore off a copy for Nehemiah. "All I know is, if this boy got mixed up in the wrong kind of trouble, I'm not surprised he wouldn't have too many friends around here. I'm awful sorry, Nehemiah. I am. I'll ask around. Let me know what you hear."

"Yes sir. I will do that." Nehemiah Thomas tucked the certificate in his jacket, and shook Dove's hand. "Fine-looking fellow," he said, meaning me.

"This is my nephew, Peter Joseph. He wants to learn the business."

"An admirable ambition, son. There's always room for new men in the field."

"Come on, Peter Joseph, let's go."

As I started for the door, the boy's eyes flickered up and caught mine, just for a moment—I felt a flash of heat. Pure hatred welled up in him and overflowed and splashed on me, burning me. Somehow the look in his eyes made me feel responsible for what lay between us on the bed.

Dove took my hand. I followed him through the room where the people were crying. David Jackson's mother was stretched out on the floor, a wet towel on her face. Two young girls held her hands, soothing her.

Outside, the neighbors muttered and stirred to let us through. We got in the hearse with Mrs. Eldridge and drove off down the bumpety lane.

"Why aren't we taking him back with us?"

"Nehemiah Thomas will take care of him," Dove said. "He runs the colored funeral home. On the south side of town."

"You can't take colored people to your place?"

Dove squinted ahead, trying to see through the darkness. "Well, I could, but that would take away Nehemiah's business. And some folks don't want their kin in the parlor next to somebody colored. I don't see where it makes any difference to the deceased, but you can't change the way people think."

"Who killed him, Uncle Dove?"

"I don't know, son. I have some ideas. There's some rough men in this county. They won't ever catch anybody."

"Howcome?"

"They catch who they want to catch."

I pondered this. "What kind of trouble was he in?"

"You know who Martin Luther King is, don't you?"

"Sure. His picture was on the wall." King was by far the most impressive-sounding Negro I had ever heard, with the recent exception of Nehemiah Thomas.

"Well some of his people have been poking around our courthouse down here, and people in Industry don't like it a bit. There's a sign out on the Dothan Highway that says 'Martin Lucifer Coon, don't let the sun set on you here.' If that gives you some idea. Folks are so scared of what's happened where he's been, up in Montgomery, up in Selma. It's like he brings a spreading disease, you know? And people in this town want to make damn sure it doesn't spread here."

I wasn't sure what Martin Luther King had to do with the dead, battered boy in the little house, the silent rage of his brother in the shadows. Was it a crime to put King's picture on the wall?

I felt scalded by the clouds of emotion rolling through those rooms. Those people were possessed by their grief. They gave themselves over to it, all the way. It scared me, how cold my own heart seemed in the presence of such a great sorrow.

11

Lucille

On the Road

At first Lucille liked Texas much better than Louisiana. The land dried out. Her nerves began to recover from all the bridges.

Then she passed a sign that said EL PASO 748, and she thought she might faint.

She wrestled the map with her free hand. Seven hundred forty-eight miles just to get across Texas? And that wasn't even halfway to California! Impossible! She had never conceived of such distances. Since she fled New Orleans she had stopped three times for coffee and twice to pee, and here it was only Houston, ten o'clock at night, thousands of miles yet to go. She felt the gray fog beginning to descend, and a strange energy in it, like someone reaching over her shoulder, taking the wheel. Probably shouldn't be driving, probably should find a motel and stop for some rest, but the rhythm of the white lines and her tires on the highway lulled her into the luminous cloud.

Someone else drove the car. Lucille held the wheel. Somehow the miles worked themselves out under her tires, hundreds of miles of flat Texas, hour after hour. Dimly she remembered that Texas once had been a country, and dear Jesus, it was truly big enough to qualify.

Somewhere west of Luling, she lost her place.

A dream came down on her, a sitting-up wide-awake dream of the time she was pregnant, her first time. The baby was weeks overdue. Lucille was a blimp with legs, a swollen weepy despondent mess, she didn't want the child, the weight squeezed her bladder so she had to pee every second. She hated the child and the father of the child. Her figure would be ruined. She would never be a star. It was a fact of life: stretch marks were forever.

Her mother said she could have had the child long ago, but she was holding it in her womb with all those depressing thoughts.

Finally her water broke and Chester took her to the hospital. Somehow the dinky twenty-room hospital in Industry became a glossy modern complex, an impersonal place with endless shiny hallways. Nurses placed Lucille in a wheelchair and rushed her down one corridor after another, taking blind turns and coming up against dead-end walls.

One wall slid away. Twenty people in white surgical gowns stood waiting for her. A soothing voice said "Come in, Lucille, it's time for your baby" and she felt the life inside clawing at her, a terrible nauseous pain threatening to split her open like a watermelon. "Get it out of me!" she cried. The people in white swarmed around her and lifted her up on their shoulders. They carried her into a vast room, laid her down on a white marble table. The light blinded her. The child clawed to get out and the doctor said, "Push, take a deep breath and push!" the incredible bulk of the head coming through oh such pain, such a terrible thing.

It was born. It was not a girl or a boy but a thing. It sat up in the palm of the doctor's hand, fully formed but so tiny and gray, an ancient expression of rage on its face. It screamed at her: "Get away from me, Mother. I hate you!"

Lucille recoiled in horror and fell from the table. She clutched a white sheet to her breasts and ran for her life. The baby scrambled after her on all fours, chasing her, calling out foul accusations.

That was the dream of Texas. When she became aware that the sun was well up and she was alive and Lucille, and not being chased by a monster baby, she was crossing the state line into New Mexico, Land of Enchantment.

This land was flat as a tabletop, harsh dry and white under a flawless blue sky. Lucille did not remember stopping for gas but she must have, the gauge showed three-quarters full.

She rubbed her eyes. What a strange dream to have while you're driving! No doubt she had been a menace to other motorists but she felt fine now, wide-awake and refreshed. No need for coffee. Her head felt wide open, a breeze blowing through. The nightmare faded to an unpleasant hum at the back of her mind.

Gradually it dawned on her that New Orleans was only yesterday. She had made it all the way across Texas in one night and part of a morning.

She peered around the Cadillac for clues to the owner's personality. A pair of fuzzy dice dangled from the rearview mirror. A box of Kleenex, an empty Schlitz bottle on the floorboard, a litter bag with Lady Bird

Johnson's face on it. On the back seat, Lucille's purse and the Maison Blanche hatbox.

Aside from the beer bottle, the car's interior was pristine, aromatic black vinyl. Lucille peered at the odometer and realized she'd had the good luck to commandeer a car with fewer than four thousand miles on it. No wonder that bartender looked so pitiful down on the floor, begging her not to take it.

Tough luck. From now on he would think before he insulted somebody.

Ahead in the shimmering light Lucille saw a squat, flat-roofed building, the red Mobil Oil flying horse, a hand-painted sign:

NAMELESS CAFE

FIRST CHANCE IN N. MEX.

IF YOU CANT STOP, HONK

That was cheerful enough. Lucille started to blow the horn, but a vision of a grilled-cheese sandwich sent her foot to the brake instead. She swung into the dusty gravel lot between two tractor-trailer rigs, and reached for her purse.

The dull gleam of the pistol showed under the sheaf of new twenties she'd snatched from the cash register at Jean Lafitte's Blacksmith Shop. She couldn't believe she had stolen all that money when all she needed was a car. What power that pistol gave her! She got drunk on that power sensation and lost all control.

She checked the clip. Seven bullets. The box of ammunition was in the Galaxie, which was now in the hands of the New Orleans police. She stuffed all the glove-box papers into the Lady Bird bag, snapped the magazine into the pistol grip, tucked it away. "You stay put, Chester. I'll be right back."

She stepped out into white sunlight. New Mexico was plenty different from Texas: flatter, with straight lines, like a Road Runner cartoon. Always she worried that the places she dreamed of going would turn out disappointing in real life, less different and interesting than she had imagined. That's how her old life had been—one long unbroken series of dashed expectations. But the landscape stretching away from these huddled buildings was chalk-white and strange as the moon.

A dog rose from the front stoop and staggered out to meet her.

"Hello, dog." She avoided its nose. "Go on, now." It was black and mange-ridden, but its eager eyes reminded her of Mama's old white dog,

Adolf. For the first time since she drove out of that yard, Lucille thought *poor Mama, I really should call her and see how she's holding up* but she stiff-armed that idea and pushed through the door of the café.

Hank Williams wailed on the jukebox, *If you looooved me half as much as I love you.* Lucille slid her sunglasses back on her head. Four old men in the corner booth glanced up from their coffee cups, brightening at the sight of her. She smiled, smoothing her hair.

Most of the tables were occupied by truckers sitting alone, working over big greasy breakfasts. The air was full of smoke from cigarettes and the griddle, where a hulking short-order man tended pancakes and hash-browns. Lucille took a seat at the counter.

"Hello, honey." The waitress moved forward with coffeepot tilted in hand. "Coffee this morning?"

"Milk," Lucille said. "Some milk and a grilled-cheese sandwich, please."

"Grilled cheese," the waitress repeated over her shoulder. Her dark-black hair was held in place by an old-fashioned hairnet. She must once have been strikingly pretty, but too many years in that hairnet with all that makeup had pulled and hardened her features. She took a drag on her cigarette. "Where you headed?"

"California." Lucille reached for a Salem.

The waitress offered a light. "Yeah, I figured. I went out there once myself."

"How far is it from here?"

"You got a ways to go yet. I hope you got a good car, if you break down in the desert it's too bad for you. You traveling alone?"

Lucille lied and said yes.

"Junie!" One of the old men in the corner. "Get some coffee down here?"

The waitress stubbed out her cigarette and went off with the coffeepot.

Lucille cast an eye around the place. The unshaven truckers stared at their plates as they ate, their jaws moving like cows chewing cud.

"Grilled cheese up!" called the short-order man.

Junie slid a plate and a glass of milk in front of Lucille. "What else, hon?"

"This looks just fine," Lucille said. "I'm starved." She took a hot, crusty, buttery bite of the sandwich. Yes. Melted Velveeta washed down with cold milk, the homeliest taste in the world, followed by a hit on her menthol cigarette. Perfect.

"Been drivin' all night?"

"I sure have. Do I look that bad?"

"A little tired, maybe," Junie said. "You going out there to be a movie star?"

"Why not," Lucille said. "Movie star, television."

"You'll take whatever work they give you, in other words."

Lucille shrugged. "Until I get established."

"My name's Junie. What's yours?"

"Carolyn Clay."

"That your real name?"

"Of course." Lucille smiled. "Why?"

"Sounds like a movie name. Mine was June Fontana, when I was in the business."

"You were—you were in the movies?"

"I sure was. I was the fourth female lead in a picture for Darryl F. Zanuck."

Lucille was thrilled by this good omen. An actual movie actress way out here in the desert! "That's wonderful! What was the movie?"

"I ended up on the cutting-room floor," Junie said. "You want another sandwich? You sucked that one down."

"Yes please." She sat up. "Look, don't take this the wrong way, but what on earth are you doing out here in the middle of—New Mexico?"

Junie lowered her voice. "Let me tell you, honey, I did it the way you're supposed to do it. I got to know every miserable producer in Hollywood, if you know what I mean. What it got me was a big fat zero. I'm lucky to be anywhere. This is a steady job and nobody in my bed unless I want 'em there, get it? You be careful out there."

"I would never let anyone do that to me."

"Hm." Junie folded her arms and looked her over. "I think you'd be better off going back to the kids and the husband."

"It's too late for that," Lucille said. "That's all over."

"Well I hope you know how to wait tables, then."

Lucille sat up straighter. "Don't worry about me. I can take care of myself."

Junie tapped her front tooth with a thumbnail. "I bet you can."

"You can wrap up that sandwich," Lucille said. "I've got to be going."

"Aw now, don't run off mad. I didn't mean anything. I know you'll do just fine out there."

"No, I'm not mad, I really do have to go. I have an audition next Tuesday." She fished a five from her purse, smoothed it on the counter, stood up.

"Wait, you got change coming."

"You keep it. It was nice talking to you."

Junie handed over a grease-spotted paper bag. "Stop in on your way back East."

"What makes you so sure I'll go back?"

"Maybe not," Junie said. "This is America, anything can happen."

Lucille said "that's right" and went out into brilliant sunshine. The mangy dog followed her to the car, waggling its rear end.

She paused to consider the phone booth at the edge of the parking lot, beside the fake oil derrick. Just a quick call to make sure the kids were all right—not long enough for anyone to trace it, or for Mama to ask any questions.

Oh, no. Cut those apron strings. That life is over. Get on with your new life. You are Carolyn Clay.

But what if Farley's sniffles had turned into something serious? What if Sandra forgot to take her antihistamines? And poor Cary, he probably hadn't quit crying yet for his mama.

What if the sheriff had taken her kids away and locked them up in some juvenile home?

One little telephone call couldn't hurt.

She coasted with the door open, crunching gravel, across the lot. She left the car in Park with the engine running and the air conditioning cranked up full, for Chester.

The phone booth was a four-sided glass oven. Lucille propped the door open with her knee and dialed O. She placed the call collect, praying Mama would answer.

On the fifth ring, she did, and accepted the charges.

"Go ahead, please."

"Oh baby, I prayed that was you. Where are you? Are you all right?"

"I'm fine, Mama, I'm—I'm in Florida," Lucille said.

"Florida? I thought you were going to California."

"I changed my mind. I thought I saw some police looking for me in New Orleans."

"Well they've been looking everywhere. They've asked me the same questions fifteen times. And poor Peejoe, they're asking him, too."

"Is he there? Let me talk to him."

"No. He's with Dove. Him and Wiley both went back with Dove. Lucille, what on earth are you doing?"

"I'm not sure. I think I'll stay down here awhile in Florida, you know, lay low for a while."

"Well how can I reach you?"

"I'll have to call you. Mama, how are the babies?"

A long silence, then Mama said: "I'm surprised you would even ask. It's just like you to dump 'em here and run off and then start in to fretting about them."

"Aw, Mama, don't be that way, I did what I had to do. Is Cary all right?"

"He cries a lot. They're all outside right now. I ran them out. They're about to drive me crazy."

Lucille felt a pang for Cary. "Did Sandra take her hay-fever medicine?"

"She did." Mama's tone was grudging, as if all of Lucille's actions had been designed to inconvenience her. "She's all right. They're upset."

"Farley still got his cold?"

"No, he's about to shake it—listen, Lucille, you've got to stop this mess and come home. You've got to let us help you. Now tell me where you are. Dove will come get you."

"It's too late for that," Lucille said. "I got to go now. I'll call you, Mama. I'm sorry."

"Wait, honey, don't—" Click, and a hum.

Lucille sank against the hot glass. If she stopped now to feel guilty for what she had done, she would never do anything else in this life.

She depressed the switch hook and fumbled in her purse for change, enough for a trunk call to California. The number was scratched on the back of her checkbook. The phone rang twice, a liquid echoing ring. A nasal woman answered: "Hall and Fliegleman."

Lucille used her actress voice: "Good morning. I'd like to speak with Harry Hall, please."

"May I tell him who's calling?"

"Carolyn Clay."

"Will he know what this is regarding, Miss Clay?"

"Yes, well—tell him it's Lucille from Alabama."

"Lucille."

"Right."

"Lucille Clay?"

"Lucille Vinson. He called me. He'll remember."

"One moment." The woman clicked off. A sprightly recorded tune took her place. Lucille mulled over the recklessness of giving out both her names in the same conversation.

An operator said, "Please deposit forty cents for the next three minutes."

Through the door of the phone booth Lucille saw a New Mexico state trooper pulling into the parking spot she had just left.

Frantically she searched the bottom of her purse for change.

"Miss Clay, I'm sorry, Mr. Hall is in a meeting right now, may I take your name and—"

Boop! "Forty cents for the next three minutes."

"Hold on just a minute!"

"Hello?" said the nasal woman. "Are you still there? Mr. Hall is in a meeting."

"I'll call back tomorrow." Lucille slammed down the phone and walked back to her Cadillac.

The lanky trooper stood with his arms folded, studying her from behind his mirrored glasses. Was he trying to read her license plate? Instantly Lucille knew how foolish she'd been to drive a stolen car without switching the plates, as car thieves in the movies instinctively know to do.

She gave him a flirty little wave with three fingers, and climbed in. Easy, calmly now, slide out of here, not a care in this world.

She pulled onto the highway, holding her breath.

The trooper pulled out behind her.

"Oh dear God. Chester, he's following me."

Of course Chester did not answer. She imagined him taking a great load of satisfaction from her predicament.

Seven bullets in the clip. If it came to a choice between going to jail and shooting a state trooper, would she do it? Was she that far gone?

She knew one thing: She had not come all this way to get herself arrested in East Jesus, New Mexico.

She needed a cool head, a plan. Some way to deflect his attention so the situation would never get that far.

She checked her makeup in the mirror. She looked a bit frowsy and undone, but still attractive enough. Maybe she could sweet-talk-and-pitiful her way out of this.

The trooper followed at a distance, matching her speed.

Lucille knew precisely what her crime was, and the penalty. Premeditated murder was the worst kind, and Lord knows she had spent these last months premeditating over Chester. If she were caught and convicted, she could go to the electric chair. Alabama's electric chair was famously defective. Every month or two you read about some poor murderer who got his hair singed by the first couple of jolts and had to sit there, dazed and smoldering, while they fiddled with the wires. It was enough to put you off the idea of getting caught.

Still, knowing she had already committed the worst possible crime gave Lucille a remarkable sense of freedom. All the rules of life had been suspended by that D-Con she'd stirred into Chester's coffee. Now she understood how these crazies get started on their killing sprees. Once you've killed one person, how much worse can it get, the punishment? Why not pile up the bodies? Why not settle all your scores and give in to every desperate urge that comes over you?

They can't put you to death more than once.

She supposed she could shoot the trooper. If she had to. She didn't want to. But she could do it. And if she did, she would not shoot to wound him or scare him. She would not leave a witness.

Just then, as if he had read her mind, the trooper flipped on his red revolving light and let out a siren whoop.

Steady hands. Nothing wrong. Pull over oh so politely.

She brought the car to a stop beneath a billboard of a man and woman floating down through the air to an open convertible: LET HERTZ PUT YOU IN THE DRIVER'S SEAT! She took out her license and left the purse unlatched on the seat, where she could reach the gun and bring it around in one smooth move. If she had to.

The trooper unfolded himself from the car, a rangy young man in a dun-colored uniform. He swaggered up, patting his pistol.

"Morning, Officer." She smiled her warmest.

"See your license, please."

If Lucille had been clever, she'd have gotten her hands on a fake license, but it was the real thing with her real name and address that she handed him.

He studied it. "These out-of-state licenses are different from ours," he said. "The numbers are in different places." He was not long out of trooper school, to judge from his pretty, bland-featured face.

"Did I do something wrong?" said Miss Sweet Innocence of 1965. "I'm sure I wasn't speeding."

"No ma'am," he said. "It's your dress."

"What?"

"Your dress." He pointed with his thumb. "You shut the car door on it."

"Oh my goodness." Lucille glanced down to discover the hem of her splashy Mexican skirt in the doorjamb. She opened the door: a grease mark and six inches of material hanging out. "So I did."

"I knew you didn't want to keep driving that way," he said, "and mess up that pretty dress."

"Well." She smiled. "Wasn't that thoughtful of you."

"May I see your registration, please?"

Lucille made a big show of checking the glove compartment. "I'm sorry, Officer. This is my boyfriend's car. I don't see anything like that in here."

"Your boyfriend, huh." His eyes were unreadable behind his mirror shades. "He's from Louisiana?"

"That's right. New Orleans."

The trooper shifted on his feet. She imagined his hard skinny body inside that roomy uniform. "He knows you borrowed his car, I guess."

"Oh yeah." She improvised a story out of thin air. "He knows. We had a big fight. I told him the car was the least he could give me after all the hell he put me through. He watched me drive it away."

"You're a sparky kind of lady, aren't you. Would you mind stepping out of the vehicle, please?"

"Thanks, but I've got my skirt all inside with me now. I've got a long way to go."

"Miz Vinson, this vehicle was reported stolen out of New Orleans on Friday."

"Well, that son of a bitch. I might have known he'd do something like that." She acted her heart out. She rested her hand on the seat beside her, toying with the fake lizard purse. "Listen, Officer, you look like a nice man. I know what you're thinking. But you can't send me back there. I had to get away from that man. You don't know what he did to me."

The trooper coughed at the back of his throat. "Ma'am, I'm sorry, but when I see a vehicle that appears on our list, I have to bring 'em in."

He didn't have much imagination, but that nervous little cough sounded like an opening. Lucille decided to pounce. She straightened her leg so the skirt slipped away from her knee. She dropped her voice way down in the seductress range. "He didn't know how to make love to a woman," she said. "He was too rough. He made me"—she shuddered—"he made me do things."

The trooper swallowed, took a step forward. "Like what kind of things?"

"Oh, I couldn't tell you. I couldn't say those words out loud. He's a bartender, you know. He drinks, he comes home, and—oh, it's too awful. I can't say it." She watched him from the corner of her eye. "Not to a big old policeman like you."

His tongue flicked across his damp upper lip. "You can tell me," he said. "It's all right."

Lucille brought her other knee up and pulled off her sunglasses. "I can't tell you, but I can show you."

He stirred. She was glad she wouldn't have to kill him. All men are alike. The way to their heart is through the front of their pants. Put them in a uniform, give them a gun and a red flashing light and they're just like other men—even more accustomed to getting what they want.

"Do you like it?" he said. "I mean, when he makes you do things."

Lucille let her eyes caress him, starting at his zipper and working up to his face. "He told me I look like a whore. Do you think I look like a whore?"

"No ma'am, I sure don't." He looked more eager every second. "I think you're real beautiful."

"I bet you know how to treat a woman," Lucille said. "I bet you're real sweet."

"Yes ma'am." He was about to pop a neck button. "I guess I am."

"Stop calling me ma'am. I'm not old. Are you married?"

He dropped his left hand into his pocket and fiddled around, shucking a ring off his finger. "Married?"

"You know. To a wife."

"Gosh," he said. "Not me." A sweat-shine broke out on his forehead.

At first Lucille had thought it might be enough to flirt with him until he got flustrated and let her go, but she wouldn't be three miles down the road before his trooper instinct took over and he came after her. No. She would have to go all the way through with it. When she thought about it, the prospect was not entirely repellent. In fact it was rather exciting.

"What's your name?" she said.

"Bill."

"Hi, Bill. I'm Lucille. Do you know any place we could go?"

"Go?" He glanced up at the Hertz couple magically levitating toward their car.

"Well we can't very well get to know each other right out here in front of God and everybody, can we?"

He grinned. "I guess not. I don't know. I've never—listen, up the road about a mile there's a dirt track that goes off to the old gypsum mine. Hardly anybody ever goes out there."

"Why don't I follow you," Lucille said. "I've never been inside a real state trooper car before."

Trooper Bill looked so gosh-golly-awful excited that he nearly tripped over his own feet going back to his car. She imagined the other troopers regaling this gangly kid with wild stories of roadside amours, he's laughing along with them all the while telling himself *someday, that will be me.* And today was his lucky day.

He drove around her with a salute and a big goofus grin.

Lucille put the Cadillac in gear and fell in behind him, feeling a little tingle herself. In all her years with Chester, she had never done it in broad-open daylight. The idea was perverse and attractive. Maybe she was born to be brazen and she just hadn't known it till now. "Stay off that radio, Bill," she whispered. "Keep your mind on what's going to happen to you."

He turned off at a pair of tire tracks heading over a hill, through scrubby, ghost-white bushes dusted with a fine white powder. Lucille steered over the rise. A clutter of ruined mining towers in the distance, white flat endless desert. The trooper slowed to a stop in the crook of the hill.

Lucille snapped her purse shut and got out. "I've never done anything like this before," she said. "I guess I just can't resist that uniform."

Trooper Bill opened his door. His grin had not faltered. "You're a bad girl, aren't you," he said, wagging a finger at her.

She sauntered up to his car, casually tossing her purse to the floorboard. "I'm pretty good, as a matter of fact."

He snaked his arm around her, pulled her in. His breath smelled sweet; he'd just eaten a peppermint, she could see little bits of it in his teeth. Then he was kissing her, kissing too hard, his teeth pressing her lips, prying at her with his tongue. He must have kissed no more than two or three girls in his life, then married a girl who didn't know how to kiss. He went at it like a horse trying to kick down its stall.

"Hold on, Tiger, slow down, not so hard. Just open your mouth and— relax." She pulled off his aviator glasses. "You have nice eyes," she said, curling back up to him, kissing him gently, to show him how.

He learned fast. His hands came around her, feeling down her sides to her fanny. "Oh baby."

She slid her knee between his legs, teased and circled his tongue with her own, keeping him busy while her fingers found the buckle of his gun belt and yanked it open and tossed it onto the floor beside her purse.

She pushed him back, crawled in on top of him. She ran the heel of her hand over the hardness in his pants. She popped the clasp, tugged at his zipper.

"Wait, let me do it." He was breathless, his voice green with enthusiasm. He wiggled out of his britches, revealing a pair of striped boxer shorts and a strong red monster nosing out of the fly.

Lucille moved up until she was straddling his waist. She plucked at his shirt-buttons, opening up his skinny chest, white as the desert. Where her fingernails touched he erupted in goosebumps. His little brown nipples stood up. His eyes had the most wonderful shine of astonished delight. He grabbed the back of her neck and pulled her down to him, kissing and purring under his breath, his fingers tangled in the elastic of her panties.

"Hold on, big boy." She pushed her skirt over his face, lapping and nipping down his chest toward his navel.

Her free hand groped along the length of the gun belt for the U-shaped leather pouch containing the handcuffs. She put the tip of her tongue in his belly-button. He moaned and writhed.

She encircled his big thing with her other hand, and hiked herself up, and came down on him, swallowing him.

"Oh, God," she cried, "oh, God!" In a flash he was thrusting up, Lucille was yelping. He trembled, the shirt went over his face and then she was riding him, *giddyup yeah, hi-ho Silver, away!* She rocked and rocked a wild flash of herself as a child on a rocking-horse, rocking and riding and where was she going? A flash and a tingle, a spreading web of nerves all firing, tiny delicious firecrackers shooting off all over her body.

Oh. Jesus God. She drove down on him, dripping sweat on his face. She loved seeing him there, underneath her, entirely under her power.

He threw his head to the side. He hummed and huffed. She locked her knees around his ribs. "Come on," she breathed, "come on, come on."

He was young and hard. Lucille took him the way she had always longed to be taken, hard and fast, yes this is what was missing from her life, a real man to take for her pleasure whenever she wanted.

Her cries came up from deep inside her, noises she had never made before, wild animal sounds in the desert. She heard him grunt, felt his jet going off.

She fell over him, keeping the rhythm while her hand stretched down to the floorboard, groping for her purse, the pistol. She found it and flipped off the safety and brought it up, aimed at the bridge of his nose.

His eyes blinked open. "What the hell!"

Lucille pushed the tip of the barrel into his left nostril. "Relax, sugar," she said. "You're my prisoner now." She gave him her lewdest grin, and tightened up her inside muscles.

He winced. His eyes widened. "Oh Jesus," he grunted, wriggling to free himself. "What—are you doing? Put that gun down." A tendril of drool from the side of his mouth.

"That was nice," she said. "That was real nice. But now you're going to have to do exactly what I say. I will kill you in a second, believe me. I've done it before." She raised up on her knees, sliding wetly off him. "Turn over on your stomach. Put your hands behind your back."

He groaned and turned his pimpled butt to the sky. She kept the gun at the base of his skull while she figured out how to unlock the handcuffs.

"You're crazy," he said. "Do you know how much trouble you're going to be in?"

She snapped the cuffs shut on one wrist, then the other. "Honey, you are the least of my problems," she said. "You wouldn't happen to have a spare set of license plates, would you?"

He made a wild lunge with both feet but Lucille got out of his way, she got off him and outside, found her underpants in the dust and stooped to put them on. The trooper struggled, flopping like a fish.

Lucille gathered his clothes, her purse, the gun belt and the shotgun from the front seat, and carried them to the Cadillac.

She hog-tied him in the back seat with two sets of cuffs, binding him wrist-and-ankle around the window pillar with his bare butt on the hot vinyl. Every moment she expected he would lash out at her, try to knock her down or something. But his nakedness and the gun at his head made him suddenly tractable.

"Thanks for everything, Bill. You were just what I needed. I'm sorry to have to do you this way."

He snarled, "I swear, I'll get you for this."

She climbed into the front seat, started the engine, and steered off the tire tracks so the car pointed straight out across the flat white desert. The radio hissed at her.

The trooper screamed curses, he called her everything. Lucille ignored him. She found a heavy rock for the accelerator. She slid the gearshift to Drive and got out.

The car moved away at two or three miles an hour, coasting off across the flat desert toward the shimmering horizon. The trooper's howls faded with the crunch of the tires.

Lucille stood for a long time watching the car creep along, growing smaller and smaller until it was just a silver speck in the distance. She got in the Cadillac and roared to the highway in a cloud of white dust.

"Hey Chester," she said, "I did it. Right out in broad daylight. And guess what else. He was better than you ever were."

She laughed out loud. She put on her sunglasses, unwrapped the leftover grilled-cheese sandwich, and went racing out over the Land of Enchantment.

12

Peejoe

Industry

The object of Monopoly, as we'd always played it with Meemaw, was
to keep the game going for hours and hours by distributing wealth
around the table. Meemaw's spirit of generosity flavored our rules; she
said the rules in the box lid were written by people who hadn't spent
much time playing and had no real concern for their fellow human
beings.

Mabel and Dove and Earlene played a whole different game. They
followed the rules printed in the box lid as if they were the Ten Com-
mandments. To begin with, they had a complicated dice-rolling ritual to
determine which player got which metal token.

"Peejoe's the dog," Mabel announced.

"I hate the dog," I said. "I want to be the cannon. I always get to be the
cannon."

"Let him be the cannon, Mabel," said Dove.

"Wiley's the cannon. He rolled for it fair and square."

Wiley said, "Don't be a baby, Peejoe."

"*Okay.*" I rolled my eyes. "I'll be the dog." It was a stupid-looking dog,
a tarnished schnauzer. Wiley looked awfully pleased with himself, placing my cannon on "Go."

"If we don't get started it'll be time for bed," said Earlene, who had
been mad at the world since discovering she was not invited to Irma Belle
Davenport's Eastern Star tea the next afternoon.

The body of old Mrs. Eldridge reclined in Parlor Six, directly below us.
All day I had been stealing down between mourners for another look at
her. Dove had worked wonders behind the gray door with the help of his
part-time cosmetologist, Randall Mulch, a high-school senior who wore

thick black eyeglasses and had a girlish flutter in his hands when he talked. Dove and Randall had transformed that sunken husk of bones into a credible imitation of an old woman asleep, complete with a rosy glow in her cheeks and a little smile that hinted of sweet dreams.

During evening visitations, we stayed upstairs. Parlor Six overflowed with Eldridges, their comings and goings supervised by old Milton. Every time the front door slammed shut, a vibration traveled up through the old house to jiggle the stack of Chance cards on the Monopoly board.

"Your turn, Peejoe." Between turns Earlene was painting her fingernails red. She picked up the dice with her thumb and little finger and dropped them in my hand.

I rolled double sixes. "All right! St. James Place. I'll buy it," I said. "I like the orange ones."

"You don't have enough money," said Mabel. "It's a hundred and eighty dollars."

"Well then give me a loan from the Bank."

Mabel had appointed herself Banker. "The Bank doesn't make loans. You shouldn't have spent all your money on those railroads."

"Come on, Wiley, tell her she's got to give me a loan."

"Tough luck, Peejoe," he said, brandishing the box. "Read the rules. Nothing in here about loans." Already Wiley had amassed a stack of prime real-estate cards, and here he was keeping me from buying one lousy orange property. I mortgaged a couple of railroads and bought it anyway.

Mabel landed on Chance, the ominous question mark. She turned over a pumpkin-colored card. "'Go to jail, go directly to jail, do not pass Go, do not collect two hundred dollars,'" she read. "Fine with me. I'll just sit there and collect rent."

Earlene rolled a nine, which landed her silver shoe smack on Boardwalk, the best property on the board. "I'll buy it, thank you very much," she said, fanning her nails with the fine royal-blue card, lording it over the rest of us.

"You always get Boardwalk," said Dove.

"Some people are born to live well," Earlene said. "Go, Wiley."

Wiley played his usual merciless game of acquire and conquer, building little green houses in earnest. Mabel arranged a trade with her mother which gave Mabel the red properties in exchange for four hundred bucks and the coveted Boardwalk-Park Place monopoly. Houses and hotels sprang up all over the board.

"Listen, Peter Joseph," said Dove, "they're going to whip us if we don't put our heads together. Now if you was to give me Vermont, and I was to give you Pacific and Pennsylvania, we could both build us some of them houses."

"That's not fair," Mabel said. "You're giving Peejoe the second-best monopoly for nothing."

"Survival of the fittest," said Dove.

We traded cards and shook on the deal. With Dove as my ally, I quickly built a row of houses on the fancy green properties. Earlene plopped down on North Carolina Avenue and had to sell all her houses to pay me. I swapped my houses for fat red hotels.

Dove took a swallow of bourbon. "Roll 'em, Wiley."

After three trips around the board I was beginning to look like a winner. Earlene hit Pacific Avenue and had to bow out, surrendering all her properties to me. She snorted disgust and went to heat a tray of Chun King eggrolls. I rebuilt the hotels on Boardwalk and Park Place, and settled in to wait for the kill.

It didn't take long. On her very next throw Mabel landed on Park Place. Her face drew up in a frustrated knot. She mortgaged everything to pay me off. "I might as well quit," she sulked.

"Aw, don't quit," said Wiley. "You need a loan to keep going?"

"Don't give her a loan," I said. "You said no loans, remember?"

Mabel shot me a murderous look. "The rules say the *Bank* doesn't make loans. It doesn't say anything about individual players. Thank you, Wiley, I think three hundred dollars should get me through until I can pass Go."

Wiley obliged. Mister Lone Wolf, Mister Go His Own Way was suddenly the picture of cooperation. I watched the power lines shifting. Since we arrived in Industry, Mabel had been my pal, and she'd kept a certain bristly distance from Wiley. Now they were working together against me.

"Oh, I get it." I folded my arms. "Y'all just love all those rules until *you* get in trouble."

"Survival of the fittest," Wiley replied. "Like Uncle Dove said."

"Come on, folks," Dove said. "It's just a game."

The loan from Wiley dribbled away; before long Mabel was in jail, fighting tears, glaring at me, without even the fifty dollars to get out.

"Here's fifty, May Belle," said Dove. "Call it an early birthday present."

"Thanks a lot," she moped. "I was winning until you made that trade with Peejoe." All of a sudden she was a charity case. I made a face at Wiley, intending to convey my opinion of this, but he was too busy gazing at Mabel with real sympathy in his eyes.

"Here's another hundred," he said. "So you won't be broke."

"Thank you, Wiley." She sniffed and settled back.

Earlene returned with the eggrolls. I bit into one and cried out and hung my mouth open, puffing and blowing on the scalding mush inside.

Earlene said, "Careful. They're hot."

"Aa nah ah ah," I said, waving my hand at my mouth. I wouldn't taste anything for days.

Mabel took up the dice, rubbed them in her palms, and tossed them. One came up a four. The other hopped off the board and landed on the furry rug.

"That's a three," I said.

"No fair, it landed crooked. I get to roll again."

"Forget it, Mabel. It's a three. Four plus three is seven. That puts you on Boardwalk. You owe me two thousand bucks. You lose."

"Ease up, Peejoe," said Wiley. "Let her roll again."

"It is kind of sitting at an angle," Dove said, bending down to retrieve the die, "but it sure looks like a three from where I sit."

"Oh sure, take his side," Mabel blurted, eyes shining. "You'll take anybody's side against me! You want me to lose!"

"Mabel, don't whine," said Earlene.

"Well it's true, Mother," she quavered. "He's helping Peejoe finish me off."

I knew just how she felt; I'd felt that way plenty of times. But for once I was winning at Monopoly, and I simply couldn't find it in my heart to give her a break. "Two thousand bucks," I said. "Why don't you get Wiley to loan you some more."

Mabel stared at the board with a terrible intensity, as if she were Supergirl trying to burn a hole with her heat-vision.

A wave of cold air passed through the room.

I will never know whether Mabel brought her knee up under the card table or performed some other invisible trick. Everything happened at once. The board flew up off the table into the air, scattering red and green plastic hotels and houses and Chance cards everywhere, flopping face-down on the rug. At the same instant we heard a commotion downstairs, a door slamming and slamming again, the house trembling under running feet.

Dove came out of his chair—"What the hell?" When he opened the door we heard shouting below, a thunder of people fleeing.

Dove ran down the stairs. Mabel regarded the wreckage of the game with an unreadable smile.

"Way to go, Mabel." I went to the door.

From the landing I heard Dove imploring: "Calm down, just calm down, these things happen." I rounded the bend in the stairs. The front door stood wide open. On the lawn, women were weeping and calling out in the dark.

"Jesus, Dove, she's alive!" a man shouted—Mr. Eldridge. "She's alive!"

"Now J.D., I am telling you—" Dove stopped when he saw me and Wiley on the stairs. We shrank against the railing and slipped past him, down the hall.

Milton stood just outside Parlor Six, rubbing his hands together. "Milton! What happened?"

"She set up," he said.

"What?"

"She set up. Take a look."

I peered around the velvet curtain. Every molecule in my body jumped back an inch.

Mrs. Eldridge must have gotten tired of lying there dead and decided it was time to sit up. Straight up in her coffin. Her hands in her lap. A little smile on her lips.

I heard Wiley's gulp from where I stood.

Then a ruckus in the hall behind us and Mr. Eldridge was pushing past me into the room. "Mama!" He shook her by the shoulders. "Mama, can you hear me?"

Dove came up beside him, murmuring into his ear, something about the muscles contracting if certain stitches didn't hold . . .

J.D. Eldridge whirled on him, wild-eyed. "Do something! She's alive! We all saw it! She heard Doris's voice and sat up!"

Dove grabbed him by the wrists, and pulled him away. Mrs. Eldridge remained perfectly upright and attentive, as if she intended to join in the conversation.

"Let her go, J.D. You go home now, let us spend a little more time with her. Come back in the morning."

"She's alive! You embalmed her while she's still alive!"

Dove shook his head. "Now, you know that's not possible."

Wiley said, "Uncle Dove?"

Dove hissed from the side of his mouth: "Get *out* of here."

We obeyed in a very big hurry.

13

Peejoe

Industry

By the next morning Mrs. Eldridge was flat on her back. Dove came up from the mortuary and found us loitering at Parlor Six. "What y'all doing?"

"Waitin' to see if she'll sit up again," I said.

"I believe she's sat up for the last time." Dove's eyes were tired. He must have been up all night with her. "She popped a couple of stitches. It happens once in a while. Listen, you boys don't need to hang around here all day, you need some fresh air. They opened the new swimming pool yesterday. Why don't you go down there and check it out?"

We said okay.

"And make Mabel go with you. She's worse than y'all for staying inside, she's white as a ghost."

We changed into bathing trunks and headed down the weedy lawn toward town. Over her swimsuit Mabel wore an ankle-length black shroud of a dress, a wide straw hat, dark movie-star sunglasses. It was a white-bright hot morning, but any ray of sun was going to have a hard time finding Mabel through that getup.

"You look like the girl on 'The Addams Family,'" I said. "I didn't know we were going to a funeral."

"Shut up, Peejoe." Wiley elbowed ahead, so that I had to walk two paces back. "I think she looks just fine."

"Thank you, Wiley."

"Aw come on, Mabel, you're not still mad about Monopoly, are you?"

"Don't be ridiculous." She tossed a superior glance over her shoulder.

I didn't like tagging along in the role of little kid, and I didn't trust this new coziness between them. They kept their heads together, muttering jokes I couldn't hear, laughing loud enough to make sure I knew I was excluded.

"Come on, let's race," I crowed, starting out at a dead run to get a head start. I was all the way to the foot of Lee Street when I realized they were ambling along way back there, paying no attention to me.

So they thought they were sweet on each other. How disgusting. They couldn't really feel that way, not really. They were kids, just like me. This had to be some new kind of game for them, a way to play grownup.

Besides. Mabel was our first cousin. Everybody knew cousins couldn't be sweethearts or they'd end up having two-headed cross-eyed babies.

I did the only thing you can do when you are being ignored: I ignored them back. I skipped on down the hill to Beauregard Avenue, the wide street that led through Industry's stretch of nice homes on its way to the courthouse square.

Rounding the corner, I heard squeals and splashing, the blare of radio on a loudspeaker—"Little Red Ridin' Hood," a slinky-sounding song sung by a wolf who said *You're everything that a big bad wolf could want* and then howled *owooooo!*

The pool was blue as the ocean on a Rand McNally map, so blue that the sky appeared washed-out and white by contrast. I admired the scene from behind the chain-link fence. Dozens of kids splashed and shrieked and leaped and screamed "Mama! Watch this!" while their mothers flipped a page in a magazine and said "I'm watching, honey."

A lifeguard with big muscles and straw-blond hair surveyed everything from a high chair near the diving board. Teenagers lolled on beach towels, looking cool in their sunglasses. I had to squint to take in the dazzling water and shiny cement and all that bare skin.

A potbellied man at the poolhouse wrote my name in a book, took my quarter, and gave me a little metal tag to pin to the leg of my plaid swimming trunks.

I headed for the snack bar to read the menu. Three noisy teenage girls bounced up, giggling, and ordered three Suicides. I asked what a Suicide was. The girls tittered and poked each other and gaped at me.

The snack-bar lady handed them three foaming cups. The girls bolted away, shrieking at my ignorance.

I fished a quarter from the secret pouch in the waistband of my trunks. "One Suicide, please."

The lady shook some ice in a cup and pressed the rim to each of the nozzles on the soda dispenser, mixing 7-Up with Pepsi with Nehi Orange with root beer with Grapico. The resulting concoction was fizzy, reddish-brown, incredibly sweet, like cough syrup mixed with Hawaiian Punch. I didn't really like the taste, but I loved the dangerous sound of its name.

"Whatcha got?" Wiley, at my elbow.

"It's a Suicide. Want a taste?" I felt hip, knowing what it was.

He took one sip and scrunched up his face. "Guh-ross. What the hell is it?"

"All different flavors mixed up together," I said. "I think it's good."

The happy chaos in the pool was irresistible. "Come on, Peejoe, let's get in!"

We started for the edge of the pool, stripping off shirts. Mabel approached from the girls' shower. "Look, Wiley, there's Jane and some of the girls from my class. Come on, I want you to meet them."

Now, the Wiley I knew would have gone to any lengths to avoid a bunch of girls on beach towels, as opposed to his first leap into a genuine swimming pool, but this was not that Wiley. This was a stranger who said "You go on, Peejoe, I'll be there in a minute" and put his shirt back on and followed after Mabel like a dog on a leash.

The lifeguard blew his whistle at two kids pretending to drown a younger boy. High-school boys performed dives off the board at the deep end; the board thrummed *racketatack* and sent them soaring in the air.

Stashing my shirt and flip-flops and Suicide at the fence, I padded to the shallow end and touched the sole of my foot to the water. It was warm.

I scooted forward, hands poised on the edge, and slipped in.

There was something special in this water, some magic mineral flowing out from the ground below Industry—or maybe it was the temperature, velvety warm in the sun, like I imagined the water in a tropical sea. It was nothing like the cold shock of the spring behind Meemaw's house. Swimming there had always been a fast shivery affair with lots of splashing and horseplay to keep from freezing to death. This water was soft, perfect. I floated in heaven. I could stay in this pool forever and be happy. I could float here all summer and never do anything else.

I supported myself with two fingers on the tiled edge, my body drifting off behind me, weightless.

Two younger kids came splashing by, shouting me out of this trance. I pushed off from the wall of the pool with both feet.

Way up in the sky a buzzard traced a wobbly circle.

Sucking a chestful of air, I flopped over on my stomach and kicked down, breaststroking underwater. All the squeals and splashing blended into a rubbery hiss. I swam down and down the clean white slope of the floor to the deep end, streaming bubbles from my nose. I was an astronaut on a space walk, a bird soaring through clear air, a porpoise propelling myself with my flipper, a Mer-Man, born with gills in my neck, free of gravity and the need to breathe air. In the liquid blue light I saw the shapes of headless humans kicking, walking, floating.

But I was not free, after all. I could not stay down. I flew up toward the mirror of the sky, bursting the glass with my head as my chest exploded.

I drew in more sweet air, and went down again.

I don't know how long I spent diving, surfacing, exploring the weightless world underwater. Sunlight streamed down in radiant shafts. Cannonballers landed on the water-sky like ten-ton bombs. I was a dolphin, a shark. I was a diving bell, slowly exhaling all the air in my lungs to sink to the bottom, where I would rest for one lovely air-starved moment before thrusting up to the air again.

Gradually I became aware that the headless humans were growing fewer and fewer. I was nearly alone in the pool.

Breaking the surface, I blinked through the rainbow chlorine haze. Everyone was standing around on the deck with their arms folded, staring at the shallow end.

The pool was empty except for me and a couple of kids splashing in the shallows. I couldn't see them for the glare. *Haaaaaang on Sloopy—uh Sloopy hang on! (Yeah) Yeah (Yeah) Yay-uh!*

Wiley stood by the diving board, waving me out of the pool.

I thrashed toward the shallow end. I didn't know what was wrong. The lifeguard was out of his chair, hastening through the spectators toward the source of the commotion.

I started up the chrome ladder, and glanced back.

Those boys in the shallow end were Negroes.

It had not occurred to me that everyone at the pool was white until I saw those two boys. At once I knew they weren't supposed to be here. Maybe they had misbehaved and I hadn't seen it, but somehow I knew their real crime was bringing their Negro skin among all this white skin.

They frolicked and splashed, unaware of all the people watching them.

I felt a chill—the breeze, and my embarrassment at having been the last one in the pool with them. Everyone must have seen me, lost in my playworld down under the deep end. I hurried to retrieve my shirt.

The lifeguard's whistle went *skreeet!*

The taller boy had his hand on the other's head, preparing to dunk him under. A second shrill blast on the whistle stopped him.

"Who let you boys in the pool?"

The boys blinked up at the lifeguard. They were skinny, very black, so much alike they had to be brothers. The older one was just about my age. I watched it dawn on them—the empty pool, the staring crowd, a stiff silence broken only by a radio jingle: "You can trust your car to the man who wears the star . . ."

The lifeguard squatted at the edge. "I said, who let you in the pool."

"Nobody." The boy's voice was a whisper. He pointed to the poolhouse. "We just, we come in back yonder."

"You didn't pay?"

"Nosuh, we—"

"You didn't see Mr. Peterson at the window?"

"No suh."

"You just snuck in."

"No suh. Nobody back there, we just, we just . . ." His voice trailed off. His hand curled protectively around his brother's shoulder. The younger boy's eyes loomed wide with fear.

"Y'all come on out of the pool." The lifeguard extended his hand. His voice was not mean, but the boys shrank back, terrified.

In slow motion they waded away to the opposite side of the pool. People stepped back from the edge as if they were unclean. Everyone watched the taller one boost himself up from the water, then turn to give his brother a hand.

". . . offers forty percent better protection against engine wear . . ."

The boys huddled at the center of the crowd, dripping. I tasted their humiliation on my tongue.

The lifeguard said "Go on home, now. It's white only allowed in this pool."

The older boy stooped for a bundle of shirts and towels, and grabbed his brother's hand. They darted for the shower room. People stepped back to let them pass. No one said a word until they disappeared through the door, then a voice in back of the crowd said "Niggers."

The lifeguard whirled, eyes flashing. "Who said that? There's no need to get ugly."

No one confessed. Some older boys guffawed, and all at once the tension went out of the moment. It was as if everyone had been obeying a singular voice, the crowd tensing up as one to drive the intruders away— and when that was done they dissolved back into harmless groups of kids and teenagers and mothers, buzzing among themselves. Sunbathers stretched out on towels. The radio music resumed.

I reached the chain-link fence in time to see the boys sprinting across the open field. The younger one stumbled and fell. His brother jerked him to his feet. They scrambled on as if pursued by a pack of invisible dogs, and vanished in the weedy jungle at the border of the park.

I kept watching. In a minute their heads poked out of the jungle, looking back. I couldn't see their faces that far away.

I lifted my hand. I waved to them.

They vanished.

Behind me, the pool had returned to its cheerful uproar. I wandered over to where Wiley sat on a blanket with Mabel and her friends. Mabel had removed her black shroud to reveal a surprisingly grownup figure; a navy-blue tank suit showed off her slim waist, pear-sized breasts, long white legs glossy with Coppertone. "Hey, Peejoe."

"Hey." I sank crosslegged to the cement, my back to the chain-link fence. Wiley ignored me. He looked very hot sitting there in his shirt.

"I wonder how they got in without paying," one of Mabel's friends was saying.

"Well I don't know, but I think it's just awful," said another. "You'd think they'd have a sign up or something. It makes me want to not get in the pool."

"Oh Jane," said Mabel, "you're *so* idiotic. What do you think, they poisoned the water?"

"Well you know they hardly ever bathe," Jane said.

"They can't float," a third girl put in. "They sink like a rock. That's why you never see them swimming."

They might have been talking about Martians or creatures in a zoo.

Wiley said, "I don't see what's the big deal. I mean, if there wasn't any sign, and the guy didn't stop them. How were they supposed to know?"

"You haven't been here very long, have you, Wiley," said Jane. "Everybody knows where they're wanted and where they're not."

The girl who had spoken first said "I mean, they have their own school, for gosh sakes."

I said "Do they have their own swimming pool, too?"

Jane rolled over on her stomach to peer at me through cat-eyed sunglasses, like Aunt Lucille's. "No, they don't have a *swimming pool*," she said. "Who are you?"

At last Wiley was forced to acknowledge me. "That's Peejoe. My brother."

"I just wondered," I said.

"Come on, Peejoe, let's go for a swim." Wiley shucked his shirt, took three loping steps and dove into the pool.

I jumped in. We came up together.

Wiley slung water from his hair. "Man, this is great, huh? The water's so warm."

"Howcome you're hanging out with all those—girls?"

"Just being polite," he replied. "They're Mabel's friends." I had never known Wiley to want to be polite to anybody, of his own free will. But I had him in the pool now, ready to play with me, so I didn't press the point. "Let's race underwater!"

I got a head start, stayed abreast of him halfway across the pool, then his long legs took over and propelled him to the far wall in three easy kicks.

I straggled up, puffing and blowing.

"I win," he said, craning around to see if Mabel had noticed. She was wrapped up in conversation with her friends.

"Okay, let's go again. This time you can use your arms but you aren't allowed to kick. Okay?"

"I don't know." He slicked back his hair. "I think I'm gonna get out for a while."

"Get *out?* You just got in!"

"Look, Peejoe, see if you can find somebody your own age to play with, okay?" He hiked himself out of the water.

"Wiley . . ."

He must have known what I was thinking. It was all in his face. "Don't whine," he said, dripping water on me.

"But I don't have anybody to play with," I whined.

"That's your problem." He sucked in his nonexistent belly and strutted over to Mabel.

I could pretend to drown and make the lifeguard come in after me, and then Wiley would be sorry. How stupid to come to a wonderful pool like this and spend your time baking on the cement with a bunch of stupid girls!

I sidestroked to the shallow end and paddled around, spurting water through my teeth, feeling sorry for myself.

When I couldn't stand it any longer, I retrieved the watery remains of my Suicide and went back to my place at the fence, the edge of their conversation.

The plumpish girl, Jane, rolled over when I sat down. "You're the one who saw your uncle's head, aren't you. We read all about it in the paper."

"Wiley saw it, too."

"Woman Flees With Husband's Head," she said. "That must have been horrible."

"It was kind of awful."

The girls shuddered and leaned in for details. I looked to Wiley for help. He lay on his back with his eyes closed, hands behind his head.

"I hear Lucille sometimes," Mabel said. "She talks to me."

"Mabel, you're so spooky." Jane's hand stopped in midair on the way to the suntan oil. Her mouth dropped open. "Oh my *God*."

The way she was staring, I thought maybe I had something hanging out of my nose. I felt with my finger but that wasn't it. "What's wrong?"

Mabel sat up. "Behind you, Peejoe."

I turned.

Across the open field, a group of Negro boys stepped from the weeds. They advanced in a ragged line across the field, coming on steadily, striding toward the pool in cut-off trousers, no shirts or shoes, a troop of half-naked soldiers.

At one end of the line I recognized the two boys the lifeguard had evicted from the pool. They'd come back for more trouble! And this time they'd brought older boys, reinforcements. I was swept with admiration. If that had been me, I would be cowering under a bed somewhere.

Mabel reached for her dress. "I don't like the look of this."

"What do they want?" said Jane.

"What do you think they want?" Mabel pulled the dress over her head. "They want to get in the pool."

The Supremes jangled on the loudspeakers, *Stop! in the name of love.* The boys kept coming. I counted thirteen. In the lead was a thin boy swinging long arms. He led them directly toward our stretch of fence.

Of course. That was the boy from Dog Junction, from the shadows of the room, the silent gaunt boy with yellow eyes. The dead boy's brother. What was his name?

Taylor. Taylor Jackson. He found his brother in the yard.

The word of their coming spread around the pool. Everyone at our end got up and moved back from the fence. The lifeguard hastened down from his chair and loped for the poolhouse.

"Let's get out of here, Wiley." Mabel pulled the black dress over her head.

"Wait. I want to see what's gonna happen."

Think it o-wo-ver. (Haven't I been good to you?)

The boys stepped up to the concrete lip of the pool deck and grabbed the chain links, as if to test the strength of the fence. They didn't try to climb over. They stood on the cement ledge, gripping the fence, peering in with serious eyes.

The music broke off. The lifeguard emerged from the poolhouse with Mr. Peterson, the potbellied man who had signed me in. They hurried through the crowd. The lifeguard blew his whistle. "Everybody out! Out of the pool!"

Swimmers headed for the ladders. Mabel's friends gathered towels and magazines, and drifted toward the exit gate with a stream of kids and mothers glancing nervously over their shoulders.

The lifeguard approached the fence, folding his arms over his muscled chest. "What do y'all want?"

Taylor Jackson spoke up: "We want to swim in the pool."

"Well you can't. I already told those two. You ain't allowed."

"Hold on, Bucky." Mr. Peterson stepped toward the fence. "I'm sure these boys don't want any trouble."

"Don't want trouble," Taylor said. "We just want to swim in the pool."

"What's your name, son?"

"Taylor Jackson."

"Well, Taylor, I'm sorry, but this pool is white only. I didn't make the rule, but there it is. Now y'all are gonna have to go on away from here."

"We ain't goin' nowhere," said Taylor. "We'll just sit right here until you change your mind." He looked down the line of his troops and abruptly sat down crosslegged on the strip of cement.

Apparently that was a signal. The other boys sat down, too.

Taylor gazed up at Mr. Peterson with a smile. "This is a sit-in."

The lifeguard lunged at the fence. "Get the heck out of here!" His voice cracked. "Don't you know you don't belong here?"

"Bucky, shut up and go call the sheriff," said Peterson. The lifeguard glared, but did as he was told.

"You boys are making a big mistake," Peterson said. "Why you want to cause trouble for yourselves?"

Taylor held the boys in place with his steadfast calm. "We just sittin' here," he said. "Y'all can go on with your swimming."

"You're trespassing." Mr. Peterson's face was turning red but he kept his voice even. "I don't want to call the law, but you're forcing me to."

The smile grew on Taylor's face—confident, arrogant, so superior it took my breath away. "We just want to swim."

Peterson looked as if he might like to reach through that fence and strangle Taylor, but instead he turned on the crowd of us gawkers. "Folks, I'm sorry. You'll have to clear out. The pool is closed for the day."

We groaned.

He held up his hands. "Now, I don't want a scene. Get your things and go home. We'll be open again tomorrow."

Wiley and I allowed ourselves to be herded with everyone else toward the open gate. We stepped out and looked back to the fence. The boys sat quiet as statues.

Just then a bronze-colored sheriff's car came sliding downhill past the Dairy Dog, followed by two more just like it.

This news raced through the crowd. The boys stayed where they were.

I felt a reckless urge to find out what it felt like, that kind of courage. I touched Wiley's arm. "We could go over and sit down with them."

"Are you nuts?"

"But—Wiley, they aren't hurting anybody. They're just sitting there."

"Well I know, Peejoe, but Jesus. It's none of our business. You want to get us arrested?"

"They won't arrest us. We're kids."

"I wouldn't be so sure. Looka here."

That was Sheriff Doggett unfolding from the lead car, surrounded by deputies drawing clubs from their belts. Mr. Peterson went over, waving his hands, explaining.

The deputies milled around, casting annoyed glances at the line of intruders.

Mr. Peterson paced in front of the crowd, pleading with us to go home. His words bounced off. We watched with eager, terrible eyes, like rubberneckers at the scene of an accident.

The deputies formed a huddle and started forward. We scrambled out of their way.

They rounded the corner of the fence. Sheriff Doggett stepped out in front with his Kirk Douglas chin. "You are trespassing on public property," he boomed. "This is an unlawful assembly. Now get up and go on home. We are not having any of this kind of thing in this town."

The boys began scooting on their butts toward Taylor. He stayed where he was. "This is a sit-in," he said.

The sheriff snorted. "Yeah, I hear you, young friend. I know just what this is. Now you get your ass up from here and disperse, or I'm going to have to disperse you."

"If you want to arrest us," said Taylor, "go ahead."

"Oh, no. I ain't messin' up my nice clean jail with you. Let's clear 'em out of here, men."

Two deputies bent over to lift Taylor under his arms. He thrashed out of their grip and flopped over in the red sand as if his legs had forgotten how to stand up.

Seven men held out their clubs and began to advance.

The other boys looked to Taylor for some clue. He hopped to his feet. "This is our pool, too," he said loudly. "We got a right to swim here."

The deputy gave Taylor a shove that jostled him back a step.

That offhanded shove infuriated me. What a bully! Wasn't it enough he had a gun and his billy club and the law on his side? Why go pushing Taylor Jackson around like that?

I don't know why I did it. I didn't even think about it first. I took two steps out of the crowd, and then another step, and another, until I was standing just behind the deputy.

I heard the gasps of the people behind me. In that instant I felt completely alone.

I don't know what I intended to say—something like *Stop! He ain't hurting anybody!*— but the deputy whirled on me, raising his stick. "You get back there," he said.

For a moment Taylor Jackson's eyes flickered over to mine. I don't know whether he recognized me, but he saw that I was somebody alive, on his side—at least until the deputy took one threatening step toward me, and I melted back into the shelter of the crowd.

Wiley's face said *have you lost your mind?*

The deputies began dragging the other boys away from the fence. A scuffle broke out, shoving, punching, kicks to the ribs. Somehow Taylor got free of his captors and banged facefirst into the fence, rattling the chain links. The men grabbed him. He coiled up his long legs and kicked, sending one of them sprawling, and then the other men were all over him.

He ducked through a hole in their arms. Something caught his foot. He stumbled and fell over backwards in a clean, curving line which brought the base of his skull down against the concrete lip of the pool deck.

The crowd surged ahead, down the fence. Someone shoved me. I shoved back.

The lawmen got rough. One of the boys broke free and lit out for the woods, pursued by a deputy waving his stick. Others staggered to their feet and got knocked down again.

Some of our crowd mixed in, now, five white teenagers surrounding one boy.

I spotted Taylor on the ground in the midst of the commotion.

It all happened too fast. The sheriff roared for everyone to get back, get out of the way. At the sound of his voice the deputies raised up, their concentration broken long enough for the black boys to untangle themselves and scramble out over the field.

Three deputies took off in pursuit, but the sheriff hollered them back. Some of the teenagers laughed and shouted "Run, nigger!"

John Doggett stood with his arms folded, looking down at Taylor on the ground. He poked with his toe. "Get up."

Taylor did not stir. He lay in the sand, his head resting against the concrete edge. He was perfectly peaceful, asleep.

The deputies gathered around him, peering down.

The crowd hushed and began to retreat. I felt Wiley's breath at my ear: "I think they really hurt him."

I swallowed. I couldn't speak.

"Peejoe." He pressed a dime in my hand. "Run call Uncle Dove. Tell him to come. Hurry!"

I ran through a blur of tears to the phone at the snack bar. Frantically I flipped through the phone book, found the number, dialed it. The phone rang forever.

Dove answered "Croaker-Moseley."

I blurted it all out, the sit-in, the sheriff, Taylor Jackson on the ground. "Uncle Dove, hurry!"

"Stay where you are. I'll be there in two minutes. Don't do anything!" The dial tone hummed in my ear.

I hung up and went to wait with Mabel and Wiley at the corner of the fence. Most everyone else had scattered out to the road or disappeared.

The sheriff hunkered beside Taylor on the ground. His men stood in a circle, looking expectantly down, as if Taylor might get up in a minute and forgive them all.

"God damn troublemakers," the sheriff said, his voice thick.

The wail of Dove's siren preceded him down the hill. The white hearse bumped across the grass, winding down to a whine. He jumped out.

The sheriff glanced up. "Dove, bring a stretcher. This boy's hurt."

Dove stalked over to their circle. The deputies parted to let him through. He knelt beside Taylor.

The sheriff said "He fell and hit his head."

Dove listened to the chest, cupped his hand over the nose and mouth. He opened one eye with his thumb. "He ain't hurt, John. He's dead."

The sheriff drew himself up. "I didn't touch him. He tripped and he fell."

Dove clenched his jaw to keep from saying anything.

"Get him out of here." Doggett stepped back. "Take him over to Nehemiah." He turned on the crowd of us. "I told y'all to get the hell out of here! Go home!"

Dove spotted us then, jerked his head—*get in the car.* He knelt and came up with the broken boy in his arms. Taylor's head lolled back. His arms dangled.

Doggett said "It was an accident."

Dove said "There's just too goddamn many accidents here lately, my friend."

I opened the rear gate and climbed in front with Mabel and Wiley. Dove placed Taylor on the stretcher in back, and strapped him down.

We drove in silence to Sycamore Street, to the Blessed Rest Funeral Home.

Nehemiah Thomas wept when he saw it was Taylor. "It's a war," he said through his tears. "It's a war."

14

Lucille

On the Road

By the time Lucille reached Harry Hall from a pay phone in Flagstaff, Arizona, she had become just the tiniest bit hysterical—and who wouldn't be, after killing her husband, forsaking her children, hijacking a car, driving halfway across the country, and making wild love to a New Mexico highway patrolman?

This had been the busiest week of her life.

In all the excitement of being on her own, there had been moments when Lucille nearly lost sight of her ultimate purpose. It didn't help that every time she stopped to call California the same nasal receptionist gave her the same line: Mr. Hall is in a meeting.

The fifth time Lucille heard this, she snapped. "He's been in a meeting for two days. Who does he think he is, the United Nations?"

"I'm sorry, Miss Clay, I'll be happy to take a number and have him call you."

"I've already told you, I'm driving to California. He can't call me."

"Could you try back in an hour? I'm sure he'll be finished by then."

Lucille bit her tongue, thanked the woman, hung up. She couldn't let her temper get in the way of her big break, not when she was so close. She'd had hardly any sleep in six days, except for a few fitful hours last night at the Crazy $8 Motel in Pima, Arizona. The pillow smelled like soured milk, and the walls trembled every time a truck blew by on the highway.

Sometime after midnight she gave up trying to sleep. She got dressed, and sneaked around the motel parking lot until she found Arizona license plate UR7717; all those sevens sounded lucky. She unscrewed the plate with an emery board and attached it to her Cadillac.

Stoked with takeout coffee from Howard Johnson, she headed into the night.

She stopped once, to fling the old plates off a bridge, along with the trooper's clothes and guns—she heard the *clank!* in a dry riverbed.

Lucille drove all over Arizona that night, searching for State Road 93. Somehow she missed a turn. When the sun came up in her windshield she realized she was all the way turned around, heading east instead of west—if she kept going she'd wind up back in New Mexico.

She stopped for a long careful look at the map, a call to California. That was when the receptionist told her to try back in an hour.

She raced west across the desert on Route 66, checking her watch every five minutes. Her conscience was throbbing now like a decaying tooth. She had thrown over her whole life on the basis of one phone call from Harry Hall, and back in the skeptical reaches of her mind she began to suspect it was some kind of joke to him, a passing flirtation, maybe he called all kinds of girls, promising auditions. . . .

She tormented herself this way to the outskirts of Flagstaff, where she phoned again. This time the receptionist said "Oh yes, he's free now. Please hold," and rang the call through.

"Harry Hall."

"Oh thank God, Harry, I was beginning to think you didn't exist."

"Do I know you?"

"Well I hope so. Lucille Vinson, remember, from Cornelia, Alabama? 'One of the beauties of spring'?"

"Oh, of course, Lucille, how are you, doll? 'Scuse my confusion. This note says it was, lessee . . . Carolyn Clay on the line."

"That's my new stage name. Do you like it?"

"Whatever," said Harry. "I've been dodging your calls for days. Where are you? I thought you were supposed to be here by now."

Thank God. It was not just a figment in her mind. "I had some things to straighten out at home," she said.

"Where are you?"

"Arizona. I'm headin' your way just as quick as I can."

"I do love that accent, darling, hang on to that," Harry said. "By the way, somebody called from Alabama looking for you. What was his name—wait, Yvonne wrote it down. It sounded like something from Tennessee Williams . . . here it is. Dove. Dove Bullis. God, what a marvelous name."

"What did you tell him?" Lucille asked, meaning *what did he tell you?*

"Yvonne took the call. She said we hadn't heard from you. Tell you the truth, darling, I was about to give up on you. You still planning to make that audition?"

"You bet I am. I'll be there Sunday at the latest. Is it still on for Tuesday?"

"Ten o'clock at Filmways. Why don't you call me Monday in the a.m. We'll have lunch. I have a good feeling about this one, and just between you and me, I'm never wrong."

Lucille thanked him abundantly and rang off, dizzy with relief. She might be crazy but she had not invented the enthusiasm in his voice. Lunch and then Filmways. Win the audition. Become a star. Prove that you deserve a better life than Chester Vinson ever dreamed you could have.

The operator put the second call through. Lucille heard clicks and static as one line linked to the next, leapfrogging all the way across the country to the funeral home in Industry. Dove picked up on the second ring: "Croaker-Moseley."

"Hey, Dove. It's me."

He sucked in a breath. "Baby Sister. Where are you?"

"Florida. Hear the ocean?" She held the phone out toward the highway, hoping the traffic would sound like pounding surf. "It's nice down here, Dove. Real hot."

"Are you all right? Mama told me you called."

"Yeah, and I heard you called Harry Hall, too. You leave him out of this. Mind your own business. I've given up on that whole idea. Things are different now."

"Just trying to find you," Dove said. "Listen, have you lost your mind, or what is it exactly with you?"

"Oh, I don't know, Dove. I just had to get away."

"Hey, we all need a vacation now and then, but Jesus Christ, Baby Sister! You left one hell of a mess. You know we found Chester."

"What's done is done," said Lucille. "I don't want to hear about it."

"They're looking for you."

"That does not mean they'll find me."

"I think you should come on back, Baby Sister. We can try to work things out."

"It's too late for that, Dove. I know it and you know it. For God's sake, I'm not stupid. They are not going to catch me."

"Well what are you planning to do? You just gonna keep running?"

"I'm taking it one day at a time," Lucille said. "What's wrong with you, Dove? You sound funny."

"What's *wrong?* You want to know what's *wrong?*"

"Yeah—listen, I've got to go. Do me a favor, don't call Harry again. Did you tell anybody else about him?"

"Baby Sister, I'm on your side. We've got some race trouble down here right now, and—"

"Thanks, Dove. I'll call you from Miami."

"Don't hang up," he said, but she did.

She climbed back in the car. She studied her face in the mirror. All the worry lines began to smooth out. "Hello," she said in her sexy voice. "My name is Carolyn Clay." She felt her heart growing lighter. She'd had more than a few bumps along a very long road, but she was long gone from where she had started, she was lifting away from the pavement now, soaring toward her future.

She felt like singing, like running downstage center and throwing her arms in the air, bursting forth *The hills are alive . . .*

"Chester, I did it," she said, "I really did. I got out. It's really happening now."

The road ran straight as a line drawn with a ruler, not a tree or a bird as far as you could see. Lucille exulted in the great sweep of the horizon. All her life she'd been hemmed in by trees, jungly woods and green leaves and brick walls, doors and windowscreens, husband and kids. Out here in the desert there was room to think, there was only her own self and nothing else, pink sand and red rocks stretching to a sharp and visible edge against the sky.

A question nagged at her ear: How had Dove known to telephone Harry Hall? Mama must have remembered the name, or Peejoe. Had they told the police? Was Harry in on it, too? What if Lucille was heading into a trap?

She had an impulse to find another dry riverbed and fling the hatbox into it. How could she ever be truly free, as long as she insisted on clinging to Chester?

Don't think about that. Think of the dazzling spotlights waiting at the end of this road, waiting to shine down on you. Think of life without Chester, or Mama, or children, or obligations of any kind. Think of Carolyn Clay. The lovely, the talented—

"Lucille."

She jumped.

A whisper in her ear.

Lord God. Her imagination running wild. Too many days and nights on the road, excitement and coffee and wild hurried sex and no sleep . . .

"Lucille."

She clutched the wheel. A live whisper. Not a voice in her head. A real voice, clearly audible in the air of the car.

She glanced over her shoulder. Her elegant Chanel hat lay beside the hatbox, which was firmly secured with black ribbons.

She switched on the radio. Twanging guitars, a hillbilly yodeler. She drew out a Salem, punched the lighter.

"Lucille. Don't do this."

She kept her eyes on the road. Traffic streamed the other way, toward Flagstaff. She lit the cigarette, blowing smoke through her nose.

"Chester," she said, "if that's you, you just leave me the hell alone."

"Lucille . . ."

Who else said her name like that, Lou-see-yul, like fingernails down a blackboard? How many times had she screamed "Lu-*seel!* It's Lu-*seel*, for God's sake!" and he'd grin that maddening grin and drive her crazy teasing Lou-see-yul, Lou-see-yul . . .

"Buddy, you better not mess with me," she said. "I'll stop this car and put you out right here."

"Don't throw me away, sweetie." A whisper. "I love you."

Now, Lucille knew there was no way she could be hearing Chester's voice through a Maison Blanche hatbox, three layers of tissue paper, and the patented press-and-lock Tupperware seal. There was no way that Chester Vinson's head, severed or not, would ever say something like *I love you*—but Lucille was wide awake now, not dreaming. That was Chester's voice, unmistakably. He might have been leaning up from the back seat to whisper in her ear.

"I love you, Lucille. I never quit loving you."

Three silvery Airstream trailers shot by, heading the other way. Lucille gripped the wheel.

"This is ridiculous, Chester. How can you say that? You never loved me."

"Don't throw me away. We can learn to be happy."

"This isn't you," Lucille said. "This can't be you."

"Lou-see-yul . . ."

"Shut up!" She pushed hair from her eyes. "I don't want to hear any more."

This must be a trick of her mind.

Her eye fell on a road heading north from Route 66, along a range of hooded blue mountains. A sign pointed the way to Hoover Dam and Las Vegas.

Hoover Dam summoned a mind-picture of an immense frozen concrete waterfall, swirling white water at the bottom. Maybe that was the place to get rid of Chester.

"Don't do it," he whispered.

Lucille took the turn. The mountains grew craggier, the land dry as chalk. The road ran past hamlets with chemical names: Chloride, Soda Flats, Alkaline City.

Maybe her crimes had made her crazy. Maybe a normal person just couldn't do the things she had done and stay in her right mind.

But if she was crazy, if the gray fog was insanity lowering itself over her, it was nothing new. She had lived in and out of that fog for years.

The real craziness was staying with him all that time, in that loveless house, that empty marriage. It was only *after* she killed him that the fog began to lift. She had never felt saner in her life than she did right now.

On the one hand, what she did was wrong: she could accept that. But now that it was done, somebody else would just have to feel guilty about it. Lucille didn't have time. She was enjoying her freedom too much.

"Chester, do you think I'm crazy?"

Of course he had no answer for that.

"I'm upset, that's all," she said. "I'm just upset. I must not be thinking too straight."

He maintained perfect silence.

"I know you're dead. I know you're nothing but a hallucination. It's like—I don't know, the voice of guilt or something. And soon as I can get rid of you, I won't hear it anymore."

Abruptly the road ascended into a gathering of brown hills.

"But I don't feel guilty," she said. "Or maybe I do. I don't know. I'm talking to myself now. I'm so awful tired of driving."

Two-legged steel towers marched across the hills, giant robots carrying the threads of power lines in their arms.

Lucille turned the radio up loud, Petula Clark taking her sassy walk downtown, *bah-na-na-baaaa-na na na* all over her lonely life. Lucille sang along— "*You can forget all your troubles, forget all your cares . . .*"

Around the next curve a huge lake appeared, a flat plain of unearthly blue, rocks rising up from the shore—a dead lake, without a twig or a spot of moss.

The road switched back. The power-line robots closed ranks, converging over the rocky hills from all directions. The road looped through a series of hairpin turns that slowed Lucille to a crawl. She came out on a bluff overlooking one end of the lake, bounded by the curving roadway. A little wooden shack advertised HOOVER DAM SCENIC VUES SOUVENERS.

The road unbent for the quick jaunt over the top of the dam. Halfway across, Lucille made the mistake of glancing to her left: a dizzying drop into space—her stomach dropped, too, free-falling. Dear Lord, this was higher than any bridge in the world!

She held her breath and clung to the steering wheel and somehow made it across. WELCOME TO NEVADA.

She pulled into a parking lot and rested her head against the wheel, drinking in air.

When she had recovered, she lifted the hatbox from the back seat and carried it to the guardrail.

From this side she could appreciate the stunning balancing act that was Hoover Dam: an immense volume of water opposed to an equal amount of thin air, with only a fragile-looking wall of cement keeping one from the other. The dam in its plummeting gorge looked too big to be real. It was the biggest thing Lucille had ever seen. Just looking at it made her nervous.

At once she saw this place would not do for Chester. Too many people snapping Kodaks and crowding the rail. Anyway she'd have to make some kind of Sandy Koufax miracle pitch to get the hatbox out past the wall of the canyon, past the transformer building at the base of the dam, and into that faraway swatch of whitewater.

She returned Chester to the Cadillac and went to the souvenir shack for cigarettes, a Coke, and a fifty-cent brochure called "You Can WIN! At Roulette!"

The woman at the cash register said Las Vegas was no more than an hour's drive north. "My advice to you is the nickel slots," she said. "You don't lose as fast."

Lucille thanked her and went to the car. She opened the booklet to the first page: "The casino employee who operates the game is known as a *croupier* (KROO-pee-ay)."

She drove into Nevada. Chester stayed quiet. Maybe he was grateful to have been spared the depths of Hoover Dam.

The highway ran down a barren slope toward a scattered-out city, tall hotels standing around in the dusk. Liquor stores sprouted along the roadside, and motels, hamburger stands, poker parlors, drive-in casinos, wedding chapels, divorce chapels, Putt-Putt golf courses, gas stations, drive-ins, used-car lots. A billboard of a glittering slot machine, tall as a four-story building, flashed the words GOLDEN NUGGET.

Lucille felt her pulse accelerating. For the first time since New Orleans, she was in a place where she wouldn't mind spending the night: Las

Vegas, World Capital of Legalized Vice. A gas station offered FREE
ASPIRIN & TENDER SYMPATHY.

Lucille surged with a river of cars onto a wide boulevard flanked by
high-rise hotels. Lights flickered on, neon and fluorescent, dazzling fields
of white winking bulbs. Giant billboards announced Joey Bishop at the
Dunes, Perry Como at the Aladdin, Frank and Nancy Sinatra at the
Sands, Patti Page at the Riviera, Dean Martin at the Stardust, Robert
Goulet and Jack Benny at the Fabulous Flamingo.

"Look, Chester, Jack Benny. Your favorite."

"Now *cut* that out," Chester said.

An enormous glowing pink flamingo pointed its beak TO CASINO,
DINING ROOM, LOUNGE AND POOL. Lucille swung into the drive.

Maybe she ought to behave like a proper fugitive and hide out in one of
those dumpy motels on the outskirts of town, peeping out from behind a
curtain. But the lights were much brighter here, the palm trees serenely
blue and fake-looking, the Fabulous Flamingo calling out Come in,
Lucille, it's KOOL inside! Come rest your weary head! Haven't you driven
all the way across the country? Aren't you worn to a frazzle?

She couldn't show up in Hollywood looking like some wild woman
who just roared in off the desert. She needed a room with a big bed, a
bottomless tub, a two-hour soak and a twelve-hour sleep. In the morning
she would be lovely and fresh just in time to go meet Harry Hall.

But first she would like to meet this handsome brown-headed bellboy
in a pink tuxedo, stepping up to her car. "Checking in?"

The sight of his perfect square jaw made Lucille feel younger. She
reached for her hat. "You bet I am, sweetie."

"Any luggage?"

"Just that hatbox in back. I'll get it."

"Allow me." He leaned in.

"No!" Lucille cried. "Wait—pick it up by the bottom. It's heavy."

His grin shot off bright as a flashbulb. "Don't worry. I think I can
handle a hatbox." But of course it weighed more than it should, and his
brown eyes crinkled up, just as puzzled and pretty. "Whoa, it is heavy.
What do you have in here, bricks?"

Lucille adjusted her hat in the driver's window. "It's my husband's
head. I take it with me everywhere."

The lad thought that was funny. He laughed. "Just his head, huh?"

"Mm-hmm. I left the rest of him home." Lucille took the box from
him. "Will you park this car for me?"

"Sure." He held out his hand.

She clasped his fingers a moment, thinking *This country is overrun with handsome young men. Where have I been all my life?*

"The keys," he said.

"Oh of course. Here, hold this."

He held Chester while Lucille dug in her purse. His sunny good looks had dried up her exhaustion. Here she was wondering how a bellhop might taste, with the taste of a state trooper still on her tongue.

You only live once, she thought. And if you are me, you have lived oh so long without ever living. You have some serious catching up to do.

"Cherry car," he said. He was a straight arrow, a college kid. Like one of those beach-movie boys, Tab or Troy or Rock.

She handed him the keys, and an appraising glance. "Maybe you could let somebody else park it," she said, "and you could show me the way to my room."

His eyes lit up. His Adam's apple bobbed in his throat. "That sounds like a real good idea, but I'm supposed to be working the check-ins."

She fingered the velvet edge of her hat. "I'm a check-in."

He glanced at the other bellhops smoking and standing around. "Listen, tell you what, I've got a break in twenty minutes. Why don't you take a look around the casino. Then I'll come help you . . . find your room."

"Maybe I will." She smiled. "Or maybe you just blew the best chance you'll ever get." She walked away up the curving sidewalk, through a vale of palmettos and fountains, lights glowing tropical colors. If anyone could see her private thoughts Lucille would be glowing turquoise and pink.

She glanced back. He was still grinning at her.

He was young and pleasant to the eye—what a smile! Lucille felt like the flower of sex, unfolding. She wanted every man she saw. All she had to do was drop the littlest hint, and they were helpless to resist her.

Then she stepped into another world: the casino: and forgot the bellhop just like that. There were miles of red carpets and green felt, swanky draperies, velvet and mirrors, banks and banks of gleaming slot machines, gamblers in evening clothes from here to the far side of there—it was better than the movies. Better than Hoover Dam. It made the Admiral Semmes Hotel in Mobile (formerly the most glamorous place she'd ever been) look like some rundown rooming-house. The air was blue with cigar smoke, the music of hard money clinking into metal pans, bells ringing, tinkling, a combo razzing out "Fly Me to the Moon."

Lucille wandered among the whirring slot machines, down the rows of horseshoe tables where men in tuxedoes were dealing cards onto rich green felt.

All the dealers shared a profoundly bored expression. The people at the tables sipped cocktails and smoked and stared at the dealers' hands flicking cards around the table. You would never guess they were winning or losing anything.

At the end of the row Lucille came upon another game, a fancy wheel twirling and flashing like a Cadillac hubcap. A white marble bounced along the rim. When it settled on a number, a man yelped and shot both hands into the air. His friends pounded his back.

The croupier pushed three large stacks of white chips across the table, and began sorting the other chips with lightning hands.

You Can WIN! At Roulette!

The gamblers leaned politely past each other to place their bets. Lucille admired the croupier's confident twirl of the wheel, the scuttling marble, the breathtaking instant before it landed . . . Roulette was a series of quiet mysteries leading up to the big moment: the jackpot, or mud on your face.

Some of the gamblers piled a whole bunch of chips on one number. Some scattered their chips in elaborate patterns. Sometimes, when the croupier gave them a big stack of winnings, they gave him a chip in return, for bringing them luck.

Lucille knew she ought to rent a room, take a bath, and read through her booklet, but the sound of money crashing into slot-machine pans made her want to try one little wager.

A gold-faced plaque stated that the minimum bet was twenty dollars.

She held her purse close, to hide the gun. She had not even bothered to count the money from Jean Lafitte's but she knew there was more than a thousand dollars. Stolen money, the devil's money. What better use for it than to gamble it away?

"Twenty-two!"

A man lost his last chips and got up in disgust.

The croupier said "Thank you, sir. Good luck."

The man stalked away, hiking his pants.

Lucille slid into his chair. She put the hatbox and purse at her feet, and gave the entire stack of twenties to the croupier. "Can I have some chips, please?"

All that money—he didn't even blink. He riffled through it once and said "Eleven hundred forty, cash in" over his shoulder.

Behind him a portly man in a tuxedo glanced at the money, and then at Lucille, a nod, a slight smile. He clicked a metal cricket in his hand.

From nowhere a waitress appeared at Lucille's elbow. "Cocktail?"

"Why not. I'll have . . . a Tom Collins."

The fat man beside Lucille raised his empty glass but the waitress was already gone. The croupier scooted over two stacks of pink chips and a stack of fancier chips stamped $100. "Place your bets, please."

Lucille waited until everyone else had done their leaning and placing, then she said, "Can I bet on thirteen, even if somebody already did?"

A murmur of amusement ran up the table. That must have been an ignorant question.

The croupier smiled. "Feel free."

Lucille took a $100 chip and placed it atop the blue chips on number thirteen.

The waitress materialized with a bright red cocktail. Lucille beamed and took a sip. "Delicious." She tried to pay, but the girl said it was on the house.

People were awfully nice here.

The croupier set the wheel spinning, cupped the white marble in his palm, and shot it around the inner edge of the wheel. It made a hollow sound like a coin rolling across a floor, then slowed and began to descend toward the whirling numbers.

"Hold your bets, please," the croupier said.

A hush fell.

The ball skipped, bounced, and landed.

"Thirteen."

"Whoo-hoo! Thank you, Jesus!" cried a man at the end.

Lucille's eyes followed the ball around. Yes, indeed! Yes! It rode in the slot marked thirteen!

The croupier pushed three stacks of powder-blue chips to the man who had hollered, and three stacks of Christmas-colored $100 chips to Lucille.

"Thank you." She took another taste of her Tom Collins, and gave him the top chip from the stack.

"Thank *you*." He rapped it smartly on its edge and stashed it away.

That was quite a pile of money in front of Lucille. Hundreds and hundreds of dollars. The other gamblers stared with genuine envy.

You Can WIN! At Roulette!

"Place your bets, please."

Lucille liked this game. It seemed absurdly easy. She took a stack of $100 chips as high as her knuckle, and placed them again on number thirteen. The blue-chip man loaded more chips on top of hers. They exchanged a glance of shared victory.

The sight of all those expensive chips had drawn a little crowd to the end of the table. The portly supervisor stood close beside the croupier, watching.

The wheel was off and spinning, the marble racing against the spin, losing momentum—"Hold your bets, please."

Lucille took a breath and closed her eyes. She concentrated: *thirteen*. She heard the ball skip and skitter.

"Thirteen."

Did he say it? A great whoop went up. The blue-chip man jumped off his stool and danced around the table to Lucille, crowing "Yes! Mama, yes!"

A sickly grin spread over the croupier's face. His boss gaped at Lucille as if she had punched his big stomach.

"Oh lady, we did it!" the other winner was shouting. "We did it! God *damn!*"

The croupier pushed eight columns of powder-blue chips to his end, and began to count out stacks of red-and-gold $500 chips for Lucille. More people wandered into the commotion.

Lucille felt dizzy. The croupier raked the whole pile across the green felt, to join the small fortune she had won on her first turn.

Good Lord. Thousands and thousands of dollars. She tipped the croupier three hundred bucks.

This time his "Thank you, ma'am" had the ring of sincerity. He bowed and turned to the table. "Place your bets, please."

Everyone was betting thirteen and waiting for Lucille. She knew she should quit but she had to see if it would happen a third time.

"She won all that in two spins!"

"Who *is* she?"

The buzz grew. People unglued themselves from the slot machines and headed over to the excitement.

Lucille knew it was probably unwise to become the center-ring attraction in a casino, but who could have predicted this luck? Who on earth could get up and walk away from such luck as this?

She counted out five thousand dollars with her thumbnail, and pushed the stack onto the number thirteen. Maybe she would become rich beyond her wildest dreams. If this unlucky number came up a third time, Lucille would know beyond all doubt that it was a direct literal sign from God, Yes! Lucille, yes! Keep going! You're on the right path!

Reams of chips in every color came to join hers, crowding out thirteen, spilling over other numbers.

The croupier stacked and restacked the pile into a small mountain of wealth. Three burly men in tuxedoes gathered behind him as he set the wheel spinning.

The waitress touched Lucille's shoulder. "Cocktail?"

She turned to say no thanks, she'd barely had time to taste the first one, when the croupier said "Hold your bets, please." She had no time to concentrate.

The ball took a bounce, and another bounce, and skipped onto the wheel.

"Twenty-seven," the croupier said.

The crowd groaned as if they'd been stabbed. The blunt rake came out and stroked that whole big pile of chips back into the croupier's trough.

All the people who'd bet with Lucille were now glaring at her.

She shrugged. That fast, she knew her luck had changed. "I guess three times is not the charm, after all." She bent down for her hatbox and purse. "Thank you all so much, I think I'll go take a bath now."

She could tell by the arch in the croupier's eyebrows that he never expected her to win that much that fast, or to walk away after losing once. He smiled. "Very good, ma'am." He swapped her chips for green money chips. His boss clicked his cricket twice.

A hefty tuxedoed man materialized at Lucille's elbow, offering a large paper cup embossed with a pink flamingo.

"My name's Ralston," he said. "I'll be happy to escort you to the cashier."

"Why, thank you, Mr. Ralston. Everyone here is so pleasant."

He helped her scoop her winnings into the cup by the double handful, and steered her through the crowd. Spectators stepped back from the wheel to let them through. A few applauded. Lucille did a little curtsy, and smiled. She decided it must be very rare to win at roulette, everyone was making such a fuss.

Ralston was a beefy, tough-looking guy with a five o'clock shadow; if he weren't in a tuxedo, he would be driving a truck. "That was some big luck, Miss, uhm—sorry, I didn't catch your name."

"Clay," she said. "Carolyn Clay."

"Are you staying with us, Miss Clay?"

"If I can get a room with a nice tub."

"I think we can handle that." He pressed a business card into her hand. "This number's private. Anything you need while you're here, just call. How long are you staying?"

"Just tonight." Lucille was under the impression she had just won a tremendous amount of money from this casino. Why was this man being so nice to her? Watch him try and hustle his money back. . . .

They approached a wall of teller cages. "Did you want that in cash?" Ralston said.

"Cash will be fine." She handed the cup through the window.

The impassive cashier poured the chips in a heap, sorted them with dazzling speed, and began laying out bundle after bundle of hundred-dollar bills bound with white paper collars.

"You're welcome to keep this in our safe," Ralston was saying. "For your peace of mind."

Lucille said "It's my money, right?"

"Right."

"Well, I think I'll just hold on to it."

"Whatever you say. Just be careful."

The cashier pushed four bricks of bills through the cage. "Thirty-one thousand, four hundred dollars."

"My goodness." Lucille blinked. As far as anyone could see, she maintained an amazing grip on herself—but inside, she was jumping up and down screaming for joy.

You!

    Can!

       Win!

          At!

            ROULETTE!!

What she said was: "My purse won't hold all that."

The cashier gave her a white canvas bag. Lucille loaded in the money, pulled the drawstring shut, and followed Ralston past a row of ritzy shops—dresses, jewelry, furs—and straight to the head of a line of people sitting on their luggage at the hotel desk.

Ralston snapped his fingers at the clerk. "Suzanne, this is Miss Clay. She'll be our guest in the Rose Garden Suite tonight."

Suzanne turned her back on her customer. "Welcome to the Flamingo, Miss Clay."

"That sounds pretty fancy, a suite." Lucille tried not to sound suspicious. "How much is that going to cost?"

Ralston lowered his voice. "It's a courtesy of the house for our special players. I beg your pardon, but—is this by any chance your first time in Vegas?"

"Oh no, I've been here lots of times. But I've never played roulette before. Usually I play cards." Lucille pictured herself plopped on the floor at home with Sandra and Cary, playing Old Maid.

"You did very well," he said. "I hope you'll join us for a game later on—we have private tables for poker, twenty-one, baccarat, whatever you like."

Lucille smiled from one ear to the other. "I like roulette."

"I imagine you do." He bowed. "If you want dinner, want to see a show . . ."

"I'll call you."

"Please do." He headed back to the casino. The desk clerk bopped a big copper bell.

Lucille's favorite towheaded bellhop appeared from nowhere. "Good evening," he said with a delicious grin.

He must have been waiting behind the slot machines for that bell. Lucille tingled all over—a bag of free money and a good-looking boy! She couldn't wait to get him upstairs and out of that pink tuxedo.

"Show Miss Clay to the Rose Garden Suite, will you, Jack?" The clerk gave him a key. "Enjoy your stay."

"Oh, I am already," she said, and silently: Hello, Jack.

Jack played his part very well. "Evening, ma'am. Any luggage?"

"Just these." She handed him her purse and the bag of money. "I'll carry my husband myself."

He laughed. She followed him to the elevator.

He pressed the topmost button. "Did you get a chance to look around the casino?"

"I sure did. I played roulette."

"Any luck?"

"Take a look in the bag."

He loosened the cinch. His eyes clicked wide open. "You—you won all this? There must be . . ."

"Thirty-one thousand four hundred dollars." She couldn't stop smiling.

"Man!" He smacked his hand on the wood-grained wall. "Lady! You are *rich!*"

"I know. I've never been rich before. You'll have to show me how to act."

The elevator door slid open. He bowed low with his hand extended, footman to a queen. "After you."

Lucille stepped out. "Your name's Jack?"

"That's right."

"I'm Carolyn."

Flash! went his thousand-watt grin. "Welcome to Vegas, Carolyn." He led the way to a door with a fancy gold plaque: Rose Garden Suite.

"I've never stayed in a room that had a name," she said.

"I bet you get used to it real fast." His hand brushed her arm as he leaned to open the door.

Well hello, had Lucille died and gone to heaven? This room was bigger than her whole house, bigger than any house in Cornelia. Dusky pink carpet stretched to a wall of windows, an artful arrangement of low-slung Danish modern furniture by a fireplace, two sofas flanked by armless chairs, a kidney-shaped coffee table—everything was perfectly sleek and new, in elegant tones of rose-pink and white.

"My Lord, it's enormous." She didn't see a bed. Maybe one of those sofas was a fold-out.

Jack went into his bellhop routine, flipping lights on and off, demonstrating the electrically-controlled curtains, the TV set concealed in a maple armoire. "That's a wet bar there, fully stocked, and if you'll step in here . . ."

Lucille had assumed that door led to a closet, but no! A whole other room! "This just goes on and on," she murmured.

And then she saw it, on a raised platform against the wall: a big pink heart-shaped bed, like the wide plushy heart behind the opening credits of "I Love Lucy." The headboard was another heart, inverted, upholstered in red velvet.

First she thought: where on earth do they get heart-shaped sheets? Her second thought made her blush. Jack was in the bathroom, splashing and flushing and turning on lights.

Whoever designed that bed was not thinking about a good night's sleep.

"This is the honeymoon suite." Jack came to the doorway. His grin made a lovely straight line with his jaw.

Lucille placed the hatbox on the dresser. "I guess that makes this my second honeymoon." She kicked off her shoes, and crossed the room wiggling her toes in the furry carpet. "Tell you the truth, it's my first. Chester and I were supposed to go to Panama City, but he went coon hunting instead." She sat on the pointed end of the heart.

Jack eased from the doorway. "You're married?"

"A widow." She liked the sound of that.

"I'm sorry. . . ."

"Don't be. I'm not." She patted the bed. "Come here."

He sauntered over and dropped the money bag on the bed. "I only get twenty minutes for my break."

"Well then I guess we'd better hurry." She smiled up.

"You are one hot-blooded lady." He slid out of his jacket. His clip-on bowtie came off in her hand. She undid his shirt buttons teasingly, one at a time, sliding her knuckles down his hard chest. A Technicolor tan, big shoulders, slender waist. Big biceps from lifting all that luggage.

"I bet you do this a lot," she said.

"Not as much as I'd like." He grinned and pushed her back on the bed. "And never with a lady as good-looking as you."

"Oh sugar, aren't you smart." She opened her arms. "You know all the magic words."

He stretched over her, the whole young length of him pressing down. He kissed her. She tasted bubble gum.

She tugged at his shirt. "Wait a minute." Something under her shoulder—the canvas bag. She felt down in it.

Jack nuzzled her neck. His fingers plied the buttons on her blouse.

She brought out a bundle of hundreds, and tickled his naked flank with the end of it.

He wiggled. "Stop!"

"Look at this." Slicing the paper collar with her thumbnail, she fanned out the bills and pressed them to her nose, breathing the green inky smell. "Here, smell."

He obliged. His eyes sparkled. "We're both lucky tonight." He rolled her over on her back. His knee sidled up her thigh as he kissed up her arm, her throat . . .

She flung the money in the air. It fluttered down all around like confetti.

"Tell me, Jack," she murmured, "have you ever made love in a whole bunch of money?"

"Huh-uh"—hot breath in her ear. He came around to kiss her. His eager young tongue swam in, then he broke off the kiss, hopped off the bed, stripped off his pants. He was wonderfully excited, breathing fast— it struck Lucille how silly a man looks with a boner, even the best-looking man. It throws them out of balance, like an extra leg. Wouldn't it look strange if one of her breasts got big and stuck out that way when she got excited?

"What is it?" he said, seeing her smile. "What's wrong?"

"Nothing." She stretched back onto the pillow. "You look beautiful."

"You too." His hands skimmed up her legs, smooth as water up under her skirt, to her waist. "No underwear?" He shook his finger at her, naughty girl, and planted a kiss on her hipbone.

"It's too hot," she said, wrestling out of the dress. She undid the catch on her Cross Your Heart bra. They were naked together on pink satin.

He kissed a warm trail up her belly. "Here I come, ready or no-ot . . ."

Lucille closed her eyes and lay back. His mouth roamed over her body like some incredibly talented butterfly fluttering silken wings. He traced the hills and slopes, treating each place to a touch, a breath, a moment.

The teasing ended, and things took a serious turn.

He circled her nipple with his tongue, sending warm waves through her. He nipped her collarbone, the side of her neck, he tasted her ear. Lucille felt her body yearning and tossing under his intricate attention. Their legs overlapped. Jack looked like a boy but he was good, a good lover, he knew what he was doing now with his fingers.

In a heartbeat his tenderness vanished. He grabbed her, opened her up, then he was booming into her like waves on a beach, rolling and crashing, retreating and crashing again, coming on. She cried out. She opened her eyes to watch him drive at it. His face surly, intent. He wanted what he was getting what he wanted. A little grunt in the back of his throat. He turned her sideways on the heart-shaped bed for a better angle.

Don't stop. Now or ever. Don't stop.

Lucille lost track. It was not like the fog. It was fast and dirty and romantic. He did everything. He took her down and turned her over so she straddled the point of the heart with her knees. There was more, she didn't remember. In the end they were up at the pillows again making wild noises as her nose mashed into the red velvet headboard and lightning ran shuddering down to her dark very middle. He shouted "Yes! Oh, God! Hunh!" and they collapsed.

For a long time, they lay breathing on each other, entwined.

"Whoo-ee." Jack rose up with a hundred-dollar bill stuck to his sweaty face.

Lucille peeled it off, and leaned over to kiss him, and knew she would never have a better moment than this.

15

Peejoe

Industry

O ne minute Taylor Jackson was a real boy like me, living breathing walking around like me, and the next minute he was dead because he wanted to swim in the pool and the sheriff did not want him there.

I had never spent much time thinking about dying, since it made me afraid, but I thought a life was a mighty big thing to give up for something as small as that.

Dove said he couldn't understand what made those boys go down there and start trouble. "They must have known," he said, "you push a man like John Doggett and he's got to push back."

"The only one who got pushed was Taylor," I said. "I saw the whole thing."

"Did you see who pushed him?"

"Not exactly."

"See there?" Dove shook his head. "You were there, you saw it, and you're not even sure what you saw. It won't help anything for you to get all worked up about it."

I wasn't worked up. I saw it all plain. I knew it was wrong. It was *wrong*. Taylor Jackson did not have to die. Anybody who saw it knew that. It was some power larger than everyone there, some deadly breeze that blew through those deputies and set them upon those boys with their clubs. Nobody meant for Taylor Jackson to die. When he did, they turned around and blamed it on him.

The rest of us stood by and watched it like something on TV. I'd been so proud of myself for stepping out to defend him, but when that deputy saw me and raised his billy club, I tucked myself back in the white part of that crowd right quick.

In most people's eyes Taylor was just a nigger, not even a human being.

His death didn't count. But I'd seen him die. It counted for me. I saw it happen, I knew it was wrong. I knew that more purely than I'd ever known anything.

Today I was looking for some visible sign, some change in the world. On Lee Street the birds sang and darted through chattering sprinklers. A woman stood at a clothesline, whacking a quilt with a stick.

Cicadas sent up a racket from the bushes, a rising sinuous hiss that came from all around to shatter the hot afternoon. A truck rumbled up Beauregard Avenue. A black dog barked and loped up to sniff my hand, wagged along after me to the edge of the park.

A boy slouched against the fence by the swimming pool, looking down at the spot where Taylor Jackson fell.

The black dog turned and went home.

I trotted across the field, wetting the toes of my sneakers in the dewy grass. The pool shone jewel-blue, a perfect glittering rectangle, deserted. A hand-lettered sign said CLOSED FOR REPAIRS.

"Hey, Wiley."

He turned, startled. "What are you doing here?"

"I just came to look."

We gazed down at the red sand, the skimpy grass, the concrete ledge: not a footprint, not a drop of blood—no sign at all of the struggle that now unscrolled itself in my mind like a bad dream.

"Looks like somebody came with a broom and swept it," I said.

"They erased him." Wiley drew a line in the sand with his toe. "Like it never happened."

I said "They ought to arrest somebody."

"You think the sheriff's gonna arrest himself? I'd like to see that."

"Well he started it."

"That's not true, Peejoe. Those nigger boys started it. It wasn't their fault what happened next, but they were the ones who sat down and wouldn't leave."

"I guess you're right."

Wiley rubbed out the line with the side of his shoe. "Let's get out of here."

We wandered up the hill toward town. Already it was hot enough that the Dairy Dog was doing big business in dip cones and Slushees. The COLORED window stood abandoned on the shady side. Five people waited in the hot sun at the window marked WHITE. Wiley and I watched a bunch of dirty kids swarming over a picnic table—and here came their big rolling mother bearing a cardboard tray heaped with corn dogs and French fries and steaming cones of soft-serve ice cream.

Wiley poked me. "Got money?"

I shook my head. I'd spent my last quarter on that Suicide at the pool yesterday.

We walked uptown. The usual old men sat on the courthouse benches, trading opinions in the shade of the trees. A row of fine, shiny cars stood in hot sunshine in front of the Planter's Bank. The Negro end of Beauregard Street was deserted.

"Where'd they all go?" Wiley said.

"I bet they're afraid after what happened."

We followed the sound of hammering down Stuart Street. For a while we watched a herd of construction workers pounding on the skeleton of the new Piggly Wiggly.

We set off along the back of an overgrown yard, where an ancient old woman was hanging out sheets on the line.

She spotted us and said "Boys!"

"Keep walking," Wiley muttered.

"You, boys! Come here!"

We stopped. We looked around. Obviously she meant us.

Wiley said "What?"

She crooked her finger. "Come here to me."

She was old. Older even than Meemaw. What if she just needed help reaching the clothesline? "Come on, let's see what she wants."

Reluctantly he followed me through the waist-high forest of weeds.

The lady wore a blue apron over a faded print housedress. Her straw hat was tied at her chin with a black ribbon. She ran a sheet out to full length along the line and pinned it with the clothespin from her mouth. "Whose boys are you?"

"Nobody's," I said. I tried not to stare at the flesh-colored mole sprouting hairs from her chin.

Her teeth clicked. "I heard there was trouble over there at that swimmin' pool yesterday." She spat the words "swimmin' pool" like a curse.

"Yes, ma'am," Wiley said.

"I heard all about it. They try to keep things from me but I hear what goes on."

That didn't sound like a question. I didn't try to answer.

"I told them they should never have put that thing in there in the first place. That was begging for trouble. There was plenty of places to swim, the crick was always good enough for us. We never needed no *swimmin' pool*. It's like that Wallace says, any time they go and change something, it's trouble." She lifted a yellowed pillowcase to the line with trembling hands. "Are y'all playing hooky from school?"

"School's out," I said. "It's summertime."

"Yes, it is. It surely is."

She seemed frail and kind of lonesome. I found myself stooping to help her lift the wet bedsheet from the basket. Wiley rolled his eyes. He wanted to get out of there.

"Said a nigra boy got killed at that place."

"Yes, ma'am," I said. "He tripped and hit his head."

She fetched a handful of pins from her apron. "That is surely too bad. This is no time to go killing them. I seen that one on the television, got 'em carrying on from here to Montgomery."

"Yes ma'am."

"Our colored people are happy down here. It ain't like Selma. Those people up there are common, if you ask me. You boys know how to run a lawn mower?"

I said yes, because I didn't want her to think I couldn't do something that simple. Wiley glared at me.

"I got a perfectly good one, but nobody's used it in years," she said. "I'd pay good money if you all was to cut down this yard for me."

My fingers felt down in my pockets. Nothing but lint.

Wiley said "How much?"

"Two dollars."

He shrugged. "This is a big yard. Look how high this grass is."

"Three dollars, then."

"Ten dollars," I said.

The old lady snatched the pillowcase from my hand. "Ten dollars? My Grady used to break his back pushing a plow from sunup to sundown and he never made no ten dollars."

"Well maybe you should get him to cut it for you," I said. "Come on, Wiley. Let's go."

"Wait," she said. "Grady's dead. Five dollars. That's as much as I can pay."

I knew she was being cheap. That was a fine old house, even if she hadn't kept it up. She probably had hundreds stashed in her mattress. "Sorry," I said. "We'd have to have ten."

"All right, but don't you dare tell a soul I paid you that much. They'll cart me off to Bryce's."

She introduced herself as Mrs. Boggs. Wiley said he was Wiley. I said I was Peejoe, and she asked what kind of name was that.

I said it was just my name.

She led us to the lawn mower, a primitive Yazoo nearly as old as the lady, with bike-sized rear wheels and the blade dangerously exposed on top. Wiley wheeled it out from under the house.

Mrs. Boggs retreated to her porch to watch.

I spilled gasoline all over my hands filling the tank. Wiley stood yanking a long time on the starter-cord. At last the old machine stammered to life.

It took one bite of that tough, fork-tongued grass, and died.

Wiley pulled and sweated and got it started again, while I stood to one side offering advice. He tilted the blade at an angle, and managed to cut out a mower-sized chunk of the weeds. Pulverized grass flew everywhere, coating us both in fine dust. Wiley sneezed. The mower conked out. Wiley sneezed again.

He wiped his nose on his shirt. "Look, Peejoe, I say we just forget this. Look at this damn jungle. I don't want to spend all day getting all hot and sweaty for five lousy bucks. You got us into this. Tell her we've gotta go home."

"You go home," I said. "That'll leave the whole ten bucks for me."

"Are you crazy? You can't cut this whole yard by yourself."

"Wanna bet? I bet you three dollars I can, and then I'll have thirteen dollars and you won't have nothing."

"Uncle Dove'll *give* us ten bucks if we ask him."

I crouched beside the mower.

"I'm going to see what Mabel's up to," said Wiley.

I pulled the starter-cord. "Have a good time."

I didn't really believe he would go off and leave me to cut that big yard by myself, but he did, and I didn't run after him. Mrs. Boggs's backyard was a job for a man, or at least two boys, but the prospects of ten dollars in my pocket and showing up Wiley made me doubly determined. I sweated and struggled and started the mower.

The blade whined, biting into the snaky weeds, slinging gobs of grass through the air. I started chewing away at the edges of the jungle, carving a thicker slice with each pass around the perimeter. I raised a great dust cloud and a racket to drown out every cicada in town.

Whenever I missed a spot, Mrs. Boggs came down off her porch to point it out. Otherwise I was alone with the job. The job swallowed me up. It made me happy to sweat and get dirty. I slaved away for hours, singing the Herman's Hermits song in the key of the roaring mower, stopping again and again to refill the gas tank. I was too busy mowing to think about anything.

I never saw the hole. I heard the yowl of the mower passing over it. Later I went back to Mrs. Boggs's yard and searched all around and found it, a shallow, fist-sized sinkhole hidden under the weeds, lined with gravel and pieces of broken glass.

As the mower passed over, it sucked up the rocks, rattled them around and sprayed them out the top at me, *pi-yannng!* ricocheting like jagged bullets.

One rock caught me just above the elbow, a sharp sting. I looked down in surprise—a red spot, a bloom of fresh blood.

While I was looking at that, something hit my eye.

That was all I knew, something hit my eye and I could not see.

My hand touched my face and came away covered with blood.

I staggered back. I must have screamed but I remember only the sputter and *pop!* of the lawn mower running downhill away from me. I tripped and fell and got up again, clutching the side of my face. Something squishy on my cheek.

I had no sensation of pain. Blood dripped onto my tongue. A black awful chill seized the front of my head, as if the pain will come but not yet, not yet, the waiting is terrible knowing how bad it will be.

I know I presented a truly fearful sight to Mrs. Boggs, reeling across her yard a disfigured monster, streaming blood down my face, my free hand stretched out to her.

She came out of her porch swing with terrorized eyes. She turned stone white, and collapsed.

I stumbled up the steps to stand over her, pleading with her to please get up and help me. Blood fell in fat splashes on her apron. I crouched down and shook her arm. Bending over brought a wild rush of dizziness that sent me lurching into the porch rail.

I had the impression that my right hand was the only thing holding my eye in. Blood ran down my elbow. I fought the urge to throw up.

I don't know who shut off that lawn mower, maybe it ran out of gas, maybe it is still running somewhere looking for me, looking to fling a rock into my other eye. I ran for my life, terror rising inside me, *oh what have I done have I done.* There was no pain but cold, deep black cold in my face. *Please somebody help me* I ran into a tree. Panic urged me on, a shrill voice shrieking *Injury! Major injury! Run!*

I tottered out to a landscape of wheelbarrows, mounded red dirt, future site of the Piggly Wiggly parking lot. I made it over the first red mound and fell to my knees.

I made some noise that stopped them all working at once. Even the men on the roof dropped their hammers and turned to see me.

Two men came toward me, reflecting the horror of my face in their eyes.

When I saw their faces, I fainted.

Many voices, strained and shouting. I felt them lifting me, the weight of two hands pressing down on my face as the other hands lifted me up. I let out a groan that only made them shout louder. No one was talking to me.

Somebody came to hold my eye in, it was more than I could do. My hands weighed ten tons apiece.

Words loomed up from the dark: "There's an old lady dead over there. Blood all over the place."

And another voice: "I want men back there. Don't let anybody get away. Move!"

I tried to move. I fainted again.

They thought I was shot. The construction men took one look at the bloody mess behind my fingers and called it in to the sheriff that way, *boy shot in the face.* When the deputies found Mrs. Boggs crumpled on her porch, spackled with blood and quite dead, they assumed we both had been shot by persons unknown, and that's how it went out over the radio. By the time the ambulance got me to the county hospital, deputies were combing the neighborhood for the gunman, and the WCOT deejay was on the air with news of a double shooting in Industry, two believed dead in the wake of Thursday's race incident at the new swimming pool.

I knew nothing of this. I was gone at the time. Some people say when they get close to death they see bright lights or lush green gardens. I must not have gotten close. I didn't see anything. I remember green masks peering down. They gave me a shot in my face, just over my eye. The pain bloomed like a white waxy flower. Then I was gone again.

Dove didn't know it was me. He was out in the country collecting on pre-need burial policies when he heard the news on the radio. He sped into town and found Mrs. Boggs's house by the wail of the sirens. In the confusion he learned that an old woman and a boy had been shot, but not who. He saw right away that the lady hadn't been shot at all—no bullet holes, not enough blood—but John Doggett was too busy directing his manhunt to listen.

Dove placed Mrs. Boggs on a stretcher in the back of his hearse, and drove her to Croaker-Moseley.

Wiley came downstairs to tell him I hadn't come back from mowing an old lady's yard.

I don't know how Dove felt when he heard this. To this day I am glad I don't know.

He flew to the hospital.

It was hot in that country, steaming hot, nothing happening. In the listless air of an afternoon like that, the story spread in circles from every house with a radio, washing down back alleys, over phone lines and fencetops, widening and improving with every telling. All afternoon I was the white unknown juvenile in serious condition. By the time Dove reached the hospital they were saying my name on the radio, my accident had gotten all mixed up with what happened to Taylor Jackson. Word got out that I had been at the swimming pool Friday. Some identified me as a white boy who'd stepped forward in defense of the sit-in. Everyone saw a connection between what happened at the pool and the inexplicable shooting of Mrs. Boggs and myself.

This was all pure invention, of course, but it was vivid enough, and the weather was hot enough. The story unfurled its wings and took off. It was just the kind of thing people wanted to believe. They fanned it along, kept it aloft, breathed it full of hot air.

Out in Dog Junction, fearful word passed from house to house: two white folks shot, two Negro boys under arrest, everybody stay home and keep your head down.

Dr. Ward, the general surgeon who was stitching my eye back into my face, heard the news on the radio when he stepped out in mid-operation to smoke a cigarette.

He padded back into the operating room. "This boy wasn't shot," he said.

The head nurse said "I beg your pardon?"

"On the radio they're saying he was shot." He took up a sponge and began dabbing my eye. "Debra, better go call the sheriff. They've arrested a couple of kids. Tell John Doggett I don't know what hit this boy, but it wasn't a bullet. I think maybe a sharp rock, or a big piece of glass. Look how it cut. Sliced right along the smooth muscle. He lost a lot of blood." His thumb tenderly traced the socket. "I hope we can save this eye."

"What did they say on the radio?"

"They said it had something to do with that mess at the pool yesterday. Hand me that clamp."

My body lay before them. They spoke in toneless voices as they stitched my eye with needles. I was in a land beyond dreams.

16

Peejoe

Industry

I woke up blind, my head wrapped in cotton. I didn't know where I was.

"Can you hear me, Sweet Pea?" Meemaw pressed my hand.

"I can't see."

"I know, honey, you hurt your eye. Do you remember?"

I did. It was terrible. I swallowed the stone in my throat. "Am I going to die?"

"Heavens no."

"My head hurts, Meemaw."

"I know it does." I felt her solid weight beside me on the bed. Her cool fingers stroked my cheek below the bandage.

I heard the squeal of a door-hinge, and footsteps, and Dove's booming voice: "You awake, big man?" He got a grip on my toe, and shook my whole leg. "How you doing there?"

Meemaw moved away from the bed.

"Am I blind, Uncle Dove?"

"Don't think so." He sounded cheerful, but not certain. "Got a big bandage around your head. You should see yourself, you look like the Mummy." He squeezed my toe. "Did you see what hit you?"

"A rock," I said. "I think it was a rock."

"Are you sure about that? Nobody took a shot at you, nothing like that?"

"I don't—I don't know what you mean."

"The boys on the scene said somebody took a potshot at you and Miz Boggs. Now, I know she wasn't shot."

"Meemaw, tell him. I was cutting her grass. Something hit my eye."

He let go of my toe. "Peter Joseph, I saw that yard and I can't figure for

137

the life of me what you were thinking. We got plenty of grass you could have cut."

"She was gonna pay me ten dollars."

"Son." He let out all his worry in one long sigh. "If you needed money, don't you know you can always ask me? You didn't have to go and put your eye out for ten dollars."

"I'm sorry." I was terrified. Was my eye put out?

Dove said "What happened to Miz Boggs?"

"I don't know, she just—she fainted, I guess. I was bleeding." Just then a terrible needle slid into my eye. "Meemaw, my head hurts something awful."

"Peter Joseph." Dove's voice was quiet. "Meemaw's not here. She's back home with your cousins. She wants to come, she's worried sick about you. Maybe she can, before too long."

"But she was just—I was just talking to her."

"No, that was me."

"But you . . . didn't you see her when you came in?"

"The nurse was just in to give you a shot," he said. "I think you're dreaming a little. It's the medicine."

"It was her," I protested. "She was here." I was blind, and here was Dove trying to make me think I was crazy.

"Listen, sport, you need some rest. And I've got a fire to put out. Here. Here's a quarter, open your hand. I'll come back at suppertime and keep you company." He leaned down to kiss my cheek, leaving a whiff of Hai Karate in the air.

The door squealed again, and he was gone.

"Meemaw. I know you're here."

She didn't answer.

"Why are you hiding?"

I heard voices outside. A shroud of darkness swept over me.

Sometime later, a nurse came in and made me swallow a pill with a cup of tepid water which I spilled all down my hospital gown. I asked who else was in the room. The nurse said "Nobody. It's the middle of the night. What have you got in your hand?"

I gave her the quarter.

"I'll leave it right here on your bedside table. Now go back to sleep."

But I couldn't sleep. I was not alone. The others were holding their breath and stealing about in the dark, taking advantage of my blindness.

I listened for the telltale sounds. I didn't know how bad my eye was. I thought it was bad.

Almost without my noticing, the pain had begun, and now it was a sledgehammer pounding away at the front of my head. I kept trying to duck out of the way, but it kept on swinging and striking.

Meemaw came in. She sat on the edge of the bed and touched my face. Where her fingertips touched, a warmth spread and kept spreading, and warmed out all the pain until I felt just wonderful. It was magic. My eye was healed.

A man said "What's the matter with you?"

"Uncle Chester?" He sounded so close—my hand groped in empty air.

"We want to swim in the pool," said Taylor Jackson.

"We have a right to be here," said a third voice.

The room was filling up with people. I wished Wiley was here to see them all, to see how Meemaw's miracle touch had cured me.

An old lady said, "I would pay good money if somebody was to cut down this yard for me."

"Are you crazy?" That was Wiley. "You can't cut this whole yard by yourself."

"I have a right to be buried here," Chester murmured. "I was born here."

"Purty a day as this is, and you in here messing around with old me."

With my hands I examined the stiff bandage encasing my head.

"Look at him." A new voice, deep and gentle. A stranger. "Isn't he fine? Just as fine as we hoped he would be."

"Poor baby, his eye is hurt." A woman's voice, somehow familiar. "I wish we could have saved him from that."

The other voices faded until I was alone with just these two.

"He'll be all right," the man said. "He'll just have to see twice as much with his other eye."

The woman sat lightly on the foot of the bed. "Does he know who we are? Do you think he knows we're here?"

"Tomorrow he'll think he was dreaming," the man said.

I tried to say something but I had forgotten how to speak.

The man said "I'm proud of how he turned out. And I'm sorry, you know, we had to go off and leave him."

Her voice was strained. "I wish he knew how much we love him."

"Don't cry, honey," the man said. "He knows."

And then they were gone.

17

Peejoe

Industry

O ne time Meemaw took Wiley and me to the eye doctor. He gave us
drops to dilate our eyes, and black-plastic wraparound sunglasses
to wear afterward. On the way home Meemaw stopped by Greer's market
to pick up some cornmeal. Wiley and I had the best time in those glasses
pretending we were blind boys—leaning on the guardrails, running our
hands over the faces of cereal boxes, waving our hands in front of us like
Helen Keller. Meemaw saw what we were doing and told us to stop. "It's
bad luck," she said, and we laughed at her.

Now I knew she had spoken the truth.

I huddled against the cool steel bedrail. Anyone could lay a hand on me
and I would never see them coming.

I managed to open my left eye just enough to see speckled light
through the gauze. My right eye was a big heavy stone mounted to the
front of my head. The pressure from the bandage made my skull ache.

I heard the squeak of rubber soles. "Hello, Pete, I'm Dr. Ward. We
didn't get a chance to meet the other night." I liked his firm grip. "I'm the
one who sewed you back together. Do they call you Pete?"

"Peejoe."

"Well all right. Peejoe." He felt my pulse, listened to my chest. "How
do you feel this morning?"

"My head hurts."

"It's probably going to hurt for a while."

"Are my eyes blind?"

"Your left eye is fine. Let's don't worry about the right one for now. Tell
me exactly what happened."

His voice was wise and sure, like his hands. I relaxed. As I told him all about Mrs. Boggs and the lawn mower, he began snipping with scissors at my helmet of cotton.

"You know everybody thought you'd been shot, you and the lady," he said.

"That's what Uncle Dove said. I don't know why. I never said that. It was the lawn mower."

"Well, for one thing, you lost a lot of blood." Dr. Ward unwound the gauze from my head. The pressure lightened with each pass around. "You cut a nice chunk in your face and you got blood all over Mrs. Boggs, nobody realized it was your blood. Apparently she had a cerebral hemorrhage."

"I killed her." I wasn't afraid to confess. "She took one look at me and dropped dead."

"Well, be that as it may," he said, "the whole thing was an accident. The sheriff's men picked up a couple of colored boys on suspicion of shooting you. They let 'em go, but now everybody's jumpy. The colored folks are having meetings and talking about marching somewhere. People tend to overreact."

"Am I in trouble?"

"Not that I know of." He removed the last stretch of bandage. Bright light washed into my head—but only one side of my head.

I squinted in the window-glare. The left side of the room was a blur, which slowly evolved into vision.

My right eye saw nothing at all.

Turning my head, I saw Dr. Ward studying me. He looked older than his voice, silver hair and amiable wrinkles in his face. "Son, you had what we call an orbital blowout. What that means is your eye came out of the socket. We put it back in." I remember the squishy thing I'd held against my cheek.

"Can you see me at all through this eye? Here. Close the good one." He put his thumb on my eyelid. "Now. Anything?"

"No. It's all dark."

"Well, okay."

My heart sank. "Is it blind?"

"I think we'll have to see. There's something called an optic nerve, it's like the main extension cord to your eye. Sometimes it'll just plug itself in. We'll see what happens when you've had some rest."

"How bad does it look?"

"Not all that bad."

"Can I see?"

"I don't know why not." He fetched a hand mirror from his satchel and held it up before me.

I flinched. A gruesome centipede scar crawled across the bone above my eye socket, held together with dozens of stitches from the bridge of my nose to my ear. The eye was black. It looked dead, like the eye of a fish.

"How long will it look like that?"

"The scar will heal pretty well, have to think up a good story to tell your girlfriends. The eye itself—we'll see. You'll need to look through this other one for the time being."

The nurse helped him construct a whopper of a gauze-and-tape bandage on the front of my head. "Now I'm going to give you this eyepatch. I want you to wear it to keep the bandage on until you come back to see me."

The patch looked like one cup of a little black brassiere with an elastic strap. I stretched it over my head. "Like this?"

"Just right. You look like Long John Silver."

When it was over, Dove drove me home in the white hearse. He made me lie down on the stretcher in back, which was hardly necessary, but I didn't object to riding through Industry on my back like some bigshot accident victim. I lay very still, so people peeking in might think I was dead.

Wiley was waiting for us in the carport.

He looked stricken. Dove hadn't said anything to me, but we all knew Wiley had left me in Mrs. Boggs's yard with that killer lawn mower, when he was supposed to be my big brother, looking out for me. He had left his post just at the moment the worst possible thing was about to happen.

I hated to think what he'd gone through since then.

"Hey, Wiley."

"Hey." He stared at my bandage. "You all right?"

"Pretty good." I turned my head to see him. "The doctor says my eye might get well."

He must have truly suffered while I lay dreaming in the hospital. But I felt a secret glimmer of pleasure: I had something on him so momentous I could hold it over his head for the rest of all time.

Dove helped me down from the stretcher. All that lying down had left me feeble, a bit dizzy and weak-kneed. I wobbled toward the house.

"Peter Joseph, you're going to stay in Mabel's room for now."

"Aw come on, Uncle Dove, I like it up there with Wiley." The top floor was *our* place! Who wanted to sleep with Mabel's creepy stuffed animals and New Christy Minstrels posters?

"Let him stay up there with me," Wiley said. "I'll look out after him."
Dove said "I don't want him falling down those stairs."

"He won't, I promise."

The world seemed only half as wide through one eye. I held out my hands for balance. "Please, Uncle Dove."

"I don't know, boy, I'm responsible for you. You don't know what it was like to call Mama and tell her what happened."

I remembered Meemaw's gentle hand on my face in the hospital room. I knew she had been there, no matter what Dove said. It was one of those mysterious moments you know in your heart is true, but you keep it to yourself since you also know no one will ever believe you.

Dove steered me through the mortuary to the front of the house. I scanned this way and that, waiting for something to spring out at me from my blind side.

A visitation in progress, the last parlor on the right. "That's Miz Boggs," Wiley whispered.

I glimpsed the edge of a casket, a pair of ghostly folded hands holding a bouquet of white flowers.

Dove steered me up the stairs—maybe he didn't want her family to see me. Maybe they blamed me for killing her.

Mabel and Earlene came out to welcome me home; they winced at the sight of me. "My Lord," Earlene said. "You look frightful."

I pleaded until Dove agreed to let me stay on the third floor where I belonged. He found me a little brass bell to ring when I needed something. Earlene brought an extra pillow for my cot and went out to have her hair done.

I gave that bell a workout all afternoon. Mabel and Wiley trudged up and down fixing a nest for me, bringing me blankets and 7-Ups and magazines and a transistor radio, tending to my every desire. I thought up lots of things for them to do.

I suppose I overdid it. By evening they were ignoring the bell; I was all alone in the vast gloom of the attic. My head throbbed. I had read every comic book in the house. I knew for a fact that there were two hundred and eleven acoustical tiles in the finished portion of the ceiling. The minutes slogged by. Earlene had gone to her Daughters of the Confederacy meeting. Dove and Milton were off retrieving the body of an old man who'd been dead on his kitchen floor for so long that his hungry cocker spaniels had gotten after him. I wanted to go along to see that, but Dove said, "Forget about it."

Struggling up from the cot, I startled myself in the mirror. No wonder everyone looked traumatized at the sight of me. Five spider-legs of adhesive tape held the bulging bandage to my face, and with the black eyepatch strapped over that, I looked like a hideous bug-eyed Cyclops monster from a Saturday afternoon movie.

I had been brave up to now, but all at once I felt horribly ugly and alone. Maybe I should go over to the nursing home and scare up more business for Uncle Dove.

The bandage would come off, but that terrible scar would never heal. And the eye: I had seen it myself. It was dead.

I got away from that mirror.

I made my way down the stairs with both hands on the rail, thinking how you take for granted something as easy as walking down stairs, until suddenly one day you only have one eye and you break out in a cold sweat trying to do it.

I stuck my head in the apartment door: the six o'clock news played loudly to an empty room.

I went on downstairs. The display caskets glowed under their spot-lights. The whole house felt empty, except for the invisible organist tweedling his mournful chords.

Up the hall, in the last parlor on the right, I found one person who was not going anywhere.

She'd had no visitors all day. It was just me and Mrs. Boggs. I lowered myself to a chair.

She looked younger than I remembered. Death had smoothed out all her wrinkles. She wore an ivory sleeping-gown edged with frail lace, the kind of fine thing she might have kept on a high shelf wrapped in paper for a special occasion. In her hand, a bouquet of tiny white roses.

Okay: I was sorry: I killed her. I didn't mean to do it.

I was all despondent about one lousy eye, while Mrs. Boggs lay here dead, thanks to me.

Still. It wasn't entirely my fault. She was so old. She died so quick. She must have been just on the verge of dying when I showed up.

And wasn't she the one who started it all, wasn't she the one who called out to me from her clothesline? If she hadn't done that, Mrs. Boggs would still be alive. And I would still have both eyes.

I sat with hands folded, hoping she would not pick this moment to sit up like Mrs. Eldridge.

I heard someone coming in the back of the house, and abandoned Mrs. Boggs to the gloom. It was Milton, rolling three boxes of embalming chemicals on a hand truck toward the forbidden gray door. "Hey there, young son! Didn't know you was up and about!"

"I'm not supposed to be. Don't tell. I got tired of laying in bed."

"I 'spect you did. You ain't had much fun here lately."

He was right about that. "Can I help you, Milton?"

"You could hold the door open while I roll this inside."

I started to tell him I wasn't allowed in the embalming room, but I caught the words on the end of my tongue. I turned the knob on the gray door, and pushed in.

"Thank you kindly, just hold it . . ." He bumped the hand truck over the sill.

I let the door swing shut behind him, and took a look around.

At the center of the room was a shiny steel table with gutters. A dead old man lay on the table with a sheet pulled up to his chin.

He didn't scare me: he was a wax-and-powder man, a reconstructed mask of a man. His lips were too pink to be true.

I had pictured this room as a dark and infernal place full of ropes and cauldrons, rows of jars, floating specimens, at least a skeleton or two. I was disappointed. This place was as bright and clean as Dr. Ward's office. A concrete floor sloped down to a drainhole at one end. A garden hose lay neatly coiled beside a row of cabinets with frosted-glass fronts. I recognized several of the plastic squeeze bottles Meemaw used at the ironing board, but these were the real thing, filled with formaldehyde—and the smell in the air was a familiar chemical tang, the smell Dove always tried to conceal with Hai Karate.

I drank in every detail of the room so I could describe it to Wiley. I'd have to make it sound more ominous than it was, to impress him.

Milton rolled the cartons to the shelves in back, and asked me to steady the ladder while he put them away. "How long you got to wear that ol' patch on your eye?"

"I don't know. Maybe forever."

"That don't bother you, does it?"

"Sure it does, it makes me mad! I mean, I'd just like to haul off and hit somebody, you know? But I can't."

"Why not?" He grunted, hoisting a box.

"It's not anybody's fault. It's my fault. I can't go hit that stupid lawn mower."

"Why not? Maybe it'd make you feel better, to kick it around a little bit."

"I'd probably cut off my foot."

"Well, maybe you would at that. But listen, young son, nobody gone blame you for bein' put out about this. Long as you don't wait too long to get past it."

I changed the subject. "I'm gonna have my own funeral home when I grow up, Milton."

"I like it here, too," he said. "It's peaceful. Mist' Dove is about the best friend a man could have. And folks like Mister Brewster here, they ain't no trouble. They ain't got no opinions. They done said everything they had to say. They happy just to lie quiet while you tend to 'em." He went to the door. "You best go lay down yourself, boy. Mist' Brewster's got to get dressed. Thank you kindly for your help."

I stepped out, taking deep breaths to clear the formaldehyde from my head. After all my anticipation, I had found nothing scary behind the gray door. Just another dead body.

I went upstairs.

On the landing opposite Dove and Earlene's apartment was a half-sized door that led into the attic over the back wing of the house. Wiley and I had poked our heads in there once—nothing but dust and old magazines. Now, as I rounded the top of the stairs, I heard a distinct sound from behind that door.

I stopped. It was too loud to be a mouse. It sounded human.

There. There it was again. A little whimper.

In the split second before I opened that door I had an inkling what I would find. I opened it anyway.

They were kissing. His hands on her breasts. I heard a scream then I saw Mabel hastening to sit up on a wooden crate, wearing only a bra and her skirt. Wiley bent over with his pants down around his ankles, showing his skinny white butt in Jockey shorts.

He scrambled for cover. "Jesus, Peejoe! Shut the door!"

I shut it, all right. I slammed it so hard the chandelier rang.

I sat down on the third step to wait. Time passed. The door crept open. Mabel flushed red, put her nose in the air and stalked across the landing to the apartment, the tail of her blouse hanging out. BAM! went that door.

I pulled myself up the stairs and flopped on my cot. My head reeled. Wiley and I had always been different, but now he had entered a realm where I could not go.

I knew about Spin the Bottle and Strip Poker, I had sneaked a look at Wiley's health-class pamphlet, "Where Do Babies Come From?" but the whole thing was still a fuzzy notion in my head—nowhere near as vivid as the sight of his hands on Mabel's breasts as they strained against her white lace brassiere. I saw that well enough through one eye. . . .

The door creaked. Wiley charged up the stairs. "Damn, Peejoe, couldn't you learn to knock before you come barging in places? You're not even supposed to be out of bed!"

"Oh, excuse me," I sniffed. "Just that I didn't expect to find you and her in there, you know, doing whatever that was."

"That was nothing."

I rolled over. I wanted him to look me straight in the eye and say that. "Oh come on, Wiley. Your face is all red."

"So what are you gonna do, tell?"

"No, I'm not gonna tell. I don't care what you do."

"Good. Then mind your own business."

"I will!"

"Good!" He threw himself down on his cot, dangling his big feet off the end. After a while he let out a sigh. "Peejoe, we weren't doing anything. Just messing around."

"You think I care? Go away and leave me alone." I rolled over to face the wall.

"It's kind of fun," he said. "You'll find out someday."

"I don't want to hear about it."

"I can't wait to show you that room, there's a place—"

"I said I don't want to hear about it!"

"All right, I won't tell you." His weight jingled the springs on the cot. "But I saw you and Milton."

I sat up. "What do you mean?"

"There's a hole in the floor in there. Mabel showed me. You scoot this tile over and you can see right down in the embalming room. I heard every word y'all said. If you tell on me, I'll tell Dove you went in there when you're not allowed."

"Wiley, you better watch out or she'll have a baby. A two-headed retarded baby."

"Shut up." He snorted disgust. "Don't be stupid. That's not gonna happen. We were just—"

"She's our *cousin!* It's gross! I can't believe you would do that."

"That's right, she's our cousin, it's not like she's our sister or something," he sputtered. "I can't help it if she likes me. I like her, too."

I pressed my bandage with both hands, but it only made the hammer strike harder. "I bet you're sorry I even came home from the hospital, huh. I'm just getting in the way of your fun."

He groaned. "You're such an idiot. I better go talk to her. You shook her up pretty good."

"I can't help it if I look like a monster."

He stared at me a minute. He got up and tucked in his shirt. "That's not what I meant. You don't look all that bad."

"Oh, right. Like you even care."

"You don't know. You scared the hell out of us. At first we didn't know if you were dead or what."

"Yeah, well, if you'd stayed to help me cut that grass instead of running off to find Mabel in the first place . . ."

"Go on, say it." His eyes blazed. "You're thinking it, you might as well say it. If I'd stayed and looked out for you, you wouldn't have got your eye put out. It's all my fault."

"Wiley—"

"Maybe it wouldn't have happened at all, or maybe it would have been *my* eye. Maybe that's what was supposed to happen, Jesus, Peejoe, what do you want me to say? I'm sorry, okay? I'm sorry. I'm *sorry*. You want me to put my eye out too?"

I couldn't stand one more minute of this. He was my brother and I loved him. I had to let him off the hook. "It doesn't matter, Wiley. You're right. It happened. It's not your fault. It just happened."

He went to the head of the stairs. "I'm going to see about Mabel," he said. And he did.

18

Lucille

Las Vegas, Nevada

Jack the bellboy fell fast asleep in Lucille's arms. She spent the night snuggled up to the curve of him.

He awoke with a start and raced around searching for his underwear. He was sure he'd be fired—his twenty-minute break had lasted all night. Lucille found his Jockey shorts wedged under the point of the heart-shaped mattress. She got him back in his pink tuxedo, slipped a hundred-dollar bill in his pocket when he wasn't looking, and sent him off with a kiss.

The moment the door clicked shut, she heard a whisper from the hatbox on the table: "Lou-see-yul . . ."

She stuffed the money back in the canvas bag and carried it into the bathroom. She shut the door and started the water running loud enough to drown out any sound.

It took forever for the giant pink porcelain clamshell bathtub to fill all the way. Lucille sat on the polished lip, rubbing her finger along the inside of her knee where it tingled from his kisses.

What a night! She'd slept for a hundred years, and awakened to find a fortune in gold and a handsome prince in her bed. With a delicious groan she settled into the bath.

She dozed and floated and splashed, thumbing through a copy of *Vogue* until it was swollen with damp. She plunged her head underwater to rinse the road dirt from her hair. Occasionally she freshened the bubbles with jets of heat from the gold-plated spigot.

After an hour she pulled the drain-plug with her toe and sank back, eyes closed, savoring the sensation of the water-line creeping down her body, cool air flooding over her where hot water had been.

She dried herself briskly, slipped into a white-terry robe with a pink flamingo on the pocket. She felt well-scrubbed and rosy and new. She ordered room-service coffee, orange juice, corn flakes, and blueberry muffins. She watched a rerun of "Have Gun Will Travel" and ate every bite.

Her gaze fell upon her old tired Mexican skirt and blue blouse, splayed out on the floor where Jack had flung them. She was sick of those clothes. They would no longer do. She was a rich woman now. A rich, wanted woman.

Of course she'd have to wear them one last time while she went to buy something else.

She left Chester in the suite and took the money with her to the elevator. The doors slid open to the casino clamor: bells ringing, the clatter of money, exactly the same sound as when the doors slid shut the night before.

Lucille resisted the temptation. Today she had another itch to scratch.

In the first boutique she bought eight pairs of shoes and a "Mademoiselle Traveler" brown-leather luggage ensemble, snap snap, thank you very much, twelve hundred dollars.

Then she set out to fill up her new suitcases with nice things. She moved like a shopping tornado through a store called Wonderful Woman: four tailored suits, seven silk blouses, a couple of clever Jackie Kennedy hip-hugger skirts, and an array of slinky underwear befitting the new sexy woman that she was becoming.

She tipped the salesgirl twenty bucks. (Now that she was rich and sexy, she was determined not to be cheap.) The girl phoned for a bellhop to help with all the packages. A dour old fellow appeared, a long face in a pink jacket. He followed Lucille with a hand truck while she stopped in Charles of the Desert for stockings and slacks and perfume, Flamingo Jewels for a pair of stunning one-carat diamond earrings, Monsieur Henri for an assortment of the latest Mary Quant makeup.

The last shop was the ritziest of all, a high-fashion furs-and-dresses parlor called Madelyn's Elegant Styles. One glance at Lucille and that overloaded hand truck, and the proprietress lit up like a little girl on Christmas morning. "Well, hel-*loo!* I have some things you are just going to *love*."

Lucille smiled. "Are you Madelyn?"

"I am." She lifted her crescent-moon glasses to her nose. "Mister Bellman, just leave those things, we'll call you when we're through. Now, dear, let's see, what are we, about a six?"

"Ten," said Lucille, "but thanks for the compliment."

"And today we're in the mood for . . . ?"

"I don't know. I think I've bought enough sensible stuff. I'm going to Hollywood for a big audition, and I want something . . . wonderful. Something that's in style right this minute. Something really expensive. Do you have anything like that?"

Madelyn lowered her glasses to rest on their chain on her bosom. "My dear, you have made me a happy woman. I see before me a lady who has style, who has taste, who is obviously not afraid to spend money. Now it's my job to make you happy. I have only one word to say to you—the single most exciting, most up-to-the-minute word in the world of haute couture."

Lucille waited.

Madelyn pursed her lips. "Pucci."

"Pucci?"

"Emilio Pucci. Italian. Simple lines. Bold geometrics. He's new, he's bright, he's perfect. He's you."

"Is he expensive?"

"Is he ever," said Madelyn. "Did you win a lot of money?"

Lucille grinned. "How'd you know?"

"Madelyn knows. And just between you and me, I think you're awfully smart to buy nice things with it instead of feeding it back into the slots. Most people, you would be amazed."

She swept up four Pucci day dresses and carried them off to the dressing room.

They were bold, all right; those big gaudy prints made Lucille feel like a circus billboard. The least gaudy one cost one thousand four hundred seventy-five dollars.

For a *dress.*

She tried it on. She turned this way and that in the three-way mirror while Madelyn exclaimed over her. Anyone could see the dress was very stylish, but Lucille was not at all sure she could actually bring herself to wear something so loud in public.

On her way back from the dressing room she noticed a mannequin in a very smart, very short dress—a space-age sleeveless jumper, crisp white, with a wide stripe of bouncy yellow linen at the neckline and hem. The mannequin wore matching white gloves and shiny white ankle-high boots, and the cutest little four-cornered sailor hat trimmed in the same yellow linen.

Lucille put her hands on her hips. "Now, that is adorable."

"That's André Courrèges." Madelyn pinched the hem. "Isn't it marvelously spare? Courrèges says a woman is never more beautiful than when she is naked."

"That's the kind of man I like," said Lucille. "Reckon whether I'd look beautiful in that dress, or just naked?"

"One way to find out." Madelyn went off to find her size.

As it turned out, Lucille looked terrific in the dress—fresh and young and rather delightful, a bright white-and-yellow daisy. With the flouncy turned-up hat she might have stepped straight out of the pages of *Life*.

"You certainly have the legs to wear it," Madelyn said. "Most women don't."

"I love it," Lucille said. "I'll take it. I'll wear it now. Also I want the gloves, and the hat, and those boots. How much?"

"Twenty-two with all the *accessoires*."

"Twenty-two hundred? Dollars?" Lucille tried to keep the shock off her face.

"That's marked down from thirty-one fifty. Believe me, it's a steal."

"Fine, that's fine, I'll take it. It doesn't matter."

"Shall I wrap up the clothes you wore in?"

"You can burn 'em, I don't care."

"Whatever you say. . . ."

When Lucille finished paying for everything and got out of there, she realized she'd spent eight thousand dollars in just under an hour. She felt daring and reckless, completely alive and in charge of her life. There was nobody around to tell her not to blow all her money, if that's what she wanted to do. She still had more than twenty thousand dollars in that canvas bag.

She marched through the ranks of blackjack tables to the concierge desk, trailing the sad-faced bellhop in her wake. "I want to go to Los Angeles," she announced. "I want someone to drive me."

"Very good, ma'am," said the concierge. "Will you want a regular sedan, or a limousine?"

"A limousine sounds nice. I'll take one of those."

The Coupe de Ville could just stay wherever Jack the bellboy had parked it. He had the keys. Maybe he'd keep it himself, or maybe he'd call the bartender from New Orleans to come get it. Lucille didn't care.

She went back up to the Rose Garden Suite to retrieve Chester, and to take one last look at that heart-shaped bed. It was magic, what happened on that bed last night. It convinced her all over again what a terrible lie her marriage had been. She and Chester had never had sex like that, never once in thirteen years. Yet she drove into Las Vegas and found it with the first boy who came to open her door.

She lifted Chester's hatbox by the ribbons. He seemed to weigh a little more every morning. She didn't want to think why.

The casino cried Lucille! Wait! You can win MORE at roulette! but she kept her shoulders up, her eyes fixed on the image of herself approaching the mirrored doors. She looked saucy enough for TV, new diamonds sparkling on her ears, swinging along as if she'd been born wearing André Courrèges. Money and sex were good for her looks. If she had enough money and sex, Lucille could be the most beautiful woman in the world. She had a hankering to find Jack, take him with her, make love to him all up and down California. . . .

Be patient. There will be more and better Jacks in Hollywood. Movie-star Jacks with blue eyes and blue swimming pools and big fat bank accounts.

She stepped out into blinding sunlight and dust, the wind blowing hot as a hair dryer. She fumbled for sunglasses. While you were inside you could forget the heat, but outside at noon all the palms and fountains in the world could not hide the fact that Las Vegas was smack in the middle of a blistering desert.

A gleaming black limousine stretched out along the sidewalk. Lucille's heart squeezed an extra beat. A small round fiftyish man in cap and uniform took a step forward. "Are you Miss Clay?"

"I sure am. Is this whole car for me?"

He smiled, showing a gold tooth in front. "My name's Norman Wirtz. I'm your driver."

She shook his hand. "This is the biggest car I've ever seen."

Norman stood straighter, as if to demonstrate that he was tall enough to drive it. The top of his cap barely came up to her shoulder. "I have your packages all loaded up. Understand we're going to L.A.?"

"That's right. How long will it take?"

"Four, five hours, depending on traffic. It's two hundred dollars, including my drive time back to Vegas. In advance, if you don't mind."

"That seems fair." She counted out the bills in his hand. "I hope you've got air-conditioning, Norman. It's hot as bejesus out here."

"Yes ma'am, of course." He held on to Chester and the money bag while Lucille figured out how to get into the car in her new, extremely short designer dress.

She tugged at the hem and flopped over sidesaddle into the deep-velvet seat. She sank back among the packages, crossing her legs.

Norman handed the hatbox through the door. "Comfortable?"

"You bet." The passenger compartment was a ritzy hotel room on wheels: glove-soft leather seats, built-in bar with crystal stemware, a bottle of champagne nodding in a silver bucket, a push-button panel to control the air-vents and windows and intercom.

They skimmed down the drive. Lucille decided she could ride around the world very happily in this car, with Norman up front to handle the bridges.

She pushed a button. "Norman, can you hear me?"

"Loud and clear," said his intercom voice.

"Can you open this thing so I can see you?"

The smoked-glass panel slid down. "There's a button on your panel marked 'Privacy Window,'" he said over his shoulder.

"We have one stop to make," she said. "I spotted the place last night. It's along here on the right." She lowered the window to look for it.

Las Vegas in the daytime was devoid of glamour. White-hot sunlight washed out those billions of lightbulb watts. The place looked dusty and faded, exhausted by the heat.

INSTANT DIVORCE $20 / FREE TOURIST INFO. "Here," she said. "Pull over to the curb. I'll be right back."

The place was not cute like the wedding chapels with their bells and ribbons and twinkling bride-and-groom signs. It was a plain blue corrugated-steel double-wide trailer on concrete blocks. Lucille carried the hatbox up the rickety steps and rang the bell.

The man who poked his head out was fifty, or forty, or maybe sixty. Hard to tell. Gray stubble, bleary eyes.

"It says 'Instant Divorce.'" Lucille pointed to the sign. "That's what I want."

He opened the door. His T-shirt was stained the familiar orange of Chef Boyardee sauce. "You got cash?"

"Of course I've got cash." Lucille supposed it didn't matter what kind of trashy person you got to divorce you; divorce was a trashy business. Somehow it seemed fitting to come to a double-wide trailer in the desert to put an end to a cheap double-wide kind of marriage.

Lucille had been in a bad mood for thirteen years, since that terrible April afternoon in 1952 when she said "I do" with little Sandra already three months inside her, making her want to throw up. At last she would stand up and say *No, I don't. I might have said I did, once. But I sure as hell don't anymore.*

She placed the hatbox atop a file cabinet. She wanted Chester to witness the proceedings.

"First you got to fill out this paper." The man offered a folding chair and the single corner of his desk that was not piled with junk. Lucille worked the form in three minutes. She even knew Chester's Social Security number, one more useless thing cluttering up her brain. Where the form asked "Reason for Divorce," she wrote "Mental cruelty."

The man poked a toothpick around his gums, watching her. "Now sign at the bottom by the X."

She signed with a flourish. "Is that all?"

"Hold on. I've got to make you a copy." He labored over his clipboard as if it were his fourth-grade homework. "You been a resident of Nevada for at least thirty days?"

"You bet I have. It seems like a year." Lucille tapped her toe and studied a calendar scene of four grinning dogs playing poker.

"Any chance your husband would want to contest this?"

"Not a chance. I guarantee you will not hear from him."

"Alrighty." He gave her the paper. "That's it. Twenty bucks."

It wasn't exactly instant, but it was fast. She gave him a twenty and fled to the limousine.

Norman opened her door. "All done?"

"Yes. Get me the hell out of here."

He climbed in, scratched off from the curb. She thought she saw sympathy in his eyes in the mirror. That was one thing she did not need, thank you very much.

She settled in among all her fancy shopping bags to examine the decree. The embossed seal under her fingertips even *felt* official. She was no longer Chester's wife. No longer even his widow. She was a legal divorcée, sworn and attested by the State of Nevada. This was a severance even more final than Chester's head from his neck.

Maybe now he would leave her alone.

Lucille untied the black ribbon, folded the decree in thirds, and tucked it into the tissue paper beside the Tupperware bowl. She permitted herself a sniff. Nothing. No odor at all.

One day, when all this was over, she would throw a Tupperware party. Truly she would. She would raise her right hand and solemnly swear to the excellence of that patented press-and-lock seal.

She couldn't shake the memory of the toolshed: it was like carving a roast with a very tough bone. The electric knife-blades rubbed together as they pried through the gristle of his spine.

She began to imagine how his head must look now, after all these days. . . .

Don't think about that.

She tucked the money bag into the hatbox, re-tied the ribbons, and returned Chester to his rightful place under all her new shoes.

Now that she was divorced, Chester had no power over her. She had no reason to hate him anymore. He was only a head in a box.

So far life without him was proving to be utterly fabulous. So far Lucille had made love to two different good-looking men and won a pile of big money, and here she was popping a bottle of Veuve Clicquot champagne in the back of a long black Cadillac, speeding across the desert toward Hollywood. The bubbles drove lovely tiny twenty-four-karat gold screws into her tongue.

She packed all her new clothes into her new luggage. She smoked a Salem. She leaned back and closed her eyes to think about Jack's face above her, the sweet grimace that brought on his first explosion. She drifted to sleep.

When she opened her eyes, she had a vision of palm trees standing guard along both sides of the highway.

The privacy window was down. Norman watched her in the mirror.

"Where are we?"

"L.A., more or less. It's hard to say where it starts exactly."

"You mean I slept the whole way?"

"You sure did. This car does that to people."

The champagne must have knocked her out. She had dropped off so fast and so hard that she didn't remember a thing.

She opened the box for a peek in the money bag. It was all there. She felt a twinge of shame for her suspicion, but only a twinge. "What did I miss?"

"The desert," said Norman. "Not too much in the way of scenery. By the way, where are we headed?"

"I'm not sure . . . What's the best hotel in town?"

"That would be the Beverly Hills."

"Is it nice?"

"Well, yes ma'am, what I've seen of it, it sure is."

"Take me there." Lucille sat back to enjoy what was left of this expensive limousine ride she had just snoozed through, thank you very much for nothing. Ranks of slender, tall-headed palms watched over eight lanes of zooming cars. She saw mile after mile of pastel houses, Disney-colored neighborhoods built on brown hills. Bright sunshine made everything sparkle. The air had a clean fragrance like Pine-Sol. Norman said that was from the eucalyptus trees.

Six highways converged in one great mass of tangled concrete spaghetti. The limousine soared up and around the maze on an improbable skyborne roadway that left Lucille white-faced, clutching the armrest. "Norman, don't ever leave me."

He glanced back. "What did you say?"

"I need you to drive me wherever I go for the rest of my life."

His eyes smiled in the mirror. He took a moment to frame his reply. "I wouldn't mind that myself, thank you ma'am."

They rounded a bend and yes there it was the vast city of Lost Angels sprawling down from the hills, from the mountains across a plain to the blue ominous Pacific hovering in the distance.

All her life Lucille had dreamed this place. Every time she put down fifty cents at the Roxie Theater, she traveled on wings of silvery light to the magic land of Hollywood. She was Margaret O'Brien pouting at Judy Garland, Elizabeth Taylor weeping over a horse, Shirley MacLaine as a winsome ingenue; for two hours she was Audrey Hepburn, Leslie Caron, Kim Novak, Shelley Winters; she was Marilyn Monroe wiggling her plump sexy bottom down the aisle of a train. And now, at long last, she was here with them all, she was here in the town where they lived and made movies.

Look out, girls. There's a new girl in town.

"Norman, where did they bury Marilyn Monroe?"

"Westwood, I think. It's just beyond Beverly Hills. Do you want to go there?"

"No, just wondering."

Poor Marilyn. She wasn't any better at handling success than Lucille had been at handling failure. Both of them had a pressing problem. Both of them went to extremes to solve it. Lucille killed Chester. Marilyn killed herself.

But then Marilyn had Joe DiMaggio to put red roses on her grave every day, rain or shine. A show of devotion like that—from your ex-husband, no less—that was almost enough to make suicide attractive.

Lucille had to face facts. She was thirty-three years old (although people said she looked twenty-seven, twenty-eight), not old for a woman with six children, but plenty old for Hollywood. She didn't have Joe DiMaggio waiting to buy her roses; God knows Chester never bought her any; she wouldn't even know what a rose looked like if she hadn't seen them growing in other people's yards. She wasn't Marilyn Monroe or even Shirley MacLaine. She was Carolyn Clay. She would have to use her own resources.

Somehow, she had to make a big splash—while evading attention from anyone who might figure out who she was and what she'd done.

That would be quite a trick. How do you become a star while you're on the run for murder?

It was, Lucille decided, a challenge that hardly anyone had ever faced before. She would just have to figure it out as she went along. Fortunately she was having a run of good luck.

Norman steered up a ramp and onto a wide boulevard. Four blond teenagers roared past in an open Mustang, laughing and waving over their surfboards. Lucille lowered the window and waved back, to give them the impression she was a big star who was also a nice person. Then she raised it again, so they'd argue all the way to the beach about who she was—Stella Stevens? Tippi Hedren?

"If you're not in a big hurry to go to your hotel," Norman said, "we could ride around awhile. See the sights."

"No, thanks. I'll see 'em later. I've got phone calls to make." Lucille pressed her nose to the glass. Sunset Boulevard meandered along the side of a hill, past chic hotels and shops, theaters, bistros. It was true what they said about California: everything was brassy and polished and new. People with glorious suntans drove shiny Lincolns, Mercedes-Benzes, red Corvette convertibles, not the beat-up old Chevies and Fords you see in Alabama. These people looked *expensive.* Even the guys pumping gas at the Texaco station had movie-star tans and white teeth.

Norman swung the limousine off the boulevard, up a steep side street, and coasted to a stop in front of a rambling house done up like the witch's cottage in "Hansel and Gretel."

Lucille peered at the pitched roof, the fake-rickety chimney, the crooked windows placed at studied odd angles. "This can't be the hotel."

Norman switched off the engine and sat gazing at the dashboard. "There's something I have to tell you."

His voice was strange. Lucille tightened her grip on the money bag. She wasn't quite sure what was happening. If he intended to rob her, she had the gun tucked right there in her purse. She unsnapped the clasp.

He turned halfway in the seat, without meeting her gaze. "I have a confession to make, Miss Clay. While you were sleeping, I—oh, I know you're gonna be angry, but you just looked so pretty lying there, and I stopped the car, and I—well, I—"

"What did you *do?*"

"I took some pictures." He tucked his chin, ashamed.

"Pictures? Of what?"

"Of you. Nothing nasty, nothing at all. Just some portraits, you know, of you sleeping."

"Well that's about the silliest thing I ever heard. Why didn't you just ask? I would have been happy to pose for you."

"No, see, it wouldn't be the same. Because then you would have known, and you'd look different—it was the way your hair was falling, and the light . . . you just had to see it." He swept off his cap, smoothed his hair over the bald spot. His eyes shone. "You're beautiful."

He had such an honest, earnest face. Lucille looked at him really for the first time, and saw a man who must have been okay to look at once, before he started losing hair and gaining weight. If he were ten years younger, or Lucille were ten years older, they might have been able to work something out.

"Why are you telling me this, Norman? Why didn't you just go on and look at your pictures? I never had to know anything about it."

"I don't know, I didn't think it was fair. Like I was stealing something from you." He produced a Kodak Instamatic with a burnt-out flashcube, and a cartridge of film. "Here it is, if you want to throw it away or whatever."

She studied the cartridge. "I don't know what to say. I've never been in this particular situation before."

He covered his heart with his cap. His eyes grew all moony. "I love you, Miss Clay. I'm in love with you. There. Now I said it."

"Oh come on, Norman. Don't be ridiculous. You don't even know me. Take me to my hotel."

He got to his knees on the seat. "I will love you forever, as God is my witness," he said. "I have never beheld such loveliness in my limousine."

"You've got to be kidding." Lucille unlocked the door in case she had to make a run for it.

"It's perfect timing, don't you see? You're a free woman now. Me and my wife split up six months ago. You and me, we were meant for each other. Come back to Vegas with me. I'll take care of you forever. I own this car, you know. I'll drive you anywhere you want to go."

"I don't want to go back to Vegas. It's taken me a long time to get where I am. So if you don't mind . . ."

"All my life I've been waiting for someone like you," he said. "I can't let you go now."

"Norman."

He put his elbows on the back of the seat. "Listen. I'll level with you, okay? I'm just a plain kind of guy. I'm not rich, but I've managed to save up enough so we can be comfortable."

"Norman—"

"I know I'm not good enough for you. I'm not as young as I used to be, and I know I'm not good-looking, I don't have much hair. But if you'd just give me a chance to show you—"

"Norman!"

"What?"

"You better turn around in that seat and start the car this instant, or else you're going to hear a sound from back here that's gonna make you balder than you already are. Do you understand me?"

His flattery was touching, but Lucille had had enough.

Norman sighed. "I'll take you. Don't worry." He started the engine. "Only I had to tell you. I couldn't let you go without telling you."

"That's all right," she said. "Just drive."

He turned around in the driveway of the witch's cottage, and headed down the hill. "One day you're going to marry me. You wait and see."

"I'm not marrying anybody," Lucille said. "I just got done with all that."

"Yeah, we'll see. I'm actually a hell of a guy when you get to know me."

"I think you've been in Las Vegas too long. I think all that heat has gone to your head."

"Maybe so," he said, peering back, "but I sure know a fine woman when I see one."

They rolled out onto Sunset Boulevard. At once Lucille spotted a discreet sign tucked in a grove of tall palms: THE BEVERLY HILLS HOTEL. "We were right around the corner all the time," she murmured.

"Here. I'll give you my card. If you think about it and change your mind you call me any time, day or night. I'll come get you."

"Thank you, Norman. I'll hang on to this." She dropped the card in one of the shopping bags.

The Beverly Hills Hotel looked like the campus of some posh, pink university: one long old building in the style of a Spanish mission, flanked by several sleek modern additions and darling pink bungalows scattered through lush tropical gardens. All the buildings were so very pink they made Lucille's face feel hot.

The driveway led up a gentle slope, under a concrete porte-cochere painted with green-and-white stripes to resemble a canvas awning. A pair of carved-stone monkeys flanked the red-carpeted entrance.

Norman came around for the luggage. "Remember what I told you."

"I don't think I'll ever forget it." She accepted his hand to get out of the car, and gave him the Instamatic cartridge. "Listen, why don't you just keep these old pictures. I don't have the slightest idea what I would do with them."

He fairly glowed. "Oh, thank you. I knew you'd understand. You're as nice as any woman I ever met. Why don't you marry me?"

She gave him a sideways look. "Norman, go back to Las Vegas."

A bellhop approached. Norman handed over the luggage and all the bags. "This is Miss Clay. You take care of her for me, understand?" He tipped his cap to Lucille, blew a kiss, and got back in the limousine.

She watched him go. Now that she knew he was harmless, she felt more pity for him than anything. Poor sweet old guy. Probably lonely all his life. Probably destined to stay that way.

And now who was this young tall thing with the Beatle-like mop of blond hair, presently handling her luggage?

Take one good long look at that, Lucille. Mm-hmm. A little piece of blond-headed heaven.

"Good afternoon," he said. "Checking in?"

She batted her eyes. "You bet I am, sweetie. What's your name and where do I sign up for you?"

He laughed and said his name was Ted. He held out his hand for the hatbox.

"Careful," Lucille said. "That's my husband's head in there. It's heavy."

Ted laughed at that, too. They walked together up the red carpet into the Beverly Hills Hotel.

19

Peejoe

Industry

I woke up with Wiley's hands around my throat. "I could kill you right
now if I wanted," he whispered, pressing his thumbs to my windpipe.

"Quit that," I croaked. "You're hurting me."

He tightened his grip. "Everybody would think your eye was what
killed you. I'd get off scot-free."

"Nuh-uh." I pried at his fingers. "They'd see the strangle marks and
put you in jail."

Wiley in his underwear had come all the way from his cot at the other
end of the room to wake me up by torturing me.

Days had passed since I caught him playing hide-and-seek in the closet
with Mabel. He hadn't mentioned it again, and *I* sure wasn't about to
bring it up. I was certain I had saved him from a terrible fate, and he
would thank me someday.

Late at night I lay on my cot, remembering his hands on Mabel's bra.
One night to my utter astonishment I popped a boner just thinking about
it. I didn't know what to do, so I lay there thinking about Jesus and Hell
and the Devil until it went down. It was an uncomfortably close call with
a brand-new sensation. I tried to put it out of my mind.

Often I found Mabel sitting up way late, alone in the casket room,
talking to the people she heard in there. Wiley agreed: She was getting
weirder by the day. She seemed to be falling deeper and deeper under the
spell of those voices.

I asked Dove if she was going crazy. He said he didn't think so, it was
just a phase teenage girls went through.

Wiley raised a pillow to smother me. "I could kill you this way. It
wouldn't leave marks."

He started to press down.

I howled "Watch out for my eye!"

Instantly he dropped the pillow.

My eye was my trusty new defense. Aside from our parents' fatal crash and the shovel that killed Grandpa Joe Wiley, it was the most serious calamity ever sustained by any Bullis. It commanded respect—and an anxious call every night from Meemaw, although she couldn't afford the long distance.

I felt dizzy and slightly nauseated most of the time. I lurched around like the Death Monster in my big white skull-encasing bandage. Everyone winced when they saw me, then to make up for that they raised a big fuss about how good I looked.

At least Wiley didn't do that. He called me Popeye and One-Eye and Helen Keller and Blindy, and every day he was adding new names to his list. "Hey Mummy Face, guess what. They're gonna bury Taylor Jackson in Dog Junction today."

I squinted up at him. "Didn't they do that already? It's been more than a week."

"Dove says colored folks like to stretch it out."

"Is Dove going over there?"

"Don't know," Wiley said.

"Maybe he'd take us."

"I doubt it. I don't think he's ever letting you out of this house for the rest of your life."

"But we saw Taylor get killed. We have to go to his funeral."

"It's a nigger funeral, Peejoe. We don't belong there."

"That's not true. Anybody can go." Trying to sit up, I lost my balance and nearly toppled off the cot.

He caught me by the shoulders. "See? You can't even sit up by yourself."

"I'm okay. I'm gonna ask Dove if he'll take us." The moment I shrugged out of his grasp, the room started spinning.

He caught me, held me swaying in place until I got my feet back under me. He held up my shirt, steered my arm into the sleeve.

Earlene called *breakfast*.

After the warm summer morning in the old part of the house, the apartment felt like dark wintertime. Earlene sat in the recliner with her feet up, eating white sugar doughnuts while she watched Governor Wallace on TV.

I said "Morning, Aunt Earlene."

She glanced up. "You're not walking so good. Is your eye worse?"

"No, it's okay. I just keep feeling like I'm going to run into something."

"Soon as you've eaten, you go right back up those stairs," she said. "I'm having Dude Cranford and Layne Reynolds and Betty Jernigan for a luncheon at two, and I don't want you underfoot." She took off one fuzzy slipper to scratch her toe.

"I think I'll—"

"Hush." She waved her hand. "I want to hear this."

The governor jabbed his finger at the interviewer. "That's the typical mush-mouthed bleedin'-heart stuff we always get from you Washington reporters," he fumed. "The good people of the state of Alabama have the constitutional right to run their own lives."

"Give 'em hell, George," Earlene said. "You know, I don't agree with everything he says, but I just love it when he takes out after these Yankees."

"I'm going outside," I announced. "Wiley brought me a book from the library."

"Just stay out of the way," she said. "I don't want to see you while we're trying to eat lunch."

It didn't surprise me that Earlene was not exactly eaten up with sympathy over my accident.

Wiley dumped a can of frozen orange concentrate into a pitcher. "Where's Mabel?"

"In her room," Earlene said. "I don't know what's got into her lately, she's acting stranger than usual."

Wiley fixed me with a look: *don't you open your mouth.*

"Peejoe, I know you're *wounded* and all," said Earlene, "but is it too much to ask you to pick up your comic books instead of leaving them scattered all over the place?"

Some days Earlene was nothing but a prickly pincushion bristling with opinions and instructions. I went to the counter for doughnuts. I closed my eye, picturing one of Meemaw's big fluffy buttermilk biscuits running over with butter and sorghum. . . .

Dove's big hands on my shoulders. "Boo."

"Hey, Uncle Dove." I squinted up.

"You looking bright-eyed this morning," he said. "Earlene, did John Doggett call?"

She shook her head, glued to the TV.

Dove moved around to tilt my chin up for a closer inspection. "How's that eye today, Skeeter?"

"About the same."

"Did you sleep any better?"

"I woke up a few times."

"You ought to hear him," said Wiley. "You'd think they were sticking him with needles."

"Well I'm sorry, I try to be quiet. I can't help if it hurts."

Dove touched my nose with his thumb. "He's right, Wiley. Maybe you ought to sleep somewhere else if he's keeping you awake."

"Naw, it's okay." Wiley looked at his knees. "I didn't mean that."

"Gotta go, I've got one hell of a day," Dove said. "What are y'all up to?"

Wiley said "I'm going to the pool."

"I didn't think they'd opened it up again."

"Yesterday," Wiley said. "They put up a big sign that says 'White Only.'"

"I want to go too," I said.

Dove washed his hands in the sink, fixing me with a sideways glance. "I don't want y'all down at that pool. Let's give everybody a chance to settle down."

"Aw come on, Uncle Dove," Wiley groaned, "there's nothing to do around here."

"You stay here and keep your brother company. Since he is not allowed to set one foot off this place—Peter Joseph, you hear me?"

"Yes, sir."

"And one more thing. I don't want you boys anywhere near Dog Junction this afternoon. I'm not going to that funeral and neither are you."

Wiley glanced at me: Had he read our minds?

Earlene said "I don't know why they should listen to you. They never listen to me."

"I'm serious about this, boys. Do you understand?"

"Yes sir," we said together.

"Earlene, have you seen my blue tie? I'm s'posed to meet the man at nine and it's five minutes of."

"It's on the hanger with your good suit."

I followed Wiley downstairs. He lowered his voice: "I don't really want to go swimming. I just said that to throw him off."

"What do you mean?"

"In case, you know, we want to go check out that funeral."

"Really? Would you go with me?"

"I don't see what it would hurt to take a look from the road."

"What about Mabel?"

"Listen. I'm not gonna hang around waiting for her to decide to talk to me. You'd think it was all my fault, what happened. She was the one who started it. She's weird."

Secretly I cheered. This meant I would get Wiley back.

That afternoon we slipped away, just the two of us. Earlene was too busy fretting over her guests, who were already half an hour late, to notice us leaving.

We followed the train tracks a mile to Dog Junction, where tarpaper shacks crowded up to the railroad right-of-way. The dirt streets were full of colored people in starched dresses and Sunday hats, white shirts, pressed trousers.

We fell in with the crowd moving up the road to the Holy Redeemer Full Gospel African Methodist Evangelical Church, where we found a much larger crowd thronging the churchyard, spilling into a broad open pasture. Apparently every Negro man, woman, and child in Cotton County had come out to pay last respects to Taylor Jackson. A long line of mourners snaked through the one-room frame church. That must be the line to see Taylor in his casket.

The pasture was jammed with people milling and talking, ladies in white gloves holding black umbrellas for shade, old men in suspenders, gaggles of young girls and young men, children running. Some people had blankets spread on the ground as for a picnic.

"I didn't know there were this many colored folks in the world," I marveled.

Wiley said, "You never see this many in one place."

Of course we provoked our share of attention, with our white skin and the big ugly bandage on my head. Some people pointed as if I were wearing a Halloween mask. One lady said "po child, what you do to yo face?" and reached out to touch my bandage. I ducked past her hand.

"Have you ever seen so many hats?" Wiley said. "Looka there, Peejoe, there goes one for you."

He pointed out a huge lady sailing by with a pile of wax fruit on her head.

Suddenly his face changed. He squinted over my shoulder. "Oh, hell. There's Dove."

I followed the line of his finger to the road, where six or seven white men stood watching the crowd. Dove was deep in conversation with a man in a brown fedora.

We hurried over behind a giant live oak spreading its limbs above the church. Wiley slapped the trunk. "Let's climb."

I got lightheaded just looking up. "Wiley. You know I can't climb a tree."

"Do you want him to see us? Here's a low branch to start on. Come on, I'll help you."

He guided me with both hands from branch to branch, until I was wedged in a junction of limbs about fifteen feet up. The leaves were dense enough to hide us, but I could see the whole pasture spread out below.

"You're right," I said, settling in, "it's better up here." From above, Taylor's funeral resembled a carnival, an ice-cream social on a summer afternoon. Although I heard folks shushing rowdy children, and here and there a woman weeping, the feeling in the air was light, almost celebratory. Everyone seemed excited by the size of the crowd. Friends greeted friends with enthusiastic handshakes: "How you *doin'*? You lookin' *good!*"

Some of them still wore their fieldhand clothes, gardener clothes, cleaning-the-white-lady's-house clothes; they must have been lured from their work by the sight of all the people in the streets.

"Wiley, this is too many people for just a funeral. This has got to be something else."

"I was thinking the same thing." He stretched on the branch above me, dangling his feet in midair. "You remember on TV, all that mess in Selma?"

It was a Sunday night, a few weeks before Aunt Lucille came along to mess up our lives. We were watching "Bonanza." The Montgomery station broke in with a special report. State troopers rode up on Negroes with horses and beat them with clubs and choked them with teargas. Meemaw made us turn it off.

Now on this sweltering afternoon in Industry I didn't see a lawman anywhere. If all these people should decide at the same moment to do something, I couldn't imagine what on earth might stop them.

"Look—" Wiley pointed. "They're bringing him out." A commotion arose in the doorway of the church, men scrambling out of the way.

Here it came, a yellow pine box on the shoulders of six men. Silence moved in a wave through the crowd, spreading out to the edge of the pasture, bouncing off the trees and returning as a wave of motion, people stirring, moving closer.

An ancient blue pickup truck backed to the church steps. The pallbearers lifted Taylor Jackson's coffin over the tailgate and onto the bed.

Someone else produced a microphone and a portable amplifier: "Testing one two . . ."

Thomas took the microphone and approached the tailgate, waving his right arm for attention. He looked taller than I remembered, in his black vested suit and red polka-dot bowtie, facing that vast congregation.

"Friends!" His deep voice settled the crowd. "Friends, I know Reverend Williams would be happy to have everybody come in the church, but there's just way too many of us."

An appreciative murmur rolled through the pasture, then a ripple of applause which built into an ovation, people clapping and whistling.

Nehemiah held up his hand: Wait.

"A boy's dead," he said. "I want you all to hold on a minute and think about that. A boy is dead. That's why we're here. His name was Taylor Jackson. He was sixteen years old. I knew him from the day he was born. This is not the time for handclapping."

The crowd fell quiet, abashed.

Nehemiah dabbed the shine on his forehead. "Taylor is my sister's boy, he's Mattie's boy," he said. "Mattie has lost two sons this year. That's more than any mother should have to bear."

"Amen."

"That's right."

"But she didn't just *lose* those two sons. They didn't just *die*. They gave their lives for a cause. For *our* cause. There were others to die before them, and there will be more before it's over."

His listeners shifted and peered around as if trying to guess who might be next.

"You all know me, I'm a businessman, I run a business. I'm not a preacher, I'm not the kind to make speeches or stick my neck out." His reedy voice filled the air. "When they burned down the house where those voting rights folk from Atlanta were staying, I didn't say anything. And when they found Isie Waters's boy Calvin beat up and bloodied out by Cooper's Creek, and he told how four white men jumped on him, I told myself Calvin must have done something to bring that on himself.

"See, I thought this place was better than Selma. I thought it was better than Montgomery or Birmingham. I thought we had good white folk down here, our good white folk who wear the badges and run things in this town. I thought they would look out for us. Friends, let me tell you, I was wrong. They are the same. When it comes to looking out for Negroes, Sheriff John Doggett is no different than Jim Clark or Bull Connor or George Wallace. He is cut from the same piece of cloth."

"That's right!"

"Now, certain white folk around here, they like things just the way they are. If we try to change things, they'll try to kill us. And Sheriff Doggett will not lift a finger to stop 'em."

Someone cried: "They can't kill us all!"

"No, brother, they can't. But they killed David Jackson when he tried to help folks get their registration to vote. And they killed Taylor Jackson when he tried to swim in a public swimming pool that was paid for with the same taxes we all pays, every one of us, Negro and white. Now people, this has got to stop. We got to stop it. Right now."

"Yes! Amen!"

Wiley nudged me with his toe. I looked where he was pointing, to the road beyond Dove and the other white men. A bronze-colored squad car had pulled up beside Dove's white hearse. That looked like John Doggett himself standing beside it, scanning the crowd with binoculars.

Nehemiah said, "Taylor Jackson went to that swimming pool and he sat down. And they killed him for that."

Wails of protest arose.

"But that's not the end of the story," he said. "People, I don't know how to swim, never been swimming in my life. But what I'm going to do right now, I am marching back down to that pool. I'm taking Taylor down there. That swimming pool is the river of freedom, my friends. I am going to swim in that river."

A murmur traveled up from the back of the crowd.

"They can kill us," Nehemiah cried, "but they cannot keep us down forever!"

The murmur swelled to a roar. The crowd engulfed the blue truck. Nehemiah waved his hands in the air.

I glanced to the road. Sheriff Doggett had departed as quietly as he'd come. Dove and the other men huddled on the hillside beyond the road, talking things over.

Wiley shinnied down the limb toward me. His eyes shone. "Man, this is better than TV!"

"The sheriff didn't seem all that worried," I said. "He took one look and took off."

"What else could he do? It's, like, a thousand against one."

Nehemiah Thomas climbed off the truck to be swept into the crowd, lifted up on shoulders, and borne like a conquering hero toward the road.

Taylor Jackson's coffin bobbed along after him, supported by six strong men, leading a sea of people. Where the sea met the road, it narrowed to a river twenty people wide, and rolled off toward Industry, swaying and singing.

> *Ain't gonna let She'f Doggett turn me around*
> *Turn me around*
> *Turn me around*

"Come on, let's go with 'em." Wiley dropped like Tarzan to the branch below, and jumped to the ground to assist in my final descent. "Here. Put your foot here." He coaxed me down one limb at a time.

I swung from a branch. He grabbed around my waist and stumbled back—we bumped the treetrunk and collapsed laughing in a heap.

A stern-faced woman shot us a disapproving look. I thought of Grandpa Joe Wiley's last funeral, and put my smile away.

We were swept along in the tide past the place where Dove's hearse had been. He must have left when he saw Nehemiah's little speech turning into this demonstration. Dove hated conflicts, people shouting or carrying signs. He liked things peaceful. He would say "yes, uh-huh, sure" all night long to stay out of a fight with Earlene.

Not me. I was fascinated by people out of control, acting on impulse, when their masks were stripped away and they were forced to show their true selves. I still felt the shiver of the time Aunt Lucille held up Chester's head for us to see—and the confusion that followed, that was horrible and thrilling. Watching the women in Mattie Jackson's house abandon themselves to their grief, watching Taylor Jackson stand down that lifeguard, nose to nose through the chain-link fence . . . I felt the same giddy sensation now, marching with this excited rabble toward something dangerous and new.

I stooped to retrieve one of the yellow flyers littering the ground.

MASS MEETING
Negro Citizens Of Industry, Awake!
Come to the Holy Redeemer A.M.E. Church Friday at 3 o'clock to commemorate the passing of the late beloved Taylor Jackson. The Rights of the Negro can no longer be trampled by those who hold the Strings of Power! All who admire the Nonviolent teachings of Rev. M. L. King are welcome.

So *that* was how the death of one anonymous boy could have provoked a whole countyful of black folks to leave the safety of their homes, to march down this road with their children. This was drastic. This could not be undone.

Nehemiah Thomas must have been busy all week, setting it up—the mimeographed handbills, the microphone and PA, the pickup truck in the right place at the right time.

"Look, those poor folks got trapped." Wiley pointed to three carloads of white people who'd been forced to the side of the road by the river of marchers.

I said "They look scared to death." A fat woman in a beat-up Rambler nudged her husband, pointed at me, and said something. I waved and kept walking.

Far ahead, Taylor's pine box led the way into town. A new song traveled back through the ranks:

> *Freedom, freedom*
> *Freedom, freedom*
> *It ain't a long ways to go*

We swept through the outskirts of Industry. The head of the column ran into some obstacle. We bunched up together in back, marking time.

"You the boy that got shot?"

I turned. A thin brown woman with close-cropped hair was inspecting me with a frown. She was the one who'd given us a dirty look for laughing, under the oak tree.

"Are you talking to me?"

"I said you the boy that got shot."

"Well no ma'am, I didn't get shot."

"Don't 'ma'am' me. I'm Lydia Combs. What happened to you?"

"I got hit in the eye with a rock."

"Naw, you the one, you and a old white lady too," she said. "I heard you got shot 'cause you stood up for Taylor. At the pool. They put your eye out."

"No ma'am," I said.

"Howcome you here, then?"

"Ma'am?"

"Am I talking too fast? I said howcome you here, if you're not the same one?"

Wiley pretended he didn't know me.

"I just wanted to come," I said.

"What's your name?"

"Peter Joseph. Bullis."

"That's you all right." She swooped her arm in the air and cried, "Hey! This the boy that got shot! This the white boy that stood up for Taylor! Look here!"

Everyone within earshot turned to stare—first at her, then at me. I reddened behind my bandage.

"That the Bullis boy?" said an older man.

"Who that?"

"You heard about him. They put Oscar Simmons and Derek Wayfield in jail for shooting him, but everybody known it was somebody white."

All the people in our vicinity seemed to have heard a little something about it. Some of them swore I'd been ambushed by the sheriff's buddies as a warning to other white boys with fresh ideas. Others vowed that a deputy had shot me while I was defending Taylor at the swimming pool. They argued the details.

I tried again: "Listen, I promise. It was an accident."

"Ain't no such thing as an accident," said Lydia Combs. "Didn't you hear Brother Thomas? They try to kill anybody who stands up to them. Don't go acting all humble, we know what you did. We proud of anybody that would stand up for Taylor, especially white. And look what it got you."

Wiley had circled around behind Lydia Combs and frantically motioned for me to get away from her.

I stayed where I was. I might have tried harder to convince her of the truth, but I rather liked her version. It wouldn't be too hard for me to start believing it myself. I *had* stood up for Taylor. For a minute, anyway.

The crowd began to move. Lydia Combs went off to find Nehemiah and tell him how brave I had been.

"What the hell do you think you're doing?" Wiley grabbed my arm.

"Let go of me! Hey, that hurts!"

"I'm not touching your eye, just get over here." He yanked me across the road. "Don't you know Dove's just spent four days trying to stop all this talk about you? Do you even know how much trouble you were in, Peejoe? The sheriff wanted to charge you with making false statements, that's a crime! He almost did it, too. And here you are standing around like some big hero."

"What are you talking about?"

"He claims you told those guys at the Piggly Wiggly somebody shot you and the old lady from the bushes."

"I didn't tell 'em anything! I passed out!"

"It doesn't matter, it's what the sheriff says. He's got it in for you, Peejoe. He saw you at the pool that day. He told Dove you're a trouble-maker. And then after he arrested those guys for shooting you, he had to let 'em go. Made him look like a fool. Of *course* he blamed you, he had to blame somebody."

"Like he blamed Taylor for what happened to him," I said.

We climbed a little knoll. Six blocks ahead, people poured into the green sunlit park. I was trying to comprehend the idea that I had become notorious while lying on my cot, counting the ceiling tiles with one eye.

"Wiley, why didn't you tell me?"

"Dove said the most important thing was for you to get over it."

The river had thinned to a trickle of families, the elderly and the slow-footed straggling up the street. Nehemiah's amplified voice echoed down the block—he was preaching again. The commotion had brought white people out of their houses. Some hung back in the shadows of their porches, watching with fearful eyes.

We rounded the corner. The swimming pool was closed, a placid blue rectangle surrounded by empty white concrete, the high chain-link fence—and hundreds of people outside, wanting in.

Taylor's coffin rested in the bed of the old blue truck, near the spot where he had fallen. Nehemiah addressed the congregation from the tailgate. "We have a right to be here!"

I spotted four sheriff's cars parked at the top of the hill beside the Dairy Dog. The deputies sat on their hoods, licking ice-cream cones. They were watching the scene below, but I didn't see what they could do in the face of such numbers.

". . . and if they think they can keep us out with a little old padlock and some chain-link fence, they don't know very much. I say we open this pool up for business."

A cry went up. The people nearest the gate began banging on the fence, rocking it back and forth. One boy took up a brick and started beating at the padlock. Another boy pushed him aside and went at it with a hammer.

The lock broke. The boys swarmed through.

Nehemiah hopped down from the truck to follow the surge through the gate. "No damage, now, come on, people, let's show respect."

Wiley and I pushed through just behind him. Little boys ran out on the diving board, screaming their glee, bouncing in their Sunday clothes.

Nehemiah shucked off his suit coat, handed it to the lady beside him, and began to unbutton his vest.

The lady looked shocked.

"Don't worry, Miss Dora, I intend to remain entirely decent." He took off his vest and his shoes and his socks, exposing his gnarled brown toes. He walked to the edge of the pool, snapping his suspenders.

The people cheered: "Jump, Brother Thomas! Jump in!"

"All right. This is for Taylor." Nehemiah pinched his nose, closed his eyes, and stepped off the edge.

He came up spluttering. The crowd approved wildly, with whistles and cheers.

Nehemiah flailed to the ladder and pulled himself up, dripping, his shirt clinging to his skinny bones. "Hallelujah, the pool is open. Somebody hand me a towel."

He made an announcement: a mass meeting Friday night, eight o'clock at Holy Redeemer, pass it on. Then he dried off and went off with Mattie Jackson and her family to bury Taylor at a church in the country.

The crowd grew solemn while the truck bearing the pine box passed among them to the road.

Then the row of boys toppled off the diving board. Just that fast, the funeral turned into a pool party. Other kids shucked off their pants and jumped in. Grown men stripped off jackets and shoes, tossed them against the fence, bounded into the pool. A race developed to see who could get in the water fastest.

Those people took over that place. Within minutes they had the PA playing Cannibal & the Headhunters' "Land of 1000 Dances." They danced in the water, on the pool deck, by the snack bar. Several hundred stood patiently outside the fence, awaiting their dip in the pool. They filed through ten or twelve at a time, hopping into the water and out again, clapping shoulders and laughing. Preachers performed on-the-spot baptisms in the shallow end.

Naked children swarmed the baby pool. Older kids swam in their underpants, men in their boxer shorts or their good trousers. The women mostly stood back from the water trying not to get wet. The few who were daring enough to make the plunge in their Sunday dresses were roundly applauded.

Nobody touched the WHITE ONLY sign on the wall by the snack bar. They left it right up there so everybody could see it.

Apparently someone decided to give the pool over to the Negroes for the whole afternoon.

The sun fell way down in the trees, shadows stretching to every corner of the park, and still the celebration went on, still dozens waiting for their turn to swim. It was a badge of honor to get sopping wet and have your picture taken by the young white man in the gray felt hat who was snapping flash photos of everything. Teenage boys took turns striking crazy poses for him.

Wiley squinted over the field. "It's getting dark. Where did all the deputies go?"

A crowd of white people watched from the top of the hill, but the deputies and their bronze-colored cars had withdrawn when no one was looking.

"They gave up, Wiley! Can you believe it?" What a change had come over this town in one afternoon! This was a big fat victory for Nehemiah Thomas and the Negroes. There was the sign on the wall: WHITE ONLY. There were the colored people swimming. They had won. The pool was theirs. Sheriff Doggett had not lifted a finger to stop them.

Vapor lamps flickered on around the pool. In the gathering dusk, the people began to feel a damp chill. Mothers rounded their children out of the water to join the stream of people across the field toward Dog Junction.

"Maybe we ought to go home," Wiley said, "just in case we're not in hot water yet."

I agreed. "It's not that much fun watching other people swim, anyway."

The man with the camera stopped me at the gate. "Excuse me, son, I need your name, I took a picture of you."

"Of me?" I backed up a step. "When?"

"A minute ago. I'm not sure they'll use it, but I need your name just in case." He whipped out a little notebook.

"It's Peter, Joseph, Bullis."

He asked me to spell "Bullis" and wrote it down. "Oh right, I've heard about you. How old are you, Peter?"

"I'm twelve. Why did you take my picture?"

"Thanks kid, gotta go." He turned away.

"Great." Wiley rolled his eyes. "Now they're going to put your ugly face in the newspaper, and Dove'll know we were here."

"You're just jealous they didn't take your picture," I told him.

"Yeah, right."

Just then the vapor light burst over the deep end of the pool—a shower of glass tinkled to the concrete, splattered like diamonds in the water. Kids squealed and ran.

"Well that's weird," Wiley said.

A note of concern ran through the crowd.

The light on the snack bar exploded.

In the next breath the light on the pole by the poolhouse exploded, *ka-bash!*

Suddenly it was dark at the pool. The squeals turned to screams. I heard someone fall into the water.

"What's going on, Wiley? I can't see!"

"They're shooting out the lights."

We pondered this notion a moment, then took off scrambling for the road. Wiley dragged me by one arm. "Keep your head down!"

Behind us people screamed, trying to jam through the gate.

The light on the pole directly above us exploded, *ka-plash!* Glass rained on our heads.

A little Negro girl shrieked and threw her arms around me so hard she almost knocked me down.

I reached around to pat her shoulder. "It's okay, you're not hurt. Go on. Run home."

From the woods to our right I heard a rumble of engines. The little girl hid her face in my shirt.

At the top of the hill, the Dairy Dog streetlight exploded.

The whole spread of the park was now submerged in darkness, except for a bright flash now and then—the man in the felt hat snapping pictures, freezing people in postures of running and screaming.

"Peejoe, come on! This way!"

I pried the girl's hands from around my waist. "Run home! Hurry!" I lit out after Wiley.

We crashed through the bushes, into a clearing full of men—three dozen at least, big guys, with guns and sticks and hunting caps, a squadron of white men advancing through the bushes toward the park. Their pickup trucks were scattered all through these trees.

This was an ambush.

Five men branched off and came toward us, waving guns.

We flung our hands in the air.

"Don't hurt us," Wiley cried. "We're white."

I stared into two holes at the end of a shotgun. They could have killed me right then.

A flashlight snapped on. The beam moved across the ground, up my leg, up the front of my shirt to shine in my good eye.

My other eye made them gasp.

A gruff voice: "What happened to him?"

"He's hurt, we gotta find him a doctor." Wiley kept his voice calm and his hands up. "We'll go this way or back the way we came. Whichever you say."

The lead man waved the gun-barrel over his shoulder. "Go on."

"Yes sir"

"Thank you sir"

I didn't dare look at them or I would surely be struck dead. We hurried past, through a litter of beer cans and Golden Flake potato-chip bags. They'd been having a little party back here in the trees, waiting for darkness to fall.

We hid behind a mud-spattered Dodge truck, papered over with bumper stickers: Goldwater '64, George Wallace—Stand Up for Alabama, Better Dead Than Red, Castro Out of Cuba, See Rock City, Eat More Pork, Impeach Earl Warren, If You Can Read This Get Off My Dam Bumper.

"You think they shot out the lights?"

"I think they laid a real fine trap," said Wiley. "Look. There they go. They're going to clean out that park."

We raised up enough to see the dim shapes of men crashing through the bushes howling, a Rebel yell answered by terrified cries.

If we hadn't come stumbling into them, that would be us screaming now, "Stop! Please, don't! Don't!" A sound like someone chopping wood.

"Wiley, we got to do something."

"You got your knife?"

I patted my pockets. Uncle Franklin had given us identical Scout knives for Christmas. "Yeah, but I'm not going out there with a knife, are you crazy?"

He unfolded his blade. "Go ahead, get it out."

He crabwalked along the bumper of the Dodge to the rear wheelwell. Gunfire rang through the trees: three shots, a pause, a shotgun blast.

Wiley buried his knife to the hilt in the tire—a loud *ffffshtt* as the burst of pressure escaped. He ripped the tire open. The truck sagged on its springs.

"Hurry, Peejoe. Do that one over there. Do both the back tires."

I made my way through the weeds to a Ford pickup.

Someone crashed through the bushes fifty yards away, shouting for help.

I stuck my knife in the tire, hammering with the heel of my hand until the handle was smack up against the rubber. I took hold with both hands and yanked as hard as I could. The tire blew stale-rubber air in my face, and collapsed.

We heard the men beating Negroes. We cut their tires.

At last Wiley said "That's enough. Let's get out of here!"

We crept through the clearing. Inhuman sounds drifted in from the park. No one could hear those sounds and stay clean. A cry arose, "No no no no!" trailing through the air.

This was nothing like Selma. Selma was a TV show in broad daylight, it was over in two minutes. This was real it was live it was happening now, it went on and on in the dark.

We stole through the bushes to Lee Street. If they hadn't shot out the lights we could have seen the whole struggle spread over the field up the slope to the Dairy Dog, but in the darkness we heard the sounds and saw a weird shadow-ballet—a mob over here, a clutch of men there—there! look there! someone running. Escaping.

The headlights of a car swept over the field where men crawled on all fours and other men surrounded them, kicking them.

20

Peejoe

Industry

W e didn't know those were Dove's headlights until the white hearse roared up and the rear door flew open and Dove said "Get in."

"But—"

"Move!"

We moved. Milton peered at us over the seat.

"Uncle Dove . . ."

"Quiet!" he bellowed. "I don't want to hear from you!"

I hung my head. He had never raised his voice to me.

Three men chased a boy past our bumper.

"See why I told you not to come? Do you understand now?" Dove swung the hearse around in a wide circle to pull up alongside an old lady on her knees. "Ma'am, are you all right? Milton, go around and open the back. Ma'am?"

She held her head in her hands. Dove got out and knelt beside her.

I shrank down beside Wiley. A big moon was rising now over the field. In the silver light I could make out the shapes of people lying on the ground or hobbling away.

The chain-link gate lay where the terrified crowd had ripped it from its hinges. That whole side of the fence was trampled flat.

The men Wiley and I met coming through the woods had broken up into smaller groups, roaming the park and the streets near the park, firing their guns in the air. They chased anything that moved.

Dove and Milton helped the old lady into the hearse. "Law, my head," she kept saying, "they sho crack my head."

Dove bumped over the curb and onto the field, steering toward the wounded people as his headlights found them. We picked up two bloody-

179

nosed teenage boys, a lady with a broken ankle, a kid we found lying unconscious by the fence, a man bleeding from a nasty cut on his head.

Over the field came a shout—"There he goes! Run, nigger!"—a fusillade of gunshots. I heard men jeering and laughing but I couldn't see them.

The county ambulance came tearing downhill past the Dairy Dog, blinking and wailing.

Dove flashed his high beams and rolled down his window.

The ambulance slid alongside. "Hey Dove, we got some wild call . . ." When the plump-faced driver saw all the Negroes crammed into our hearse, his voice trailed off. ". . . What the hell?"

"It's a damn race riot out here, Eugene," Dove told him. "We got people shooting and beating on folks, and where the hell is John Doggett?"

"Don't know." The ambulance driver stuck his thumb over his shoulder. "Take a look, some joker uptown just busted out my back window."

"This is out of control," Dove said. "This is just what he wanted to happen."

Eugene eyed our passengers. "Where you taking all them?"

"To County. Quick as I can unload 'em I'll come back for more. There's plenty out there for you."

"They ain't gone take 'em at County," said Eugene.

"What do you mean? They're hurt."

"Don't matter. They won't take all these niggers out there." Eugene fished a cigar from his pocket. "Believe me, I know. They'll take one or two, maybe, but not all these."

"Well hell, Eugene, this is your job, not mine! What should I do?"

"The ones that can walk, I'd take 'em on home. The rest of 'em, I don't know. Your best bet is probly Doc Hollis in Dog Junction." He revved his engine. "See you."

"Wait! Eugene, those are people out there."

"Yeah, I know what they are. I ain't fixin' to get mixed up in this." He rolled up his window and sped away.

"Mist' Dove, this fella's head is surely bleeding," said Milton.

Something struck our rear fender with a *chunk!*

I saw a gang of dark figures approaching the hearse. One of them hollered "Go home, niggers!"

At that moment I tasted the water in the nigger cup. I tasted the iron tang of blood in the water. I was huddled in that hearse with them, breathing the smell of their blood, sharing their fear.

A rock smacked the window.

"Cracked it," cried Wiley. "Uncle Dove, get us out of here!"

One man managed to get his hand on our tailfin just as Dove mashed the pedal to the floor. The mighty V-8 took us out of there slinging dust. "Sit down, Peter Joseph, I'm trying to drive! Milton, how's he doing back there?"

"Still bleeding."

"Keep pressure on it." In the dashboard light I saw the sweat-beads on Dove's face, his eyes flicking from the road to the mirror, and over to me. "You all right?"

"Yes sir. I'm sorry—"

"We'll talk about it later. What the hell happened down there?"

"Nehemiah took everybody to swim in the pool," I said.

"And there was a bunch of guys in the woods," Wiley put in. "And they shot out all the lights."

"And then they just started beating on everybody," I said.

"They come from the devil," said a man in back.

All down the Old Goshen Road, people loomed suddenly in our headlights, staggering up out of nowhere. Dove had to swerve to keep from hitting them. That part felt like a movie to me, dodging those people as they popped up in our windshield like ducks in a shooting arcade.

The old lady groaned. Dove swung onto Sycamore Street, shrieking tires. "Milton, can't you do something for her?"

"My hands are full. It's just a li'l ol' knot on her head."

"All right now, folks," Dove said, "I'm taking you to Nehemiah's, he can fetch Dr. Hollis for you. I don't know what else to do. There's still a lot of hurt people back there."

The old lady said, "Jesus will bless you."

Lights blazed in every window of the Blessed Rest Funeral Home, a dignified one-story house with a wide front porch. Nehemiah's battered Lincoln hearse sat in the yard.

Through the windows it looked like a party or meeting under way in the house, people standing around.

"I need help!" Dove called. "I got injured people here!"

A woman in the doorway said something to those inside. Four young men came trotting out to help Dove and Milton unload the wounded.

Nehemiah hurried up. "We've just heard what happened. Are there more people hurt?"

"A hell of a lot more," Dove snapped. "That's real fine, Nehemiah. Start something like that, then take off and leave it to blow up in everybody's face. I hope you're satisfied. This is all your doing."

Nehemiah gazed through his glasses, unblinking. "Now Mr. Bullis, you know that's not true. I didn't hurt anybody."

A vein throbbed in Dove's temple. "Don't play dumb with me, Nehemiah. I never had any idea how smooth you were till today. One speech and you think you're Martin Luther King. Well, you got 'em whipped up, all right, you got 'em in that water, you sure did. Then you went off and left 'em to the sharks."

"We had to bury the boy. I had no idea—"

Dove jabbed his finger in Nehemiah's chest. "You started it. You should have stayed to finish what you started."

"Wait a minute." Nehemiah took a step back. "It started a long time before me, Mr. Bullis. This is a fine thing you're doing, helping these folks. I'll follow you down. Ben? Ramsey? Let's go."

His coolness blew back over Dove. They regarded each other.

Dove slammed us in, fished the red emergency light from under his seat, licked the suction cup, stuck it to the dashboard.

Milton wiped blood off the seat. I got up on my knees to watch Nehemiah following close on our bumper.

Dove said "We're not hanging around here one minute longer than we have to. Wiley, you help Milton get the people in the car. Peter Joseph, keep a lookout as best you can."

We jounced into the park, siren wailing. Our headlights swept the field and found a huddle of wounded people near the collapsed section of the fence.

Their eyes came up into our lights, a moment of terror—then they spotted Nehemiah in the second hearse, and opened their arms to receive us. Nobody had to help them get in. By this time every able-bodied soul had long since fled; we gathered up mostly old folks. They swarmed both cars, scrabbling at the door-handles. The ones who could walk dragged the others in through any available door. The air rang with sobbing and grateful cries. They were cut, bruised, scared to death—but not dead, at least no one we could find.

"I don't see anybody else," Nehemiah called.

We headed out to the road. Everyone started talking at once. They said the white men all broke off the attack at the same moment, as if on a signal, and melted back into the trees.

Dove steered around a jacked-up pickup truck half in the ditch. Two men were on their knees in the dirt, changing the tire.

An electric tingle ran over me. I tugged Wiley's elbow.

He put a finger to his lips: shh.

"That's the man!" cried a woman in the jumpseat. "That's the one was hittin' on my Dolphus! Stop this car!"

"No stopping." Dove speeded up.

We jolted into the yard beside Nehemiah's hearse. I groped up the steps to open the door for the wounded.

A man shouted into a telephone. I pressed myself against the wall, breathing the rubbing-alcohol smell. All the furniture had been shoved against the walls to make room for people on the floor. That must be Doctor Hollis, that brown wizened man with the stethoscope.

"Coming through!" Dove shouldered in with the old lady in his arms. He set her down gently against the front wall, out of the traffic.

Nehemiah followed him in. "I think everyone's inside now. It's a miracle, all that shooting and no one is dead. Mr. Bullis, I want to thank you again."

"Listen, I don't want your thanks. I want a straight answer."

Nehemiah folded his arms. "All right. What is the question?"

"The question is, what do you want? Exactly what the hell do you want from all this?"

Nehemiah pondered the question.

"Freedom," he said at last. "That's all I want."

"Yeah, right, I heard that already. That and what else?"

"That's all," said Nehemiah. "It may not sound like much to you, but it's something I've never had."

"Do you want to turn this town into Selma? Is that it? Want to go to jail, get yourself on TV? Because I can guarantee you, whatever you come up with, John Doggett will rise to the occasion. He's as stubborn as you. He will match you every step of the way."

"Absolutely. I'm counting on that." Nehemiah stepped aside for a woman with a steaming kettle. "You can be a big help to us, Mr. Bullis."

"Not a chance." Dove shook his head. "I am washing my hands of this mess. I'm gonna let you and John go ahead and throw the biggest old civil-rights party anybody ever saw. Meantime this town will just go straight to hell."

"It's hell *now*, Mr. Bullis. It's hell *already*. Look at this! This is a funeral home, not a hospital. I got twenty people bleeding on my floor because the sheriff won't protect 'em and the hospital won't take 'em. That lady you carried in here, that's Miss Bessie Stringfellow, she taught me second grade, she's—how old are you, Miss Bessie?"

"Eighty-three," Miss Bessie crowed proudly.

"Eighty-three. And they hit her in the head with a rock. I say this place is long past going to hell."

"You're wasting your preaching on me," Dove said. "You forget, I know you're just a lousy undertaker."

Nehemiah smiled. "Sometimes the undertakers have to lead the way."

"Yeah, where angels fear to tread," said Dove. "You be careful."

Maybe he shouldn't have said that. When I think about what happened next, it always seems to me Dove saying "be careful" was the trigger that set everything in motion. First I heard the noise from outside—an engine gunning and popping, backfiring. I turned. My eye recorded a slow-motion picture of Doctor Hollis and his helpers bobbing among the people on the floor, the plastic-lace curtain, the strip of translucent yellow flypaper coiling down the screen. A flicker of light in the trees.

The boys on the porch flung themselves down facefirst.

Dove came at me from the blind side. He caught me in one arm and Wiley in the other and threw us to the floor with all his weight. A pickup truck zoomed by *pop! pop! pop!* I saw two muzzles flashing. I buried my face in Dove's side.

Bullets thudded into the house, marching down the porch wall, ripping into boards, shattering windows.

All around us people crashed to the floor, and the screams, oh the screams will come back in my worst dreams forever, those people went clean over the edge of fear into some other place.

A hoarse whisper: "Get those lights out!"

Dove scrambled across the doorway and shot his hand up to the switch, plunging the room into darkness.

The boys scuttled in from the porch on their elbows.

Dove cried, "Stay down!" And here came the truck again careening in the other direction, blazing away with both guns. Bullets spattered down the house. I heard a ricochet *piyaaiiing!* like on "Gunsmoke." Everyone screamed as if they'd been shot.

The truck screeched around the corner and into the night.

For the longest time we stayed on the floor without moving. Gradually the screaming subsided to whimpers, kids crying.

Dove crawled over toward us. "Boys? You all right?"

We said we were. He felt us to make sure, hugged us close. His back was soaked with sweat.

My teeth chattered. I listened for the sound of the truck.

Nehemiah moved through the house with a candle. "Did they hit anybody?"

"They did." That was Doctor Hollis, on his knees beside Miss Bessie Stringfellow.

She looked all right to me, propped against the wall where Dove had left her, but when the doctor took his hand away I saw the blood. The bullet had come through the wall straight through her heart and killed her.

Sheriff Doggett arrived with two backup cars. They pulled up in the yard to shine their headlights on the riddled face of the funeral home.

The sheriff swaggered to the porch, where some of the men were counting bullet holes. "We had a complaint of some shooting out here," he began—then he saw Dove standing just inside the door. His eyebrows went up.

"Evening, John."

"What say, Dove. What you doing over here?"

"The question is, where the hell have *you* been?"

"Had some trouble in town," Doggett said.

Dove opened the door. "Tell me about it."

"Let's get some lights on in here," the sheriff boomed, reaching for the switch. He did not expect to see all those people laid out on the floor. "What the hell is this?"

Nehemiah glanced up from Miss Bessie. "Sheriff."

"Brother Thomas. I been looking for you. I got a outstanding warrant for you."

"First you might want to look at Miss Bessie," Nehemiah said, touching her hand. "Your friends shot her in the back. She was nothing but an old lady."

"I want to know what all this shooting is about," said the sheriff. "We got complaints."

"You should take it up with the ones who did the shooting." Nehemiah stood. "You just missed them. They were driving a Ford pickup, brown with a white stripe down the side. I didn't get a look at the license plate."

Doggett frowned. "How do I know you didn't just shoot the place up yourself, to get some publicity? That's what you're after, ain't it, Nehemiah? Publicity? Now I got orders to bring you in and that's exactly what I mean to do."

Dove said "Aw for Christ's sake, John. On what charge?"

"You name it. Unlawful assembly, inciting a riot, parading without a permit, disturbing the peace, destroying public property . . ."

"That's ridiculous," Dove said.

"You think so? Go take a look at that nice new pool. They tore down that fence like a bunch of damn animals."

"John. You got guys riding around shooting guns, you got a bunch of people hurt and one old lady shot dead. You mean to tell me you're worried about a chain-link fence?"

"I'll tell you something, Dove. I care more about that fence than I do about these niggers. See, I don't care how many of 'em gets hurt. They don't concern me, people like this. I'd just as soon let 'em pile up. It don't bother me even a little."

"That's fine," Dove said. "That is just fine."

"I let 'em have their way today," the sheriff went on. "When this rabble-rousing little sonofabitch got up and talked 'em all into marching down to that pool, I sat back and let 'em have at it. I let 'em swim the whole afternoon, didn't touch a hair on their heads. What happened to them after that, I don't know and I don't care. They oughta be thankful I didn't chuck 'em all in jail." He unclipped handcuffs from his belt. "If some good law-abiding people decided to teach 'em a lesson or two about how to get along in this town, well, that's just dandy with me." He made Nehemiah stand with his hands crossed before him.

"I get it now," Dove said. "You came here to make sure they got him. And now you see they missed, you're gonna put him away. Who all was in that truck, John?"

"I don't know about any truck." He snapped the cuffs on Nehemiah's wrists. "I told you, he probably shot up the place himself."

Dove said "I was here. I saw it. All these people are witnesses. You're not God, you know. There are judges, there are people who can come here and force you to uphold the law."

The sheriff turned Nehemiah by the shoulders. "You hear that, Brother Thomas? He's gonna sic the judges on me. See how scared I am?"

"What I mean is, you better start doing your job. This town is about to come unraveled."

"Don't you worry about me. I think *you* better make up your mind right quicklike whose side *you* are on."

"I'm trying to stay off of sides," Dove said. "I just want all this killing to stop."

"Howcome? It's good for your business." The sheriff cracked a smile. "You take care of the dead ones, Dove, and leave the live ones to me."

"Mr. Bullis," said Nehemiah, "I know it's a lot to ask, but since I'm apparently going to be—indisposed, I wonder if you might take care of Miss Bessie for me."

Dove hesitated. "That's a little hard right now, Nehemiah, that puts me in an awkward position," he said. "I'll see what I can do."

"Come on, Preacher Man. Let's go." The sheriff tugged at the hand-cuffs. No one made a move to stop him from marching Nehemiah to the deputy's car, and locking him in the back seat. We followed them out.

"Take him down and hold him," Doggett told the deputy. "I'll be there in ten minutes."

Nehemiah peered out the window. He held up his hands so everyone could see the cuffs as they drove him away.

The sheriff said "Listen, Dove, one other thing. Some friends of mine had trouble with some vandalism tonight, seems somebody cut the tires on just about every last one of their vehicles. You happen to know anything about that?"

Dove said "No, why should I?"

I did not dare look at Wiley. I concentrated on freezing my face in a neutral expression.

"These fellers said they saw a couple kids out there. Said one of 'em had a big ol' bandage on his head. That ring a bell?"

Dove clenched his fists. "That's really low, John, that is low even for you. You leave these kids out of this. They've been with me all day."

"Whatever you say. I guess that feller was wrong. I guess he just made it up."

"Go pick on somebody your own size," said Dove. "Boys, get in the car."

The sheriff roared off. Dove stood looking after him, with his hands on his hips, arguing some question in his head. Then he turned and went back in the Blessed Rest.

I told Wiley I was sorry. "This stupid bandage gave us away."

He stuck his finger against his temple, and pulled the trigger. "It's okay. I don't care. I don't mind Dove knowing what we did. I'd do it again."

Injured people streamed out of the house, limping off down the road. Apparently they thought they would be safer somewhere else.

Just an hour ago it seemed Nehemiah had won such a big victory. Now his people were scattered and wounded and shot, his house riddled with holes, Nehemiah on his way to jail. He had won the day, but the sheriff and his friends won it all back in the night.

Dove and Milton emerged from the house with Miss Bessie on a stretcher. They rolled her out to the hearse and put her in back.

Milton got in beside us. Dove rode alone up front. "All right, boys, which one of you was cutting tires?"

I swallowed hard. "We both did."

"It was my idea." Wiley leaned up in the seat. "Those were the guys that were beating on people, Uncle Dove! We saw 'em doing it! The sheriff ought to go arrest them, if he wants to arrest somebody."

Dove glanced over his shoulder. "What exactly did you have in mind, son? Did you want to keep 'em all there for some reason?"

"I don't know," Wiley said, "I guess I wanted to help catch 'em. I guess nobody really wanted to."

Milton said "Did y'all really cut them men's tires?"

I grinned. "Yeah, we did."

"Ought to give you the prize," he said, with a grin.

"Don't encourage 'em, Milton. The one time I give these boys a direct order, and next thing I know they're out slashin' tires." In spite of himself, Dove smiled. "I bet they were mighty pissed off."

He switched on the radio. We rode home with Brenda Lee wailing "Emotions."

I did feel proud, because I had cut those tires and I had come through a race riot and a hail of gunfire without getting beat up or shot. There were not many boys my age who'd done that. I felt sorry for Miss Bessie Stringfellow lying back there dead, but that was our job, taking care of dead people wherever they might appear.

They shot at me and missed. I was excited. I was still Peejoe, one-eyed but alive and ready for what might come next.

We found Earlene waiting up, pacing the floor. "I have been worried sick," she snapped. "The telephone has not stopped ringing."

Wiley and I flopped on the sheepskin rug in front of the TV. We turned on "Shindig" with the sound off.

"I heard there was a riot," Earlene said. "I heard there were people killed."

"One lady is all we have so far," said Dove. "Milton's bringing her in the back. She was one of Nehemiah's old schoolteachers. Shot in the back."

"You don't mean a colored woman."

"John Doggett took Nehemiah off to jail," he said. "The lady was dead, there's nobody else to handle the embalming. Nehemiah asked me, professional courtesy. I didn't see any choice."

"Dove Bullis, you brought a colored woman into this house?"

"Oh relax, Earlene, she's not going to bite you. We just won't say anything about it and nobody will have to know she was here."

"Well, you better hope not. I can't believe you would do that with everything that's happening in this town."

"Earlene. What's the matter with you? You're all up in the air about something."

"I've only had the worst day of my life," she blurted, suddenly on the verge of tears. "I worked my heart out getting all ready to have a nice luncheon, and then an hour after they were supposed to be here Betty Jernigan called and said they were afraid to go out of the house on account of what-all they were hearing about the Nigroes. That left me with four dozen little pimento cheese sandwiches gone entirely to waste. I swear, Dove, sometimes I just don't think I can take it." She began to cry.

Dove put his arm around her shoulder. "It's all right, Earlene, we'll eat the sandwiches."

She stiffened. "I threw 'em in the garbage. What right does she have to call me at the last minute like that? I don't think they even wanted to come in the first place. I think it was just a stupid excuse and they were all three over at her house laughing at me."

Dove peered down at her. "You threw away four dozen pimento cheese sandwiches?"

"Well I was so mad," she said, wiping her tears. "We are never going to have any decent friends in this place!"

21

Lucille

Beverly Hills, California

Lucille wished she had thought to take some little souvenir from each man when she finished with him, snip off a lock of his hair maybe. Four men in one week, and a fifth one head-over-heels in love with her. She was beginning to lose track.

The New Mexico state trooper was fading to a hazy memory. She scanned the papers every morning but never saw any mention of a trooper hog-tied naked in his car. She decided he had freed himself somehow and been too ashamed to tell anybody.

Then there was Jack the Las Vegas bellboy, he was sweet and athletic, and very attentive with his tongue to certain locations that had never before been explored. And also Ted, the blond bellboy in Beverly Hills, an afternoon's diversion.

Already poor Norman, the lovestruck chauffeur, had sent red roses, chocolates, and champagne, each new gift accompanied by the same card: "Miss Clay, I will always adore you. Sincerely, Norman Wirtz."

She had to count the man from last night, though she didn't know his name. She hadn't even seen him clearly. She blushed when she thought about what she had done. She could almost hear her mother saying *that is so cheap.* And it was. Cheap and dirty. She liked it.

Lucille had never pictured herself as a slut but she was certainly carrying on like one. Maybe that New Orleans bartender had seen into her future. It was thrilling to get everything she'd always wanted, and more of it, again and again, from a new man every day.

The only one from whom she'd kept a souvenir was Chester, and of course she had snipped off more than his hair.

It turned out Chester was a highly defective representative of the male sex in almost every way. His idea of lovemaking was to lick his lips and climb up on top with a groan (not from pleasure but from his bad back), heave-ho back and forth, rocking always in that same sluggish rhythm like a washing machine on the gentle cycle. He had no idea what made sex exciting: he was incapable of the suddenness and mystery and teasing and energy that went into it.

Why had it taken so long for Lucille to find out these things for herself? Why hadn't she cheated on him once in all those years?

God knows she'd had chances. That neighbor man Lewis Abernathy used to walk his eyes up and down her at the backyard barbecues, he tried to kiss her in the kitchen every New Year's Eve. And there was that towheaded college boy who came to fix the roof the time Chester took the children to visit his sick mother. Lucille talked to that kid, she drank in the lovely solidity of his muscles, she got him alone in her kitchen three mornings in a row, she made him coffee and stood close to him—but when he made a move to kiss her, she turned huffy and cold and sent him away and hired another man to finish the roof.

Why had she done that? She couldn't remember. She was a dead woman then. She was walking around dead all the time. Being married to Chester had killed everything alive inside her, like pouring poison into a lake year after year, until all the fish float to the surface. Lucille raised his children and oh, she supposed she loved them, but most of the time they drove her crazy. They were the visible result of her marriage to *him;* she couldn't escape a certain feeling of revulsion, no matter how hard she tried.

She was never meant for that life. She was born to be a fabulous Hollywood star, and yes, a slut. She felt more at home in Bungalow Six of the Beverly Hills Hotel than she'd ever felt anywhere within the state of Alabama.

Also, she was learning: the more sex you get, the more you want.

Yesterday she ate breakfast at a little round iron table by the swimming pool; she lounged on her private patio in her smart Jackie Kennedy sundress; she read *Glamour* and *Modern Screen* and soaked up the sunshine, waiting for Harry to call. She drank three daiquiris and fell asleep.

When she awoke it was twilight, a coolish breeze starting up. She shivered, wrapped her damp hair in a towel, hurried to her bungalow. She had just stepped inside when the telephone rang.

"Hello?"

"Hi, baby." A man's dark voice. Quiet.

"Harry? Is that you?"

"No. Who's Harry?"

"Who is this?"

"I saw you." His voice had a dangerous rumble, like a motorcycle. "I watched you sleeping by the pool."

"Oh, come off it, Norman. You're very sweet and I thank you for all the presents, but it's not going to work, all right? I told you. You're just not my type."

The man said "What *is* your type?"

He didn't sound much like Norman: his voice was darker, mysterious. Interesting.

"Listen, who is this?" she demanded. "What do you want?"

"I want to make love to you."

"Oh my." Lucille took the phone away and glared as if it had just stuck a wet tongue in her ear. For a minute she didn't know what to do. Then it came to her: hang up, stupid.

She hung up.

She stared at the phone. She found herself thinking *please call back.*

She did not say that out loud, but the phone rang as if she had. She flinched.

Do not answer that, Lucille. Let it ring.

She lit a cigarette. The phone rang, and rang, and rang.

She thought she could outlast him, she thought she could stand the ringing longer than he would stay on the phone, but after counting the thirty-fifth ring, she grabbed it. "What do you *want?*"

"I saw you wake up. You were beautiful. You stretched your arms like a cat. I liked how you wrapped that towel around your hair." His voice tickled some part of Lucille. "I want to kiss you."

"Listen, buster," she sputtered, "I don't know who you think this is, but you've got the wrong number." She slammed down the receiver.

She counted: one, two, three, four—

The phone rang.

She snatched it up. "If you don't quit bothering me I'm calling the manager! I mean it, now, leave me alone!"

Of course she should have hung up right then, and left it off the hook. She did not do that.

She dropped the receiver on the table and kicked the bathroom door shut with her toe, to simulate the sound of leaving the room. Then she leaned down to the phone, just close enough to hear him say "I know you're there, baby. Open the curtains."

Gently cupping her hand over the mouthpiece, Lucille lifted the receiver to her ear.

"Be a good girl. Go to the window and open the curtains. Let me look at you."

She began to imagine a man to go with that voice. He would have to be tall. His voice was strongly persuasive.

"Come on, little baby. Do what I tell you."

For an instant an image of Chester flickered across her mind. She turned to make sure the hatbox was still on the dresser where she'd left it.

Not even Chester could make a telephone ring from beyond the grave.

She uncovered the mouthpiece. "Who is this really?"

"This is the man of your dreams."

"I'm getting tired of this game. Is this Ted?"

"No, it's not Ted, or Norman, or Tom, Dick, or Harry. You have a lot of boyfriends, don't you."

Lucille snapped off the lamp and parted the curtains an inch. Warm lights glowed in the neighboring bungalows. She didn't see anyone out there.

"Ah, now I see you," he said. "Why did you turn out the lights? Are you shy?"

"I am not listening to one more minute of this . . ."

Lucille thought of those cartoons where a cat uses a piece of cheese to lure a mouse from its hole, the vaporous aroma of the cheese assumes the form of a snake-charmer, paralyzing the mouse into walking stiff-kneed and glassy-eyed toward its doom with its little arms stuck straight out. At this moment Lucille was behaving like that mouse.

"It's all right," he was saying, "leave it dark. I like it better in the dark."

"I don't know who you think I am," Lucille said.

"Unlock your door, and go on to bed. Just go to sleep. I'll come visit you in a while. I'll come into your dreams."

A click, and a hum.

Lucille hung up.

She peered into the darkness, burning with curiosity. What if he *was* the man of her dreams? Would he just announce himself like that?

His voice was captivating.

Lucille took the gun from her purse and tucked it under the night-table where she could reach it in an instant. She unlocked the door and stretched out on the bed, just to think about things.

What could it hurt to see what he looked like? What could it possibly hurt? If he wasn't nice, she would scream bloody murder and run him out of there with the pistol.

She shouldn't be sleepy, she'd had such a long nap in the sun. She yawned and tucked her toes under the covers.

After a long time she heard the click of the door, the rustle of someone coming in. She pretended to sleep. She heard him undoing his shirt buttons, shucking off his undershirt; the tinkle of his belt buckle, the *zzt!* of the zipper, coins rattling as the trousers came down.

Then he was on the bed beside her, his hand stealing up to her breast. Hot breath in her ear. "Wake up, little baby."

She rolled over. In the darkness he was only the shape of a big strong man. She ran her hand up his chest. "I've never done anything like this before," she said.

"I'll show you how." He bent to kiss her neck. He was clean-shaven, with a fresh crewcut and a smell of Old Spice. They came face-to-face and thank God he was handsome, with a square jaw, like an Army man . . . maybe it was the crewcut. He was familiar somehow. It was too dark to see him very well.

She traced the line of his shoulder with a fingernail. "Who *are* you?"

He kissed her ear. "Were you dreaming about me?"

Lucille wrapped him in her arms and pulled him under the covers with her. He was warm, and handsome, and hard, he was here and on fire with her. All her life she had dreamed of a handsome strong man in the dark, and now he was here, and she gave herself to him.

They kissed. The cinnamon tang of Dentyne was real enough, it gave her a moment to think *Lucille, what on earth are you doing?*—but she shoved that thought away and kissed him again. Their tongues clashed in a lovely way.

She stroked the fine brush of his hair. He was not in a hurry. He worked his way down her body. After nibbling and tasting a while he would come up to her lips for a kiss, as if drawing his oxygen from her.

Then he moved her around and began to angle in for what he wanted. His tenderness dissolved into something hard. She resisted him, she put herself in his way and he came at her relentlessly.

When it was over he kissed her, and slipped away into the night. Lucille slept without dreams.

That was last night. Today the hotel pool was the center of a hubbub, although no one dipped so much as a toe in the water. All the action took place at tables with pink-and-green umbrellas on the terrace. White-jacketed waiters scurried around with trays of cocktails and fancy luncheon salads. Well-dressed people with shiny jewelry peered at each other through sunglasses. Some of the tables were tucked into pink-canvas cabanas arranged on one side of the pool like tents in a sheik movie.

Every few minutes a Philip Morris midget in a red costume would come through calling "Mr. Silverstein, Mr. Elliot Silverstein, telephone please." Mr. Silverstein never seemed to be within earshot, his name would trail off in the distance, and in a minute another page would appear, crying "Mr. Mankiewicz, Mr. Joseph Mankiewicz . . ."

Lucille stretched out in the chaise, took a sip of her strawberry daiquiri, and unfolded her map of the stars' homes. With her lipstick she made red dots on the ones she especially wanted to see: Elvis, Gregory Peck, Lucille Ball, Julie Andrews, and of course Marilyn Monroe.

All the stars lived within a couple of miles of each other, along twisty streets with names like Viewmont and Hillcrest and Wonderland Drive. If they ever dropped a bomb on that neighborhood, it would put an end to the movies.

Wouldn't it be fun to live there between Mickey Rooney and Lana Turner, with Kathryn Grayson across the street and Marlon Brando at the end of the block? You could have a very festive backyard barbecue with neighbors like that.

A sensationally blond woman strutted past wielding a cigarette holder, a pair of dinky chihuahuas scuttering along behind her. From the size of her sunglasses and the prideful way she carried herself, Lucille supposed she was somebody famous.

"Lucille? Darling, is that you?"

She nearly jumped out of the chaise. She hadn't seen the big man approaching.

"Don't move!" He made a frame in the air with his hands. "I want to remember you exactly like this. My God, you're a vision!" He was a great beaming bald man in an iridescent blue sharkskin suit, black open-necked polo shirt, and tiny Gandhi-style spectacles with green lenses.

"Harry?"

He unfurled his fingers. "Who else? Welcome to Hollywood. Give us a hug." He embraced her, a kiss in the air on both sides. His cologne smelled of jasmine. "Look at you! Here you are!"

"Here I am." She smiled.

He cocked an eyebrow. "You have fabulous taste in hotels. You didn't tell me you were loaded."

"Well I'm not, really. I just wanted to stay in a nice place for once in my life."

Harry looked like the sultan of some obscure Near Eastern kingdom, with his shiny moon head and those funny little sunglasses. "Listen, darling, I'm right over here with some people. Come join us!"

Lucille followed him down the poolside with her hatbox and her copy of *Glamour*. She was glad she had put on her spiffy white clamdigger shorts and an expensive silk blouse, since Harry led her to a table surrounded by some very swanky people. They all had golden tans and sunglasses. One of them was the tall flashy blonde with the big breasts and the tiny Mexican hairless dogs wrapping their chains around her chair leg.

Harry said "Everyone, like you to meet my latest discovery—darling, what's that new name?"

"Carolyn Clay," said Lucille.

"Ladies and gentlemen, Miss Carolyn Clay from Alabama!"

"Lovely," said the man with gold chains lying in his forest of chest hair. "Did you come with a banjo on your knee?"

Lucille grinned. "Sorry, I left it at home."

Harry settled onto a deck chair, and waved her to a white cast-iron bench. "Come sit at the feet of the master, my dear."

"Harry, where on earth did you find her," said the blonde.

"Isn't she stunning? It's the first time we've actually met. These blind dates always do a job on my nerves. You can never be one hundred percent sure from a photograph."

The woman sipped smoke from her cigarette holder. "What does she do?"

"I'm an actress." Lucille tucked Chester under her feet.

Harry said "Walter Weitzman at Filmways took one look at her eight-by-ten and got all worked up about it."

"Mm," said the blonde. "Television."

"Don't turn up your nose, Joan," Harry replied. "You may be glad to get television before it's all over."

The distinguished gray-haired man lifted his shades for a better look at Lucille. "Well she's simply marvelous, Harry, I don't know where you find them. I see Veronica Lake obviously, the hair and the sultry pouty thing, Gloria Grahame, a hint of Novak, but there's something else there, something new. A certain sense of, I don't know, danger—*femme fatale?* I can't put my finger on it. Can she act?"

"We shall see," Harry said.

Lucille felt like a new pet or a car, some object to be discussed but not addressed directly. As long as they were saying nice things, though, it was probably wise to sit there and smile.

"Have you shown her to Hitchcock's people?" said the furry-chested man. "He's looking for another long blonde for his new picture."

"Bernie, I'm up for that part," said Joan.

"Oh excuse me, your highness. I sometimes forget that Joan Blake is the only blonde in town."

"Time to go, Alexander." She stood abruptly. "Harry, it's been fabulous as always."

The gray-haired man set about untangling the chihuahuas' chains.

Harry kissed Joan's hand. "I'll call you *mañana*, darling. Don't fret, this is not the first time a big star has had to make a studio sit up and beg."

"Harry, please! Don't discuss my business in front of strangers!" She shot a look that might have killed Lucille if it had hit her head on.

"Nice to meet you," Lucille ventured.

Joan smiled with her lips together. "Good luck in television." She went off, clicking spike heels. The gray-haired man trailed after with the dogs.

"I know I should recognize her," said Lucille.

"You must not go to Westerns," Harry said. "Joan Blake. Lady Peroxide. Generally you'll find her in a prairie dress on a horse with her tits bouncing up and down."

"Harry, don't be a schmuck," said the man with gold chains.

Harry smiled. "I'm sorry, Lucille, I must sound awful. She's made me a lot of money through the years. Just promise me when you get to be a star you won't turn into a rattlesnake."

"I promise," Lucille said. A star! Yes!

Bernie said "I thought her name was Carolyn."

"Stage name," said Harry, "her real name is—"

"It's just Carolyn now, Harry," she said quickly. "I meant to tell you. I'm not using my old name anymore."

"Already she talks like a star." Bernie got to his feet. "What are you doing about that accent?"

"I think it's part of the charm," said Harry. "You know, the Southern thing."

"Maybe so, I understand Southern is big right now." Bernie put on his cap. "Carolyn Clay, it was a pleasure."

"Bye, now," said Lucille.

" 'Bah, now,' " Bernie mimicked. "Don't you love it? I love it." He went off chortling.

Harry rattled his ice at a passing waiter. "I'm having the driest possible martini. My dear? What for you?"

"The strawberry daiquiris are mighty tasty."

The waiter bowed and went away.

Harry said, "So. Tell me everything. How was your trip?"

Lucille said, "It's a long way to come by yourself."

"Didn't you say you have a husband?"

"I did, the first time you called." She nudged Chester with her toe. "I'm a widow now."

"Oh, my God! Oh, no! Darling, I am so sorry. What happened?"

"My husband died."

He peered over his green lenses. "No, I—I meant, how? If you don't mind my asking."

"Not at all," Lucille said. "I gave him rat poison in his coffee."

For a moment Harry was startled, then a smile broadened out on his face. "Well. Okay. I'll play. Why'd you give him rat poison?"

She smiled back. "Because he was a rat."

He guffawed. "Oh, that's rich! I've never represented a *murderess*. I think I'm going to love you."

Harry explained that he worked on an agent's commission, a flat ten percent of any money Lucille might make. No contract, strictly a hand-shake deal.

"Do you really think I have a chance, Harry?"

"Sweetheart, if I didn't think so, you'd still be daydreaming over there by the pool."

"I sure hope you're right. I gave up an awful lot to come out here."

"You just leave everything to me."

They sat in the sunshine, laughing, sipping cocktails. Harry seemed to think Lucille was the most charming creature on earth, and she found herself becoming more charming by the minute. Her stories from home cracked him up. He found it hilarious, for example, to hear about Aunt Sister, who was married to Uncle Junior.

"It's so gothic!" he exclaimed. "You're perfect for comedy, but I don't know whether you should play in it or *write* it." He glanced at his watch. "Well, time marcheth on. Let's go take a look in that closet of yours. I want you to look perfect for Walter Weitzman tomorrow."

She led him along the curving pink walkway, through the jungle to the door of Bungalow Six.

He whistled. "Wait a minute, this is two hundred dollars a night!"

"Two twenty." She unlocked the door. "I know I've got to look for another place, but it's so nice here." She led him into the living room, bright with fresh tulips and Japanese paintings and banana-leaf wallpaper.

"I'm serious, I don't want you to burn up all your money the first week. It may take us a while to get started."

"I don't have a while, Harry. I'm in a hurry. If it's going to happen, it's got to happen fast."

He sank to the sofa, folding his hands on his belly like Buddha. "Well quit standing around, then. Let's have that fashion show."

Lucille fetched her new outfits one at a time. Harry kept shaking his head. "No, too sophisticated. I want innocent. Fresh. Like a daisy."

"Hold on. I think I've got it." She brought out the sleeveless Courrèges jumper, white with yellow trim, which had summoned up the very picture of a daisy to her own mind when she bought it.

"Perfect." He beamed. "It's simple and it doesn't look nearly as expensive as it is."

"You got that right," she said. "See, and it has these matching boots, and this hat."

"Skip the boots." Harry got to his feet. "Wear the hat."

There were no lines to learn in advance. Harry said the producer wanted a candid impression. They arranged a rendezvous for nine the next morning. "Off to fight the wars of art and commerce, my dear. Get your beauty sleep. Don't poison anybody else tonight."

"Don't worry. I've turned over a new leaf."

He chuckled all the way out the door.

Lucille stood at the mirror holding the dress in front of her. She'd always known she was pretty in a normal way, a nice-looking woman with good long legs—not "stunning." And yet Harry Hall had used exactly that word, and none of the fancy people at his table had laughed. They seemed to agree. That snobby Joan Blake even took a dislike to Lucille because of all the attention she was getting from the men.

Back in Cornelia Lucille used to catch a glimpse of herself in the hall mirror, on her way to the basement with a basket of smelly laundry, her hair frowsy and flyblown, dark circles under her eyes. These accidental encounters were scary as hell. *Is that me? Do I really look like that?* She would straighten up and try to remember everything she'd learned about posture and bearing and sparkle and capital-P Personality, but it was hard to get around that vision of the tired, beaten-down woman in the mirror. One blast of "Mom! He hit me first!" was enough to wipe the sparkle off anyone's face.

This was a different woman standing here now. The dark circles were gone, and the lines around her eyes. Maybe it was the radiance from inside, the heat of these passionate nights beginning to melt the ice floes in her heart. All her beauty was welling up to the surface. She smiled at her mirror-self.

Is that me?

Do I look like that?

"Lou-see-yul . . ."

She went into the bathroom and shut the door. Chester carried on in the other room. She ignored him. She would not let him ruin this wonderful feeling.

She unlocked her door before she went to bed, but the man of her dreams did not come back.

She got up early to fret about the audition and her hair and her nails and the freckles on her arms, which would show all too plainly in the sleeveless Courrèges jumper. Room-service coffee only made her more jumpy.

Chester muttered indecipherable things in the hatbox. He was starting to get on her nerves again—who would think a severed head could get on your nerves?

He did.

Divorcing him in Las Vegas had satisfied Lucille in some deep-seated way, but it had no effect whatever on Chester. He kept quiet when anyone else was around. The minute he and Lucille were alone he started up the same nonsense, he loved her, always had loved her, blah blah blah.

Any minute now she was going to get serious about getting rid of him. A little chime went off in her head when she read in the tourist guide about the La Brea tar pits, but on further reflection that seemed entirely too gradual a fate for Chester.

Any old place would not do. It would have to be a place where he would disappear swiftly, irrevocably. A place with height and distance and drama and water to sweep him away, so far away and so deep that Lucille would never hear his voice again. In the meantime he was keeping fresh in his Tupperware.

She painted her nails, brushed her hair until her scalp tingled. She spent most of an hour experimenting with makeup effects. In the end she wiped it all off and settled on a hot-red lipstick and a hint of Mary Quant cerulean shadow to bring out the blue in her eyes.

She couldn't leave Chester untended all morning in the bungalow. What if he decided to say hello to the maid? It would be just like him to announce himself the first time she dared to leave him alone for more than one minute.

"Don't torture me this way, Lucille," he was saying. "I love you so much."

"Shut up, Chester." She should have tossed him off Hoover Dam when she had the chance.

The telephone rang. "Miss Clay? Mr. Hall is here to meet you."

She straightened her sailor hat, blew herself a good-luck kiss in the mirror, and carried the hatbox along the jungly pathway to the lobby. She stepped between the stone monkeys and down the red carpet. Harry sat at the wheel of a splendid white Rolls-Royce convertible, his arms open to her. "Darling! Let me get my dark glasses! The dress is too wonderful!"

She did a little pirouette. "You like it?"

"Why, you're cute as a little old Alabama bug. Come get in my cah, heah." He leaned forward to open her door. He was himself resplendent in a black double-breasted suit with striped shirt and natty red tie. "What do you have there?"

"My lucky hatbox." She placed it on the floor at her feet. The Rolls's interior was all gleaming wood and buttery leather. "Nice car, Harry."

"Thanks, it's a present from a client. They should all be so happy. Are you happy this morning?"

"I'm happy. I'm ready to go."

"That's good, we've got work to do." The car glided down the corridor of palms onto Sunset Boulevard. "I think we'll get this part easy, it's just a walk-on. Just to get your feet wet. But those gentlemen you met yesterday, those are a couple of very big boys in theatrical features, and they liked you. A lot."

"I liked them, too," Lucille said.

"No, I don't mean it like some kind of social thing. See, they don't like *anybody*. Maybe one or two faces a year, they see and they like. Boom boom. Bernie Metzenbaum wants to bring you to Fox for a test."

He gave her a few auditioning tips. Try not to act, he said. Be natural. Acting for TV is the opposite of stage acting; the camera exaggerates every little movement. "It doesn't hurt to flirt with the producer, you never know. If he asks, you're twenty-six, single, no kids. Let me do most of the talking. That's what you're paying me for."

"I'm just so grateful to you, I don't know what to say." Lucille's heart swelled with visions of riches and fame. Oh, to be wealthy enough to buy your agent a Rolls-Royce as a *gift*. "How did you happen to see my picture in the first place, Harry? I can't imagine you reading the *Montgomery Advertiser*."

"I have a friend in Atlanta who sends me clippings from all over. He looks for faces he thinks I might like. Your face just leapt out at me from the top of the stack. I picked up the telephone instantly." He fired up a cigar as he waited for the green light. "Everyone in this business has a specialty. Mine is finding hometown girls and making them into stars."

"That's me," said Lucille. "A hometown girl."

"I wonder." He glanced over. "Hometown girls generally don't stay at the Beverly Hills Hotel, and they don't wear André Courrèges couture lines that cost two or three grand apiece. You see I know my designers. There's a lot more to you than you've told me so far, isn't there, Lucille?"

She smiled what she hoped was an enigmatic smile. "What do you want to know?"

"Everything," he said. "But not now. Now we concentrate on making a good impression."

Lucille had half-imagined they might roll up to the gates of that fancy French-looking mansion from "The Beverly Hillbillies," but they stopped at a nondescript gray-brick building on a treeless industrial block. She fought her disappointment. This was the business side of show business.

"You're taking your hatbox to the audition?" said Harry. "That's a new one on me."

"It's my good-luck charm."

He held the door. "Remember, don't try to hide that wonderful accent. They're looking for an accent. Let it flow."

"I don't think I can help it," Lucille said.

"'Don't thank you can hep it'? Perfect. This way."

They walked through a modest foyer to a suite of offices. Lucille spotted the Filmways logo etched in the glass door and recalled Elly May's closing line: "This's been a Filmways presentation!"

The matronly receptionist smiled ear-to-ear when she spotted Harry. She got up and came around the desk to receive his embrace.

"Maxine, you are younger and more beautiful than is moral for a woman in your position," he teased. "I want you to stop it at once."

"Oh be quiet, Harry Hall. Where have you been? Such a stranger."

"Oh, it's just too tiresome, I'm in constant demand," he said. "All the time in my heart I've been right here with you."

Lucille smiled, admiring this performance. Harry had the kind of warmth that reached out and wrapped its arms around you.

He was smart, too. It wouldn't do to pique his curiosity. She was playing a dangerous game, telling him she had poisoned her husband, telling those bellboys exactly what was in that box they were holding . . . but besides the little thrill it gave her, there was a weird backward security in this strategy. The truth was so outrageous that nobody believed it. Nobody even suspected it. Neither of the bellhops actually tried to look in the hatbox; a severed head was probably the last thing they'd expect to find. Harry didn't even wait for Lucille to finish telling how she'd poisoned Chester before he turned it into a joke. People simply did not believe a nice-looking woman like Lucille could do something like that. She almost didn't believe it herself.

That's how she was getting away with murder. She didn't have to worry about being caught in a lie, because she told everybody the truth.

"You've brought a pretty one this time, Harry." Maxine punched a button on her phone, and winked at Lucille. "Love your little hat."

She smiled and said thanks.

"Carolyn Clay, this is Maxine Dandridge, keeper of dark secrets."

Maxine nodded hi and spoke to the phone. "Harry Hall and a Miss Clay to see you, sir." She hung up. "He's all yours."

Harry marched to the door. "Walter? Go sit in your chair. No, put your putter down and sit down, I want your absolute and undivided attention."

"Come in, Harry," a man said. "I need a laugh."

"I'll give you something better than that," Harry said, waving his hand.

Lucille straightened her shoulders and strode into the room.

Harry said, "Walter Weitzman, genius producer of television, allow me to present Miss Carolyn Clay."

Weitzman bent over a putter, concentrating. With a mild stroke he sent a golf ball skittering across the rug and into a ballcatcher shaped like a dustpan. The gadget caught the ball and spat it back across the rug toward him.

Lucille smiled. "Hole in one."

He looked up—a slender, late-fiftyish man with quick glancing eyes and touches of silver at his temples. His oversized glasses gave him a vaguely owlish expression. "Yes, indeed." He put out his hand to Lucille. "Carolyn, is it? Even prettier than your picture. Lovely dress."

"Well thank you, Mr. Weitzman." She shook his hand. "Real nice to meet you."

He leaned the putter against his desk and pressed a button on the intercom. "Maxine, would you have Cy and Marty step in here, please?"

"What did I tell you, Walter?" Harry plopped into an overstuffed chair. "You tell me 'Harry, I have a tiny part for a blonde.' And what do I bring you? A goddess."

Weitzman smiled. "Are you a goddess, Carolyn?"

Lucille placed the hatbox on the floor behind Harry's chair. "I'm whatever Harry tells me to be."

"Good answer. You listen to Harry. He's the best in the business—wait, I never said that."

"Good God, let me get a notary public!" cried Harry. "Let me get a court reporter! I have a witness!"

"Now Carolyn, this part is only two days' work, maybe three," Weitzman said, "but I'm involved because we see a possibility this Patsy Belle might become a recurring character. If we find the right girl. I don't know if Harry's told you the bit."

"Just the one-sentence pitch," Harry said.

"Are you familiar with the show?"

"Of course, it's my favorite," Lucille said. "My—I watch it every week. It's so clever."

"Thank you, we're proud of it. Anyway, the script calls for Patsy Belle to arrive out of nowhere, she's a schemer, heard about the Clampett fortune and she's come to Beverly Hills to trick Jethro into marrying her. She knew him back in Arkansas, she was a real sexpot, most popular girl in school, never gave him the time of day. All of a sudden she's in Hollywood, hot to trot for him, and of course it gives Max a lot of great reaction shots. It's a cute script."

"Who's Max?"

"Max Baer. Jethro," said Weitzman. "We considered having him play Patsy Belle himself, he's very funny in drag, but he already plays his own sister Jethrene and we don't want to overdo it."

"This girl has everything you want, Walter," Harry said. "Look at her, she's lovely, she's fresh, a completely new face—and as Alexander Powell was saying, she also has the slightest hint of something dangerous. Besides which, you don't have to teach her the accent. Say something, darling."

"What do you want me to say?" said Lucille.

"Listen to that. Is that perfect?"

"Very authentic," said Walter. "Where are you from, Carolyn?"

"Alabama," she said. "I'm twenty-six years old and I've never been married."

Weitzman said, "You let Alex Powell see her first? Harry, for shame."

A rap on the door—two young men popped in with a chorus of "Good morning, Walter." They were nearly identical, a couple of anxious-looking fellows, prematurely balding with black horn-rimmed glasses, white shirts, loud ties.

Weitzman said, "Cy, Marty, this is Carolyn. What do you think? Is she right for Patsy Belle?"

The men inspected Lucille up and down as if she were an artifact in a museum case.

"Looks right," said Marty.

"Can she act?" said Cy.

"Get her to read something," Marty said.

Weitzman rummaged around on his desk and came up with a script. "All right, Carolyn, read Patsy Belle's lines starting with 'Jethro, you're such a big old piece of man.' Marty, you give her Max's lines."

"I don't read lines, I'm an assistant producer," said Marty.

"For God's sake," said Weitzman. "Cy, you read it."

Cy took the script. " 'Golly, Miss Patsy Belle, I can't believe you'd come all the way out here to California just to see me.' "

Lucille cleared her throat. "Should I start now?"

"Start," the men said.

" 'Jethro, you're such a big ol' piece of man, of course I came to see you!' Wait. Can I do it again?"

"I don't know about this, Walter."

"Let her do it again," Cy said. "Mm-hmm, 'can't believe you'd come all the way out here to California just to see me.' "

Lucille put on a sexy smile and slung her arms around Cy's neck. His eyes widened. "Why Jethro, you big ol' hunk of man, of course I came to see you!" she cried. "I was so lonesome back home—I just *couldn't* stop thinking about you!"

"Wait." Cy wrestled out of her arms. "It's not 'hunk of man,' it's 'piece of man.' She changed the line."

"She's not supposed to change the line," Marty said.

"It's better the way she did it." Weitzman folded his arms. "Keep going, Cy."

"Okay. Uhm . . . couldn't stop thinking about you, and then he says, 'Well did Granny see you yet, she'll be plumb tickled to see somebody from home.' "

" 'Oh, she saw me all right,' " Lucille read. " 'She tried to give me a dose of her medicine. She's such a sweet little thing.' "

"Hoo-ee, you didn't drink that stuff did you, Uncle Jed says one dose of Granny's tonic is enough to put hair on a—"

"That's fine, Cy, thank you," Weitzman said. "So what do you think?"

Cy said, "I don't know . . ."

Marty shrugged. "She's okay. But I got four writers who'll kill her if she steps on the lines."

"I don't think she's okay," Weitzman said.

Lucille's heart sank.

"She's terrific," he said. "We'll use her in this show and make a decision about the character after we see the film."

Lucille lit up. A string of Christmas lights blinked on and off inside her body.

"Terrific," said Cy. "That's the word I was looking for."

"Come on, Cy," Marty said. They went out.

Lucille was amazed at how fast it happened. "Is that all there is to it?"

Harry beamed. "What did I tell you? She's a natural."

"Rehearsal tomorrow," said Weitzman. "You'll start shooting Thursday at seven-thirty, that's General Services on Las Palmas, Maxine will fill you in. We had a show drop out of the rotation, so this one'll go on next week. I'll talk to your holdup artist of an agent about the money. Don't get excited, it won't be much."

"That's okay, I don't care a thing about that. I'm just so excited I can't stand it." She pressed his hand. "Mr. Weitzman, how can I ever thank you? This is my big break."

"Just do a good job," he said. "Learn your lines and don't piss off my actors."

"Oh, no, I'm *real* easy to get along with." Lucille didn't realize how forward that sounded until she saw Weitzman's smile.

"I'll bet you are." He winked. "Maxine will have a script sent to your hotel. Leave a number with her."

Harry said "Carolyn, get your hatbox, we don't want to be late for our next appointment."

"Don't show her to anybody else until we talk, Harry," said Weitzman. "There's something about this girl."

Lucille retrieved Chester and followed Harry out.

When they were out in the sunshine, she said "Did I flirt too much, Harry?"

"You had him eating out of your pretty little hand."

"I liked him." She strode down the steps. "I think he's handsome."

"Sweetheart, with an attitude like that you will go far."

Lucille remembered that waitress in Nowhere, New Mexico, who warned her of the perils of the casting couch. Now she knew that if it ever came down to making love with a man like Walter Weitzman or missing her big chance to become a star, she'd be the first one on that couch with a smile on her face.

Harry quizzed her some more on the way to the hotel. She fed him morsels of the truth to throw him off track: She told him she'd won big money at roulette in Las Vegas, which explained her stylish new clothes and the ritzy accommodations. Without exactly saying so, she gave the impression she'd left Chester at home with the children. She never actually said she'd left *all* of him there.

"Family has never been all that important to me, Harry. My career has always come first."

"That's the only way to do it, sad but true. Success and family are a difficult mix. I must say, you're very confident for someone with no experience."

"It's the only thing I ever wanted, to be a star. I've always known I could do it. I've worked my whole life for this chance."

"A lot of people say that, but the minute they get in front of a producer, someone with real clout, they fold. You were as cool as any actress I've ever seen."

Lucille thought: but I *am* an actress. For thirteen years I have played the part of a happy housewife who loves her husband and children. I should have won an Academy Award. Try living through a loveless marriage sometime; after thirteen years of that, a couple of lines in a script are no problem.

"I practiced a lot at home," she said.

"I wish you hadn't said you didn't care about the money," said Harry. "That's what I meant when I said let me do the talking."

"Oh, sorry, I guess I got carried away. If it's not enough money, I'll pay you."

He grinned. "I don't think that'll be necessary. You're adorable, Lucille. This really isn't an act, is it. You really are this way. We don't see much of the genuine article out here."

"Remember, it's not Lucille anymore. I want you to forget all about Lucille."

"Sorry, darling. From now on, I promise, it's Carolyn Clay. Before you know it we'll have it up in lights."

They drove along an avenue flanked by ridiculously tall palm trees waving green pompons at the top of their sticklike trunks. Harry invited

Lucille to a party Saturday night—"everybody will be there, so I want you there, too"—then he steered the car up the hotel drive, under the porte-cochere.

"Congratulations, my dear. Let's hope the rest of your career goes as well as the first day. You just concentrate on learning those lines."

"Thank you for everything, Harry. I'll see you tomorrow."

"Oh no, tomorrow you're on your own. I just negotiate. You have to do the work by yourself." He must have seen how that unnerved her. "Darling, don't worry. You're *won*derful. I'll ring you in the morning with the details. Bah, now."

"Bye, Harry." She retrieved Chester from the back seat, and watched the Rolls-Royce roll away.

Everything was better than she'd ever dreamed. Lucille was in Hollywood with eighteen thousand dollars of the devil's money tucked in the hatbox with Chester's head. She'd landed an appearance on national TV her very first try. She sashayed up the red carpet feeling just fine.

"Good evening, Miss Clay!" sang the front-desk boy. "More flowers for you. Shall I have them sent over to your bungalow?" He indicated a bright-yellow chrysanthemum spray.

"Yes, please." That Norman. Any time now, he would just have to give up this absurd campaign. . . .

Lucille had to admit she'd be a little bit sorry when he did. Between Norman's flowers and lusty bellhops and secret men stealing into her bungalow, Lucille was beginning to feel a lot like Marilyn Monroe. She was finally getting the attention she'd been craving.

She stopped in the gift shop for a pack of Salems. Among the postcards of beaches, smiling bikini girls, orange groves, and Disneyland, the cover of a magazine caught her eye: a disturbing photograph on the new issue of *Life*.

It was a black-and-white picture of a race riot, a horde of colored people fleeing in panic. In the foreground a white child and a black child huddle together in fear. The white boy is wearing a hideous bandage and a black eyepatch, his arms around the little pigtailed Negro girl. Frightened tears roll down her cheeks. The camera has captured it all, the terrified crowd blindly fleeing, the miraculous instinct of those children reaching to comfort each other at the heart of the uproar.

The caption said "A Southern Town's Night of Agony."

It was the kind of picture that summed up the whole race question in one vivid image: two children, one white, one black. The fear in their faces was identical.

Lucille had little patience for troublemaking Negroes, but she had no patience at all for the ignorant white crackers who had managed to turn the thing into a shooting war.

Hold on. Hold on just one minute.

Lucille knew that boy. The boy with his face half-hidden behind the bandage.

That boy was Peejoe.

Had to be. Her hands trembled as she flipped past ads for Polaroid and Gaines Burgers to the contents page. Sure enough—

> On the Cover: Peter Bullis, age 12 (at left), injured in myste-
> rious shooting incident after he defended Negro youths try-
> ing to integrate Industry, Ala., municipal swimming pool,
> attends the funeral of Taylor Jackson, 16, killed at the spon-
> taneous May 14 sit-in. When Jackson's funeral erupted in
> violence, young Bullis shielded 9-year-old Josie Ella Davis
> (right) from flying glass. Photo © 1965 by Mike Clemmer.
> (Story on page 45.)

"Jesus H. Christ," said Lucille.

The cashier looked up from his book. "Can I help you?"

"Oh. Yes, a pack of Salems, and this—this magazine. I'll take all of these."

She hurried back to her bungalow with all six copies of *Life* hidden against her side as if the picture of Peejoe might reveal her identity.

She locked the door, closed the shutters, flopped on the bed.

How could this happen? She had talked to Dove a week ago from Arizona, and he'd never mentioned—whoa, wait a minute, maybe he had. Maybe he had tried to tell her something about some trouble in Industry, and she'd been too wrapped up in her own adventures to listen.

That whole world back home had ceased to exist for Lucille, until Peejoe's face peered out at her from that magazine rack.

She fought a pang of jealousy at the idea that her twelve-year-old nephew had made it onto the cover of *Life* before her.

Poor Peejoe! Look at his face! She whipped through the pages. Apparently Cotton County had exploded into some kind of Selma situation the minute Lucille departed. Here was the evidence splashed in stark black-and-white for the whole world to see.

Lord, there was Sheriff John Doggett himself looming big-bellied and mean on the steps of the courthouse, with an inch-high headline: 'WE GOT NO PATIENCE FOR UPPITY NIGGERS,' SHERIFF EXPLAINS.

The next spread was a series of photographs of colored people jumping fully clothed into a swimming pool, and the tag "Wild Plunge Into 'Freedom River' Ends In Tragedy."

And then more pictures like the one on the cover, a night riot frozen in time, mobs of white men jeering and laughing, bloodied victims. Lucille didn't see Peejoe in any of these pictures, but she spotted Dove's hearse in the background of one.

She turned back to the first spread.

It's a quiet town, Industry, Alabama—quieter than the name might lead you to believe. Tree-shaded seat of Cotton County, farm center, and rail junction, Industry is home to 2,000-odd souls, roughly half Negro, half white.

Until last week, the Negro half of Industry has always remained largely silent and invisible.

Last week the town's Negroes found their voices, and their voices were heard. In the latest demonstration of the civil-rights revolution spreading like brushfire through Southern hamlets (see *Life,* April 18), the Negro citizens of Industry erupted with a local version of the quasi-religious fervor and nonviolent determination promoted by Rev. Martin Luther King, Jr., in his famous Selma and Birmingham campaigns.

A grassroots effort to desegregate Industry's spanking-new municipal swimming pool provoked a full-fledged race riot. Under cover of darkness, while local lawmen averted their gaze, roving mobs of white supremacists attacked and beat demonstrators for more than forty minutes. Two were killed, at least 20 injured.

Negro mortician Nehemiah Thomas, self-proclaimed leader of Industry's fledgling desegregation movement, now languishes in the Cotton County jail on unspecified charges. "Our battle is only beginning," he says.

Four-term Sheriff John Doggett (above) offers a succinct explanation for the violence: "We got no patience for uppity niggers and outside agitators coming into Cotton County," he says. "We have always had our own way of doing things down here, and we don't welcome anybody that would try to change that."

Doggett and his 14 deputies were nowhere to be seen on the evening of May 21, Industry's night of terror and shame . . .

Lucille read the story three times. There was nothing about Peejoe. Only that haunting picture on the cover.

She put it off as long as she could stand it, because she was Carolyn Clay now, the transformation was almost complete. It was dangerous to give clues of herself to anyone back in her old life.

Then she couldn't stand it anymore. She flung the magazine across the room and reached for the telephone.

22

Peejoe

Industry

C rowds of Negroes gathered every morning at the courthouse with "Free Brother Thomas" signs. White boys gathered to taunt them and spit on the pavement.

With Nehemiah in jail, Dove had quietly taken over embalming all the colored people who died in Cotton County, in addition to his white clientele.

This was dangerous business, and Aunt Earlene didn't like it a bit, what with all the marches and speeches and prayer meetings every day now, the rumors running through town.

In the first place, Earlene reminded Dove, it was against the law to operate an integrated funeral home in the state of Alabama. "In the second place, it's none of your business. Why can't they take care of their own?"

"Oh, leave me alone," Dove said.

"Swimming pools and lunch counters are one thing, baby," she went on, "but people should be able to put their dead kinfolks in whatever kind of place they want."

"What about the colored ones?" said Dove. "They're just as dead. What am I supposed to do about them?"

Earlene said "Lately I wonder if you're not just looking for trouble."

"I don't want to argue with you, I know that," said Dove.

"If people find out you're sneaking colored bodies in the back door while their old white grannies are laid out in the front parlor, why, honey, they'll run us out of town. God knows at the very least you'll go out of business and we'll never be invited anywhere again our entire lives."

"What do you want me to do, Earlene? The man is in jail. I can't just put off embalming these bodies until John decides to let him out."

"It's none of your concern."

"Well it sure as hell is, I'm the county coroner. And I'm the only board-certified mortician in town that doesn't happen to be behind bars."

"Well whoop-tee-do, Doctor Kildare. This is not a life-or-death situation, Dove. Those people are dead, it won't hurt them to stay in the cooler an extra day or two."

"What do you know about it? People need to get on with their grieving and burying. It matters to them."

"That's right, pour yourself another drink," she said. "Drink yourself to death on top of everything else."

Somehow they struck a truce. In the daylight hours, Croaker-Moseley remained to all appearances a White Only funeral home. Between midnight and two, Nehemiah's sons Ben and Ramsey delivered any colored people who had died that day. Dove and Randall Mulch worked all night in the embalming room so Milton could deliver the bodies back to the Blessed Rest before dawn.

Earlene stayed mad at Dove; Dove was mad at the sheriff and Nehemiah Thomas, who were mad at each other and had crowds of people getting mad on their respective behalfs. Mabel was mad at Wiley; Wiley was mad at the world. I wasn't really mad at anybody, but I was amazed that those shadowy men could come out of the woods, beat people and shoot up the Blessed Rest and get away with it clean (except for the matter of their tires). I saw no reason on earth why those men were not in jail instead of Nehemiah Thomas.

The sheriff made no effort to catch them. Even Dove said it was no use tracking them down, there would always be more men just like them.

But that night at the Blessed Rest had changed Dove. From the moment he brought Miss Bessie Stringfellow into that hearse with us, he was walking on the side of Nehemiah Thomas and the Negroes.

He camouflaged his choice with a lot of sneaking around under cover of darkness; he may not have realized himself that his decision was irrevocable, but it was. He never explained this to me, never said a word about it. I saw it all in his eyes.

I saw it way late one night when I peeped through the secret hole in the attic floor and discovered him reeling about the embalming room, singing at the top of his lungs: "Waltzin' Matilda, waltzin' Matilda, Matilda, Matilda, with me . . ."

The corpse of a middle-aged man lay on the table. He must have been white before the lightning hit him. He lay there charred and greasy, like some underdone barbecue. He looked bad. I didn't see how Dove in his present condition could make him look any better.

Dove sang with gusto, careening off the table. He and Earlene had been fighting again, I'd heard them over the roar of the air conditioners. I knew how Dove hated to fight.

He cried "goddamn it!" and ran into a cabinet, toppling a stack of metal pans.

I put my eye to the hole. Dove sprawled on his butt beside the embalming table. He bleated and pushed his hands against the floor in an ineffective attempt to rise.

Flopping over on his side, he got one hand up on the table and pulled himself to his feet—face-to-face with the barbecued man.

Dove gave a little grunt of surprise, lurched back into the wall, and slid down to the floor.

I couldn't stand seeing him like that. I loved him. I was embarrassed for him.

I felt my way downstairs. The Muzak organist droned through the laying-out parlors. I groped down the wall to the mortuary wing.

I opened the gray door.

The lightning-struck man was much more vivid at eye level. Mixed with the formaldehyde stench was a faint smell of cooked meat that sent me swaying back into the hallway for air.

My first job was to cover that man so I could stand to be in there.

I took a deep breath and rushed in, grabbed a tarpaulin and shook it out over him like a crackly black bedsheet, all the time keeping my eyes to the floor. When I grew up and became a funeral director I would have to look at such things, but for now I knew I was better off not looking.

"Hello, Peer Joseph. What the hell do you want?" Dove squinted up. "It's a middle the night."

"I know, Uncle Dove." I knelt beside him on the concrete floor, one knee on the drain. "It's time for you to go to bed."

"I dunno," he said. "I dunno. I think I gotta do, jus', jus' a little more work, an' then I can go . . ."

"You already worked too much tonight. See if you can get your arm around my shoulder."

He snorted, and pushed my hand away. "That's ridiculous, you're hurt. Your poor li'l eye, oh my God. You can't be helping me."

"You can't just sleep here on the floor! Come on, at least try, okay?"

He tried. Together we got him onto his feet with his back against the wall. "Whoa . . ." He rocked on his heels.

We took one step. He brought his face so close that I felt woozy from the fumes. "I dunno, boy, I dunno. Where we goin'?"

I heard the *chunk!* of a car door out back. Dove slipped out of my hands.

My heart slid with him to the floor. What if that was Ben or Ramsey with a late delivery? I couldn't let them see him like this.

He snickered, as if his inability to stay on his feet was a wonderful game. I got down on my knees and tried lifting under his arms, but he was too big for me. "Oh come on, Uncle Dove, please? Somebody's coming!"

"We got company?" His arms went limp.

The door squealed. Milton's smile of greeting faded as he took in the situation. "Evenin', Peejoe. You up mighty late."

"I'm sure glad that's you. Can you help me get him to bed?"

"Well I don't know, do he want to go?" Milton crouched down. "Mist' Dove, do you want to go to bed?"

"Naw."

"See there? He don't want to go."

"Well we can't leave him here!"

"Most times when he . . . tired like this, I put him on his sofa back yonder," said Milton. "He sleeps real good back there." He clamped his arm around Dove's shoulders, and brought him to his feet in one practiced motion. "Mist' Dove workin' too hard these days. He gets wo' out."

Dove murmured "I am sho' nuff wo' out, Milton."

The telephone rang.

"Mist' Peejoe, you answer that? I got my hands full."

I slipped past him to the office, lined with mortuary science books and piled-over file cabinets and realistic scale models of caskets. I picked up the phone. "Hello?"

A woman's voice: "Who is this?"

"Peejoe. Who's this?"

"Peejoe? My God, are you all right?"

"Aunt Lucille? Is that you?"

Long silence. "Who's there with you?"

"Just Dove," I said. "And Milton."

"Is anybody else there? Anybody listening on the phone?"

"No. Where are you?" She sounded far away, a hiss on the line like a seashell held up to my ear.

"Let me speak to Dove."

At the moment Milton was steering him through the office door. Dove beheld the black-vinyl sofa and staggered toward it with his hands out.

"I don't think he can talk right now." I watched him collapse in slow motion on the sofa.

"Is he asleep, or just drunk?"

"I reckon he's drunk."

"Well Jesus, Peejoe, I saw the picture tonight and I got so worried! What's happening back there? What in the world did they do to your face?"

"What picture?"

"You mean you haven't seen it?"

"No ma'am."

"Well hold on to your hat, little boy. You're on the cover of *Life* magazine."

"I'm what?!"

"It's the new issue, what is it, May . . . twenty-fifth. There's a picture of you on the cover. You didn't know?"

"Well no ma'am," I said, "I don't know anything about"—then I remembered the man in the gray hat with his flashing camera, the night of the swimming-pool massacre. "Wait a minute. Oh no. Did he really—you saw my picture?"

"Me and everybody else in the world," said Lucille. "What kind of mess are you in, child? Who has been shooting at you?"

Of course I had about five billion questions for Aunt Lucille, but she wouldn't let me ask even one until I had explained the whole thing, starting with Taylor at the swimming pool through my accident at Mrs. Boggs's and right on to the shootout at the Blessed Rest.

"Well it says it right here," she insisted. " 'Peter Bullis, age twelve, injured in mysterious shooting incident.' Why would they put that in there?"

"I don't know, it's what everybody's saying but it's not true." I couldn't believe it—my face on *Life* magazine! I could not wait to tell Wiley.

Dove snored. Milton watched me with puzzled eyes.

"Aunt Lucille, where did you go?"

Another long pause. "I went to Florida, Peejoe. I went to the beach. I'm having a wonderful time. Listen, by the way, I'm sorry you and Wiley had to leave Mama's and go with Dove. It was something I just couldn't help."

"Do you still have Uncle Chester's head?"

"Shh, don't—I don't know what you're talking about. Don't you know somebody might be listening?"

"It's okay. Everybody's asleep but Milton."

"Has the sheriff been asking you questions about me?"

"He did, at first. He's been kinda busy with this other stuff."

"Did you tell him anything?"

"Not much. I remembered the name of that guy you were going to see, but I didn't tell him. I wanted you to get away."

She made a little sniffling sound. "Oh thank you, Peejoe. Someday I'll make it up to you. Listen, I've got to go. Tell Dove I'll call him, I don't know when. I have to be careful. I know you understand."

"Are you ever coming back, Aunt Lucille?"

"Not if I can help it, honey."

"Will I ever see you again?"

"Well now that may be a different story. I want you to take care of that eye in the meantime."

"I will."

"Okay, sugar, goodbye now." She hung up.

Milton said "Who was that?"

"Aunt Lucille."

"I thought that's who you said. Where she at?"

"She's in Florida. At the beach."

"Mm, mm. She ain't comin' back here, I reckon."

"I don't think so. I wish she would."

"Oh, not me." He shook his head. "No thank you, suh."

"Howcome, Milton?"

"You seen what she done to Mister Chester."

"She was mad at him. She's not gonna hurt anybody else," I said. "If she came back, me and Wiley could go home."

It was the first time in a long time that I'd made that wish. Lucille's voice on the phone brought it all back to me, what a sweet easy life Wiley and I were having until she came to Pigeon Creek and turned everything upside down. Life with Dove had not turned out like I'd imagined. Look at him there on the sofa, one hand dragging the floor, his mouth hanging open, leaking a snore.

Milton said, "I'm gone on to bed."

"Don't we need to cover him up or something? He looks cold."

"He's all right."

"I'll go get him a blanket," I said.

"You good to look after him this way. I know he would thank you. Goodnight, now." Milton went to his room.

I heard a noise in the casket room, and peered around the velvet curtain. Mabel didn't see me. She muttered to herself. Her hands floated out to the sides like wings.

I trudged on up to the attic, where Wiley was sawing logs of his own, and came back trailing my rough woolen Army blanket down the stairs. I found Dove flopped over on his other side, with his face buried in the vinyl back-cushion. I tucked the blanket around him the best I could.

At last I'd seen the terrible secret behind the gray door, the thing he never wanted me to see—Dove himself, out of control.

I snapped off the light and went to the bathroom upstairs to gather all the towels I could find. I went back to my cot and lay down and spread those towels out over me in a patchwork arrangement. My eye didn't hurt anymore and it wasn't really cold, and it wasn't Dove's idea that I should sleep under towels while he snored under my blanket. But I surely did feel pitiful, and I let myself wallow in that feeling awhile.

Then I remembered: *Life* magazine!

23

Peejoe

Industry

D ove held his face in his hands. "What did she say?"
"She said she's in Florida. She's not coming back."
He squeezed his temples. His face was puffy and red. A cup of coffee sat untouched at his elbow. "Did she say where in Florida?"

"No sir."

"I think she's lying, I think she went straight to California like she meant to all along. Did she say whether she was alone?"

"She didn't say. I asked her if she still had Uncle Chester's head, but she didn't want to talk about it."

One eye peered at me between two fingers. "You asked her that?"

"I thought maybe she'd tell me, if she left it somewhere."

"But she didn't."

"No sir."

I told him as much of the conversation as I could remember.

"Why didn't you wake me up and let me talk to her?"

If he didn't even remember what shape he'd been in, I wasn't going to be the one to remind him. "Well, you were sleeping pretty good, Uncle Dove. She said she'll call back. I didn't tell you the best part, why she called." All morning I'd waited for Dove to wake up and Wiley to come in from batting fly balls so I could make my big announcement.

I didn't get the chance. At that moment Earlene came storming up the stairs and burst in, waving a sheaf of mail in one hand, a magazine in the other. "Look at this!" she shrieked. "Look! Look at it!" She charged across the room and flung the magazine on the table.

Oh Lord. There was my face, big as *Life*.

Why hadn't Lucille told me how ghastly awful I looked? God! I had envisioned something like last year's school photo, with my hair combed and a nice fakey smile. She hadn't mentioned that I looked like a scared wounded animal, with a little colored girl clinging to me and terrorized marchers stampeding in the background.

I groaned. "Oh no. I didn't know it would turn out like that."

"You *knew?*" Earlene snatched the magazine from my hand as if she might smite me with it. "You knew about this and didn't tell anybody? Who gave you permission to be in *Life* magazine?"

"What the hell are y'all talking about?" Dove held out his hand. "Earlene, let me see that."

Wiley got up from the sheepskin rug and came over. He saw the picture. His mouth fell open.

Earlene's voice trembled with rage. "I am not believing this, Dove. It's too much! Here we are trying to keep our heads down and come through this thing with some kind of a decent reputation, and this boy—*your* kin, living under *our* roof—look at him! Hugging a Nigra on the cover of *Life!*"

Dove whistled. "Well now, you know, I believe that is you, Peter Joseph."

"That's what I been trying to tell you. That's why Aunt Lucille called last night. She saw this picture down in Florida."

"Who's this little gal hanging on to you?"

"I don't know. She grabbed me when they were shooting out the lights. It all happened so fast—I didn't even see him taking that picture. You remember that guy, don't you, Wiley? We thought he was from the newspaper."

Wiley said, "This is the real *Life* magazine? Like, with Jackie Kennedy on it?"

"We are ruined," said Earlene. "We might as well start packing. I will never be able to hold up my head in this town again. Look what it says, Dove, 'Night of Agony'! Oh, I'm so ashamed."

Wiley said "My gosh, Peejoe, you're famous."

"Look, he got your foot in the picture." I pointed to the edge of the frame.

"It sure makes you look pathetic, son." Dove thumbed through the magazine. "See who else they—ah, look here, Earlene, you think Peter Joseph looks bad, look at John Doggett with his belly hanging over his belt."

"Dove, you're going to call your mother tonight." Earlene was suddenly calm, and deadly serious. "She'll have to take them back, that's all. I'm sorry, boys, I've been as patient as I could, but this really is the last straw."

"Don't be silly, Earlene, Peter Joseph can't help it if they took his picture."

The telephone rang. Earlene huffed off to answer it.

"Listen to this." Dove held the magazine up to the light. "'Jailed protest leader Nehemiah Thomas reports that Rev. Martin Luther King, Jr., has offered to come to Cotton County to speak in support of the swimming-pool desegregation movement.' See, now it's a 'movement.' That'll scare everybody to death. I bet Nehemiah's out of jail ten minutes after they read this downtown. And I bet George Wallace will holler like a stuck pig."

I heard Earlene trying to sound cheery. "No, Barbara, we didn't know anything about it until we—well, we're just as surprised as you, but the whole thing's an awful mistake. Dove didn't even—what's that? Slow down, Barbara, I can't understand you."

"Ah-oh, listen to this," Dove said. "'On the cover, Peter Bullis, age twelve, injured in mysterious shooting incident after he defended Negro youths trying to integrate Industry, Alabama, municipal swimming pool.' Peter Joseph, they're just damned and determined to get you mixed up in all this."

I studied it over his shoulder. "I promise I never told anybody that, Uncle Dove."

"I believe you. This is a hard story to stop. It's like that snake-headed monster, you know? You chop off one head and it sprouts two new heads."

On the page after Sheriff Doggett I spotted the thin, sharp-boned woman who'd accosted me at Taylor's funeral, what was her name?—Lydia Combs. There she was on page 47, holding a "Free Brother Thomas" sign on the courthouse steps. She was quoted below: "We will not rest until every one of us is free." She must have told the photographer all that stuff about me.

"I warned John Doggett this would happen," said Dove. "He can't blame this on anybody but himself. I bet he had no idea this guy was roaming around takin' pictures."

"I don't know why you should say that, Barbara, it's none of our doing," Earlene shrilled. "Well now—well, that's hardly fair, is it? Maybe we should get together and see if we can't try to—hello? Hello?" Earlene turned with the phone in her hand. "Good Lord. She hung up on me."

"What did she want?" Dove said.

Earlene put the phone on the hook. "She's seen it, they all have. It's all over town. It came in everybody's mail this morning. Barbara's mother called her first. She said we were nigger lovers, Dove."

"Barbara said that?"

"Her mother. But Barbara said we've brought shame on the whole town, posing for a picture like that, and if we don't like it here we should go somewhere else."

"I didn't pose," I protested.

"I can't believe she would say that," said Dove. "That's downright ugly. You don't need friends like that, Earlene. You should have hung up on *her*."

"She said everybody knows you've been taking in bodies for Nehemiah," Earlene went on. "She said from now on when anybody dies they'll use Brown Service in Dothan. I told you this would happen."

"Aw, that's a bunch of hot air," Dove said. "It's a hundred miles to Dothan and back. This'll blow over in a week."

I studied my face on the magazine. I looked as scared as that little girl clinging to me, "9-year-old Josie Ella Davis." If that wasn't me, if I was a stranger looking at that picture, I would think *oh, those poor kids*.

"I look so ugly," I said.

Earlene whirled on me. "I want you out of this house. Dove, it's your choice. Him or me."

"Oh be quiet, he's not going anywhere. He's had a rough enough time—"

"I said I want him out of here, and I want you to stop this insane foolishness with Nehemiah Thomas before you ruin whatever is left of our good name."

"Earlene. These boys live here now. They're my family, whether you like it or not. And I will continue to do exactly whatever I want to do, just like I always have," Dove said. "If your yackety friends don't like it, *they* can go somewhere else. And if you don't like it, well honey, the door is wide open."

Earlene bristled. "Dove Bullis, don't you threaten me."

"It's not a threat." His voice was cold as a mouthful of ice. "It's a fact. Sometimes you seem to forget you're my wife. You're not my mother, or my boss. I wish to God just once you would get behind me when I'm trying to do what I think is right."

"Y'all don't fight," I cried. "If she doesn't want me here I'll be glad to go back to Meemaw's! I want to go back!"

Wiley gave Earlene the evil eye. "Me too."

"You ain't going anywhere," Dove said.

"Oh yes they are," said Earlene.

"Oh no they ain't."

They glared at each other.

"I can't stand it!" Earlene cried. "I can't stand the idea of everybody talking about us!" She stomped off to her room.

Dove rapped on Mabel's door. "Mabel, it's Daddy. Open the door now." No answer from inside. He tried the knob.

"Mabel, unlock the door for me, honey."

The door flew open. Mabel wore a dirty nightgown and a wild look in her eyes, rivers of black mascara smudged down her deathly-white face. Her hair floated around her head in a frizzy cloud.

Dove backed up a step. "Jesus, honey, when's the last time you combed your hair?"

"Go away," she spat. "Leave me alone."

She was frightening to see. I backed up, too.

Dove said "What's the matter with you?"

"I *hate* you," she cried, her eyes burning. "I hate all of you! Can't you see I'm dirty? Leave me alone!"

Wiley bit his lip and stared at the floor.

Dove said, "Mabel, what on earth? Stop this nonsense and put on your clothes. I got enough trouble around here without this from you."

Mabel slammed the door. We heard the *click!* of the lock.

Dove reached for the knob, rattled it. He tapped on the door. "Maybelle, come on, honey." Tap, tap. His hand dropped to his side. "I wish somebody would tell me what I have ever done to deserve this."

The telephone rang. He seemed grateful to answer it.

I remembered those hide-and-seek games long ago, when Mabel would fade into thin air and reappear at home base by magic. She had always been skittish, a bit strange. As a child she was terrified by the tests of the Emergency Broadcast System; she thought the high-pitched radio tone meant an atom bomb was on its way to Alabama to kill her. Wiley discovered that the high "E" on Meemaw's pump organ produced exactly the same piercing tone as the atom-bomb test. We would wait until Mabel was alone in the next room, reading a Nancy Drew mystery. I'd get down on the floor to pump the pedals with my hands while Wiley held his finger on the E. Mabel would run out shrieking every time. That cracked us up.

I turned. "What's with her?"

Wiley shook his head. "I mean it, Peejoe, things are getting really weird around here. I wouldn't mind taking off. If we had to."

"I guess we could go stay at Meemaw's with Sandra and Cary and Farley and all them," I said. "We'd have to sleep on the floor."

Dove said "I can't really talk about that, I don't know what I'd do in that case. I can meet you somewhere if you want to discuss it. Somewhere out of the county."

My ears pricked up.

"Yeah, part of it, one of Nehemiah's boys saw the first three digits. Five oh seven. It was a brown Ford pickup, white stripe down the side, an older one, I'd say fifty-seven or eight."

Wiley whispered "Who's he talking to?"

I shrugged.

"I don't know if I could do that," said Dove. "I'd be willing to meet you and, you know, discuss it, but I won't promise anything. It's a sticky situation here. As you might imagine."

He noticed us listening and told whoever it was to call back in fifteen minutes. He hung up and sat regarding us with bleary eyes. "Boys, I'm going to let you in on something. I don't want you telling anybody just yet, not Mabel, not Earlene, nobody. It could get me in real serious trouble, understand? I'm not fooling around this time."

"Yes sir," we said.

"I been talking to a man who wants to stop all this beating and killing. He wants me to help 'em try and punish the ones that's responsible. He might want your help, too. It's not gonna be easy, or safe. We'd be sticking our necks out all the way."

"What does he want us to do?" said Wiley.

"Well, if it comes down to it, he might ask you to testify. That means you get up in court and tell what you saw."

"I know about that," I said. I'd seen "Perry Mason" countless times.

"I'm not sure you realize what it means. Nobody in this town is gonna thank you for it. We'd be going up against some powerful folks, starting with Mr. John Doggett himself. And you've seen what an easygoing guy he can be."

"Why do they need us, Uncle Dove?"

"You saw what happened to that Taylor, and that night they busted up the crowd at the pool. And at Nehemiah's. I saw some of it myself, but you boys saw it all. And you got no reason to lie about it. As the man said, you're young enough and white enough that a grand jury might believe you over anybody else who was there."

I wondered if I would break down under cross-examination and confess some dreadful crime, as witnesses did every week on "Perry Mason."

"This man wants to meet you," Dove said. "He wants to hear what you saw. Now listen to me, boys. You don't have to do this. This is not fun and games. I'll gladly take you back to Mama's, if you want to go. She's wanted you back all along. I'll understand whatever you decide. I have a feeling it's gonna get hard around here before it gets easy."

"What about Aunt Earlene?" I said. "She hates me."

"You are not the cause of that problem, Peter Joseph, believe me. You let me worry about her."

When I thought about it later, I realized Dove had us boxed in. He knew what our answer would be. That wasn't any real choice—to be brave and stay there and help him catch the bad guys, or go off and leave him to do it alone. We were just kids, and it wasn't really fair of him to set us up like that, but the way he laid out the question made me feel important and wanted. I was sitting at the grownups' table at last.

Wiley said "What do you think, Peejoe?"

I thought it was my selfless and heroic nature that led me to say, "We ought to stay here and help Dove."

"Yeah, I think so too."

Dove said "Thank you, boys."

"What are they gonna do, arrest the sheriff?" said Wiley.

"I'm not sure. First you've got to get it real clear in your head what you saw, else it's no good to anybody. They got no use for 'maybe' in a court of law. And Peter Joseph, see what you can do to keep your face off the cover of the damn magazines, okay?" He shook his head. "You are truly something else."

The phone rang again. Dove waved us out of the room.

I went off to study my face on *Life*. I imagined Meemaw seeing that picture: she'd be mortified by the dirty bandaged-up eyepatched mess that was my face. Certainly I was embarrassed enough for us all. But also I was thrilled that the people of *Life* had picked mine among all the possible faces in the world for the cover of their magazine. People all over the country were looking at me right now thinking *oh, look at that poor kid*.

And all along I had supposed I would have to grow up and actually *do* something to become famous.

Every house in Alabama received its copy of *Life* on Wednesday morning. The phone at Croaker-Moseley rang all day. Some people yelled "nigger lover" and hung up. Others were friends of Dove's: neighbors and fellow funeral directors offering condolences and opinions.

Earlene came out of her room in late afternoon, pinched and tear-stained, her baby-blue Samsonite suitcase in hand. "I want Milton to drive Mabel and me to Goshen. I'm going to Erma's. I can't stand another minute of this."

"Fine," Dove said. "A change'll do you both good."

"Is that all you have to say to me?"

Dove glanced up from his newspaper. "Have a nice time. Say hello to your sister. Call me when you want me to come get you."

I said, "Aunt Earlene, I'm sorry. I didn't mean to get my picture in there."

She ignored me. "Dove, where is Mabel?"

Wiley said "She's downstairs talking to herself again."

Earlene disappeared into Mabel's room and came back in three minutes with another suitcase. "Well," she said, "I suppose this is goodbye, then." Obviously she thought Dove would beg her to stay.

He said, "Take care," and went back to his paper.

She turned on her heel, and marched out.

Wiley stood at the window to watch them go.

"Don't worry," said Dove. "She'll get about twenty miles before she makes Milton turn around and bring 'em back."

Two hours later Milton returned without Earlene or Mabel.

Dove said the full moon always makes females peculiar. He poured a big glass of whiskey and fell asleep in front of the TV.

Dr. Ward unwound the last layer of gauze. He winced when he saw my eye. At once he recovered himself, he said, "looking much better," and smoothed my hair with his hand, but that involuntary wince told me everything I needed to know.

Dove said "He's already learned to get along pretty good with just the one, haven't you, Peter Joseph?"

"There's no reason you can't live a perfectly normal life," said the doctor. "You've got twenty-twenty in your good eye, the only thing you're lacking is depth perception. And you can learn to compensate for that. The only difference between you and everybody else is you'll probably want to wear a patch on this other eye."

"Does it still look that bad? Let me see."

He held up the mirror.

I felt a jolt, like when he touched it with his finger. Since I'd last seen this eye, it had turned the color of a bruised rotted plum. It was terrible to see.

I swallowed. "Will it always look like that?"

"You broke a lot of blood vessels. Turn around and hold still, now, let me put this on." He had constructed a thick disc of gauze with a rim of white surgical tape, which he sealed around my eye-socket with his thumb. "Wear your patch over this. Maybe next time we can skip the bandage."

Dove said "Son, go on out with Wiley, let me talk to the doctor a minute."

I went out. Wiley glanced up from his magazine. "You look better without that big ol' bandage on your head."

"Thanks."

"What'd he say?"

"My eye's blind. I'm probably never gonna see out of it."

"That's okay," said Wiley. "You've got the other one."

We drove the old state highway through Eureka Springs and Hamlet, through Vinegar Flat and Pine Ridge, to a crossroads under a great spreading oak tree in the exact center of nowhere. Dove had brought crackers and Vienna sausages, apples and candy bars and Nehi soda. We ate lunch on the warm hood of the hearse.

"Peter Joseph, you get the extra Three Musketeers since you were so brave at the doctor's."

"You think my eye could get better, Uncle Dove?"

"I tell you what, son. I don't see why not. I think the Doc did us a favor, he laid it out about the worst it could be. So now you know the worst, and you just go on and see what comes next. Think positive. That's what I try to do."

Wiley said, "Is this him?" but the sedan roared on by without stopping.

"We're early," Dove said. "He'll come."

I bit into the candy. "Are Earlene and Mabel gone for good, Uncle Dove?"

"Naw, you watch, they'll be waiting for us when we get home."

"That's what you said yesterday."

Wiley said "Shut up, Peejoe."

"Let me tell you something about women," said Dove. "They don't play by any set of rules I've ever been able to make out. You can go crazy trying to figure out what they're gonna do. Now, I know she's sitting on the telephone over there waiting for me to call her, but the minute I did, she'd hang up on me. That's the way they do. I'm gonna leave her to make up her own mind."

I didn't say it, but I wasn't missing Earlene or Mabel at all. Wiley and I had the run of the house, and I had Wiley to myself again. We still ate Pop-Tarts for breakfast and Chef Boyardee for supper; nobody nagged us or made us sit through "Ben Casey" when Alfred Hitchcock was on. . . .

The song of a car's tires, from the north. A dark-blue Ford Fairlane came slowly around the curve and pulled into the shade of the oak.

"Here we go." Dove got down from the hood.

The man who stepped out was big, burly like Dove. He wore a heavy gray wool suit, a short-brimmed gray hat with a three-toned band. His big loby ears flattened against the sides of his head; those ears were big enough to gather in everything. He had a big jowly face, a stern chin, a downturned frown-line, but his eyes were friendly enough. He came over with his hand out. "You must be Mr. Bullis."

"Friends call me Dove. How you getting along." They shook hands.

"Tell you the truth, I'm burning up. I didn't bring the right clothes for this heat."

"These my nephews you were asking about," Dove said. "This here is Wiley, and that's Peter Joseph."

"Right, I recognize you from the picture." His hand enclosed mine. "Hiram Murphy, I'm a special attorney with the Justice Department. Do you know what that is?"

"I'm not sure," I said.

He explained that it was part of the Federal Government in Washington, D.C. "We've been keeping an eye on the situation in Industry. Lately we've had some luck bringing cases where the local law enforcement appears to have broken down. We try to keep these demonstrations from getting out of hand. Do you follow me?"

Wiley nodded.

"Industry is a hot spot. Cover of *Life,* all three networks sending in crews, in about two days you're going to be crawling with press people and your Freedom Rider types. George Wallace is raising hell, and we have information the Reverend King might be planning to make Cotton County his next target of operations. If we can get in there and defuse the situation, he won't have to do that."

"In other words you try to keep one step ahead of him," Dove said.

"That's about it." Sweat trickled down Murphy's face, but he did not take off his jacket or hat. "The good Reverend thrives on people like the governor or your Sheriff Doggett. He won't come here unless he's sure he'll have somebody hostile to confront him and keep the news boys interested. It's my job to try to neutralize the sheriff before that happens."

"How you gonna do that?" Dove said.

"I think if we play our cards right we can have him indicted for murder."

That word hung in the air for a moment, like smoke from a gun.

"Murder," said Dove.

"We have the incident with the older boy, David, and the second with his brother at the pool, that establishes a pattern. I have a man who can place Doggett in that pickup truck with a gun on the night Mrs. Stringfellow was killed."

"You're kidding," said Dove. "Who?"

"Another passenger in the truck. He's given us plenty of names. You don't need to know who he is, any more than I'm going to tell him about you. I want to keep everything quiet for now. Grand-jury proceedings are secret for a good reason."

"You think John Doggett was in that truck?" Dove was skeptical.

"I think you and the others can give enough evidence to support an indictment."

"Are you sure about that?"

"Mr. Bullis. I'm only gonna say this once, and if you repeat it I'll deny it. The government has a policy of trying to keep little brushfires from turning into big ones. My job is to move Sheriff Doggett out of the way. I think I can prove he was in that truck, at the very least he knew what was going to happen and allowed it, and that's as good as pulling the trigger. If I can do that, I can go home. Are you going to help me?"

Insects chanted in the grass.

Dove smiled. "You're a Yankee, aren't you, Mr. Murphy?"

"Well, yes, I'm from Pennsylvania. I guess I am."

Dove said, "Down here we don't usually lay all our face cards on the table the first time we meet."

"I don't have a lot of time," said Murphy.

"I think you better take off that jacket. This might take a little longer than you thought."

"Fair enough." Murphy shucked it off, revealing sweat-rings under his arms. He hiked himself onto the fender of the hearse. "All right, boys, start at the beginning. Tell me everything you saw."

Late that night, when I was alone on my cot, I wept for my eye. I let go all the tears I had saved up all day. I couldn't escape the feeling that I had been punished for the terrible things I had seen: Uncle Chester's dripping head, the bodies of Taylor and David and all the others. My eye was the price I'd had to pay for seeing too much.

24

Lucille

Hollywood

Lucille spent a whole afternoon choosing just the right outfit, having her hair twisted up in an elegant chignon. The minute she walked into the General Services Studio they whisked her off to costume and makeup, took her apart, and started over from scratch. They washed out her hair and blew it up into a great shiny bouffant. They pasted fake lashes on her eyelids, painted her cheeks with rouge and her lips with red gloss. They put her in high spike heels and a tight dress with a frilly bosom. Of course she was playing Patsy Belle, the sexpot of Sibly, Arkansas; the hairdo and dress were part of the joke, but she felt silly—as if they'd seen through to her recent indecent behavior and dressed her as a whore on purpose.

Lucille had to remind herself that "The Beverly Hillbillies" was the number-one television comedy in America, thank you very much. She was lucky to be here.

She met most of the stars at the read-through rehearsal, Buddy Ebsen in a Hawaiian shirt and Bermuda shorts, Irene Ryan looking about half Granny's age, in a sweater and skirt, with lovely auburn hair . . . if these normal-looking actors weren't afraid to put on ridiculous costumes and act silly in front of America every Wednesday night, Lucille wouldn't be either.

Max Baer was just as cheerful and lunky as Jethro, but not the least dimwitted—in his tweedy clothes and horn-rimmed glasses, he seemed rather intellectual. Donna Douglas was sweet-natured like Elly May, with a twinkly smile and a sharp sense of humor. These people read through the lines with assurance, every one a real professional. Lucille was starstruck, she stumbled a time or two trying too hard, but Max Baer just smiled and said, "Let's do it again."

At the end Buddy Ebsen said, "Honey, you'll do fine. Just relax."

Now she towered in her heels over the little foreign woman who kept trying to put on more makeup. "They vant a heavy look, much rouge," she said.

Lucille said "If you put any more rouge on me, I'll look like I've got the flu."

A boy stuck his head in. "Carolyn Clay? Wanted on the set."

"See there? Thank you. I've got to go."

The boy pointed her across the lot to a pastel-blue barn of a building. She wobbled along in spike heels past a knight in armor, three clowns, and some kind of rubber-faced monster that reminded her of Chester with a hangover. At the door to Stage Three she met Max Baer in his Jethro costume: checked shirt, tight blue jeans rolled up at the ankles, rope belt, and that gee-whiz grin on his face.

"Morning, Carolyn! God, look what they've done to you."

"I know. I feel just like a floozy."

"Well that's what you're supposed to be. Don't worry, I'm the big stupid idiot every week and it hasn't hurt me yet. What's in the hatbox?"

"My hat." She was taking no chances today.

Baer ushered her past familiar sets with banks of lights instead of ceilings—Mr. Drysdale's office, the Clampetts' driveway, the entry hall with the curving staircase, the "courtin' parlor," the kitchen, the cement pond. Workmen scurried everywhere polishing floors and furniture, climbing ladders to hang lights. It was strange to see these rooms lined up beside each other, the Clampett mansion disassembled and overrun by strangers. On TV it all meshed into a seamless make-believe world, but in real life you could step from the cement pond into Mr. Drysdale's office, and directly into Granny's kitchen.

Max Baer introduced Lucille to Nancy Kulp, the tall, plain-faced actress who played Miss Jane Hathaway. "This is Carolyn, from Alabama."

"At last, a real Southern girl," she trilled in her Miss Jane voice. "We haven't had many actual Southerners on the set."

"It's so good to meet you, I really love Miss Jane," said Lucille. "She's got that wild streak in her. You remember when she—"

"Nancy, Ray, places please," called Bob Weed, the director. Lucille found a quiet spot behind two lightstands to watch Nancy Kulp shoot a scene with Raymond Bailey, who played Mr. Drysdale.

"And . . . action!"

"Miss Hathaway," Bailey sputtered, "if you think this golddigging blonde is gonna get her hands on one dime of the Clampett fortune, you don't know Milburn Drysdale."

"Don't be so sure, Chief." Nancy Kulp pressed her hands together like a schoolmarm. "I didn't know Jethro was capable of such tender sentiments. I wouldn't be surprised if we're hearing wedding bells in the Clampett home before long. And after that, who knows? Maybe the patter of little feet?"

"If those two get married," Bailey snarled, "the only patter you'll hear is your little feet on the way to the unemployment line."

"*Chief!*"

"Cut! That's great, people. Next setup."

Yesterday, reading through the script, the actors had time to laugh at some of the jokes, but on the set nobody laughed. They shot it in snippets. The director yelled "cut!" and a buzzer went off and they moved on to the next camera angle.

The story was complicated for a twenty-six-page script: the golddigger Patsy Belle arrives from Arkansas all a-tizzy over Jethro, flirting and scheming to get him to marry her. After some comical misunderstandings involving Granny's secret love potion—a jug marked XXXX—Patsy Belle wins the trust of the Clampetts, who undertake elaborate preparations for a wedding Getting wind of all this, the ever-suspicious Drysdale sends the prettiest girl in his secretarial pool to make an even bigger play for Jethro. In the end, all the fussing and flirting frightens Jethro. He bolts from the altar. The last joke is when Granny tries to persuade Jed to go on and marry Patsy Belle, since he's already wearing his Sunday suit.

The girl playing the pretty secretary came to sit beside Lucille on the prop crate. She batted gorgeous blue eyes. "Hello, we didn't get to meet yesterday. I'm Sharon."

"Carolyn," Lucille said. "Isn't this exciting?"

"I guess so. If you don't mind sitting around all day."

"At least they gave you a nice dress to wear," said Lucille. "I look like something from the circus."

"But you've got a real part. My character doesn't even have a name, see? 'Pretty Girl.' That's me."

"I'll be glad to trade you," Lucille said. "Tell you the truth, I'm a little nervous. I've never done this before."

"Don't tell me that," said Sharon. "It's taken me three years of hard work to get a part this lousy."

A script girl appeared. "Sharon? Your scene's next."

"Good luck," said Lucille.

"You too." Sharon followed the script girl to the Drysdale office set. She was a real California beach girl with a lanky, carefree swing to her stride. Lucille watched her work through her scene in ten minutes, three takes, no problem. "Anything you say, Mr. Drysdale," she chirped, as Raymond Bailey mugged and leered.

"Miss Clay? Follow me, please."

Lucille carried the hatbox to the set representing the Clampetts' front door. She placed it on a fake-granite pedestal out of the way.

"Places, everybody!"

Lucille stepped under the hot lights, and here was that foreign woman again, reaching up on tiptoes with her powder puff. "A little shine on ze nose."

Bob Weed came hustling down from the other set. "Morning Max, hello Carolyn, ready to go to work?"

"Oh, yes sir."

"You know your lines?"

"I sure do." She'd stayed up till two a.m. learning them; she had the twists and turns of Patsy Belle engraved forever on her brain.

The stage manager pointed out the chalk mark where she was supposed to stand. The cameras were big hulking hooded machines with men riding their backs.

Max Baer sat in a director's chair marked MAX BAER, reading a book called *The Philosophical Indifference of Sin*. When all the lights were in place and adjusted, he put down the book and stepped to his mark. His face grew serious. "Okay, Bob, give me my motivation here."

"Let's see, you've had a big crush on her for years," said Bob Weed. "You're a little flustered by her aggressiveness, but you're happy about it too. Kid in a candy store."

Max Baer closed his eyes to fix this idea in his mind. He took a deep breath, flexed his arms in the air. When he opened his eyes he was Jethro with a big googly smile.

Bob called "Okay, roll 'em! Aaaaaand . . . action!"

"Golly, Miss Patsy Belle," said Jethro, "I can't believe you'd come all the way out here to California just to see me."

Lucille grinned her sexiest grin and slung her arms around his neck, just as she'd done at the audition. "Why Jethro, you big ol' hunk of man, of course I came to see you!" she cried. "I was so lonesome back home—I just *couldn't* stop thinking about you!"

"Aw, gee," he stammered, "did Granny see you yet? She'll be plumb tickled to see somebody from back home!"

"Oh, she saw me all right," Lucille said. "She tried to give me a dose of her medicine. She's such a sweet li'l ol' thing."

"Hoo-ee, you didn't drink that stuff, did you? Uncle Jed says one dose of Granny's tonic is enough to put hair on a bald-headed possum!"

"I don't care, Jethro," Lucille breathed. "Just as long as I can have a dose of those big old muscles of yours."

"Cut! Okay, that's good, but I want another take," said the director. "Carolyn, go ahead and touch him while you're flirting with him. And Max, she makes you a little more uncomfortable, I want all the awshucks you can give me. Load it on."

They did three takes in quick succession. Lucille forgot about the cameras and concentrated on playing Patsy Belle to Max Baer's Jethro. It was just like acting on the stage at Cornelia Baptist, except in place of Dooley Simpkins as Captain Von Trapp she was playing opposite a real TV star.

When that camera switched on, Max Baer had no shame at all. He became every bit as sweetly stupid as Jethro—besides which he was cute, in a low-rent Elvis kind of way. Lucille flirted and simpered and hammed it up, just as she saw him doing.

"Cut! Print it! That's really good, people. Let's keep that energy going. Next setup . . ."

"You're doing great," said Max Baer. "Having fun?"

"I am having a ball," said Lucille.

From the corner of her eye she spotted a cameraman making off with the hatbox. "Excuse me . . ." She ran after him. "Excuse me, that's mine."

"Okay, lady, but keep it out of my shot," the man said.

"Carolyn, we need you," said Bob Weed. "Remember, time's money, let's go."

"Sorry." She stuffed Chester under a light rack and hurried to her mark.

Making television was hard work. Before long Lucille was grateful for the little woman stepping in between takes to dab powder on her face. She flubbed several lines, but Max Baer flubbed his share, too. Mostly it seemed a matter of facing the right way for the camera and keeping your gaze focused in the scene instead of letting it drift over to some stagehand pushing a dolly in the semi-darkness.

They shot four scenes before lunch, and six scenes after. Bob Weed liked Lucille's performance so much he added a couple of lines to her scene with Granny.

They did five takes of the scene where Patsy Belle kissed Jethro. Max Baer showed her how to do a movie kiss with your lips closed, but on the last take he winked and slipped her the tongue.

Weed yelled cut.

Lucille bopped the actor's shoulder. "You better watch it, buster!"

He grinned. "Couldn't help myself."

Late in the day they put Lucille into a big fluffy wedding dress for her left-at-the-altar scene. The whole cast was dressed for the wedding, Irene Ryan in a lace bonnet, Buddy Ebsen in an old-fashioned parson's suit with his hair slicked back, Donna Douglas in a pink-organdie bridesmaid number. Max Baer looked silliest of all in a tuxedo cut three inches short, so his hands and feet stuck out and looked enormous.

"Okay people, if we can get this scene it's a wrap and everybody goes to the beach tomorrow," said Bob Weed.

The wedding took place in the Clampetts' entry hall. The script called for Patsy Belle to enter down the curving staircase, three beats behind Elly May in her bridesmaid dress.

To reach the top of those stairs Lucille had to go around behind the façade of the entry hall, onto a rickety scaffold and up a narrow spiral staircase. Somehow she made it to the little platform in that voluminous hoop-skirt.

"Careful," Donna Douglas said, "these steps are a bitch."

"Thanks." Lucille swept her train around with one hand, and took a deep breath.

"Roll 'em!" The strains of a recorded wedding march echoed through the soundstage. "Aaaaand . . . action!"

Donna Douglas put on a big gooey smile and moved into the blaze of lights, tossing rose petals from the basket in her hand.

Lucille tossed her veil and stepped out, intending to be the most beautiful bride anyone ever saw.

The first stair was steeper than she expected. Her heel caught the lining of her skirt, she lost her balance and went somersaulting down the stairs head over heels crash bang past Elly May, flat on her ass on the floor.

"Weeee doggie, Jethro, that gal shore is in a hurry to get down here and marry you," Buddy Ebsen cracked.

The set exploded in laughter.

Lucille pushed up on her elbows, dazed, her veil askew. "Cut!" Bob Weed rushed over. "You okay?"

"I think so." She'd snapped the spike heel off one shoe; nothing else seemed to be broken.

"Great fall!" Bob enthused. "I'm gonna keep it! Buddy, what a line! We're keeping the whole thing. Greg, did you get that?"

"Sure did, Mr. Weed, that was swell."

"You get the wide shot on Buddy's ad lib?"

The actors gathered around Lucille. Buddy Ebsen knelt to help her. "Little lady, you all right?"

She got to her feet, her ears ringing. The crew clapped and whistled.

"I tried to warn you about those steps," said Donna Douglas, patting her shoulder. "If I was you I'd sue somebody."

"Don't say that, I'll make sure she gets a bonus for stunt work," Bob said. "Carolyn, that was inspired."

He went off to huddle with the writers while two ladies from the costume department helped Lucille put herself back together. When the director returned he'd added a scene in which Patsy Belle samples some of Granny's XXXX tonic before the wedding, resulting in her tumble down the stairs. This meant she had to act the rest of the scene drunk. "Do you think you can do that?" said Weed. "It'll play much funnier."

"Yeah, I can act drunk." She would just picture Chester on one of his Friday nights, and the rest would come.

"Okay, Maureen, put her back like she was, total disarray. We'll start from when Buddy helps her up, and Carolyn, your line now is 'I'm not as think as you drunk I am.' You got that?"

Lucille's heart was still pounding, but she did her best to play the scene just the way he wanted, reeling and tottering on her broken shoe.

Everyone pronounced it hilarious. Bob said it was much stronger than the original finish. They did four takes before he got it just the way he wanted, and after that they had to shoot the new bit with the jug of moonshine.

By the time he called, "Cut! Thank you, folks, that's a wrap!" Lucille was so exhausted she was swaying on her feet for real. She had no idea acting was such hard work. Watching movies and TV, she had imagined that a movie star's job was to stand up, say a few lines, and ride home to her mansion in her limousine.

Technicians began snapping out lights. Bob Weed took Lucille aside. "I know you didn't mean to fall, but you were a real trouper, you took it in stride. The show will be a lot better for it."

"Thanks a lot, Mr. Weed. Do you need me in the morning?"

"No, tomorrow we just clean up odds and ends. You'll get paid for the full three days. Hope we'll be working together again. Good luck."

Lucille looked around for someone to wash out her hair, but the makeup people had gone home. She found her street clothes in a locker with "C. Clay" masking-taped on the door. She changed quickly, and peeled off the tape as a souvenir.

She was almost out the door before she remembered Chester.

She hurried through Granny's parlor, around the edge of the cement pond—then she saw the hatbox under the lightstand where she'd left it, and allowed herself to breathe.

"Come on, Chester." She grabbed him up.

"Lou-see-yul," he whispered, "I love you, honey."

"You shut up."

It was dark outside. The only human being in sight was the guard in the booth at the gate.

Lucille rapped on the glass. "Can you call a taxi for me?"

"Sorry, no outside line. You can walk up to the corner and wave one down."

"Thanks." Her toes ached from those pointy-toed shoes, but she felt pretty damn good about the job she had done. Nobody would nominate her for an Emmy—but nobody had pointed her out as a rank amateur, either. They hadn't had to stop a scene on her account more than three or four times. Even her inelegant pratfall had turned into the comedic high point of the day.

Her tailbone was sore, and also her shoulder where she'd hit the stair-rail. She couldn't keep a big smile off her face. She had done exactly what she'd set out to do, that very first moment when the skull-and-bones winked at her from the can of D-Con, when the devil's voice whispered the idea in her ear. She threw over her whole life and came to Hollywood and made good. Chester never believed she could do it. She'd brought him along to witness the whole thing. Now his humiliation was complete. Lucille had won a monumental victory over him and everyone else who'd ever doubted her.

Anything that happened after this was pure gravy.

Traffic raced in both directions. The occasional taxi seemed to speed up when the driver saw Lucille out in the street, waving.

This neighborhood was nothing like Beverly Hills: blank-faced ware-houses, vacant lots, arc-vapor streetlamps casting everything in a violet light. She should have arranged for a car from the hotel.

Where was Norman when she needed him?

A police car slowed down for a look. The cop's face swiveled to follow her as they drove past.

Lucille quickened her step down the block.

A pair of Yellow Cabs cruised by. She waved both arms over her head but neither driver slowed down.

The cop car swung into view at the next corner, coming back around for another look.

Lucille set off down Las Palmas toward the studio gate, keenly aware of the hatbox in her hand.

She felt the headlights on her back. *Don't run, Lucille. Do not run.* The gun was tucked in the tissue paper alongside the money and Chester, just where she could not get at it.

The black-and-white car slid up alongside. "Good evening."

The cop had a bland, chubby face, curly blond hair. Also he had a partner, so the gun wouldn't be any use even if she could get at it.

"What's the problem, Officer?"

"You got some identification?"

"No, sorry. I left it back at my hotel."

"Where would that be?"

"The Beverly Hills."

He looked her up and down. "You don't say."

Suddenly she saw her image reflected in the glass of the back window—Patsy Belle's big poufy hair and the layers of garish makeup. She'd been standing out in the street waving at cars. . . .

"Oh my God—oh, I see what you're thinking. You know, it's the strangest thing how many people have been making this mistake lately."

"Really?" he said. "How long's it been since the last time?"

"No, listen, Officer, you've got it all wrong. I'm an actress. I was in this studio here shooting 'The Beverly Hillbillies' today. This is stage makeup."

"What's in the hatbox?"

Lucille saw that her only hope of escape was a swift counterassault. She would have to brazen her way out of this. "It's a hat. What's the matter, is that against the law?"

The partner spoke up: "I think this *is* a studio, Ed."

"You're damn right it is," said Lucille. "Haven't you got anything better to do than going around bothering innocent women?"

"That guy up there," said the first cop, indicating the guard in the booth. "Can he vouch for you?"

"Well he better, he just sent me to the corner to find a cab. I couldn't get one to stop." She marched toward the gate.

The cruiser edged along after her.

"Hey Mister," she called, "would you please come out and tell these men I've been working in there? They seem to think I'm working out here."

It was more than the makeup and hair. It must be something about the way Lucille carried herself, something that revealed her awakening to the power of sex in these last few weeks. Or maybe it was all in the eyes of men, maybe they saw whores everywhere they looked, maybe they thought all women were whores except their mothers and the Virgin Mary.

The guard stepped out with his hand up to block the headlights. "She was on Stage Three. I signed her out myself." Lucille stalked back to the cruiser. "I hope you're satisfied. You owe me an apology."

"Listen, lady," the cop said, "it was an honest mistake, in this neighborhood. We have to keep an eye on things."

"Not only do you owe me an apology," she said, "but I think you ought to give me a ride to my hotel."

Lately she could not resist flirting with danger every time it wiggled a finger at her. The best defense, as Chester used to say, is a good offense.

"Can't do that," the cop said. "We're on duty."

"Yeah, you're real busy, I can tell." You Can WIN! At Roulette.

"Aw, let's give her a ride, Ed. It was our mistake."

"It sure was," Lucille said, "and I can't wait to tell my lawyer about it."

"Get in the back," said the first cop.

That is how Lucille came to ride from the studio to the Beverly Hills Hotel under the protection of the Los Angeles Police Department, with Chester's head and a gun and eighteen thousand dollars in a box on her lap. It seemed like a pretty good joke. The cops were friendly. They wanted to know inside stuff about Jed and Granny and especially Elly May.

The doorman at the Beverly Hills did not bat an eye. He stepped to open the back of the black-and-white car as if it were a limousine. "Good evening, Miss Clay. Welcome back."

"Thank you," she said. "Thanks for the ride, boys."

The cops waved and rolled off down the drive.

"Wasn't that nice," Lucille said. "They gave me a ride home. Everybody is so friendly out here."

Harry Hall called for her in his white Rolls-Royce on a warm summer Saturday night. He looked splendid in his tuxedo at the wheel of that car. Lucille twirled to let him admire her latest fashion splurge, a black sparkly party gown with sequins and a filmy shawl to cover her bare shoulders. "You like it? It's new."

"It's marvelous," he said, "but haven't your ill-gotten gains begun to run out on you yet?"

"Not yet."

"And of course the hatbox, as always." The Rolls purred off into the soft summer night. "It's one of my great ambitions to have a look at that hat one day."

"It's not just a hat, Harry. I keep all my important things in here."

"Most girls I know get by with a purse," he said.

She smiled. "I'm not like most girls."

"You can say that again. Walter Weitzman called me, all excited. Apparently you had some kind of mishap, and they were able to use it?"

"I fell down the stairs." Lucille drew the shawl around her head to protect her fancy French twist from the wind. "They thought it was funny."

"They sure did. From what Walter says the film is hysterical. He's offered us a contract. They want to write Patsy Belle into four shows for the fall season."

"You're kidding! Oh Harry, that's terrific."

"Yes and no. It's terrific they liked you, but I'm not sure we want to lock you into anything just yet. It may turn out Alexander Powell has something bigger for us at Paramount. This is his party tonight. Be nice to him but don't promise anything."

They followed a narrow, winding road into the hills. The smell of eucalyptus washed through the car. City lights sparkled in the distance, twinkling like the string of Christmas lights inside Lucille. These days in Hollywood had been the very best of her life. Every day she tempted fate, and every day fate handed her another plump bundle of good fortune wrapped up in shiny paper. While the people back home were fighting and marching and dying and having their eyes put out, the old ways of life unraveling, Lucille was forging a wonderful new life for herself. She didn't know how long her luck could go on getting better and better, with no price to pay for what she had done.

For days now she had sensed a shadow trailing her, a dark silhouette running along underneath her happiness. She knew this was not her real life but only a wonderful vacation from life, a vacation now moving toward its inevitable end. She had stayed on in her bungalow because she had a feeling this part of her journey was almost over, and she wanted to savor every moment.

Lucille had some terrible qualities—she was vain, selfish, quick-tempered, with a certain late tendency toward violence and sex—but stupidity was not one of them. Along with the glow of her sudden success came the knowledge of the huge risk she was taking, living out her dream this way. She could not hide her face in the gray cloud now. The cloud was nowhere in sight. She knew what would probably happen Wednesday night when her face was broadcast onto twenty million television sets. She could not put herself out over the airwaves of America and hope to remain anonymous.

She clung to the vague hope that Patsy Belle's makeup and hair might have transformed her so completely no one would recognize her, but that was a very slender thread.

She had her bags all packed in the closet of Bungalow Six, ready to go at a moment's notice.

She didn't know when, or where. She knew only that she had to stay one step ahead. She could do it, she could keep going, if only she could find the right place to get rid of Chester. She simply had to stop dragging him around. The load was becoming intolerable. That hatbox must weigh fifty pounds by now.

"You're quiet tonight," Harry said.

"Just thinking. I'm so lucky, here, lately."

"You make your own luck, kiddo. Take me, for instance. I started out with nothing. I worked for everything I've got."

She lit a Salem. "Listen, Harry, if anything should happen, if I should decide to take off for a few days, don't make a big thing about it, okay?"

"What do you mean, take off. We're just getting started! Two days' work and you want a vacation?"

"I'm not sure." She breathed smoke. "I might have to go someplace for a while. I have some unfinished business."

"What's going on, Lucille?"

"Please, Harry, don't ask me questions. And remember it's Carolyn now."

"No, I want to talk to Lucille. Face-to-face, Harry to Lucille. What are you up to? Are you going to quit and go home just when I'm about to make things happen for you?"

"No, I'm not going home. I probably won't go anywhere. I just wanted you to know not to worry. If I did. And also how grateful I am."

He touched the brake. "You're serious, aren't you. What is this all about?"

"Nothing! I'm sorry I mentioned it."

"Because the truth is I've invested quite a bit of time in you already. I have a stake in this now. If you've got something up your sleeve, I want you to tell me. I don't like surprises."

"Look Harry, no sleeves." She tried to turn it into a joke.

He drove uphill in silence, glancing from the road to her face.

"Don't do anything without talking to me," he said. "I don't say this to

everyone, but I see a real future for you. You're not a leading lady, you're a
year or two on the wrong side of thirty for that, but you have the makings of
a really fine comic actress. Walter said you took that pratfall like Lucille
Ball."

"I didn't mean to, believe me," she said. Hollywood! The only place on
earth where you could become a fine comic actress by falling on your ass.

They pulled up to a stone gate which swung open as if by magic. The
driveway led over the ridge to reveal a magnificent white stone palace
spread in a natural bowl on the hilltop, a kingdom of gardens and pools
glowing with people and music and lights in the trees.

From this ridge, Hollywood stretched out forever, a glittering carpet of
lights and possibilities. The lights overwhelmed all the stars in the sky.

Lucille gaped. "This is his *house?*"

"One of them. Alexander has houses in Malibu, Paris, Cap d'Antibes.
Also a flat in New York."

A snappy young man came to park the car. Lucille and Harry walked
up a stone path. "You mean that nice-looking gray-headed man? The one
who was so busy looking after his wife's little dogs?"

"That's the one."

"I should have paid more attention to him," she said.

"Don't pay too much attention," he said. "Joan bites. She never lets him
out of her—whoa, hello, Alexander, good evening!"

"Harry, you scoundrel, welcome! I see you've brought your lovely Miss
Clay."

"Well hey, Mr. Powell," she said. "Thanks for inviting me to your party.
I just love your house."

"Well, thank you, we like it too. Make yourself at home—oh there you
are, Bob! Dolores, don't you look lovely!"

Dear Lord, that was Bob Hope coming up the sidewalk with his wife,
not five paces from Lucille. She had an urge to find a phone and call
Mama. Mama always had a big thing for Bob Hope.

Harry clasped her arm. "Come along, dear, close your mouth, now,
that's good. There will be a lot of film people here tonight, I don't want
you to stare. They hate that."

"Okay. I'll try."

A waiter floated by with champagne in long flutes.

"Oh my God," Lucille said, "Cary Grant."

"And don't point. Hello, Cary."

"Harry Hall! How are you?" They shook hands. He was gorgeous,
though a bit older than Lucille had imagined.

"I'm fine. This is Carolyn Clay, a client of mine."

"And a lovely one, too." Cary Grant took Lucille's hand in his, and kissed it just above the knuckles.

She melted. "Oh thank you, Mr. Grant. I've watched you in so many movies I feel like I ought to kiss *your* hand."

"By all means." He extended his hand.

She bowed to the kiss. She would always carry the moment: her lips against Cary Grant's hand.

"A charming custom," he said, "I must teach it to all my friends. Good to meet you, Miss Clay. See you, Harry." He smiled, headed off to the bar.

She wanted to tell him she had named her second son for him, but she'd been too shy. "I could die right now and be happy, Harry. Did I embarrass you?"

"Not at all. Kiss all the hands you like. But do me a favor and stash that hatbox somewhere. Just for ten minutes."

"All right . . ." The house unfolded as Lucille stepped down into it, ever larger rooms opening out to a wall of plate glass, a glowing turquoise pool, the shimmering city beyond. A pianist in white-tie-and-tails sat at a white grand piano playing "Rhapsody in Blue" for the glamorous people smoking and drinking and talking.

"Harry, I'll find someplace to put this."

"Don't get lost, now."

All the rooms were designed in a severe super-modern style, bare white walls with white furniture and white carpets, no decoration at all. Lucille carried Chester down a long empty corridor, checking in each door. If these people owned anything that wasn't white, they had hidden it well.

At last she found a room with a welcome clutter of fur stoles and evening wraps on a bed, handbags lined up along a wall. She tucked Chester under the bed and whispered for him to keep quiet.

She nodded at the uniformed maid coming down the hall with an armload of furs. This place seemed more like a sleek new hotel than somebody's home. Lucille could not begin to understand why you would have such a big house with nothing in it. She supposed it was elegant, in a cold, empty way—but can you imagine what a couple of kids would do to all these white rugs?

Of course the dazzling people at this party had no kids and never spilled their drinks. Lucille had finally gone above her raising: She was in a room full of movie stars and people who knew how to talk to movie stars without gushing and turning red. No one was making a move to have her thrown out.

She spotted Harry near the fireplace in a group that included Joan Blake, the tall blonde from poolside at the Beverly Hills. She looked very flashy in a gold-beaded dress and a huge platinum bouffant, not altogether unlike the hairdo that had nearly gotten Lucille arrested on Santa Monica Boulevard. Joan's chihuahuas were off their chains, snapping and yipping at everyone's ankles as if they were on diet pills.

Lucille gazed upon the spectacle of Richard Chamberlain, Donald O'Connor, and Mitzi Gaynor in the same end of one room. Richard and Donald shared a private joke. Mitzi held forth in a circle of admirers, telling a story that had everyone's eyes dancing. The pianist played "Taking a Chance on Love."

Lucille held up her shoulders and moved through with her glass poised in one hand, as she'd learned from the movies. Harry said "Joan, you remember Carolyn, don't you?"

"Of course I do."

"Your house is just beautiful, thank you for having me." Lucille felt a tug, and looked down to find one of the chihuahuas yanking at the hem of her new dress. "No, doggie," she said, trying to shake it off. "Go on, now." The dog wouldn't be shaken lightly. It bared its teeth and tugged harder.

Lucille managed a smile. She bent over, tried to shoo it away. She heard the *zzt!* of cloth ripping.

Joan's voice turned squeaky. "What's the matter, Binkums, you smell something? Huh? Does he smell sumsin?"

The dog growled and ripped a three-inch strip of hem from Lucille's new dress.

"Get *away* from me!" She gave a backhand swat to its hind end. The dog shrieked and let go.

When she thought about it later, Lucille could have sworn that dog gave her a dirty look. There was something mean in its little black eyes.

The second and third chihuahuas entered the fray, yarping and jumping up on their hind legs.

Joan Blake said "Well you didn't have to hit him!" She knelt down and let the dogs jump all over her. "Come here sweetie, did she hurt you, no, he's okay. He's okay."

"Joan, have you ever given any thought to having actual children?" said Harry.

"Shut up, Harry." She drew herself to full height. "Excuse me. I'll go put them away." She stalked off to the back of the house, trailed by the trio of yappers.

"Damn dog tore my new dress," said Lucille. "Sorry, Harry, I guess I shouldn't have hit it."

"Don't worry about it. She used to have four of the little bastards. One of them bit my ankle once. But only once."

Lucille laughed. "You killed it?"

"No, no. It died of natural causes, I think. Maybe one taste of my leg was fatal. Listen, darling, I see two or three people I must speak to, then I'll introduce you around. Will you be all right just to mingle?"

"I'm fine, Harry. I'm just wonderful."

She went to stand beside the piano man. He glanced up from his keyboard with a wink. She wished someone would take her picture right now, so she could remember forever how she looked in that gorgeous black gown reflected in the wall of glass, while the city lights trembled in the distance and the man played "Whatever Lola Wants" just for her.

Someone stepped up beside her, a hand on her elbow. She turned with a smile but it was not Harry.

"Hello, little baby."

A shock: It was him. The man of her dreams, in a tuxedo.

His smile was brilliant, his face more handsome than she had ever realized in the dark.

"Oh my Lord." She took a step back.

"I can't believe you're here," he said. "I thought my eyes were playing a trick on me."

She blushed. "Go away," she whispered.

"Did I startle you?"

"Someone might see us."

"Oh, I get it." He backed up a step, his hand upraised. "You're married. Sorry. Forget I was here."

"No, wait, that's not it." She wished the pianist would play louder; she felt as if the whole party had ground to a halt and everyone was looking at her and the man who had come to her bungalow, the man whose name she did not even know. "I just—I didn't expect to see you again."

"Me either, what a stroke, huh? I'm not staying at the hotel anymore, I've rented a place just above Sunset." He dropped his voice. "Are you still in your bungalow?"

"Well, yes, but I'm leaving any day now."

"Where?"

"I don't know, Japan. Argentina. Somewhere far."

He said, "I'm Toby Clark. I don't think we ever . . . I mean, we didn't introduce ourselves, did we."

"I'm Carolyn." She cleared her throat, forced a smile. "Listen, would you mind getting me some more champagne? All of a sudden I'm dry as a bone."

"Of course, give me your glass. I'll be right back." Even in his formal suit he looked like a soldier, built solid and close to the ground, with that pink scrubbed face and the boyish crewcut. And now she knew why. He was Toby Clark. Lucille had made love to Toby Clark. Oh, if the women of Cornelia ever heard that, they would drop dead from pure envy.

She'd known his face since he was a second banana in all those beach movies, but he'd only lately became famous as Private Dolan in *The Last Man Standing*, the World War II picture that won all the Oscars. She remembered his big dying scene, when his leg was blown off above the knee and he thought he was back home in Kansas. He cried out for his mother. Lucille had wept for him then.

Just think—Toby Clark, that poor wounded all-American boy, was in real life the kind of man who would call up a perfect stranger in her hotel room, talk his way into her bed, make wild love to her, and leave without saying his name.

But then, Lucille was the kind of woman who unlocked the door to let him in. Didn't that even things out, pretty much? What gave her the right to cast judgment on him?

Here he came with that grin and two glasses of champagne.

"You should have told me who you were the other night," she said. "Now I'm embarrassed. I loved you in *The Last Man Standing*."

"It didn't seem important at the time, but thank you." He lifted his glass. "Cheers."

They clinked.

Lucille said, "If you'd told me your name on the phone, I would have invited you over for a proper introduction."

He grinned. "Oh, but I liked the way it happened. Didn't you?"

"Yes. I did." There, she'd said it. The truth was out of her mouth. "It was a different kind of evening for me."

"Me too. I'd love a return engagement sometime."

"Uhmmm . . . no, I don't think so," she said. "I'm not staying here long."

"That's right, Argentina. You told me." He clinked her glass again. "To Argentina."

"Listen, would you mind if I got an autograph? It's for my—my niece, she's a big fan of yours."

He smiled and said okay, but she could tell it pained him. Just that fast she had become just another fan searching for a pen and a cocktail napkin. The moment was ruined.

"Make it out to Lucille," she said. "Put something, you know, kind of mushy."

He wrote "For Lucille—yours from here to eternity—Love, Toby Clark." "Here you go."

"Oh, that will make her so happy." Lucille folded the napkin. "I'm sorry, I know you must get tired of that."

"Never," he said, with a professional smile. "Listen, Carolyn, I see my producer over there. I'll come back and see how you're doing in a bit, all right?"

"Sure. That's fine. It's—it's nice to see you again." She smiled and watched him walk away. What a fool! She'd had Toby Clark in the palm of her hand, in her very own bed—the same Toby Clark whose pretty face made thousands of women warm and squirmy in the darkness of the matinee—and she'd run him off, just that fast.

She wished he had stayed in her dreams instead of materializing out of nowhere, only to lose interest in her.

At that moment there came a scream from the back of the house—a wild harrowing scream that silenced the piano and froze conversation to the far side of the swimming pool.

Everyone turned.

Joan Blake appeared in the door at the top of the room, shrieking, flailing her arms as if hornets were stinging her to death. She stumbled and got up and ran blindly through the room, pursued by some demon no one could see.

People stepped back to get out of her way. Propelled by her desperate screams she ran clawing at the air, tripped and fell, got up again and ran full speed through the plate-glass wall at the end of the room.

The glass burst over her in a dazzling white downpour.

Joan Blake toppled, bleeding, into the pool.

When something like that happens, one person reacts by instinct and everyone follows. Lucille always liked to remember that it was Toby Clark who dashed through that shattered glass and leapt to Joan's rescue in the pool, leading everyone else to rush after him out of the room—everyone except Lucille, who went the other way.

She hurried down the hall toward the sound of dogs yapping. She had an idea what she would find, and she braced herself—

Yes.

Chester was out of his box.

He was out of his box and his Tupperware, he was on the floor by the bed, encircled by chihuahuas barking their little lungs out. One of them had Chester by the hair and was trying to drag him across the rug.

It startled Lucille: he still looked so much like himself. That was his face. His skin wasn't the right color, he was purplish-black, but those were his features, unmistakably. She did not linger on the sight of him. She kicked the dog loose, grasped Chester by his greasy hair, and stuffed him back in the Tupperware bowl with a squishing sound that made her stomach flop over.

She had to push down to wedge him back in there. She swallowed the acid taste in her mouth. A dark fluid had spilled from the lettuce keeper all over the immaculate carpet.

The dogs barked and barked.

Holding her breath, rummaging among the furs on the bed, Lucille found the plastic lid and snapped it back on. She ran her thumb around the press-and-lock seal, wedged the bowl back into the hatbox, and crammed on the box-lid just as Harry Hall rushed to the door.

He stared at the stain on the rug. He caught a whiff of Chester and paled. The Tupperware seal had worked wonders, it surely had, but Chester had been in there for weeks now and you could not deny that smell.

"Hello, Harry." She fumbled to tie the ribbons. "I guess Joan didn't care for my hat."

"Yeah, but—but—"

"She was poking around where it wasn't any of her business." She snatched up the hatbox, kissed Harry's cheek, and slipped past him down the hall, past the noisy confusion around the swimming pool and the tuxedoed men running through the house. She marched straight out the front door to the first limousine in line.

"I'll give you one hundred dollars to take me to the Beverly Hills Hotel," she said to the driver. "I mean right now."

His face lit up. "Get in!"

She jumped in beside him. The big engine roared to life. The car jumped ahead with a screech.

Lucille got the hell out of there.

25

Peejoe

Industry

O nce *Life* did the Industry story, reporters and photographers and camera crews came from all over the country to shoot pictures and ask questions.

You could see them every morning at the courthouse, as determined with their flashbulbs and notebooks as the Negroes with their "Free Brother Thomas" signs. You could find them at lunchtime in their white short-sleeve shirts and skinny ties, eating at the café on the south end of Beauregard Avenue. Townspeople went out of their way to walk down there at noon, just to see the white reporters eating at the Negro café.

When they finished their lunch, they went to watch the picketers form up a line and march down the street singing "We Shall Overcome," past the Dairy Dog, down the hill to the swimming pool. The chain-link fence had been repaired, coils of barbed wire strung along the top. A hand-painted sign said CLOSED UNTIL FURTHER NOTICE. The water was murky, down three feet from the top, filled with leaves and sticks from last week's thunderstorms.

No one had been allowed in the pool since the day Nehemiah led his people to the plunge, but the fence made a fine backdrop for pictures and speeches.

Every day it was somebody different making the speech, a Negro preacher or one of the civil-rights workers who'd come from Atlanta and Birmingham to join the protests. Every day they recited this list of demands:

1. Immediate freedom for Nehemiah Thomas and all demonstrators jailed since his arrest.

2. Immediate integration of the Industry swimming pool, soft-ball field, all stores, cafés, lunch counters, public restrooms and drinking fountains, the Ritz Theater and the Star-Lite drive-in.
3. Immediate justice for the killers of David Jackson, Taylor Jackson, Bessie Stringfellow, and three others whose murders had gone unsolved in the past year.
4. Allow Negroes to register and vote in Cotton County.

The *Progress* printed this list every day, along with a little calendar showing how many days Industry had been under siege. Far from welcoming the invasion by their fellow members of the press, the editors of the *Progress* shared white Industry's shame at suddenly finding their town portrayed in *Time* and *Newsweek* and on *Huntley-Brinkley*—not as a sleepy, pretty little place with flowers and trees and nice folks, but as a hotbed of violent ignorant racists who attacked and beat defenseless Negroes in the dark, having first shot out the lights.

The letters to the *Progress* glowed with outrage at Negro agitators and Yankee reporters and most of all Sheriff John Doggett, who kept the confrontation alive with a new and inflammatory statement just about every day. The letter-writers called him "pig-headed" and "dangerous" and "asinine" and other words excised by a scrupulous use of the "X" key, as in "Doggett is a worthless XXX XX X XXXXX who has brought mortification upon us all." Most of these letters were signed something like "Angry Citizen."

There were other letters, too, arriving at the funeral home in batches now, every day eight or ten more, addressed to "Peter Bullis, Industry, Ala." They all sounded pretty much like the first one:

Dear Peter,

I just saw your picture in the magazine. I felt so sorry for you. I think you must be very brave and am sorry you got hurt. I hope the enclosed will buy you a new toy or some medicine, whatever you need most and will use.

Tell your mother and father they are lucky to have such a brave son. Have faith in the Lord He will show you the way.

Sincerely,
Mrs. Mavis R. Fain
Elgin, Illinois

A five-dollar bill fluttered out of that first envelope. So far my haul came to one hundred thirty-two dollars, four Bibles, two framed pictures of Jesus, and a book called "The Autobiography of Malcolm X." (I read a few pages but it didn't even try to explain how a guy could wind up with a name like "X" so I lost interest.)

Most of the letters came from ladies up North. I conjured pictures of them from the curvy handwriting, the flowered notepaper. At first Dove said I'd have to send the money back, but when the letters continued to arrive without any return address, he said it would be okay if I saved it for college.

Dove was trying hard to act as if everything was normal, although Earlene and Mabel had not come back, and Mabel had turned very peculiar since she left Industry.

One day she started crying and couldn't stop. Earlene had to put her in the Goshen hospital for observation. She got hold of a pair of scissors and tried to stab a candy striper in the leg. They put her in a room with a lock on the door and started talking about Bryce.

"She's had what they call a nervous breakdown," Dove told us. "Sometimes it just happens and they get right over it. Sometimes it takes longer."

I asked what caused it. Dove said he didn't know. Wiley asked if we could visit her. Dove said no, and went downstairs for a drink.

"What did you do to her, Wiley?"

"Nothing! When you saw us—that was the only time, I swear. It was all her idea. We didn't really do anything, but when you saw us it scared her. Real bad. After that she was weird. Like she was afraid of me."

"Are you gonna tell Dove?"

"What am I s'posed to say?—sorry Uncle Dove, I was necking with Mabel in the closet, I won't do it again? What good would that do?"

"But Wiley, he knows something happened."

He blew out his breath. "I hope she's okay."

Meanwhile business at the funeral home had dwindled away to nothing. Dove said it was a good thing he had Negroes from the Blessed Rest to embalm; all the white people were taking their funeral business over to Dothan, except for a couple of accidental cases in which nobody had a choice—a hobo run over by a freight train, a family from Ohio killed in a crash on the highway. Dove was still the coroner, of course, he still went out at all hours to sign death certificates, but generally he came back with an empty hearse and a long face.

He drank plenty of Old Grand-Dad. After a couple of belts he would start cussing the sorry sonofabitches who were responsible for his troubles, starting with Sheriff Doggett and Nehemiah Thomas, and working around until he'd cussed just about everybody in Cotton County.

In one of these moods he snarled once too often at Randall Mulch, his part-time cosmetologist. Randall got huffy and red in the face and shouted "I'm the only one in town who even speaks to you anymore! If you're gonna yell at me, I quit!"

This outburst took Dove by surprise. He blinked. "Don't quit, Randall. I'm sorry. You're right. You've always done a fine job for me."

"I don't know, Mr. Bullis," said Randall. "I've been meaning to talk to you anyway. My mother doesn't want me working here anymore. She says it's asking for trouble."

"Do you always do what your mother says?" Dove said.

Randall squirmed. "Of course not, but—"

"You think it's wrong to give these colored folks the same consideration as white folks when they die?"

"No, I don't, you know that," Randall said. "I've done everything I could to help you. I ordered that whole line of cosmetics just for them. But then she yells at me, and you yell at me, and I don't know what to do."

"I shouldn't have yelled, I apologize," Dove said. "If she wants you to quit, I guess you should. I can't afford to keep you anyway, business like it is."

They looked at each other. Randall scuffed his toe on the floor. "I'm sorry. It's been nice working here."

Dove poured another drink. "If you change your mind," he said, "you call me."

Randall gathered up his tackle boxes of makeup, and left.

We were alone in that big old house. Dove drank. Milton stayed in his room. Wiley and I watched TV. Aunt Lucille did not call.

One morning Dove got us up before daybreak and put us in our Sunday clothes, clip-on neckties, hard shoes. We drove the white hearse two hours up Highway 31 to Montgomery, to an imposing judicial building just down from the shining white dome of the state capitol. Half-columns sculpted into the façade gave the building a solid air. Carved over each door was a phrase in a mysterious language: FAVETE LINGUIS and FESTINA LENTE and PRO BONO PUBLICO. I rolled the strange words around on my tongue.

Hiram Murphy met us in the lobby and led us upstairs to a little room with a table and chairs and a rattly oscillating fan. We waited for hours playing Hearts and leafing through back issues of *American Lawyer*.

Murphy returned around noon. "Fellows, I'm sorry for the delay, but this is our crucial witness, and he's giving good information. Why don't you go find some lunch and I'm sure I'll call you by one-thirty or two."

We walked down the street to a snazzy restaurant called the Elite. We sat in a sculptured black-vinyl booth and ordered the Blue Plate Special, which turned out to be pork chops with mashed potatoes and peas—the finest meal I'd eaten since I left Meemaw's.

Dove said "I wish they'd get on with this thing. There's nothing I hate worse than sitting around waiting."

We went back to our little room in the federal building and waited some more. The smoke from Dove's Camel curled up through a high window.

After a while Hiram Murphy came for Dove.

"Boys, you wait here and behave," Dove said.

"We will." I immersed myself in the Legion of Superheroes. The Flash was my favorite. He could run clean across the country in a minute or two (and never get sweaty!) and he had the finest bright crimson future-suit with gold wings on the helmet.

I read the comic book three times, down to the fine print in the ad about how you could win a Murray bicycle by selling 1,350 packets of zinnia seeds.

The doorknob rattled. I turned to see Dove through my good eye. "Peter Joseph, you're next. Don't worry, it's a piece of cake."

Wiley said, "Don't make stuff up."

Hiram Murphy led me down a long corridor, his heels striking an echo on the marble floor. "Now Peter, the reason the grand jury is secret is so you can tell the truth. The jurors are just regular people. Relax and do the best you can."

We stopped at a tall door. Murphy opened it. The buzz of conversation ceased.

This was a long, dusky room with high ceilings. Shafts of sunlight streamed in through tall windows. Eighteen men sat around a long table staring at me. Murphy led me to a chair at the head of the table. He held out a Bible. I put one hand on top and swore to tell the whole truth.

Murphy asked if I'd been in Dog Junction with Dove the night he signed the death certificate on David Jackson.

I said I had.

"Now Peter, when you arrived at that house, was David Jackson still alive?"

"No sir. He was dead."

"Did anyone tell you how he died?"

"Mr. Thomas said some men threw him off the back of a truck."

"Did he say who?"

"He said they were friends of the sheriff."

Murphy led me over the details of that night, and the day at the pool when Taylor Jackson died. I told how it all started: The lifeguard ordered two colored boys out of the pool. Taylor and his friends materialized from the woods and sat down by the fence. The sheriff and his deputies showed up all at once. Taylor refused to budge from his spot and the deputies grabbed him and he tried to get away, fell, hit his head on the concrete ledge.

"Now think carefully, Peter," said Murphy. "Did he fall? Or did somebody trip him?"

"I know they had him by his arms. It seemed like he was trying to get loose."

Murphy kept returning to this question from different angles. I had to keep saying I didn't know. He wanted me to say yes it was Sheriff John Doggett himself who pushed Taylor down and killed him, but I couldn't swear that on the Bible or I'd go to Hell. Certainly the sheriff had *acted* guilty enough, standing over Taylor's body making excuses—but that didn't mean he *was* guilty.

Murphy led me on through the day of Taylor's funeral, the march on the swimming pool, the night riot, the attack on the Blessed Rest. I tried my best to remember the sheriff's exact words to Dove: I don't care how many of 'em get killed. I don't care if the bodies pile up, that's just dandy with me.

"One last question, son. Does the injury to your eye have anything to do with these events?"

"No sir. It was an accident."

"Thank you, Peter, you've been a big help. Ladies and gentlemen, we'll take five minutes."

I got up from the chair. It was spooky that none of those men had said a word the whole time I was in there. They sat listening, forming their judgments in silence.

Hiram Murphy led me down the corridor. "You did a good job."

"I'm sorry, I'm still confused about Taylor. I'm not sure what happened. I think he just kind of fell."

"You'll remember better as we go along. We needed to establish the pattern, and we've done that. We've got our indictments. I could see it in their eyes when you told them what Doggett said at Nehemiah's that night. I won't need to call your brother."

Wiley was crushed. All day he had pretended to be bored to death with the whole thing, but when he heard he wasn't needed, he snatched off his necktie and sulked out to the hearse.

I went after him. "Don't worry, Wiley, it wasn't that big a deal. Just a bunch of old guys in a room. He asked me the same question twenty times."

"Shut up," he said.

Dove started the big V-8. "Boys, I'm equal proud of you both. It takes guts to come up here and do what's right."

Wiley said "I didn't do anything except sit in a room and read a stupid magazine all day."

"You were there in case you were needed. That's what's important. Now comes the hard part."

"What do you mean?"

"Nothing secret from here on out. The whole thing goes public. John Doggett's no fool. As soon as they hand down these indictments, he'll know who's been talking behind his back."

"Do you think he'll try to hurt us?"

"He wouldn't dare. Hiram Murphy represents the federal govment of the United States. That's a much bigger deal than a county sheriff any day. But we have to be real damn careful we don't give him any excuses. I want you boys home, I don't want you hanging around up at the courthouse— now don't look so innocent, Peter Joseph, I know you've been up there every day. And I don't want you bragging about this to your friends."

"We don't have any friends," Wiley said.

"Well, your enemies, then." Dove fished under his seat for the whiskey, uncapped it, took a slug. "We can come through this thing if we just stick together."

26

Peejoe

Industry

I t was almost dark when we flashed into town. The courthouse square had been deserted at night ever since the trouble started. There were evening meetings in the colored churches, and sometimes the rednecks in their pickups would come to roar around the square, honking, waving Confederate flags, and giving the Rebel yell. Mostly the white folks stayed home with their window-shades down.

We pulled up the long drive to the funeral home. Sheriff Doggett leaned against the hood of his car, waiting.

"Don't say anything, boys." Dove coasted to a stop and opened his door. "Evening, John. Saw you on the news last night."

"Hey, Dove. Y'all all dressed up. Where you been?"

"Had some business in Montgomery," said Dove. "I took the boys with me. What's up?"

"I think you know," said the sheriff. He laid his hat on the hood and folded his arms. I had never noticed how big his arms were; he could break me in half if he decided to. "It's all over the goddamned radio. Grand jury indicted thirteen people this afternoon, ninety-eight counts. I got seven counts myself. What you think about that?"

Wiley and I climbed out to stand behind Dove.

"What's the charges?" Dove said.

"Something about conspiracy, violating some civil rights. I didn't get all of it. I figured you could fill me in on the details."

Dove shrugged. "They subpoenaed me to come up and testify as to cause of death in a couple of these cases. I told 'em exactly what I saw, just the way I wrote it in my reports. Which read when I wrote 'em."

"They're saying I was in the truck that shot up Nehemiah's place. You tell 'em that, Dove?"

"No, I didn't. They got that from somebody else. Is it true?"

The sheriff snorted. "I never touched a hair on anybody in my life, except in the line of duty."

"Well then, that should be easy to prove," Dove said.

"The FBI had an informer in that truck," said Doggett. "A rat. I know who was there, and I know what they done, but it wasn't me. This man is lying when he says it was me."

"I don't know anything about that," said Dove. "I went up there as coroner, like I told you. That's all."

"That ain't all. They called these boys, too. What did they want with them?"

"You sure have a good spy in Montgomery," Dove said. "Grand jury's supposed to be secret."

"It pays to have friends," Doggett said. "It might have paid you to think about that."

Dove turned. "Peter Joseph? Tell the sheriff what they asked you."

I said "They asked me about you."

"And what'd you tell 'em?"

"They wanted to know if you pushed Taylor down, you know, when he hit his head. I told 'em I thought he tripped and fell by himself."

"You damn right he did." The sheriff studied me through ice-blue eyes. "You hear that, Dove? They're trying to blame me for every nigger that ever hit his head in this county. Somebody is out to get me."

"It ain't me," said Dove.

"Maybe not. But you're helping them. And you know, Dove, I just cannot allow that."

Dove stiffened. "I don't know what you can do about it."

"Oh, I can come up with something." Doggett reached for his hat. "I got plenty of friends. When the word gets out on this, I bet you won't even have one."

"I'm not worried, John." Dove folded his arms. "I sleep real good at night."

Doggett said "I'm sleeping pretty good, myself. You know these charges'll never stick. There's plenty of judges that hate a nigger as much as anybody."

"If you're not worried, why'd you come out here bothering me?"

"Just wanted to make sure you got home safe." The coldness of his smile sent a shiver through me. "And also to tell you—they found that car

Lucille stole in New Orleans. She abandoned it in Las Vegas. We're getting close to her, Dove. I can smell it. We're gonna bring her back in. I can't wait."

"If that's all," Dove said, "I got work to do."

The sheriff tipped his hat and slid behind the wheel.

We watched him drive away.

"He's scared," Dove said. "Scared to death. I never would have expected it."

"He didn't look scared to me," Wiley said.

"Oh, but he is. He's got nothing to threaten us with. He knows he's in over his head."

We followed Dove into the old part of the house. He stopped in his tracks. "Wait a minute. Something is different in here."

"Look, the grandfather clock." I pointed to the unfaded stretch of wallpaper in the corner.

"What the hell?" He went to the door beneath the stairs and knocked with his fist. "Milton? You in there?"

No answer. Dove hastened up the stairs.

The door to the apartment stood wide open. Milton stood in the middle of the living room with a broom in his hand, a little mound of dust at his feet. The room had been stripped down to the floors and walls.

The blue-velvet sofa was gone, and the sheepskin rug, the armchairs, the Jetsons coffee table, lamps, pictures, barstools, the aquarium, all the bookshelves and books, the Jetsons chandelier, the air conditioners from the windows. Everything was gone except Dove's easy chair, the console TV, and the telephone.

Milton said "Hey, Mister Dove."

"Hello, Milton."

"Just sweeping up a little before y'all got back."

"I guess Earlene was here today, huh."

"Yes suh, she was. Her and that brother-in-law, what's his name? Mist' Francis? Him and a couple other fellas, they brung a truck."

"Well I reckon they did." Dove stepped into the room. "She flat cleaned me out, didn't she, Milton?"

"Yes suh, she did."

"Reckon why she left the TV?"

"She said she didn't have no place to put it. I tried to tell 'em, Mist' Dove, I sho did, I tol' 'em you'd want to have something to say about it, but you know what a sharp tongue that lady has. Shoo-ee."

"You're right about that. God knows I'd never expect anybody to stand in her way when she gets on a jag like this." He blew a heavy sigh. "How you like that, boys? Looks like we'll have to take turns sitting down."

"It's okay." My voice sounded hollow and wrong in the empty apartment. "There's all those folding chairs upstairs, remember?"

Wiley said, "Did all that stuff belong to her, Uncle Dove?"

His shoulders sagged. "I guess it did. Seems to me I remember paying for it." He went to the bedroom door. "She left me a bed, anyway. Thank you, sweetheart."

Milton tilted the dustpan in his hand, searching for someplace to dump it. Earlene had taken the garbage can from under the sink.

Wiley said, "I'll get those chairs," and hurried out.

Dove and Milton headed off to Vinegar Flat to pick up an old lady who'd died of the Chinese flu.

I sank into Dove's chair, easing the elastic band off my head. I could go for hours now without noticing the patch, but at night it felt like a steel cord that had squeezed on my brain all day. I reclined in the chair, rubbing my ears with my thumbs.

Wiley came in to watch "The Patty Duke Show," in which Patty played a set of identical cousins. I liked her in that movie about Helen Keller but this show was stupid. When they did one of those shots of her standing next to herself, she looked like a pair of awkward, uncomfortable girls.

"The Beverly Hillbillies" came on, brought to us by Kellogg's of Battle Creek.

Wiley did toe-touches while we watched TV. He was trying to build up his muscles. He seemed to have grown at least two inches since we came to Industry. That smudge-colored moustache grew in a little every day. He was beginning to resemble our daddy in the photograph.

"Peejoe. Tell me I'm seeing things."

I followed his finger to the television, where Jethro Bodine flirted with a poufy-haired blonde. He ogled her eye-popping figure in the snug, frilly dress.

"The blonde." Wiley moved to turn up the volume. "Tell me who that is."

"I don't care, Jethro," she said, "just as long as I can have a dose of those big old muscles of yours."

Oh, I'd know that voice anywhere. That voice told me a story I would never forget.

The makeup and hair made her look a little older, but yes oh yes sir that was Aunt Lucille in vivid black-and-white, snaking her long fingernails up the front of Jethro's checkered shirt.

They cut to a corn flakes commercial. I jumped out of my chair. "She swore she was going out there to get on that show, and she did it! Can you believe it?"

When the "Hillbillies" resumed, Mr. Drysdale the banker was all in a snit about something, Miss Jane smart-mouthing him as usual, Granny making preparations for a wedding. Elly May's critters kept getting in the way.

"Maybe that wasn't her after all," Wiley said.

But she appeared in the very next scene, confiding her scheme to a woman who was lacing her into a hoop-skirted wedding dress. "As soon as I'm Mrs. Jethro Bodine, that forty million is mine," she said. "It's only a matter of time before I have every one of these Clampetts wrapped around my little finger."

"It *is* her," I marveled. "She's pretty good!"

Wiley agreed. "I can't believe she did this."

"Well she's always said she would be a star—shh! Here she is again."

Lucille in her wedding dress glanced around to make sure no one was watching. She uncorked a jug marked XXXX, and took a slug from it. She made a very funny puckered-up face, followed by a slow woozy grin.

Then came a scene with all the Clampetts gathered in the entrance hall in their Sunday clothes, gazing expectantly up the curving staircase. Jethro looked nervous in his groom suit; he kept thinking up excuses to slip off, and Granny kept yanking him back into line. Someone played the "Wedding March" on a tuneless piano. Here came Elly May, beaming, tossing rose petals from a basket—and lo and behold, Aunt Lucille squeezed through that door in that wide wedding dress.

She took one step, lost her footing and tumbled all the way to the foot of the stairs, tumping Elly May over in the process.

We burst out laughing.

"Weeee doggie, Jethro, that gal shore is in a hurry to get down here and marry you," said Uncle Jed.

I clapped my hands. "Wow, she's great!"

Wiley shook his head in wonder. "Look here. She's drunk."

We watched and wondered, and laughed louder than the laugh track. That was our very own Aunt Lucille with her bridal veil at a funny angle, hiccupping and trying to stand up straight while the preacher spoke the wedding vows. She was the star of the show.

At the last moment Jethro got cold feet and ran off with a secretary from Mr. Drysdale's bank, leaving Lucille wailing at the altar. Granny patted her shoulder and offered another sip from the jug.

Then we were all invited back next week to that locality to have a heaping helping of their hospitality. "This's been a Filmways presentation," said Elly May.

Wiley and I stared at each other.

The phone rang.

I got there first. "Croaker-Moseley."

"Who is this?"—a rough voice.

"Peejoe. Who's this?"

"Let me talk to Dove."

The sheriff. The glow of Lucille's magical appearance winked out, all at once.

"Dove's not here."

"Yeah, where is he?"

"He went to pick up a body."

"Y'all happen to catch 'The Beverly Hillbillies'?" said the sheriff.

"No sir."

"Well I be damned if I didn't see Lucille Vinson on there," he said. "I been looking at her picture for a month, I'd know that face anywhere. She may be fast but she ain't too bright. Soon as I hang up this phone I'm calling my cousin Eddie in California. You tell Dove we'll have her back by the end of the week." He hung up without saying goodbye.

The moment I put down the phone, it rang again. Wiley grabbed it this time. "Hello? Oh hey, Meemaw," he said. "Yeah, we sure did! Did you see her? We couldn't believe it! She was good! Uh-huh. Uh-huh. Yeah, I think she called Peejoe the other night, she said she was in Florida. Mm-hmm. Yep. Oh, I guess he's okay for an idiot. The doctor—no, I don't know. Wait a minute. Here he is." He rolled his eyes, put the phone in my hand.

"Hey, Meemaw."

"Oh Sweet Pea, how are you? I've been so worried about you."

"I'm all right. I miss you."

"How's your eye today?"

"I think it's better. It doesn't hurt so much."

"Did you go to the doctor?"

"Yeah. He says it's blind."

"Well, Dove told me that, but I don't believe it. You'll see through it when it gets better. Are you being brave?"

"I guess so," I said.

"Let me talk to Dove."

"He's not here. He had to go get a body."

"Well put Earlene on, then."

"She's not here either. She moved out."

"Moved out? Child, what on earth is going on down there?"

"Oh, she got mad and took Mabel to her sister's house in Goshen. And Mabel's in the hospital. And Earlene came back today and took everything out of the house."

"You boys are there by yourself?"

"Yes ma'am. We're okay."

"Good Lord, honey, I just don't believe that you are," she said. "I had no idea things had come to such a pass. Dove hasn't told me any of this."

"The sheriff just called," I said. "He saw Aunt Lucille on TV, too."

"I daresay he did," she said, her voice rising. "The whole blessed world saw her making a fool of herself. I like to had a heart attack. Peejoe, Aunt Seale brought me your picture off that magazine. I don't like the idea of you down there all alone in all that."

"I'm not alone. Wiley's here."

"You tell Dove to call me the minute he walks in the door, you hear me? You wait up till he gets home." I heard children crying, and bossy old Sandra telling somebody what to do. "I'm going to sit by this phone until he calls me, you understand?"

"Yes ma'am."

"All right, Sweet Pea, goodnight now. Sweet dreams."

"Night, Meemaw."

I put down the phone. I don't know what ever made me think I wanted to be back at Meemaw's with all those Vinsons bouncing off the ceiling.

Wiley and I made Tater Tots and Kool-Aid for supper. We watched "The Danny Kaye Show" and dozed off on pillows we'd brought from upstairs.

Uncle Dove came home and found us asleep on the floor. "You boys go on up to bed."

"Meemaw called." I yawned, stretching up. "And the sheriff too. He saw Aunt Lucille on TV."

"He *what?*" He woke me up all the way and made me tell him everything. "Are you sure it was her?" he kept saying.

"It was her. I saw her, and so did Wiley, and Meemaw, and the sheriff, and . . ."

Wiley nodded his sleepy head in assent.

Dove said, "Baby Sister will never cease to amaze me."

27

Lucille

On the Road

Lucille counted out fourteen thousand eight hundred seventy-three dollars on the plush-velvet seat. She organized the bills into neat stacks, snapped rubber bands around them, and stuffed them into the canvas bag.

"Lou-see-yul . . ."

"Be quiet, Chester. I do not want to hear a peep out of you. I've had enough of your tricks."

"But honey, I love you so much," he purred. "I always loved you."

"The one glamorous evening of my entire life, and you had to ruin it. I'm just about through with your mess."

Once again Chester was sealed in his translucent bowl. Lucille should never have left him alone. She vowed to make certain the patented press-and-lock seal was not violated again. She couldn't quite get that odor out of her nose.

This latest exposure had changed her opinion of Tupperware's miraculous powers. Chester was unpretty in life, and a month in that plastic bowl had worked no improvement. He didn't seem hideous enough to send someone crashing through a plate-glass wall. But then again it wasn't Lucille's first look at him.

Maybe it was too much to ask any container to keep a head fresh and clean-smelling that long.

"It was the dogs," Chester muttered.

"I know you said something to them, or to that woman." She tucked the money bag into the tissue paper. "You couldn't have just sat quietly for an hour, could you."

"Little dogs," he said. "Little dogs with no hair."

"I could have stayed right there and become a fine comic actress," she said, although she knew it could never have happened that way, she'd been prepared to flee almost from the moment she arrived in Hollywood. All along she had known her luck was running entirely too fine to keep on that way.

Too bad Joan Blake had to wind up cut and bleeding in her swimming pool, but that would teach her to keep her big nose out of other people's hatboxes.

Once again Lucille was scanning the morning papers for reports of her criminal activity. Either Joan hadn't told the police what she saw, or Harry Hall had managed to keep it out of the papers. The only story of interest was an Associated Press interview with John Doggett, the famous racist sheriff of Industry. "We intend to keep this town the way it is for the benefit of our decent white people," he told the reporter. "It ain't my job to protect these outside agitators who come in here for the thrill of getting on Walter Cronkite."

If that was the man in charge of her pursuit, maybe Lucille didn't have so much to worry about.

The privacy window slid down. "Did you say something, Miss Clay?"

"Just talking to myself."

Norman stole a glance over his shoulder. "You're lovely today. That color brings out the blue in your eyes."

"That's enough, now. Remember our agreement." She smoothed the pink cashmere skirt. "Put the window up and drive on."

Lucille had checked out of the Beverly Hills as quickly as possible without appearing to be a panic-stricken murderess in flight. She paid the bill in cash. She had no idea where she would go next, or how to get there.

When she stepped out between the stone monkeys and saw Norman leaning against his limousine, it struck her as a literal signal from God and she took it. She told him she'd be glad to accept a ride—as long as he stayed up front and left her alone and dispensed with all his talk of love. She told him to drive north.

That first night they took rooms at opposite ends of a dreadful beach motel near Santa Barbara, with chintz-rose wallpaper and filthy rag rugs. Norman went out for Kentucky Fried Chicken, which they ate on a concrete picnic table overlooking the great pounding Pacific. A chilly breeze off the water raised gooseflesh on Lucille's arms.

Norman said he'd sold his trailer home in Las Vegas so he could follow Lucille to the ends of the earth.

"I know I'm just your driver, for now," he said, gnawing a chicken wing, "but I mean to be much more than that."

"Don't start in." Lucille spooned mashed potatoes from a Styrofoam cup. "You can take me as far as San Francisco, and then we have to go our separate ways."

Lucille had an idea, and San Francisco was the place for it. Norman offered a way to get there, nothing more. She was using him, using his doggish eagerness and his limousine—but at least she was honest about it, she hadn't given him any illusions.

The next day they drove a hundred miles out of the way to take a look at the home of William Randolph Hearst, a great stone pile looming at the top of a mountain. Herds of giraffe and springbok roamed the vast grounds.

They checked into the Hearst Castle Motel, near the main gate. They sat outside at twilight, eating burgers and fries, reading the tourist pamphlets. Lucille thought it would be wonderful to be so rich you gave your house to the state of California when you died, because no one on earth could afford to buy it.

"I'd like to be that rich someday," she said.

"Stick with me and maybe you will," Norman said. "I get these lucky streaks at craps sometimes."

"I'm tired, Norman. I'll go on to bed now. Goodnight."

"Sleep well. I'll stay out here awhile."

She didn't tell him what was coming on TV in six minutes. She didn't want him to watch it. What if her performance was awful? She would see it in his eyes. He would pretend she was good, but she would know.

She put the chain on the door. She switched on the set, adjusted the wire coathanger for a clearer picture, and settled down on the stiff mattress. This place was a long way from the Beverly Hills Hotel.

The "Hillbillies" came on. Lucille watched herself moving and talking onscreen, a luminous electric dream.

To her surprise, she was not awful. She looked silly with that huge hair and the clunky costume jewelry, but she seemed just as competent as anyone else on the show. The editors had clipped the scenes together so everything happened quickly. Even her tumble down the stairs looked like smart comic timing; a quick cut to Buddy Ebsen and the laugh track exploded. Lucille wanted to call her mother and crow about it, but she was sure they'd have a trace on that line by now, and she was trying seriously now to avoid getting caught.

She knew Norman was out there sitting on his hood, smoking cigarettes and gazing at the light in her window. In some ways, he was the perfect traveling companion: He anticipated her moods, he understood when she wanted to be left alone, he never complained or got tired of driving. He could have taught Chester a thing or two about traveling.

She snapped off the bedside lamp and peered out at the comfortable glow of his cigarette. She heard a soft chuckle in the darkness; the whinny of zebras settling in for the night beyond the walls of the Hearst place.

There wasn't much joy in seeing her Big Moment on TV all alone in this strange place, far from the people who cared about her. What good did it do to become a star when she couldn't share it with anyone? She had thought just doing it would be enough of a thrill, but when it came time to enjoy it she was hiding out in a knotty-pine room with traffic whizzing by on the highway.

28

Peejoe

Industry

Wiley and I were fighting a duel with curtain rods in the attic. He stopped in mid-lunge. "Listen to that."

Voices carried on the breeze from the swimming pool, ten blocks away—a chorus of hundreds raised up singing "We Shall Overcome."

I took advantage of the distraction to make a parry which knocked Wiley off balance and flat on his back. I put the tip of my sword to his throat. "I could kill you right now."

"Yeah, you're getting pretty good with one eye." He got up. "Wait till I start fighting for real."

The sea of voices rose through the window. "Sounds like more people today, Wiley. Let's go down there."

"You know what Dove said."

"He's not here." Lately Dove spent his afternoons off with Milton at Bates's Pond, drinking bourbon and fishing for croakers. "Let's go see if Huntley-Brinkley's still in town."

"You better hope the sheriff doesn't see us," said Wiley.

"I'm not afraid of him." I was Mr. Big Talk since the indictments, although the prospect of John Doggett actually spending a night behind bars was looking pretty dim. The district judge in Montgomery just happened to be Doggett's first cousin's next-door neighbor. He delayed Hiram Murphy's federal charges until Doggett and the others could be tried for misdemeanors in Industry, "site of the alleged crimes."

A lawsuit to force the integration of the swimming pool was stalled on the desk of a second judge.

The waters of protest were rising faster in the streets of town. Once the sheriff saw that ignoring the marchers wasn't going to make them go away, he began arresting them in big batches, dozens at a time. The cells on the second floor of the courthouse overflowed with prisoners, as did the National Guard Armory on Cornelia Road and jails in four neighboring counties.

As fast as the sheriff could arrest them, fresh busloads of demonstrators arrived from the North to take their places on the marching line. Industry had become famous across the nation, like Selma and Birmingham, made even more notorious by the spectacle of the sheriff and his twelve grinning co-defendants at their preliminary hearing: feet propped on the courtroom rail, taking chaws from pouches of Red Man, they looked like good old redneck boys who weren't the least concerned about the charges against them.

Already so much had been written and said about Industry that my face on *Life* was no longer a big deal, except to me. (I still received a couple of sympathy letters every day.) The story of Taylor Jackson's spontaneous sit-in at the swimming pool was printed up in all the shiny magazines as a Profile in Courage. "He was barely sixteen, hardly the sort of boy you'd expect to start a revolution," wrote Shana Alexander in *Look*. The sorrowful face of Nehemiah Thomas peered through the bars of his cell in the pages of *Newsweek*. The *New York Times* ran a four-part series: "Industry—Town on the Brink."

At first, the white citizens of Industry reacted as if General Sherman was lobbing artillery shells at them from the Old Goshen Road. They locked themselves tight in their homes and came out only for supply runs to the Piggly Wiggly. But as days passed and the demonstrators marched harmlessly from the courthouse to the swimming pool and back again, producing speeches and mass arrests and plenty of noise but no real danger, the people began to get used to it. They began to go about their business as if what was happening downtown was some kind of long-drawn-out county fair.

Some of them even enjoyed the attention. Along with the hordes of reporters and marchers came a rumble of trucks bearing the CBS eye and the NBC peacock. Half the town had turned out to see David Brinkley broadcasting from the parking lot of the Dairy Dog.

It became fashionable to have been interviewed by Brinkley or Frank Reynolds or one of the other big-name TV reporters, to say something moderate about how Industry didn't deserve its reputation, a few bad apples et cetera. Dove said he wished Earlene could be here to see the ladies competing with each other to invite the best newsmen to dinner. It was widely believed that good Southern cooking would melt the heart of the chilliest Yankee reporter, although there was no sign of that happening yet.

Even George Corley Wallace was fuming and sputtering the name of Industry from his mansion in Montgomery. He issued proclamations vowing to maintain law and order and the rights of the state. In a speech to the legislature, he warned that the "kid-glove treatment" afforded the Selma-to-Montgomery marchers was a thing of the past. "We will no longer tolerate these unwarranted, unjustified, Communist-inspired intrusions on our great way of life here in Alabama," he said. "If the good people of Industry want to swim in their swimming pool with people of their own race, I say it's none of Washinton's business. And if I have to go down there personally to show 'em what I mean, I will."

Wiley and I ambled down Lee Street. The singing gave way to an amplified voice, someone making a speech. We had tried to keep our promise to Dove, but this excitement was too much temptation. The funeral home was empty, too quiet. There weren't even any dead people now. The ghosts had departed with Mabel. The Muzak organist had fallen silent and nobody had bothered to fix the machine.

Bluejays screamed from the trees. An old colored man was down on his knees, edging a sidewalk with a hatchet. He nodded hello as we passed. A voice echoed down the street, ". . . in the name of freedom and justice, we call upon them to do that which they were elected to do . . . " and a roar of applause like a football game.

The old man cocked his ear to listen.

We passed among television vans at the corner of Beauregard and Lee. Black cables snaked along the ground, and a generator throbbed, as on a carnival midway. The field around the swimming pool was a sea of marchers, preachers, church groups, reporters, earnest young men in dark suits, girls with multiple pigtails, Yankee nuns bearing placards, pasty white people in sunglasses, schoolkids, old colored ladies, white students, vagrants, journalists. Dignitaries crowded a plywood platform at the fence. Everyone milled about or ate fried chicken on quilts on the ground. Children chased dogs. A line of state troopers and Cotton County deputies watched everything from the Dairy Dog hill.

The speaker railed on about injunctions and court orders. Wiley and I found a place to stand, a patch of trampled grass to one side of the stage, not far from the spot where Taylor Jackson fell.

I recognized Lydia Combs on the platform. In her colorful ankle-length African robe and white turban she was impossible to miss.

As if I had reached out and touched her shoulder, she turned and noticed me there—she waved over the heads of the crowd. I waved back.

The people nearby turned to stare. When they saw the patch on my eye, they edged away whispering.

Everyone seemed to be waiting for something. People glanced back to the rear of the crowd, the troopers on the hill, the street.

The speaker wound up his talk to a nice splash of applause. The Eufaula A.M.E. choir led the crowd singing "Over my head I see freedom in the air."

A line of cars appeared at the top of the hill, cruising slowly down toward us. A shiny black Chevrolet led the way. It turned at the gate and nudged into the crowd, which parted like the Red Sea in the movie. Heads turned. The freedom song trailed off in midair. An excited mutter raced through the crowd—"The king is coming! The king is coming!"

The motorcade circled through the park, heading toward the fence through a rising ovation. The black Chevrolet crept to a stop within ten feet of Wiley and me. The crowd swelled with the thrill. Everybody dropped their fried chicken and jumped to their feet, craning to see.

Then I understood what they were saying: *Doctor* King is coming.

A bunch of colored men in dark suits piled out of the cars and gathered around the Chevrolet. They were preachers, you could tell from the self-important way they hiked their trousers and gazed around with their thumbs in their lapels.

I saw him step out of the car.

He looked just like on TV, maybe a little heavier, low to the ground. His skin was brown and shiny as an old church pew, his features strange and beautiful and oddly Oriental somehow, the striking almond-shaped eyes and the strong, broad nose, skinny Fu Manchu moustache emphasizing the fullness of his lips.

He slipped into a dark suit-jacket held for him by one of the preachers. He glanced over the crowd, sizing it up. Someone whispered in his ear. He said, "All right, let's go talk to these folks," in a commanding voice that stood my hair up like static electricity.

The men arranged themselves around him and ushered him through the cheering throng.

Wiley said, "So that's what this is all about."

I was awestruck. "Man, we were that close to him! I could have got his autograph!"

My whole life I had heard his name spoken with fear or disgust. Now I saw a special light around him, a spotlight from the clear blue sky that touched him when he stepped from that car, and followed him up to that stage.

He greeted Nehemiah's sons, Mattie Jackson, Lydia Combs, Preacher Williams, the choir. He took a moment with each person, grasping hands, hugging necks. People flocked toward him, trampling blankets and treading on toes in the rush. Photographers ran clanking cameras.

He turned to acknowledge the cheers of the multitude with a modest smile and his hands up, a teacher trying to quiet an unruly class—then, failing at that, he clasped his hands behind his back and stood patiently waiting for the uproar to subside.

At last he moved to the microphone. "Thank you very kindly, my friends." His voice rang over the field, golden and clear. "I'm delighted to see so many of you here today, and delighted to be here myself. Brother Lambert was reminding me on the ride into town that I preached a sermon down the road here in Lowndes County in nineteen fifty-five, and as he said, I've come a mighty long way around to get back to where I started."

Appreciative laughter rippled the crowd.

"My friends," he said, "the news of what is happening in Industry has sounded and resounded around the whole world. As I stand here and look out upon your faces, I am reminded of the great peoples throughout history who have stood up against the forces of tyranny and oppression. I see the faces of the people of Israel, hiding behind the bloodstains on their doors that first Passover evening. I see the face of Moses as he cried 'Let my people go!' and led the Israelites into the desert of a doubtful future. I see the faces of Negro slaves in the last century, right here in this very land, the sweat-stained faces of our forefathers who were sold and traded like cattle, who seized upon the proclamation of an uncertain President as a means to achieve their own freedom."

His words flowed like improvised music, the pitch muted at first but rising above the rapt congregation. Every face tilted up to him. "And my friends, when I look out upon you I see the great heroes who have made their mark upon our own time. I see a shy and soft-spoken lady in Montgomery who refused to move to the back of the bus. I see the young students in Greensboro who sat down at a segregated lunch counter and declined to get up, for forty-three days. I see the elderly lady on our march from Selma to Montgomery, who turned down the offer of a ride with these words: 'My feets is tired, but my soul is rested.' I see all the thousands who have marched—in Alabama, in Georgia and Carolina and Tennessee and Mississippi, in all the great and tormented states of the old Confederacy, in this historic movement to win the full measure of our freedom."

The crowd burst into applause and shouts of "Amen!" The sun blazed down from the top of the sky. Martin Luther King mopped his face with a white handkerchief from his breast-pocket.

"Now today we are here, as Abraham Lincoln once said, we are met on a great battlefield of our own war. Thousands of boys died at Gettysburg for our right to be free. Only one boy, a Negro boy named Taylor Jackson, died at this pool. But I have come today to tell you that just like those boys at Gettysburg, Taylor Jackson did not die in vain. And our war is not over yet."

Mattie Jackson burst into tears.

King's voice rang to the trees: "Taylor Jackson's act of courage was the great and immortal last act of a tragically foreshortened life. By this singular act, Taylor Jackson has awakened in all of us who seek freedom the desire to keep moving, the desire to keep marching, the desire to keep struggling, to keep scaling the walls of injustice—no matter where we find them, no matter how high they may be."

I had never heard preaching like this. He pronounced each word like a separate note from a fine brass trumpet. His voice soared to the heights of a sentence then flew back down to rest at the end, gaining strength for the next flight. He held me in a spell. I was alone on that field. He was speaking only to me.

"Now, I may not have been here with you to fight this battle," he said. "I may have been off tending to battles on other battlefields, but today I am here. Today I have come to bring you news of a sweet victory. Today your efforts have overcome another wall of injustice. Today I bring you word that Judge Johnson in Montgomery has issued an order for the integration of the Industry municipal swimming pool."

A wild cheer went up. People hollered and stomped the ground, embracing, waving signs. I peered through the fence. The pool had been drained of its water, the sloping floor littered with leaves.

"Today I bring you the news that Judge Johnson has further ordered the release of our brother Nehemiah Thomas and all the other peaceful demonstrators within thirty-six hours."

The crowd erupted all over again. The celebration went on for a long time before he was allowed to continue.

"Now, these are glad tidings," he said, "but our work is not done. Our work is only beginning. We will have hard times ahead. We will have trials ahead, we will have tribulations. But today I have come to Industry to make a promise to you. We *shall* overcome."

An ovation started at the back and washed up, crashing over the stage. King seized the wave at its height.

"We *shall* overcome the highest walls of hatred and oppression that men can build in this land!" he cried. "We *shall* overcome the tyranny of men like Sheriff John Doggett, men like Jim Clark and Bull Connor and George Wallace, who seek to destroy us and in so doing sow the seeds of their own destruction. We *shall* overcome the walls that keep one race divided from another, to the everlasting shame and detriment of both. We *shall* overcome the arrogance of power and the indifference of wealth—and with our golden sword of nonviolence we *shall* overcome the violence of those who would try to stop us. God is on our side. Mine eyes have seen the glory of the coming of the Lord! Glory, glory hallelujah!" He swept his hand up in the air and stumbled back a step, overcome by the power of his own words.

The crowd went delirious. A lady beside me cried "Lawd Jesus!" over and over, slapping her hands together. Babies screamed at the uproar.

It was all so simple when King explained it. How could anyone hear him and fail to understand? It was as plain as the difference between a white man and a Negro, between night and day, sight and blindness, right and wrong.

On one side was this man with his mighty words and a thousand people roaring for him.

On the other side, at the top of the hill, a clutch of lawmen with guns, a few redneck teenagers in pickup trucks—they didn't stand a chance. They would lose. They were wrong, and they were bound to lose in the end.

I took Wiley by the arm and pulled him through the crowd to the black Chevrolet. I didn't understand the feeling, but I knew I had to put myself in the path of that man. I had to get near him, to touch him, to get myself a piece of that light shining down on him.

He was mobbed coming down from the platform. His escort of preachers broke apart in the human surge. Mothers held out their babies. Old ladies embraced him. Young men strained past each other to touch his hand. King took his time, greeting everybody, carrying the mass of people along with him down the fence. Lydia Combs steered him by the elbow, introducing him to people in the crowd.

Suddenly a hole opened up.

Lydia spotted me there.

"Doctor King," she said, "this is the boy who was on *Life* magazine, remember? This boy stood up for Taylor Jackson."

The world took a deep breath, and held it.

He reached out to my face—a soft, tentative touch, almost a caress. "Young friend," he said with a smile. "You keep doing good things and you'll come out all right."

I tried to say *thank you*. My mouth wouldn't work. His fingers brushed my cheek and then he was gone, moving off through the crowd.

I felt a glow where his fingers had touched me. I felt a warmth spreading out from that spot, over the front of my face. He was a holy man. He touched me. He healed my eye with his touch.

I floated over to the fence, sat down with my back against the chain links. I yanked off the eyepatch.

Wiley followed. "What's the matter?"

"Nothing. Wait a minute."

Closing my good eye, I prayed: *let it be true*. I put my thumb to the adhesive tape and unstuck one corner of the bandage. I opened the bad eye, straining to see . . .

Nothing. Only that blank greenish mist. I lifted the flap of the bandage.

The eye was still blind.

I smoothed the tape into place.

"Is it hurting you?" Wiley said.

"Nope." I hid my disappointment. It just wasn't going to be that easy. Just because that man walked onto a field full of people and worked them up to a pitch of exaltation, just because his voice had the power to raise the hairs on my head—that didn't mean he had worked a miracle on my eye.

From the podium a man cried "What do we want?"

The crowd roared the answer: *Freedom!*

"And when do we want it?"

Now!

Wiley insisted my eye must be bothering me or I wouldn't be messing with it. I didn't tell him what I had imagined.

"What do we want?" *Freedom!* "When do we want it?" *Now!*

"Jesus, Peejoe, look at these folks." The speech had detonated over their heads like a bomb, scattering them across the field, but the rhythm of the chant was pulling them back together, drowning out the questions until all I could hear were feet stomping and people shouting *Freedom! Now! Freedom! Now!*

The motorcade bumped across the field to the road.

A gang of boys chased the Chevrolet to the top of the hill. When they flagged and dropped back, a formation of state troopers peeled off and swung in behind the last car.

Preacher Lambert announced that Doctor King would speak again at a mass meeting Saturday night to welcome Nehemiah Thomas out of jail. All were invited.

Lydia Combs hiked her robe to step up to the stage. I studied her proud profile, her piercing dark eyes sweeping the congregation as she held up her hand and began to sing:

> *Oh-h-ho freedom,*
> *Oh freedom,*
> *Oh freedom over me*
> *And before I'd be a slave*
> *I'd be buried in my grave*
> *And go home to my Lord and be free.*

It was a day for stunning performances. Lydia's deep strong voice carried those words out over the park and the pool and the assembled masses. She called a new line for the second verse—"No more segregation!"—and the crowd swelled to join her.

> *No more segregation,*
> *No more segregation,*
> *No more segregation over me . . .*

Wiley and I headed the long way around the empty pool. I thought of the distant afternoon when I came up from the deep end to find myself alone in the water with two black boys. Who would have imagined that before the summer got really hot I would stand beside that fence to hear Martin Luther King preaching about what happened that day?

The world is strange, in strange ways.

King had not healed my eye, but he'd given me a new way of looking at things. Now I saw that the trouble in Industry was part of an old, old trouble, a war that had been going on everywhere for a long time now. It was an amazing idea: the Civil War had never really ended, it had just died down for a while. Now it was back, skirmishes breaking out all around us. Everybody was fighting on one side or the other.

At last I understood what made Taylor Jackson so important. He died just as dead as those boys in Gettysburg, and *for the same cause.* When those soldiers fell, when Taylor sat down by that fence, when Dove put Bessie Lou Stringfellow in his hearse, when he put me in front of that grand jury to tell what I'd seen—we were all fighting our own battles in the same war.

Dove and Wiley and I were fighting on the side of the Negroes, the Yankees, Hiram Murphy, Lyndon Johnson, and Martin Luther King. Dove had led us into this fight as Taylor Jackson had stepped up to that fence, blindly risking everything by the simple act of doing what he thought was right. Dove was a hero, like Taylor, like the heroes in King's sermon. Nobody knew this but me.

We cut through the bushes where we had encountered the men with their guns. Wiley said "Man, I've never heard a speech like that. He almost made you want to be black."

"Did you hear what he said to me?"

"I heard. You like everybody making a fuss over your eye, don't you?" He leaped in the air to swat at leaves.

"I got to meet him, didn't I?"

"I could have too, if I'd wanted," said Wiley. "I noticed you didn't have much to say."

"You're right. My tongue got stuck."

We walked up Beauregard Avenue. The old man was still on his knees, edging the same stretch of sidewalk. He greeted us as if nothing had changed.

29

Lucille

On the Road

L ucille lowered the windows to see the fat oval sun hanging low on the shining Pacific, the green mountains folding to the east. California seemed too beautiful to be part of the same country as Cornelia, Alabama. She wished she could build a house on one of these cliffs overlooking the rock-littered ocean, a rounded-off house of pink adobe like the houses she'd seen in New Mexico, with a courtyard and New Orleans–style cast-iron railings. But she could not afford to linger anywhere now. The open road was her home.

Tonight she would rid herself of Chester once and for all. Tomorrow find a ship and book passage. She would sail west toward the sun, so far west she would reach the Far East, and then she would lose herself among the numberless peoples of the earth.

For a while there in Hollywood, Lucille had allowed a certain fatalism to undermine her confidence. She felt powerless to keep the doors from slamming shut in front of her, one after the other. She had to goad herself into finding another way out. Everything she'd done, every sweet moment in these weeks of freedom had been the direct result of her spontaneous actions. She renewed the fierce vow she had made to Mama and Dove: *They are not going to catch me.*

Every cop, every innocent bystander in every coastside town was in danger as Lucille rolled through, on the run from the law, the loaded .45 tucked within easy reach between the seat-cushions. Just let somebody try to stop her.

Lucille had discovered the very slim line dividing a basically sweet-tempered woman from a desperate killer. She knew just how easy it was to step over that line and step back. She felt sure she could do whatever she needed to do. She feared nobody and nothing in the world, except maybe this highway threading so close to the cliffs that the limousine threatened to take off and fly.

She pressed the intercom button. "Norman, for God's sake slow down."

"Don't worry," his voice crackled back. "I'm a very good driver. Never even had a speeding ticket."

The dizzying curves gave way to a long easy stretch through the beach town of Santa Cruz. Lucille relaxed her grip on the armrest to admire the lacy rollercoaster, the long pier, the expanse of grayish sand. Way off on the horizon was the cardboard silhouette of a cargo ship, bound for Japan.

The glass panel eased down. "How about a little stroll on the beach?"

"No, thank you," she said. "I'm getting anxious to get there. How much longer?"

"About an hour, I think."

"Let's keep going," she said. "Do you mind?"

"I guess I'm just not ready to say goodbye yet." Norman wore a fresh white shirt, a striped green tie, a red cap to cover his bald spot. "I've been enjoying myself so much I don't even want to think about saying goodbye."

"Have you ever been to San Francisco, Norman?"

"One time, with my first wife Doreen. We took a cruise from there to Hawaii. It's a great-looking city, or it was then. Lots of steep hills, the cable cars. This was years ago."

"How many wives have you had?"

"Three. Three wonderful ladies. I wasn't worthy of any of them."

"Did they clean you out?"

"Only the last one," he said. "The first two treated me all right, considering what a trial I can be."

She sought his eyes in the mirror. "Did you ever want to kill one of 'em?"

"Oh you bet, plenty of times. Matter of fact, with my third wife Barbara, just about every night for the last couple years."

"You never did anything about it, did you."

"Oh no. I guess you had some rough times with your husband, too, huh."

"I surely did."

"What'd he do, hit on you?"

"Sometimes. Not that much. It was more like he kept me in a cage. Like some pet of his, some dumb animal he trained to do his tricks. He laughed at every good idea I ever had. He thought I was silly."

"I don't know how a man could think that," said Norman. "I think you're just about perfect."

"If that's what you think," Lucille said, "you don't know me at all."

She raised the privacy window and settled back in the seat to decide what to do about Norman. Sometimes his infatuation got on her nerves. Other times she was grateful. Without knowing exactly what he was doing, Norman had aided and abetted her escape, and Lucille felt she owed him something for that.

She couldn't just settle a nice chunk of money on him and send him off with a wave, could she? Didn't he deserve something more than that?

She could think of only one thing that might really satisfy the requirements of this transaction. She wouldn't have to give him the whole caboodle—with men of his generation a round of flirting and making out would provide sufficient amusement for a lot of cold winter nights. Maybe tonight, after she was rid of Chester, she would share a bottle of wine with Norman at dinner and give him something warm and sweet to remember her by. She smiled at the joy that would bring him.

All that remained was her farewell to Chester. Since the moment she found him in the back seat north of Mobile, she'd clung to him as resolutely as he had clung to her. The thought of discarding him had flickered through her mind a hundred times, but every time she passed up a chance to act, it became more impossible.

Once, Lucille had managed to convince herself that D-Con in Chester's coffee was the only way out of her misery. Lately she had come to believe that the presence of his head was somehow connected to her good fortune. She had grown comfortable sharing her adventures with him. They got along much better than at any time when they were married. Until the party in the Hollywood Hills, he had brought her nothing but wonderful luck.

Then in one sordid moment he revealed himself, and her crime. He lit up her foolishness like a stroke of lightning in a dead nighttime landscape. She saw that hanging on to Chester was taking her nowhere but down.

She'd had the courage to kill him, and to get that head off the body, but after that, her nerve had failed. She hadn't been able to take the final step: living without him. She carried him around as a token of her accomplishment, the way a child proudly carries her Crayola drawings and swim-meet ribbons and Girl Scout honor pins.

Lucille knew she had no choice but to lose him in a way that would make sure he never came back.

She chose the place from a souvenir postcard book called "Great Sights of California." She bided her time, approaching San Francisco by the most circuitous route, preparing herself to face her two largest fears: the fear of high places, the fear of discarding Chester. If she could conquer both these fears she would truly be free.

The road wound among treeless brown hills, like the backs of great sleeping animals, and down to a wide stretch of beach. The ocean pounded big waves on the sand. On the other side evergreen trees bent like old people leaning out of the wind.

This wildness abruptly gave way to the city, flat-roofed rowhouses painted bright blue and saffron and rose. This place was like an illustration of a fantastic kingdom from a fairy tale, its colors warmed by the setting sun. Wispy dream-clouds blew in from the Pacific, grazing the tops of the hills. Pink cliffs rose up sheer from the beach.

Norman steered the limousine up a steep road carved into the cliff. Lucille turned in her seat to watch the ocean drop away.

A sign announced: THE PRESIDIO, US ARMY PRESERVE, ALL VEHICLES SUBJECT TO INSPECTION.

They went over a rise. On the left side the earth fell away to a stunning view, two majestic ranges of hills separated by the wide, wide mouth of a bay, and spanned by the grandest structure Lucille had ever seen: the Golden Gate Bridge. In power and grace it was greater than the Pontchartrain Bridge and the Hoover Dam and all the bridges and roads and cities of the West put together—a pair of soaring red towers spreading their wings between two distant shores, bearing a glittering river of traffic at an unimaginable height over the water.

Lucille mashed the intercom button. "Pull over."

Norman eased the limousine to the curb. Lucille stepped out. Of course she had seen pictures, but the pictures couldn't convey the incredible drama of those hills plunging into the sea, a roadway suspended on gossamer threads.

Far below, a huge tanker steamed out to sea, insignificant as a toy.

Norman's window glided down. "Quite a sight, huh?"

Lucille got back in the car. "That's where I want to go. Take me there."

The privacy window slid down. "You want to go to the Golden Gate Bridge?"

"There's something I have to do," said Lucille. "It won't take long."

He drove on. "You're not thinking of taking off on me, are you, Miss Clay?"

"No, Norman, not yet. Not till tomorrow, I promise. I thought tonight we might go out to dinner. You know, our last night and all."

He glanced over the seat. "You mean it?"

She smiled. "You've been awfully nice to me. Keep your eyes on the road." She reached down in the floor, lifted the hatbox by its ribbons.

The bridge was too awful high, just looking at it made Lucille queasy. But she had to do this. This was the time and the place. Dozens of people made a pilgrimage every year to fling themselves off this bridge, because of its height and the view and the certainty that anybody smacking that water would die instantly, be swept out to sea and never found. That was what Lucille wanted for Chester: a hard smack, followed by a strong current sucking him out into the deep where he would never bother anyone again.

It seemed easy enough. The bridge builders had provided a wide sidewalk all the way across, with only a chest-high railing.

Now Lucille had to summon the nerve to walk out on that bridge by herself, and do it. She gathered the memories of all the brave and foolish things she had done. The towers peeped at her over the tops of fir trees. She felt the Golden Gate Bridge daring her to walk on it.

There were earthquakes out here in this country, the kind of great shakes that could plunge a city into rubble and send a bridge like this to its knees. Wouldn't it be some kind of justice for an earthquake to strike while Lucille was out there disposing of the evidence?

That would be justice beyond any argument. There was no use speculating about something like that. If you want to get rid of a nightmare, you have to trust the bridge, you have to trust the men who built the bridge, you have to trust God not to shake the bridge down while you are out on it.

Norman pulled in at a gift shop shaped like a flying saucer. The bridge towers gazed down at Lucille, winking red lights.

She checked out the nice clean drop from the railing to the black water. She was glad she had waited for this place.

"You sure you want to stop here?" Norman said.

"Oh, yes. I've thought about this a long time," Lucille said. "I just hope I have the nerve."

He turned with an odd look on his face. "The nerve for what? What are you gonna do?"

"I have something to get rid of, Norman. I should have done it a long time ago, but I've waited and waited, and now I don't have any choice."

She opened the rear door and stepped out with the Maison Blanche hatbox in hand. "It would take me too long to explain."

Norman got out, too. "Let me go with you."

"No. I have to do this by myself. You stay right here. I'll be back before you know it."

A few tourists in the parking lot turned to stare at the limousine. Lucille hurried up the steps to the walkway. A cold wind was blowing up here—she wished for one of the mink coats she'd seen in Maison Blanche—but she intended to make quick work of this and get back to the limousine.

The sidewalk provided a clear view of the toll plaza with its big neon-handed clock and the cars bustling through. The roar and bluster of all those cars put Lucille off balance for a moment. She grabbed the guard-rail to steady herself.

The bridge was cold to the touch. She felt a current in the steel, a vibration. She could do this, as long as she thought of it as a sidewalk beside a busy highway and ignored the terrifying truth of the matter.

She tightened her grip on the hatbox. "Okay, here we go," she said aloud, to get herself started. A truck blew by, sending her skittering ahead with the force of its wind. Lucille followed up those steps with actual steps of her own, one foot in front of the other, the first steps of her march toward freedom.

The sun had slipped into the ocean when she wasn't looking. The sky glowed pink and soft blue. Ferryboats sparkled in the bay; a beacon flashed on an island of rock. As Lucille made her way from the approach onto the bridge itself, the full glimmering panorama of San Francisco slid into view. For a moment she forgot Chester and everything else in the thrill of that city encrusting the hills like a forest of jewels, polished, fitted together.

Stepping up to the rail, she dared a peek down. She was still over land, looking straight down into the courtyard of a star-shaped brick fortress. She could see tiny people walking around down there, a rim of white surf beating against rocks on the shore.

She kept walking.

Where the bridge passed out over open water, Lucille felt her knees weaken. She swallowed hard. Trucks and buses roared by. She drew a line with her eyes down the middle of the sidewalk, and walked straight ahead on that line, counting until she reached forty.

She stopped.

She had planned to go all the way to the middle of the bridge, but that looked about a mile away, there were lights around that first tower. Anyway she must be three hundred feet above the water right here.

She had an urge to heave the box over and make a run for it, but after days of pondering she had decided she'd have to take the Tupperware bowl out of the hatbox and pop open the lid before consigning Chester to the deep. Otherwise that press-and-lock seal would keep him afloat on an air bubble, and Chester would bob right up to the next boat that happened by.

She thought she heard his whisper "Lou-see-yul" but it was lost in the rush of wind. Out here the vibration was strong. The bridge swayed for real.

Lucille fumbled with the ribbons. The box-lid whipped off in the wind and sailed down, down into darkness. She followed it down with her eyes.

A car horn blared.

She scooped her hand down in the box—oh but Chester was so heavy now. She got a grip underneath and brought the Tupperware bowl up from its nest of tissue paper.

Too late she noticed the drawstring of the canvas bag tangled around her hand. When she lifted the bowl from the box, the bag dropped away.

Oh dear God.

She stuck her head over the railing. Just below the sidewalk was a steel beam about eighteen inches wide. Fourteen thousand dollars now rested on this ledge, an inch or two from infinity.

"Son of a bitch." She placed the hatbox on the sidewalk, and wedged Chester down in it to keep him from rolling away.

She returned to the rail. Now wasn't that pretty. Lucille's entire fortune on the wrong side of a railing.

The next gust of wind might blow it all away.

This was more of a test than Lucille had imagined for herself.

She could do it. She could. It was like acting. She was on Mama's place back home. The steel railing was the split-rail fence in the back pasture. Inside the fence was an angry bull, pawing the ground. All Lucille had to do was leg-up and over the fence, keeping a tight hold at all times, crouch down, retrieve the canvas bag, and hop the fence to the safety of Mama's yard before the bull started to charge.

There was never any question that fourteen thousand dollars was enough money to send her over a railing on the Golden Gate Bridge. That money would buy her freedom.

She put one toe in the bottom rail and hiked herself up. As she swung her leg over she heard the screech of tires. She looked down to find a place for her foot, gripping the rail so tightly that her hands would ache for days.

She willed her left hand from the top rail to a supporting rung, and groped for the bag. She found it at once, thank you Jesus. She brought it up, dropped it over the rail, then slowly raised herself to a standing position.

She heard a shout from a passing car: "Jump!"

For a moment she forgot where to put her hand, she forgot how on earth she'd ever managed to swing her leg over that rail. Jump, he said. Perfect stranger. No idea at all about her, nothing other than "jump!"

Don't look down, Lucille. Get a grip. Bring your leg up and over. You are on the wrong side of Mama's fence and the bull is stampeding.

Maybe she should take the stranger's advice. Maybe she should let go and sail over backwards and fall through time and space to the hard smack on the water she had planned for Chester. But no, that made her furious! How dare he tell her to jump! He just wanted the pleasure of watching her fall!

Gritting her teeth, Lucille brought her leg up and over, and dropped to the safe side of the rail. She seized the canvas bag and slowly got to her feet, too wobbly to see the man in uniform who sailed out of the darkness and tackled her.

They landed thud! on the sidewalk. Traffic screamed to a stop.

"Let me go!" Lucille struggled. He held her fast in his strong arms, front to back, a long lanky man in a blue uniform. His cap and glasses had come off in the tackle. On the cap was a patch, Golden Gate Bridge Patrol.

"I won't let you do it," he said. "I saw you change your mind once. You know things aren't that bad. There's plenty to live for."

"For God's sake I'm not trying to jump," she cried. "Get off me! You're breaking my ribs!"

"Not till I get some backup out here."

Every car on the bridge was stalled, blowing its horn. People got out of their cars to see what that man was doing to Lucille.

"Listen, I dropped something and I had to get it back," she begged. "I promise. It's the truth. Let me go. See that bag? That's every bit of money I have in the world and it fell on that little ledge over the rail."

He relaxed his hold. "You're not serious."

"Look inside. It's fourteen thousand dollars. I had to get it back before it blew away. I'll give you some of it if you'll just let me go!"

But her plea came too late. Three men ran up the walkway, two of them real cops with nightsticks and guns. "What have we got?"

"She says she wasn't jumping, but I saw her go over the rail and come back."

"Don't let go of her," said the third man. "They always try it again."

"I'm sorry, ma'am," said the burly cop, "we'll have to put these cuffs on for your safety, till we're off the bridge."

Lucille said "I swear to you, Officer, I was not trying to jump."

He stood her up and locked her wrists together in front of her.

"What's this?" His partner stooped to retrieve the canvas bag. He loosened the cinch, peered inside, and let out a whistle. "Big money here, Frank."

"It's fourteen thousand dollars," said Lucille. She tried explaining about Las Vegas, subtly edging them away from the spot on the sidewalk where Chester in his Tupperware sat for the whole world to see. She thought she was getting away with it, she had them ten feet from the box and moving away when Mr. Nosy Policeman caught sight of it and said, "Is that something of yours, ma'am?"

Lucille blinked. "I've never seen it before in my life."

Of course that was the wrong answer, that made him curious. He went to the hatbox, crouched down.

Here came Norman puffing and blowing, his eyes wild with concern. "Oh thank God you're all right! I'm sorry, Miss Clay, I just couldn't let you do it!"

"Norman," she said, "you're such a fool."

The cop put his thumb on the press-and-lock seal, and popped it, and lifted the lid away. He reached down with his fingers to feel Chester's hair, and then the smell came up into his face. His eyes rolled up in his head. He keeled over backwards.

"Don't worry, honey," Chester whispered. "You'll be all right. I'll take care of you."

30

Peejoe

Industry

D ove hunched over the phone in his office. He answered whoever it was with "uh-huh" and "nuh-uh" and little else. "Okay, then. Call me back and tell me what time. Meanwhile I'll get hold of a lawyer. Listen, John. Take it easy, all right?" He hung up without saying goodbye. "They caught Baby Sister."

"Oh no!" My heart sank.

"It's all right, Peter Joseph. She's safe. They're bringing her home. It had to happen sooner or later."

"Where is she?" said Wiley.

"San Francisco." He sipped his coffee. "They caught her on the Golden Gate Bridge. The police say she was about to jump off, but that doesn't sound a bit like her."

The phone rang. Dove picked it up. "Hello? This is he. Who? Who did you say?" He frowned. "No, I don't think I'd want to say anything about that. Nope, huh-uh. Well, because I just wouldn't. All right? Thank you." He hung up. "The *Los Angeles Times*. All different ones have been calling. I guess this is big news out there." He rested his chin in one hand. "Thanks a lot, Baby Sister. I really needed this now."

"They're bringing her here?"

"They wanted to keep her in California, but John's got somebody in Montgomery pulling strings. They're flying her in there tonight. I have to go meet the plane."

I had a vision of Lucille coming to take her children away from Meemaw's so life could go back like it used to be. "Will you get to bring her home?"

"John will bring her to the jail here. I have to pick up Chester's head."

"She still had his head?" said Wiley.

"Love works in mysterious ways." Dove stretched up from the chair. "You boys want to go with me?"

On the way out of town he asked where we'd been all day. I blurted the truth: we'd been down at the swimming pool listening to Martin Luther King.

Wiley shot me an exasperated look. Dove was too amazed to be mad at us. "You mean to tell me, while John Doggett was busy trying to get Baby Sister back from California, Martin Luther King waltzed into town and made a speech?"

"You should have heard him, Uncle Dove."

"Well, *you* shouldn't have." He eyed me sideways. "We had a conversation about sticking close to home."

"It's okay, we just listened to him and came right back."

He sighed. "You boys are never going to mind me, are you."

Wiley said "I was watching out, Uncle Dove. It was safe."

"There's nothing safe now, son. Not for us. Everyone is watching us now. Let's face it, Peter Joseph tends to stand out in a crowd."

"Yeah, Martin Luther King came right up to him," said Wiley. "Tell him, Peejoe."

I told him what King said about doing good things.

Dove rolled his eyes. "Wiley, I believe we've got us a regular Martin Luther King–lovin' Freedom Rider here, what you think?"

In the afterglow of my encounter with the great man, Dove's teasing hit me in the face like cold water. Suddenly all my big ideas about him and me and Martin Luther King fighting side-by-side in the war against oppression seemed foolish. "But he's on our side, Uncle Dove. He came to help us."

"He came because the TV cameras were here," Dove said. "You can't fault him for that but it's true. He likes his publicity every bit as much as George Wallace."

That closed the discussion. We rode along to the piercing wail of Brenda Lee: *You tell me mistakes are part of bein' young . . .* Violins mimicked the breaks in her voice. The casket-carriage rattled in back.

"I talked to Earlene this morning," Dove said. "Mabel's worse."

"I got to tell you something, Uncle Dove," Wiley said.

"What's that, son?"

I pressed flat into the seat.

"It's about Mabel." He looked sick to his stomach.

"I think I already know, Wiley."

"You do?"

"Mabel talks a lot. I figure maybe the two of you was fooling around a little, and she got carried away in her head. Is that about what happened?"

"Well, yes sir."

"You didn't do anything serious, did you?"

"No sir."

"Thanks for telling me. I'm sure you would never take advantage of Mabel."

"We used to tease her, too, Uncle Dove," I confessed. "All the time. We were really mean."

"This is a real sickness, you know, what she's got. The doctor says it's schizophrenia. You boys might have helped set her off, but you're not the reason why. I'm not blaming you."

Wiley swallowed. "I just wanted to tell you."

We rode awhile in silence. On the flat stretches Dove pushed the hearse up to eighty-five, ninety.

Wiley said "Are you gonna dig up Chester and put him back together before you bury him?"

"I think we'll just bury his head with the rest of him. Let the Lord work it out."

"Maybe we could break Aunt Lucille out of jail," I offered.

"They'd just catch her again, and then it'd be worse," he said, as if he'd considered that line of action himself. "Some part of her knows she has to answer for what she did. Or else spend the rest of her life looking over her shoulder."

"I don't know, Uncle Dove. She didn't sound sorry when I talked to her."

"I didn't say she was sorry, Peejoe. But she's guilty, and she knows it. That's different from being sorry. It's stronger. It's the kind of thing that keeps you awake at night."

On the radio Elvis sang "Peace in the Valley." Dove slowed at the sign for Dannelly Field.

The runway lights were eerie blue connect-the-dot lines in the distance. Small planes huddled in pools of light.

Dove pulled up a circular drive and parked at the curb. We followed him into the terminal, where a lady at a ticket window pointed us out through glass doors, down a covered walkway toward a commotion at the last gate.

I admired the shiny luggage-carts, the big rolling stairways parked on the tarmac, leading nowhere,

Dove said, "Whoa, look what we got here." In the waiting crowd I saw reporters and photographers who'd been hanging around Industry— and, at the center of the circle, Sheriff John Doggett himself, combing his hair in a little mirror held up for him by a TV reporter. In his black dress uniform, surrounded by his deputies, he looked the very picture of law and order.

Dove held us back in the shadows.

TV floodlights snapped on. John Doggett sucked in his belly. The newsman raised a microphone.

"This is Bob Ingram, WSFA-TV, at Dannelly Field. We're speaking with Sheriff John Doggett of Cotton County, who's certainly become a well-known figure in recent weeks. Sheriff, tell us the purpose of your visit here this evening."

"Bob, I'm here on behalf of the citizens of Cotton County to take custody of a dangerous fugitive. This is a proud moment for me and my men. We've had this case under investigation from the beginning, and we're happy to have an arrest."

Dove looked away in disgust.

"Of course now we're speaking of Lucille Vinson," said Ingram, "the television actress and mother of six from Cornelia accused of killing and decapitating her husband. This sensational case has everyone's attention tonight, Sheriff. Why do you consider Mrs. Vinson dangerous?"

Doggett puffed up his chest. "She's shown herself to be ruthless, Bob. We've taken every precaution to make sure she doesn't escape. She'll be escorted by myself and three of my men to a maximum-security cell. She won't be hurting anybody else, I can promise you."

"Any word on a motive for the crime, Sheriff?"

"None that I know. It seems completely senseless to me. I understand the suspect has refused to make any statements."

"Do you expect to seek the death penalty?"

"That's not my decision. I'm here strictly to take custody of the prisoner."

"Any comment on the indictments returned against you by the grand jury?"

Doggett looked straight into the camera. "I can't say much, but when I get my day in court you'll see this is nothing but one Yankee lawyer trying to make a name for himself."

"Thank you, Sheriff." The floodlights died, leaving a hot crimson glare. The sheriff pumped the reporter's hand. He looked pleased with his performance. He hadn't had to say a word about niggers or outside agitators or Martin Luther King. He'd managed to turn all the attention onto Aunt Lucille, the famous murderess.

Dove stepped from the shadows, with Wiley and me at his heels. A reporter recognized my eyepatch and signaled his photographer, but Dove put himself between the camera and me. "Hey, fellas, let's leave the kids out of this one, okay? They've got nothing to do with this."

John Doggett grinned. "Men, I'm sure you know Dove Bullis, our county coroner. Dove already promised me that Miz Vinson being a member of his family won't interfere with this investigation, didn't you, Dove?"

"You know I did."

The reporters gathered around, pencils to notebooks. "Mr. Bullis, can you tell us why Lucille Vinson killed her husband?"

"I'm not gonna talk about any of that," said Dove. "I'm here to perform my official responsibilities."

"Have you talked to her?"

"No."

"Why did she cut off his head?" "Spell your last name, please." "Did you see her on 'The Beverly Hillbillies'?"

Dove turned all the questions away with polite non-answers. Wiley and I hung back against the white-metal railing, admiring his coolness under fire. He had come at the sheriff's request, he said, to receive certain remains for burial. Beyond that he said almost nothing. If the reporters wanted a real story, he said, they should go down to Industry and have a talk with Martin Luther King.

That brought a frigid smile from the sheriff. "Yeah, Dove can tell you all about that," he said, setting the pencils to scribbling. "He's a first-class A-number-one nigger lover. He's been on their side from the start."

"You see, boys, the sheriff can't control his big mouth any better than he can run things down in Industry," Dove said. "I think he's getting cold feet about what he started down there. Judge Johnson just ordered him to turn every one of those demonstrators loose. He's come up here tonight hoping to get y'all to talk about something else."

A high-pitched whine in the dark. Way out over the treeline to the east, two brilliant lights wobbled toward the field.

The shape of a jet became visible, a giant silvery bird swooping in with its belly inclined. The whine grew into thunder. The plane scratched on the runway and roared by us.

Two men rolled a stairway to the gate. Another man took up a stance, with glowing orange-cone flashlights in each hand. A yellow tractor puttered up, trailing a string of luggage carts.

An enormous Eastern airliner materialized out of the gloom, lumbering toward us. I marveled that something so massive could ever have left the ground.

The TV crew flooded the scene with light. Sheriff Doggett strutted with his men to the foot of the stairs.

Bob Ingram addressed the camera: "We're at Dannelly Field this evening . . ."

I remembered a scene on Meemaw's wavery black-and-white TV: a big jet rolling out of the darkness into a blaze of TV lights. A dead President in a coffin, a bloodstained widow in the cargo door, a sad dog-faced President at a cluster of microphones, telling us everything would be okay.

Ingram's words were drowned out by the scream of the engines, which peaked and began to wind down.

". . . expect to see her at any moment, arriving tonight from San Francisco, California, where she was arrested Thursday . . ."

The reporters edged through the gate as the forward hatch popped open. A stewardess in a navy-blue uniform raised her hand to fend off the glare. She said something to the people inside, and they came filing past her down the steps—baffled businessmen clutching briefcases, families returning sunburned from vacation.

After the last passenger there was a long moment of nobody else. I held my breath. Maybe she had escaped. . . .

Then a man in a dark suit appeared in the doorway, and behind him— oh yes there she was.

She wore a white sleeveless dress trimmed in yellow, white shiny ankle-high boots, a big smile for the cameras. Her hands were bound with silver cuffs. She tossed her hair, posing at the top of the stairs. She brought her hands to her lips, and blew a big movie-star kiss.

The photographers jostled each other, flashing. Flashbulbs tinkled to the pavement.

Carefully Lucille picked her way down the steps, showing her long legs to best advantage. I half-expected someone to rush forward with red roses. She looked tanned and rested and young, not at all like the nervous chain-smoking wreck who had showed up in Meemaw's side yard with that Tupperware bowl. This was someone entirely new.

The sheriff made an announcement on behalf of the citizens, blah

blah, do hereby officially accept transfer of custody of this prisoner. The dark-suited man unfolded papers for him to sign.

Reporters shouted at Lucille: "Why'd you do it?" "Why'd you cut off his head?" "Do you feel any remorse?" "Were you trying to jump off the bridge?"

Lucille smiled. "It's so good to be home."

"Are you guilty?"

She tossed that lanky blond hair. "Not in the least."

"Will you make a confession?"

"I didn't do anything wrong."

"Did you kill him?"

"I didn't do anything wrong," she repeated, with a smile.

"Did you love your husband, Mrs. Vinson?"

She blinked. "I don't know what you mean."

"Where'd you get all the money?"

"I got lucky."

The sheriff stepped up. "That's enough. She'll have all the questions she can answer at her trial."

"Oh hello, Sheriff," Lucille said. "I saw your picture in *Life* magazine. I see you still need to lose that twenty pounds."

The reporters laughed. Doggett's eyes tightened. His hand closed on her arm. "Little lady, I've been looking for you a long time."

He ushered her out of the lights, toward the spot where we were standing.

I called out, "Aunt Lucille!"

"Oh my Lord—Peejoe! Hey, Wiley! Hey, Dove!" She tried to wave but the handcuffs got in the way.

"Baby Sister," Dove said, "you all right?"

Doggett hustled her right past us without slowing down. "I'm fantastic," she called over her shoulder. "Come see me in jail."

The deputies hurried her off to the terminal, trailed by the herd of flashing cameras. The other passengers drifted along, plainly amazed to have been on a plane with a notorious criminal.

Lucille's dark-suited escort stood at the foot of the steps, riffling through his stack of papers. We followed Dove across the tarmac.

He stuck out his hand. "Dove Bullis. I'm her brother. I hope she didn't give you trouble."

"Detective Rubacky." The man shook hands warily. "Not at all. Compared to the type of prisoner I usually deal with, she was a day at the beach."

"I'm here to claim some remains," Dove said.

"Oh, right. We had to check that as baggage. That was the one time she got difficult, she wanted that thing riding up in the cabin with us, but she straightened up when she saw I meant business." He pulled out a page. "Here. You'll need this to claim it. And there's a couple suitcases, her personal effects."

Dove thanked him for his help and led us to the terminal. In one corner a conveyor belt carried luggage and parcels around a continuous loop. Dove stood at one end, inspecting each item as it came through the doorflaps. He hefted two brown leather suitcases, matching them with the tags in his hand, and then we all saw the plywood crate riding toward us: two feet square, plastered with red FRAGILE labels.

Dove lifted the crate with a grunt, set it down *chunk!* on the floor.

"It feels like they packed him in lead," he said, waving for a skycap to come with his hand truck.

"Evenin', Cap." He helped Dove tip the crate to get the hand-truck blade under one edge; they set Lucille's expensive suitcases on top of that and got it rolling.

We followed them outside. Already the sheriff had whisked Aunt Lucille into the night. The reporters around the hearse perked up when they saw us coming, but Dove shrugged them off and set to work strapping the crate onto the casket-carriage.

Wiley and I were confirmed members of the death club. Dove let us see everything. Most men would have kept us away from these things. Dove wanted us to see.

I dozed in his lap on the way home. As we crossed the Cotton County line, a pickup truck flashed out of the dark. Dove swerved.

The right front tire dropped off the road to the shoulder. Dove shouted and whipped the wheel around, brought it back on the pavement. I woke up while he was still twisting around in his seat to see what we'd almost hit.

A pickup truck vanished in our taillights.

31

Peejoe

On the Road

Wiley swore someone had tried to kill us. His face was pure white. Dove told him not to be so dramatic, it was probably some old drunk poking his nose out in the road without looking both ways.

His eyes strayed up to the rearview mirror. He took the next turnoff, a badly paved country road through miles of unpopulated pine woods.

I was wide awake now. I crawled over the seat for a better look at Uncle Chester's crate, hammered together from plywood and two-by-fours, labeled FRAGILE and HUMAN REMAINS and ATTN D. BULLIS, CROAKER-MOSELEY FUNERAL HOME, INDUSTRY, ALA. Chester was strapped to the carriage like Gulliver in the land of the little people.

I caught a splinter from the lid and sat sucking blood from my finger while I read the fine print concerning Interstate Transportation of Remains. Like Martin Luther King, Uncle Chester had come a long way around to get back where he started.

"We're sitting ducks in this hearse," Wiley was saying. "Anybody can see us coming a mile away."

"Uncle Dove, what do you reckon his head looks like now?"

"I don't know, Peter Joseph, and I don't intend to find out. Don't you mess with that box."

Wiley said "He didn't even have his lights on. He just rolled out of nowhere."

"I'm telling you, son, it was nothing. Will you stop? You're making *me* nervous."

I said, "Can we help dig the hole?"

"As a matter of fact," Dove said, "I brought three shovels."

"All right! Wiley, you hear that? We're gonna dig a *grave*."

Dove slowed at the lights of a trailer park, and pulled under the wrought-iron archway for MEADOW ACRES MEMORIAL PARK. "Son, want to open the gate?"

Wiley hopped out to swing it back on its hinges.

Dove steered past the caretaker's hut, the statue of Jesus with his arms upraised as if he'd made a touchdown. He coasted to a stop.

The crickets were singing full tilt, the treefrogs honking, a three-quarter moon racing along behind fast-moving clouds. A faint radio song carried over from the trailer park.

Dove's flashlight beam played on the bronze grave-markers. I spotted a mound of ruined flower arrangements near a tall crepe myrtle. "He's over here!"

Wiley struggled up, clanking three shovels.

Dove set his flashlight on the marker, CHESTER ARTHELL VINSON 1923–1965. The beam split apart at our feet, casting wild giant-shadows across the grass. Dove traced a circle with the point of his shovel. "Start digging here. I'll go get him."

I set my blade on the circle, pushed down with my heel, turned a spadeful of earth. It was barely a month since we buried the other part of Chester; the dirt hadn't packed, it made for easy digging. Every thrust of the shovel produced a nice loamy shovelful to add to our mound.

Dove swore and muttered, trying to drag the crate across the grass. He went back to the hearse for a hammer. I left off digging and went to hold the flashlight for him.

He wedged in the claw-end of the hammer and pried up one corner of the lid, plucking out nails like embedded teeth. He repeated this proce-dure at the other corners, and lifted the sheet of plywood away.

I turned the flashlight down in the box: wadded-up newspaper. Dove bent for a sniff. He shrugged and began pulling out handfuls of news-paper, revealing a glossy white octagonal box with a makeshift cardboard lid, tied on with fancy black ribbons.

"A hatbox," said Dove. "Well, that's unique."

The breeze welled up, scattering newspapers over the graves.

Dove got his hands under the hatbox, brought it out of the crate, staggered to one knee under its weight. "Jesus! Wiley, give me a hand with this."

It took both of them to carry the box twenty yards. They set it down hard beside the mound of fresh dirt. "That hole's wide enough," Dove said, "but it needs to be deeper."

We set to work digging until the hole was too deep for more than one person at a time. Wiley took the first turn standing down in the hole to dig while Dove and I sweated and rested. He turned about ten shovelloads, then his blade struck something hard.

"Pay dirt," said Dove. "That's the casket. Peter Joseph, give him your hand."

I helped Wiley out of the hole. "Are you gonna open the casket?"

"Not a chance. We'll just kind of lay him right down on top of it." Brushing dirt from his hands, Dove squatted beside the hatbox. "All right, let's see what we got."

He untied the ribbons, lifted away the lid, and pulled back layers of flimsy green tissue paper to reveal the green Tupperware bowl with something dark inside.

"You recognize that, Peter Joseph?"

I nodded. I remembered what Meemaw said when she first saw it: *Isn't that nice. Tupperware.*

Dove burrowed his hand down in the paper—he let out a whistle, and drew forth a blunt-nosed pistol, barrel first. "They missed something out in California. No wonder Baby Sister wanted this thing riding up in the plane with her."

He snapped the magazine from the pistol grip, spilled out a handful of bullets, tossed the bullets and the pistol into Chester's grave. "If anybody asks, you boys didn't see me do that. You never saw any gun. Understand?"

We said we did.

A thin cloud blew over the moon. On the breeze, I heard a sound—just a whisper, the shadowy ghost of a sound: "Lou-see-yul . . ."

Dove put the sole of his shoe against the edge of Chester's container, and started it rolling toward the hole. It took a skip and bounced in, landing on the casket with a thud.

"Lou-see-yul . . ."

Dove kicked the hatbox in after it. He picked up a shovel and began tossing dirt in the hole. "Come on, let's finish up and get out of here."

Spurred on by the raving crickets, we put the dirt back in that hole a lot quicker than we had dug it out. I caught a snatch of music in the air.

I straightened up—a guitar, a wild man screeching on the trailer-park radio: *Luciiiiii-yul! You don't do yo daddy's will!*

Maybe that was what I had heard, but I tell you I was purely glad to stomp the last dirt on that grave and say goodbye to Chester.

32

Lucille

On the Road

Killing Chester and cutting off his head was the most extreme and irreversible thing Lucille could think of to do—and even that was not enough to set her free. Chester had her in his grip, he was dragging her back down to Alabama. She could hear him down in the luggage hold, softly crying her name.

You could not just throw your old life away and go find a new life for yourself. The old life would come to get you every time.

Detective Rubacky was a dark, husky man of few words. Lucille had tried crossing her legs a few times, hoping to provoke some interest—she had a vague notion of enticing him into the bathroom, snatching his gun, commandeering the plane—but he wasn't taken in. He'd settled in with a paperback copy of *Psycho.*

She had begged the sergeant in San Francisco to let her change from the shapeless jail dress to her André Courrèges for the flight home. "They'll be taking my picture," she pleaded. "It might be my last chance to wear something nice."

He couldn't find any rule against it in his rulebooks, but he drew the line at the matching sailor hat. "Don't push me," he said. She didn't.

Lucille nibbled smoked almonds and gazed out at patchwork America sliding underneath the plane. If only she'd known how easy it was to fly. In five hours they covered a distance that had taken her a solid week on the road.

The detective was smart to put the handcuffs back on for the change of planes in Atlanta; his attention drifted to a noisy argument at a ticket-counter and Lucille saw a perfect opportunity to bolt through a cargo door. She would have done it, too, if she could have figured a way to get those handcuffs off before somebody spotted her.

The stewardess on the hop to Montgomery took one look at LUCILLE VINSON on the ticket and blanched. After a hurried conference with the crew, she ushered Lucille and the detective to the very last seats, blocking off three rows in front of them.

The flight to Montgomery was a quick up-and-down. As the wheels touched the runway Lucille saw television lights at the gate. The warm humid smell of Alabama came in through the fresh-air intakes, a grassy green aroma of fields and trees and insecticide.

The stewardess came to tell them to wait, they'd be last off the plane. "I've had lots of famous people on my flights," she volunteered. "Let's see, I've had Gregory Peck, and Soupy Sales, and Dion. Dion was the nicest. He gave us all autographed photos."

"And now me," Lucille said.

"And now you."

"I'm sorry I don't have a photo to give you," said Lucille.

The girl blushed. "My goodness, that's not what I meant."

Lucille struggled up from her seat. "Come on, Mr. Detective. Let's go meet my public."

Rubacky held up her jacket, intending to drape it over the handcuffs, but she pulled away. "No. Let them see. I want them to see what they've done."

She followed him up the aisle, and stepped out into the dazzling lights. She blew the newsmen a kiss. She posed for their pictures. She made her way down the stairs, taking pains not to re-enact Patsy Belle's pratfall in front of all these cameras. She held an impromptu press conference on the tarmac, tossing them little scraps of nothing.

Sheriff John Doggett sashayed up like the biggest rooster in the barnyard, throwing his weight around, making pronouncements. She put him in his place with that remark about his belly. He grabbed her arm and rushed her out of there.

She heard a cry, "Aunt Lucille!" and Lord, there were Wiley and Dove and poor pitiful one-eyed Peejoe watching the whole spectacle.

She had only a moment to wave before Doggett whisked her past them, through the terminal to his squad car. He waited for the cameramen to catch up and switch on their lights, then he made a big show of loading Lucille in the back seat between two deputies. He took the wheel himself and roared off, siren screaming.

"Well my goodness," she said, "is that what you call Southern hospitality? I want you to know you've probably left a big old bruise on my arm."

"Tell it to the judge," Doggett said.

Lucille considered a smart comeback, but decided against it. She concentrated on the not-altogether-unpleasant experience of being in a car with three men. She hadn't smelled this clash of perspiration and after-shave since she used to ride around with Dove and Franklin and their high school buddies in that '39 Dodge.

The sheriff pulled to the shoulder and switched off the siren. "Billy, you drive, and Melford, come up front. I want to talk to Lucille."

Everybody changed places. When they got rolling again Lucille held up her wrists: "Is it too much to ask you to take these off? I promise, I won't try anything."

"I can't do that," said Doggett. "You're my prize. I can't let anything happen to you."

"Well I sure hope you got the key from that man. I would hate to get stuck in these things."

"I got it. You just take it easy."

The sheriff wasn't as homely as his picture in *Life*. Anybody's belly would look huge in one of those fisheye lenses. Lucille liked the fact that he had worn his dress uniform to meet her. Biceps bulged through his sleeves. She began to calculate the peculiar conjunction of the stars and her wiles that might lead her to consider this man attractive, and to use that attraction to get out of jail.

"I hear your jail's pretty full these days," she said. "Listen, Sheriff, you're a busy man, and I sure don't want to share a cell with a bunch of Freedom Riders. So why don't you just let me go, and let's forget all this ever happened."

Doggett's smile turned into a smirk. "You been reading about me?"

"Of course I have. You're all over the papers in California."

"You hear that, Melford Junior? I'm famous in California." He fairly wiggled with pride. "My phone has been ringing off the hook. There's people telling me I oughta run for lieutenant governor."

"You're famous enough," said Lucille.

"It's not that I'd want the job so much," he said, "but nobody else seems to be willing to stand up and say what the people really think."

She said "Yes, I know exactly what you mean" while thinking *what an idiot*. She couldn't believe she was hearing this. Since she realized she was a wanted woman, Lucille had imagined the man in charge of her pursuit as a relentless force lurking out in the darkness, waiting to pounce on her first mistake. Then when she saw him in the papers he seemed like a white-trash ignoramus who couldn't shut up. Now she saw he was an overgrown boy playing boy games, cops and robbers, big bad white racist sheriff, would-be politician.

She would tell him exactly what he wanted to hear, until she could figure out some other plan.

"Never mind what you did," he was saying, "I'm hoping you got more sense than that brother of yours. Me and Dove have known each other for years, we've got along fine. But lately he's lost his mind."

"What's he done?"

"He's mixing it up with these niggers, these nigger-loving Justice Department lawyers."

"I'm sure he's just trying to do somebody some good. Dove was always like that."

"He ain't doing me one bit of good," said Doggett. "You're gonna talk to him. You're gonna tell him, depending on what him and those boys of his says to the jury in my case, we'll see what happens to you."

"I'm not sure I understand." Lucille crossed her legs, blinking attentively. "Explain it to me."

"It can go hard for you, or it can go easy," he said. "Depending."

"Well honestly, Sheriff, I don't see how it could go any harder on me than it's already going to. I mean, unless you decide to beat me up or something."

"I've never hit a woman in my life," he said.

Lucille smiled. "Let's keep it that way."

"The county solicitor is a friend of mine," the sheriff went on. "He'll take his cue from me. If Dove plays along, and you act crazy for a headshrinker, I believe we could keep you out of prison. That guy in New Orleans got his car back, I've got him agreed to drop the charges if you pay back the money. We'll get you a nice quiet room up at Bryce's."

"That sounds just delightful," she said. "I'll talk to Dove about it."

"He's stubborn. You may have to persuade him."

"So let me ask you something. That's what happens if it goes easy for me. What happens if it goes hard?"

His cold smile told her the answer. "Well, I'll bring those people in from California, the trooper from New Mexico, I'll bring 'em all in—your children, your mama, Dove and them boys—everybody you ever liked, or was close to. I'll make every last one of 'em get up and testify against you. And then when that's over, I'll see that you fry. I know the man who pulls the switch at Atmore."

"I imagine that does come in handy," said Lucille. "Let me talk to Dove and my lawyer and see what they say."

"This got nothing to do with lawyers," he said. "This is all between us."

"I see. Kind of an inside arrangement."

"You scratch my back, I scratch yours."

The deputies strained not to listen.

"What could Dove and those boys say to get you in so much trouble, Sheriff? What did you do?"

"It's a frame-up. The FBI has a stool pigeon singin' away. He's accusing me of things that I never did. They're trying to push this integration down everybody's throat, and they want me out of the way. And Dove Bullis is helping them."

"If you did something wrong, I understand," Lucille said.

"Yeah, I bet you do. How did you cut off his head, anyway?" He intended to knock her off balance with the question, but she batted it right back at him.

"Sheriff, look at me. Do I look like the kind of person who would do something like that?"

"Sweetheart, I know exactly what you did. I followed you every step of the way. No use to sit there and bullshit me."

"I wouldn't dare. Do you mind if I smoke?"

"Go ahead."

"They're in my purse. That man has it."

"Melford, get the lady a cigarette."

Lucille discovered how depressing it is to smoke a cigarette in the back of a squad car with your wrists cuffed so you have to rest elbows on thighs and bring the cigarette to your lips with both hands. She reminded herself of the first lesson of surviving captivity, the trick that kept her alive all those years with Chester: Go somewhere else in your mind. She leaned back in the seat and breathed the smell of eucalyptus trees on the Pacific Coast Highway.

For the first time since New Mexico, she sensed the gray fog hovering above her, beginning to descend. The sheriff asked her questions but she did not answer. The gray fog came down to separate her from everything.

She rode for miles in the fog.

When it lifted they were on the dark edge of a town, cruising a back street of old houses. The air smelled of honeysuckle. The radio crackled.

Lucille peered out. "Where are we?"

"You don't recognize Industry? Billy, take her around the back way, let's don't wake up the niggers." He turned to her. "They got a damn candlelight vigil going round the clock right out on my front stoop. I'm too tired to arrest anybody tonight."

"I suppose you're going to leave me in your nasty jail and go home to bed," she said.

"Yep, that's what I'm gonna do."

They drove along Beauregard Avenue. Now she knew where she was—that was the Ritz Theater, where a freckled boy named David Pardue gave Lucille her very first kiss at the exact moment Robert Taylor kissed Greer Garson on the screen.

That boy never knew what he started.

The deputy pulled to a sheltered doorway on the dark side of the courthouse. As Lucille swung her legs out of the car, she heard singing.

> *Freedom . . .*
> *Freedom . . .*
> *Freedom in Alabama now.*

The song came from the front of the building, and also from the tiny barred windows on the second floor. Rich voices echoed through the square like Sunday morning on the colored radio station.

"Oh my Lord," Lucille said. "You can't lock me up in here with all these people. This is cruel and unusual punishment."

The sheriff steered her inside to a bright room, where at last he produced the key to the handcuffs.

Lucille rubbed her wrists to get the blood going.

The desk sergeant grinned up. "Hey, I know you. I saw you on 'The Beverly Hillbillies.'"

"Why, thank you."

He had an Adam's apple the size of a peach pit. "You're lucky. We got a full house tonight, had to turn people loose so you could get a cell to yourself."

"I hope you didn't go to any special trouble."

> *Rollin', rollin',*
> *Rollin' down the freedom road . . .*

The sheriff said "Tyrone, do something about that goddamned singing."

"What you want me to do, Sheriff? They won't hush. I can arrest the ones out front, but we got no place to put 'em."

"Is the armory full?"

"Yes sir. They're sleeping on the floor." Tyrone pressed Lucille's thumb to an ink pad, rolled it on a card, then each finger in turn. Afterward he gave her a dry napkin to wipe her hands, and a paper to sign.

He positioned her at a line on the floor, and aimed a folding Polaroid camera. "Look at me." Flash. "Right profile, please."

"Well hell," Doggett said, "I guess we'll just let 'em sing, then."

"They'll run out of breath after a while," said Tyrone.

"Fine. I'm going home," said the sheriff. "Lucille, good to have you back. You talk to Dove, you hear?"

"Sweet dreams," she said.

Tyrone gave her a blue cotton jail-dress like the one in San Francisco, and showed her into a curtained alcove. Out there she'd been stripped and searched, patted by a burly impersonal jail-matron, but thank God this was the South, even a murderess was permitted a bit of privacy, if she was a lady.

Tyrone contented himself with a quick two-handed frisk down her sides. Lucille handed over her André Courrèges and cringed when he balled it up and stuffed it in a Piggly Wiggly bag with her jewelry and her watch.

Too bad she had nothing to smuggle in. They took her money away in San Francisco and gave her a receipt, and she hadn't seen it since.

"Do you have a sandwich, some crackers or something?" she said. "I couldn't eat that mess on the plane."

"Sorry. Breakfast is at seven. We don't have room service here."

"Don't I get a phone call?"

"In the morning. The switchboard is closed." He walked her through double doors, up to the second floor. The freedom song poured from the cells on both sides of the hall. Lucille fixed her gaze on the empty cell straight ahead. She was aware of a ripe smell, unwashed people packed together, dozens of eyes turning to follow her.

Tyrone opened the grate on the last cell and ushered Lucille inside.

Jericho
Jericho
And the walls come a-tumblin' down . . .

The door clanged shut. The song lingered on the sidewalk out front.

Lucille sank to the cot. "My, this is every bit as nice as the Beverly Hills Hotel."

"All right, then." Tyrone headed down the hall. "Y'all better quit singing and get some sleep," he said amiably. "It's mighty late."

"God will forgive you, Tyrone," said a deep voice.

"I hope he will." He went downstairs.

Lucille kicked off her shoes and stretched out. Her cell was set back from the others; she could hear people breathing, she could feel them straining to see her. She was a dangerous animal locked away from the other animals in the zoo.

Someone called, "'Go down Moses!'" and they started up on that. The chorus spread up through the windows and all through the jail.

Lucille was suddenly glad for the singing. It kept her from giving way to the dark despair welling up inside her. She would be damned before she let a bunch of black protesters hear her cry.

Let my people go.

Up to now Lucille hadn't had much use for uppity Negroes, but she was more like these people than she would have ever believed. She wanted to be free. Like them, she had done something radical to set herself free—and ended up in jail.

"Sst—" She heard a whisper—"Sister."

She didn't answer.

"Sister Vinson." A hoarse, urgent voice, from the nearest cell.

"I don't know who you are, but I'm not your sister." She wiped her eyes. "Leave me alone."

"I'm Nehemiah Thomas. I'm a friend of Dove's."

She remembered his picture in *Newsweek,* his wire-rimmed glasses and stern eyes peering through these iron bars. "What do you want?"

"I just want you to know your brother is a good man, he's done me many a favor. And I'm sorry for your troubles. We're supposed to go free tomorrow. If there's anything I can do for you . . ."

"No, thank you very much. Unless you happen to have something to eat." Her stomach was so empty it hurt. Three days ago she was riding in the back of Norman's limousine; now she was reduced to begging food from a black mortician in jail. How far the mighty have fallen.

A candy bar landed with a soft plop on the floor just outside her cell.

"Oh, thank you." Lucille put her face to the bars and dragged it in with one finger. Snickers. She could smell it through the wrapper.

She snatched off the paper and took half of it in one bite, it was heaven, sugar peanuts chocolate goo, soft and warm from someone's pocket. It was the very best candy bar ever.

She settled back against the cold concrete blocks, savoring each little nibble. The singing dwindled away. From every cell came sounds of people settling in for the night.

"God bless you all," Nehemiah called.

Someone said, "God bless Martin Luther King."

"And our enemies, too," said Nehemiah.

Lucille pulled the blanket around her. The candy filled her with sweetness. Her life was not over. Only Carolyn Clay was dead. Lucille was someone else now. This was another new life. She needed to make a new plan.

33

Peejoe

Industry

A mud-crusted Dodge waited behind the white hearse in the carport. "That's Francis's car," Dove said. "That means Earlene. I wonder what else she's decided to take."

"Don't let her take the TV, Uncle Dove," Wiley said.

"You boys act nice to her, now."

We followed him in. Earlene was upstairs pacing, dressed to kill in a burgundy moiré suit with hat and veil. Her brother-in-law Francis, a big dough-faced country man in Big Smith overalls, sat in Uncle Dove's recliner with his feet up.

Earlene tapped her toe. "Where have you been? We were supposed to meet you here an hour ago."

"I forgot," Dove said. "I had other business. I guess you heard Lucille is back."

"You bet I heard. I can't tell you how glad I am not to be associated with you and your trashy family."

"What do you want?"

"You have to sign these papers, I told you," she said. "We're both still her parents, like it or not. Hello, boys."

We mumbled hello.

Dove took a sheaf of papers from Earlene. "I'd ask you to sit down," he said, "but you took all the chairs."

"I'm very happy to stand," she said.

Dove studied the papers. "What's this about the guardian, here."

"Just sign it," she said.

"The hell I will. What does this mean?"

"I've already explained it to you," she said. "If I'm going up there to Tuscaloosa with her, I've got to be able to make decisions. I can't be calling you every twenty minutes to see what you think."

"I don't know why not."

"Dove, it doesn't mean anything, it's like a power of attorney. You're still her father, for God's sake."

"I'll sign this other part," he said, "but I'm not signing that."

"All right, then you go up there with her," Earlene said. "I'll sign her over to you."

"You know I can't take off and go up there."

"I don't know why not. You haven't got any business left to save. You've ruined yourself. You still don't see that, do you."

Francis said, "Y'all had much rain here lately, Dove?"

"No, Francis, it's been pretty dry."

"Sign the paper, Dove."

Dove snatched the pen from her hand. "It's not enough you take the damn furniture," he said.

He signed.

"Thank you very much." Earlene tucked the papers away. "Come on, Francis." She snapped her purse shut. "I'll call from Tuscaloosa. Come *on*, Francis!"

Francis ambled up from the chair, nodded to us on his way out. "It's been dry up around home, too," he said.

We reached the courthouse just in time to witness a commotion on the steps.

"Look, it's Nehemiah," Dove said. "John finally had to let him go." A crowd swarmed around him. A stream of demonstrators emerged squinting into the sunshine. Some of them knelt to kiss the steps. They were free, as Judge Johnson had ordered, as Martin Luther King had promised. They surged down the steps, pumping hands and embracing each other.

They formed ranks and joined hands and began a spontaneous march to the pool.

The man on duty buzzed us through two doors and took us up to the jail, a long bleak corridor with cells on either side. In the cell on the end Aunt Lucille sat crosslegged on a metal cot, brushing her hair. She wore a blue square-cut dress, like a hospital gown.

"Hello, Baby Sister."

She glanced up. Her face came alive. "Oh, God, it's good to see friendly faces."

The deputy locked us in there with her. "Peejoe, come here and give us some sugar. You boys are getting so big!" I slipped from her grasp and went to examine the stainless-steel toilet, the sink. I sat down on the cot. I was a desperate criminal headed for the electric chair.

"Peejoe, you look very dashing in that patch. Like Errol Flynn. I wouldn't worry a minute about it." She turned. "On the other hand, Dove. You look terrible. What's wrong?"

And he told her: Earlene gone, Mabel gone crazy, the whole town turned against him, his business ruined, everything falling apart. He laid it out coolly, as if describing someone else's life.

"And then I land right smack in the middle of everything, huh," she said. "Lousy timing, brother. I'm sorry. It's just awful about poor Mabel. You don't have any idea what started it?"

Wiley edged closer to the wall.

"She hears these voices," Dove said. "Earlene is convinced it's my fault. She says I always ignored Mabel. And I guess she's right. I never did know what to say to her."

"They say if you've got a problem the thing to do is get professional help," said Lucille. "I'm sure she'll get better up there. Who knows, I may be going up there with her. If I'm lucky."

A silence fell. Dove cleared his throat to end it. "I'm glad you brought that up, Baby Sister. That's the line we have to take on this."

"Yeah, I heard," said Lucille. "The sheriff wants to make a deal."

"What's the deal?"

"You give up whatever this is, this trial against him. You don't testify. He makes it easy on me. I plead guilty and they send me to Bryce instead of Atmore."

"I knew he would use you to get at me," said Dove.

"I'm not about to make a deal with that man," she said. "The thing about it is, Dove, I'm *not* crazy. I knew exactly what I was doing. I think I can explain it so people will understand. That's what's important to me. I want a chance to explain. If somebody wants to say I'm crazy, they're gonna have to prove it. After that, they can kill me or put me away, it's all the same."

"It's not the same to me," said Dove. "I'd a lot rather have you alive. Looking at you, you don't seem insane to me. But you don't want to go to prison. I've already talked to Larry Russell about this, he'll be your lawyer, he agrees with me. We can't pretend you didn't do it. All we can do is try to show what you were thinking at the time."

"You go on and testify against the big bad sheriff. I can take care of myself." She smiled. "Did you see me on TV, Peejoe?"

"I sure did, Aunt Lucille. You were great."

Wiley said, "Did you mean to fall down those stairs?"

"Well, you know, I didn't." She told us the whole story, the Beverly Hills Hotel, Harry Hall's white Rolls-Royce, Buddy Ebsen and Max Baer and Irene Ryan, a hoop-skirted wedding gown and a narrow curving staircase.

"You're lucky you didn't bust your head open," said Dove.

She grinned. "They said they'd pay me extra for stunt work, but I didn't stick around to get my check."

Dove plopped beside her on the iron cot, his big arm around her shoulders. They seemed younger together—I could see them as children, piled up just this way in a bed at Meemaw's.

"You should have got rid of his head," Dove said.

"I know. I kept trying to, but—I waited too late." She shrugged. "I can't explain it. Even now it makes me nervous not to know where he is. They put him down with the luggage! Talk about not showing respect."

"I already took care of him," Dove said. "Me and the boys buried him."

"I'm sorry you had to get involved. Where did you put him?"

"Meadow Acres. With the rest of him."

"You didn't by any chance happen to save that hatbox."

"No."

"I've still got the hat. Did he say anything?"

Dove pulled away for a good look at her. "What?"

"Did his head say anything to you?" She was serious.

"Not that I heard," Dove said.

I started to tell about the song I'd heard floating in from the trailer park, as we shoveled the dirt in the hole—but Lucille spoke first.

"He talked to me sometimes," she said. "I know it sounds incredible, but it's true. That's why I couldn't throw him away. He was talking to me right up to the end."

"Uh-*huh*." Dove scratched his head. "You know, Baby Sister, if you don't want people to think you're crazy, you shouldn't go around telling that."

"I wasn't trying to kill myself on that bridge, Dove. I was trying to get rid of his goddamn head, to shut him up once and for all."

The deputy came back.

"Take the boys," Lucille told him. "Give me ten minutes alone with my brother, okay? Boys, thank you for coming to see me."

We exchanged awkward hugs and followed the deputy downstairs.

We waited by the door until Dove came. "What do you think about that. I believe she's just about the cheerfulest of anybody in jail I ever saw."

We followed him to the hearse.

"I thought I'd feel awful to see her in jail," he said, "but you know? She seems almost content. She said Nehemiah's folks sang her to sleep last night."

We drove away from there, down the hill past the pool, where Nehemiah Thomas addressed a cheering crowd from the stage. Dove didn't slow down. I glimpsed the words FREE AT LAST on a couple of hastily scrawled placards. We turned onto Lee Street.

"I'm glad he's free at last," Dove said. "Maybe now he can handle his own business and things can get back to normal around here."

I had trouble remembering what normal was like. Seemed to me it involved a lot of dead bodies. The big sagging funeral home looked a lot grander to me then—but then I was seeing it with both eyes.

"You boys come in my office," Dove said. "I have a call to make. You have to hear me make it."

We followed him in. He settled back in his chair, fished a slip of paper from a file box. "Hello howdy. I'm calling for Hiram Murphy. Yes ma'am. Dove Bullis. I sure will." He covered the mouthpiece with one hand. "About time we got a few things straightened out around—hello, Hiram. Hey, how are you. Fine. Listen, Hiram, talking to my boys, and to tell you the truth, well, they're not so sure what they saw anymore. You know, it's been so long since it happened. That's right. Mm-hmm. No, I think the grand jury's just gonna have to do it for us, we can't help you out anymore on this. I know you understand."

We could hear Hiram Murphy's angry squawk from where we sat.

"Slow down there, Hiram, you're talking too fast," Dove said. "You can subpoena anybody you want, but if you subpoena me, I'll just have to say I don't remember. The same goes for my boys. I don't think you understand, my friend. It's just not worth it. I got a life to get through, you know what I mean? Fellow tried to run me off the—what's that? No, you going back to wherever, Pennsylvania, but I got to try and live with these people. Listen, this is the last word for me. You'll just have to use whatever else you got. I am out of this thing, as of now."

He held out the phone, and hung up.

"There. I been wanting to do that since the first time he called me. We're getting it all straightened out now."

"We're not gonna testify?" Wiley said.

"That's right. It was none of our business in the first place. Earlene was right. It's about time we started living like everybody else in this town. Don't look so long-faced, Peter Joseph. It's not the end of the world."

"It's Aunt Lucille, isn't it," I said. "You made that deal with the sheriff."

He stared hard at me. "She's family, Peter Joseph. She's my sister."

"You said we could stop him!" I felt betrayed. "You said we could put him in jail."

"Maybe Hiram still can. But he'll have to do it without using us," Dove said. "Sometimes in life you have to make compromises."

Just that fast, we were out of the war.

The trial of John Doggett and his twelve co-defendants lasted forty-eight minutes. Hiram Murphy's star witness, the FBI informer who was in the pickup truck that fired on us at the Blessed Rest, refused to appear at the trial. Dove said he feared for his life. The judge dropped all charges. The men went grinning out into the sunshine to pose for the cameras.

34

Peejoe

Industry

I was bewildered by Dove's easy surrender. For two days I stayed mad at him. If he wanted to cave in, that was his right. But what gave him the right to use Wiley and me as his excuse? I hadn't forgotten all he had taught me about standing up for what you believe—even if he had forgotten teaching me.

He cut a deal to keep his Baby Sister out of the electric chair. Anybody could understand that. Even I understood it, and I was a dumb one-eyed kid. Dove invoked the word like a Bible commandment: She's *family*, Peter Joseph. There was never any doubt that it was more important to keep Lucille out of prison than to put the sheriff in it.

But why did he have to lie about it?

I still loved him more than anybody but Meemaw (and maybe Wiley, on a good day), but now I saw the desperation, the dark failure looming on every side of him. There was no money coming in; Nehemiah was embalming the colored dead, between marches and speeches; either nobody white in Industry was dying, or word hadn't got out yet that Dove was back to running a White Only funeral home. He sat for hours drinking Old Grand-Dad with the telephone cradled in his lap, and I wonder now what he was waiting for—a call from heaven, maybe, a direct line, "Hello Dove, this is God, you're a good man and I like you, I see you're having some trouble down there so I'm sending down a series of miracles to straighten it all out for you." The call never came.

When he was in one of these moods Wiley and I carried our TV dinners down to Milton's room under the stairs. I would have gladly swapped my Swanson Ranchero Fiesta Deluxe for a plate of the sausage and eggs Milton fried for himself on his hotplate, but I figured he was poorer than we were, so I never asked.

We always listened to the Chicago White Sox on the radio while we ate. We'd hear the crack of the bat and Milton's inevitable cry, "There she goes!" If it was a safe hit he'd say "That man *hit* that ball." If it went foul he'd shake his head and say "Well, almost."

I asked Milton why he never went to the mass meetings.

"I don't understand how you 'posed to make white folks appreciate you more by going around shouting in their faces," he said. "I'll leave that to the younger ones."

"But what about freedom?" I said. "Don't you want to be free?"

"Listen at you, boy. Free? What do you think I am? I come and go. Mist' Dove pays me good. I got a nice place here, a roof over my head, and what else do I need?"

"Don't you want to go downtown and eat at the Woolworth lunch counter?"

"Now, why would I want to do that when I can cook up the same grilled-cheese sandwich right here?"

"Don't you want to go swimming in the pool?"

He laughed, and went to rinse his plate. "I get as wet as I want in my bathtub," he said. "I tell you, young son, that's the thing about white folks. They think all the colored man wants is to be just like them."

"Peejoe's a Freedom Rider now," said Wiley. "Ever since Martin Luther King shook his hand."

"Now that Dr. King, now, I wouldn't mind going to hear him. I understand he gives a good talk." *Crack!* went the bat. "There she goes!" Milton cried. "Well, almost."

You would never know from listening to Milton that the whole town was holding its breath for Integration Day. The swimming pool had been drained, scrubbed, and filled with fresh water to prepare for reopening, by order of Judge Frank Johnson. George Wallace thundered from Montgomery, vowing to come to Industry to block any Negro or Yankee lawyer who tried to integrate the pool "against the will of the people." Hiram Murphy thundered back on behalf of the Federal Government, vowing to enforce the court order with United States marshals. Nehemiah Thomas and Martin Luther King announced a People's Swim-In for Saturday.

King's presence and the governor's defiance had brought every Rebel-flag-waving redneck pickup-truck driver in Alabama on a run. The streets of Industry resounded with their unmuffled engines. Gangs of them showed up at every march to hoot and throw rocks and yell nigger and get on TV. Nobody knew where they stayed at night, but they'd been spotted in large numbers eating barbecue at the all-night place on the Dothan Highway.

The newsmen were overjoyed to find two big stories unfolding in one little town. They could cover a civil-rights protest on the front steps of the courthouse, then stroll around back to interview the jailkeepers of Lucille Vinson, the Beverly Hillbillies killer.

Lucille's trial was set to start tomorrow, the eve of Integration Day; Dove said the city fathers were using her to distract attention from the Negro crisis. Since Sheriff Doggett allowed no interviews with Lucille, the reporters were making do with jailhouse gossip and pieces of the story flooding in from points along her journey west.

Every storekeeper between New Orleans and California who'd been robbed in the last three months claimed Lucille had done it. It made for exciting reading: She was said to have kidnapped a four-year-old girl for ransom, robbed a bank in Des Moines, hijacked a Brink's truck at the Phoenix airport, knocked over three liquor stores in Arizona, and masterminded the theft of a priceless bronze statue from a museum in Fort Worth.

The *Atlanta Constitution* called her a "modern-day Bonnie, with Clyde's head in a box." Lucille was especially thrilled with that clipping. She made Dove press it in Saran Wrap to keep it from turning yellow.

Dove spent hours huddled with Larry Russell, the slow-moving beetle-browed lawyer, trying to devise ways to get Aunt Lucille to go along with the deal. After the sacrifice Dove had made—slipping out of his promise to Hiram Murphy, letting the sheriff off the hook—Lucille had her own idea. She wanted a trial. She wanted to get up on the witness stand.

"She acts like this is one of her plays," Dove said. "She wants to put on a performance. She's determined to have it. She *loves* this attention."

The jury was chosen: seven men and five women, all white. Dove said we were lucky to get so many women. Tonight he was down at the jail for one last huddle with Lucille and the lawyer.

The White Sox won, four to nothing. Milton switched off the radio. "I got to pick up something for Mister Dove. Y'all want to come with me?"

"Where?"

"Just come on and see," he said, a secret glimmering in his eyes. We bugged him all the way out to the hearse, but he wouldn't tell us a thing.

"I get the window!" Wiley shoved me over.

"Stop it!"

"Hold on now, wild Injuns." Milton started the car.

"Can we run the siren, Milton?"

"No suh, we have plenty of time."

"Time for what?"

"Wait and see." Milton drove at a crawl, like a very old lady. Years of driving in funerals had convinced him that you get there just as fast going slow.

The swimming pool was deserted, picket signs stacked on the stage beside the fence. Someone had turned on the underwater lights, as if to promote an atmosphere of tranquility with the cool blue glow of the water. At this hour, the demonstrators at the Holy Redeemer A.M.E. Church were warming up for the big day.

Downtown Industry looked like a police convention. State troopers sprawled on the courthouse steps, playing cards. Another bunch sat at the picnic tables under the stone-gray gaze of the Confederate soldier. A gang of sullen teenage boys hung out with their pickups on the north side of the square, eyeing the trooper cars parked around the other three sides.

Milton pulled to the curb.

A Greyhound bus lumbered into the square, destination MOBILE, honking, spewing a cloud of smoke.

The bus stopped midway between the scruffy-looking pickup-truck gang and the congregation of troopers. The doors folded open with a hiss.

First off the bus was an old, heavy woman in a battered straw fishing-hat, lugging a barefoot toddler on her hip.

I squinted to be sure.

It was Meemaw.

I dashed across the street. A car swerved, blowing its horn. I dodged around it and ran to her. She saw me coming and slid little Marilyn down her leg to the sidewalk, opening her arms to me.

I pressed my face to the bosom of her faded dress, breathing her musty powdery smell. For a while I thought I'd never smell that again—

"Hey, Sweet Pea. Look who all came to see you!"

Marilyn tugged at my pants leg. Sandra came down the steps, and Farley, Cary, Marlon, and Judy, the entire Vinson collection, runny-nosed, towheaded, scratching and whining as they emerged into the open air. "Where are we?" "What time is it?" "I gotta pee!"

Meemaw took little Judy by the hand. "I wouldn't let her go to the bathroom on the bus. I was afraid she'd get sucked down the hole."

"Hey, lookit Peejoe," said Sandra. "He looks like Popeye!"

"I bet you never went that far on a bus," Farley said.

Milton watched for our reaction with his eyes dancing. "I told you I had a surprise, didn't I, Peejoe." He reached for Meemaw's satchel. "Miz Bullis, how you gettin' along?"

"I'm wore out, Milton. There's three more bags back yonder. Did you tell Dove we were coming?"

"No'm, I did like you said."

Wiley straightened up to look tall. "Hello, Grandmother." He leaned to kiss her cheek.

"Come here to me, you're not too big to give your Meemaw a hug! Oh it's so good to see you boys!" She embraced us, smushing us together.

Cary tapped my arm. "What's the matter with your eye?"

"I already told you, now hush," Meemaw said. "Milton, where's Dove?"

"Up yonder." He inclined his head toward the second floor of the courthouse.

I pointed out Lucille's tiny barred window, five cells from the end.

"My poor baby," said Meemaw.

Freed from the confines of the bus, the Vinson boys turned cartwheels on the sidewalk, raising hell, whooping it up. Milton went to stow the bags in the hearse, chuckling with pleasure at having kept his big secret.

"How in the world did you get taller than me, Peejoe?" Meemaw said. "Did I shrink?"

"No, I grew."

Judy hooked one ankle on the other and twined around herself like a telephone cord. "Meemaw, I gotta *go*."

"You better hurry up," Sandra said.

"Well Miss Smarty, take her and go find a place. Go around the front door, there's bound to be a bathroom in there."

That brought Milton from the shadows. "Aw now, Miz Bullis, you don't want to do that." He stuck his thumb toward that end of the square. "There's all kind of folk runnin' around here tonight."

Meemaw fished her glasses from her pocketbook to take a good look at the pickup trucks, fat boys in T-shirts, cops all over the place, the rumble of something waiting to happen. "My goodness, there's too much trouble down here."

"Marlon?" A cry from above. I glanced up: a head popped into the fifth window from the end. "Marlon Vinson, is that you down there making all that racket?"

The children froze. Marlon let go of Farley's hair. "Mama?"

"Do you have any idea what time it is?" Lucille hollered. "You better hush that mess this instant or I'm gonna come down there and slap you into the middle of next week. Do you hear me?"

"Yes ma'am."

The troopers laughed at this exchange.

"Mommy?" Sandra stood on tiptoes to wave. "Hey Mommy, it's me!"

Lucille's head disappeared from the window.

The door banged open and there was Dove, out of breath. "Mama? Jesus, what are you doing here?"

"Well that's a fine way to say hello."

"I'm sorry. It's good to see you." He stooped to embrace her, knocking her hat to the ground. "Why didn't you tell me you were coming?"

"You would have said no. I'm sorry to bring them all with me, Dove, but I tried and I couldn't find anybody to stay with them. Rusty Carew's keeping Adolf for me."

I retrieved her hat.

"I could have done something to fix up the house, get some furniture in there at least," Dove said. "We don't have enough beds. Earlene took everything."

"We'll make do," Meemaw said. "I just couldn't not come to her trial, Dove. She's my only daughter." She put on the hat. "I want to see her now. Take me up there."

"It's too late." He steered her away from the door. "We'll see her in the morning. Let's go home. You must be worn out from your trip."

Moths fluttered around the streetlight, casting jerky shadows. The black hearse was jammed with Vinsons having a fine time with the electric windows. Dove went around to lean in the driver's window. "Little surprise for me, huh Milton."

Milton cackled. "Yes suh, Mister Dove."

"Fine. It's your job to look after 'em. See you back home."

Milton grinned miserably and pulled away at a crawl. All six windows slid up and down at erratic intervals.

I climbed in the white hearse between Meemaw and Dove. Wiley crawled in back, acting cool about everything.

"I promise we won't be a burden," Meemaw said. "I bet it's been weeks since you had a decent meal."

"Y'all can stay a day or two," Dove said, "and then I think you'd better go on back home."

"Dove, now you listen to me. I am going to this trial, I'm going to every minute of it, and I'm taking those chillun with me," she said. "I want that jury to see us. I want them to see that Lucille's a real person, she's got a family that loves her and needs her."

"Mama, you can't expect those kids to set still in a courtroom all day."

"I've got them behaving. You'll see."

"Yeah," he said dryly, "I could hear that all the way from the second floor."

"Well my goodness, they've been cooped up for hours! We went all over south Alabama to get here." She squeezed me tight. "Oh sweetie, I've missed y'all so much. Did you miss me?"

"Uh-huh."

"Wiley, you miss me?"

"Sure." He leaned up from the back seat to pat her shoulder. "But Uncle Dove's been taking good care of us."

"I know he has." The headlights flashed across the weedy lawn of the funeral home. "Oh, look how you've let it go down," Meemaw said.

"No, I haven't." Dove pulled up the drive. "I just need to cut the grass, is all."

"I guess I remembered it different," she said.

35

Peejoe

Industry

The Vinsons ran wild through the laying-out parlors, shrieking in horror at the casket room, thundering up and down stairs.

Wiley said "I'm glad to see Meemaw, but I sure as hell could've done without the rest of them."

"Let's hope this trial is over with quick," I said.

Dove came upstairs with a stack of blankets. "Hello men, caught you hiding up here. Help me lay these out, will you?"

"You're not gonna put 'em up here!" Wiley said. "This is our room!"

"Well, we've got the two older girls in Mabel's room, Milton brought up the rollaway for Mama and the little one. I figured you'd want the boys up here with you, right?"

We didn't answer.

"Aw come on, fellas, they won't stay long. Look at me. See? I'm smiling." He put on a grin, and reached out to ruffle my hair.

Meemaw supervised a mass brushing of teeth, and rounded the Vinson boys up the stairs. She came around to give us each a goodnight kiss.

She stopped to finger the elastic on my eyepatch. "Do you sleep in this thing, Sweet Pea?"

"Tonight I am." I was mindful of Cary and Farley and Marlon on their pallets at the other end of the room. All day they'd been begging me to take off the patch and show them what was behind it.

She bent to kiss my nose. "I'm sorry that ever had to happen to you," she murmured. "I wish I could make it better."

I told her about my dream in the hospital, when she came to heal my eye with her touch. "I could've sworn you were there. It was so real."

"I was, Sweet Pea, I've been here with you all the time. You never doubted that, did you? Get some sleep now. Tomorrow's a big day."

"Night, Meemaw."

The lights went out. Wiley buried his head under a pillow. Cary poked Marlon, Marlon poked Farley, Farley swatted at Cary. It went on like that until I grew accustomed to it and fell asleep.

I awoke to the whisper of voices around me, way deep in the night— someone shining a flashlight—I jumped. The eyepatch snapped *thwack!* against my face.

Farley yelped. The other two collapsed laughing. They'd been standing over me, trying to get a peek at my eye.

"You want to see it?" I grabbed the flashlight and turned it straight up my nose, casting Halloween shadows on my face. I grasped the edge of the tape and pulled the bandage loose; it hung on my cheek like a flap of dead skin. "Here! Take a look!" I turned the beam directly into my dead eye.

From their screams I knew it must have looked truly hideous in that light.

Wiley woke up—"What the hell . . .?"

Cary backed away. "Guh-*ross.*"

"They wanted to look at my eye." I snapped off the flashlight. "So I let them."

The Vinsons crept back to their pallets. I stuck the bandage in place and smiled to myself. I don't know if they ever went to sleep that night. I know they didn't bother me again.

Meemaw gave off an air of Blue Grass body powder and churchly propriety, squeezed and girdled into her pale-blue go-to-meeting dress, with a string of big plastic pearls at her neck and a white pillbox hat. Her thick ankles in nylon stockings looked like a map of blue roads.

"You look nice, Meemaw."

"Well thank you, Sweet Pea, and don't you boys too. Marlon, you need to wipe your nose."

Somehow she got us all outside and into the hearse, which Milton had buffed to a blinding white gloss.

This had to be the hottest morning of the summer, steamy hot, and the sun still coming up through the trees. Dove brought a blast of cool air from the dashboard. Meemaw said she didn't know when she'd ridden in such fine style.

Everybody chattered until the courthouse loomed before us. Today the Alabama red-X-on-white flapped above Old Glory.

"Now you children listen to me," Meemaw said. "As quiet as you are this minute, that's how quiet I want you in that courtroom today."

"Your grandma's right," Dove said. "This is a court of law. There's a judge up there who can send you to prison for making the least little noise."

Marlon sat up. "I want to go to prison. Mommy's in prison."

"No, now, Marlon, that's not the way it works," said Dove. "That's a different prison."

"I want to go too," Judy said. "I want my Mommy!"

"See what you started." Meemaw turned. "Nobody's going to prison. We're all going to sit there and act like perfect angels."

The clock in the tower said quarter to nine, but the courthouse square bustled like Saturday noon. These were mostly white people milling on the hot stretch of concrete at the flagpole, Buicks and Oldsmobiles and beat-up trucks taking every available space at the curb. There were reporters and the usual old men in suspenders, but also dozens of ladies dressed up like Meemaw, younger women in housedresses, whole families from out in the country. I recognized a passel of Earlene's ladies'-club friends standing together.

"My goodness," said Meemaw, "there's certainly a lot of folks out early."

Dove pulled over to let us out. "Now Mama, take a bench near the back in case anybody has to go." He went off to find a parking place.

If I'd been Dove, I might have had an urge to keep going and drive that hearse right out of town, away from all this. But I guess Aunt Lucille had already tried that approach without much success, which was why we were gathered here today.

We blended with the people flowing toward the doors. One of Earlene's friends spotted my eyepatch and pointed me out to the others.

I pretended not to notice their gawking. We swept up the steps, into the echoing entrance hall. Aunt Lucille's trial had attracted lots of ladies; it looked like a wedding reception, all the women in hats greeting each other. The room rang with their exclamations. I paused a moment to watch Sheriff Doggett in a corner, giving an interview.

Already spectators had jammed all but the three rows in front. Meemaw marched us down the aisle and sat us in the very first pew.

This courtroom was much grander than the grand jury room, with twenty-five-foot ceilings and a gallery around three sides for colored spectators. The windows were open all the way, but the only breeze came from cardboard hand-fans provided by Liberty National Life Insurance. Already the ladies were waving these fans like mad, spreading perfume through the air.

Wiley and I sat near the window, with Meemaw at the opposite end, and the Vinsons arranged boy-girl-boy-girl between us. I craned around to watch the spillover of white folks heading upstairs to fill in the empty seats in the Negro gallery.

Among a sea of strangers I saw familiar faces: Mrs. McGuire and Myrtle Yelverton from Earlene's bridge circle, J. D. Eldridge and his pinch-faced wife, a couple of the Cornelia Baptist ladies who'd come to Chester's funeral, Mr. Peterson from the swimming pool.

A shrill protest arose in back, where the bailiffs were trying to shut the doors on several dozen people loudly wanting in. Dove squeezed in just as they got those doors closed. He stood in back, scanning for us. I waved.

He made a face and came down the side aisle. "What are y'all doing all the way down here?"

"These were the last seats left."

He surveyed the room. "She's got her an audience, all right. Would you look at this? Earlene would love this. She thought all these old biddies didn't give a fig about us. We're the number-one ticket in town."

Wiley scooted over to make room, but Dove said he'd be sitting at the defense table with Aunt Lucille.

A court clerk and stenographer came in, followed by Sheriff Doggett with the county solicitor, a mild-faced man named Hubert Mackie, earnest-looking, balding, sincere. He carried his briefcase under a pinned-up jacket sleeve concealing what Dove said was a withered right hand that he used to win sympathy from juries. Sheriff Doggett followed him to the prosecutor's table, whispering in his ear.

The door beside the jury box swung open, and twelve citizens filed to their seats, blinking in wonderment at the packed house. Two housewives in print dresses, two worthy matrons, one hawk-faced middle-aged lady with very short hair. Seven men in white shirts and skinny neckties.

I don't know what it was about those men, maybe the fact that they looked so much alike, but I wouldn't have wanted them sitting in judgment on me. Especially if I was as guilty as Aunt Lucille. I couldn't imagine any one of them having his own independent opinion.

A stir from the back of the courtroom—all the ladies went "ahhhh." There she was: the star of the show.

As a defendant in open court it was Lucille's constitutional right to wear whatever she pleased, and she had made the most of it. She was the world's most glamorous widow: tailored black suit cut snug at the hips and just above the knee, black silk stockings, high heels, a dramatically wide hat of black velvet framing her blond hair, exotic cat-eyed sunglasses studded with rhinestones. She stepped ahead of her deputy-escort, stood there until she had the complete attention of everyone in the room, then hooked her arm through Larry Russell's and took her long walk down the aisle.

She wasn't smiling, but I saw pleasure in her stride. She reached around Russell to open the latch on the gate, and that's when she saw us all sitting there: Meemaw, her children, Wiley and me.

She took off the sunglasses. "Come to me, babies."

Sandra jumped to embrace her, and all the children surrounded her, mewling and hugging—all except Farley, who sat beside Wiley staring at the floor.

The audience went "awwwww," as in *look, how adorable.* Larry Russell glanced over to make sure the jury was watching.

"Y'all sit down now and behave." Lucille leaned past Sandra to kiss Meemaw's cheek. "Hello, Mama. I'm glad you came."

"I wouldn't have missed it for the world," said Meemaw.

"I met Bob Hope, I can't wait to tell you about it."

The deputy escorted Lucille to the defendant's table, ten feet in front of us. Dove whispered something and she laughed, a light tinkly sound.

In that hat she looked like Marlene Dietrich, like Ingrid Bergman, like every dangerous blonde who ever stepped off a train on the late show. She saw me watching and gave a sly little wink: hello, Peejoe.

I closed my good eye, and opened it—the best I could do.

A bailiff emerged from the door behind the American flag. "All rise!" We rose.

"Oyez, oyez, oyez, the Criminal Court of Cotton County, State of Alabama, is now in session, the Honorable Lewis S. Mead, Circuit Judge, presiding. God save this honorable court."

Judge Mead entered on cue—a small, dapper, angular man with a pronounced beak and inquisitive blue eyes behind wire-rimmed glasses. A cheerful red polka-dot bowtie peeked over the collar of his flowing robes. He sprang up to the bench and settled in his green-leather chair. "Be seated, be seated," he said, waving his hand. "I must say I am *unused* to such a display of interest in the proceedings of this court, but I'll allow you all to remain as long as you follow a few simple rules." His vivid blue gaze turned to us. "I see we have quite a few children here today. I don't want any talking, any kind of disruption. Mothers, I'll ask you to remove any youngster who can't remain perfectly quiet. And the same goes for all the grown folks in the room."

An approving chuckle washed through the crowd.

"That's precisely what I do not want," the judge said. "Pay attention to what I say: no talking, laughing, whispering, crying, muttering, wheezing, or any other audible disruption. Do you understand me?"

You could have heard a Kleenex hit the floor.

"Very well. Ladies and gentlemen of the jury, you've been sworn and instructed as to courtroom procedure . . ." He talked for a while in his raspy, musical voice. Right away I felt I could trust this man.

"Mr. Russell, I believe your client has entered a plea of not guilty?"

Larry Russell stood up. "That's correct, your honor." He put his hands in the air as if to say *What can I do?*

"Counsel, approach the bench, please. Mr. Mackie, you too."

They went up and stood around whispering, which I thought was rather unfair considering what a big deal the judge had just made about talking in court. Other people must have felt the same way; the buzz of conversation began to rise again—and was swiftly killed by one glance from Judge Mead.

He sent the jury out of the room. "Will the defendant please rise," he said.

Lucille stood.

"Mrs. Vinson, am I to understand you've instructed your attorney to enter a plea of not guilty, irregardless of your prior conversation with Sheriff Doggett?"

"That's right, your honor," said Lucille.

"You intend to show you're innocent?"

"The way I understand it, Mr. Mackie has to prove *his* case, not me," she said. "Anyway I can't plead guilty. I'm not guilty. By reason of sanity."

The judge hunched forward. "Do you mean to say 'insanity'?"

"No sir. I'm not the least bit insane. Everybody wants me to act like I am, they all got together on a deal to send me up to Bryce and get this over with. But nobody consulted me, and I'm not going to do it." She straightened her shoulders. "I'm not crazy. And I'm not guilty."

Hubert Mackie exploded. "Your honor, I move for a mistrial!"

"Don't be silly, Mr. Mackie," the judge said. "I'm simply talking to the lady. Any discussions she might have had with the sheriff are perfectly admissible." He turned to Lucille. "Mrs. Vinson, there's no such plea as not guilty by reason of sanity."

"I know, Judge. I think those people will understand, if you give me a chance to explain."

He propped his chin in his hand, studying her. "What's your reasoning?"

"If they find me guilty, you send me to Atmore Prison, right?"

Mead's eyebrows angled up. "In Alabama the sentence is left to the discretion of this court. The jury delivers a verdict, and the court hands down the sentence."

"Okay, and if I plead insane, you send me to Bryce. But I don't want to go to either of those places. I want to go free. The only way I can possibly go free is to plead not guilty and let the jury decide, isn't that true?"

"Only way I know of," the judge said.

John Doggett watched Lucille through narrowed eyes, a cryptic smile on his face.

"Mrs. Vinson, I'd advise any defendant in a capital case to listen carefully to her attorney's advice," the judge said, "but I'm going to allow this plea. It's the right of the defendant to mount any defense you choose, as long as you understand the consequences, which you obviously do. Bailiff, let's get the jury back in here."

Lucille smiled in triumph. She swept her hair over her shoulder, and sat down. Larry Russell studied her, shaking his head.

Hubert Mackie requested a recess. "Your honor, if I'm now expected to establish the facts of this case, I'll need time to line up witnesses."

Judge Mead said it was hard enough to get a trial started and he wasn't about to stop it now. "An effective counselor is prepared for any possibility, Mr. Mackie," he said. "Proceed."

Mackie consulted a yellow pad, and stepped up to the jury box. The evidence would show, he said, that "Marjorie Lucille Bullis Vinson did knowingly and willfully cause the death of Chester Arthell Vinson on or about the third day of May, 1965, within the borders of Cotton County, Alabama, that the defendant committed the crime with premeditation and malice aforethought, that she did mutilate the body of the deceased in a cold-blooded fashion, and then did engage in a pattern of criminal behavior which established her guilt beyond any reasonable doubt."

Aunt Lucille folded her hands on the table and cocked her head to one side, as if all this was too fundamentally silly to be believed. Dove conferred with Larry Russell behind her back.

I'd never known her first name was Marjorie. That was Meemaw's name, too.

Holding his bad arm against his chest, Hubert Mackie leaned his good hand on the rail of the jury box. "They're going to try to play on your sympathy," he said. "You see they've dressed up all these children and brought them into court and put them right here in front of you."

I straightened in my seat. Meemaw had bright tears in her eyes and a handkerchief balled in her hand; she was all set to cry. All the Vinsons were watching their mother: Marilyn reached out chubby fingers, waving hi; Sandra and Judy and Marlon drank in the sight of her, without reservation; Cary looked skeptical, curious, like a member of the jury, and Farley—oh, Farley was taking every word like an arrow to the heart.

"As you'll discover, ladies and gentlemen, this defendant likes to gamble," Mackie was saying. "She's hoping the sight of these children will make you forget the terrible crime she's committed. But I know you're smarter than that. I know that every time you look over here at these children, you'll see their father, Chester Arthell Vinson. You'll see what their mother did to him. You'll see his severed head in a box. And I know that when we're done here, you'll reach the right verdict. Thank you." He bowed and sat down.

Larry Russell got to his feet. "Your honor, my client has a statement of her own, but with the court's indulgence I'll make a few observations first."

Mackie jumped up. "Your honor, this is all just highly unusual, to say the least. Counsel is obviously willing to let his client make a mockery of this proceeding, for some reason I don't understand."

"If Mrs. Vinson has prepared a statement," said the judge, "I for one would not want to miss a chance to hear it."

"Thank you, your honor." Larry Russell shuffled to the jury box and draped himself along the railing. "Ladies and gentlemen, I have a strong-minded client, as you've already seen. I've never met anyone quite like her. Now that doesn't bother me, the Constitution gives everybody the right to be strong-minded. It also gives these children the right to come here and witness their mother on trial for her life without some lawyer trying to make something sinister of it."

The dull mutter made it plain that the spectators agreed.

"Now Mr. Mackie says Mrs. Vinson is taking a gamble. I'll let you in on a secret: she is. She's come here to tell you the truth, the whole truth, nothing but the truth. And then she'll leave it up to you to decide whether she should go to prison or not. She's willing to gamble on you."

He appeared to have more to say, but he dropped his hands in his pockets and went to sit down.

Aunt Lucille carried a sheaf of papers to the jury box. "Good morning.

I don't believe I've met any of you, but I wanted a chance to talk to you, so I made a list of what I wanted to say." She cleared her throat. "I sat up real late in my cell, and I started with the night I got married, and I wrote down every single thing I could think of that my husband ever did to me. It's a long list, see here? Nine pages, and I ran out of ink in nineteen sixty-two."

Hubert Mackie got to his feet. "Your honor, I fail to see the relevance of this."

"Oh sit down and be quiet," said Lucille. "You've already had your turn."

Laughter broke out. The judge lifted his gavel and let it fall. "Mr. Mackie, I'll let her continue."

"Thank you, Judge." Lucille brandished her list. "Don't worry, I won't make you listen to the whole thing. I'll just read a few. Number one, April the seventh, nineteen fifty-two. That was our wedding day. Chester got so drunk at the reception he forgot about me and ran off coon hunting with his buddies. He stayed gone three days. When he came back he was mad because I'd already opened the wedding presents, which meant he couldn't take 'em back to the store for the cash."

The housewives were nodding. No doubt they had husbands at home who were capable of something like that.

Lucille glanced at the page. "Two weeks after that, he got tired of seeing my stockings hanging in the bathroom. He threw them all in the trash."

A murmur ran through the room. Judge Mead warned them back into silence.

Aunt Lucille ran down her list, month after month through the years, ticking off incidents of Chester's meanness and pettiness and hatefulness. She warmed to her audience as they warmed to her. She told about the time she was pregnant with Cary, her waters broke while they were at the Cornelia-Vinegar Flat football game. It was the conference championship. Chester made her sit there in the bleachers with water running down her legs until halftime before he took her to the hospital.

She told about the time she made a pineapple upside-down cake from scratch and Chester threw it out in the yard for the dog because he said he didn't want Chinese food in the house.

"He kept me pregnant for fifty-four months of my life," Lucille said. "He liked it when I was pregnant because that meant I had to stay home. He would punch holes in my diaphragm with a pin."

I wasn't sure what that meant, but the ladies knew: I saw the shock on their faces. I began to comprehend the wisdom behind Aunt Lucille's strategy. Dove had explained that any verdict had to be unanimous. One person could deadlock a jury, so that the prosecutor had to give up and start all over. Aunt Lucille was looking for one woman on the jury who could sympathize with her—one woman who could hold out against all those men.

Hubert Mackie said "Your honor, I respectfully submit that this is not a divorce proceeding. Why are we listening to this?"

"It goes to state of mind of the defendant," said Russell.

"I'd have to agree," said the judge, turning to Lucille. "You said you weren't going to read the whole list."

"And I won't." Lucille folded the pages. "I'll go right to the end, the week before—before Chester died." She proceeded to lay out the whole story, just the way she'd told me in Meemaw's side yard—her picture in the *Advertiser* and Chester's insults, the phone call from Harry Hall, the big chance of her life. "Excuse the language," she said, "but he told me to kiss his ass. And I told him that was exactly what I had been doing for thirteen long years."

The laughter started in front and rolled all the way up to the gallery.

Judge Mead pounded his gavel. "I'm not going to warn you people again. Mrs. Vinson, please."

"I'm sorry, your honor. It's the truth." Lucille turned to the jury. "I'm sure anybody that's ever been married could write out a list. Maybe it would be as long as mine. I quit writing because I ran out of ink. And that's just how it was between Chester and me. It was always like hell, you know? and still I was always able to take it somehow. And then one day I just stopped being able to take it. I realized there are other ways a person can kill you than with a gun. There are slow ways. Chester had been killing me the slow way for thirteen years. You spend all day cooking a meal for a man and he gobbles it down in five minutes, and never says thank you, and a little piece of you dies. Every time you try to talk to him and he moves his head to get a better look around you at the TV, he's killing you. He's got you barefoot and pregnant, and helpless, he's watching you grow old and die. He's just using you up."

She shook her head. "I never did anything to make Chester treat me that way. If he made a list about me, I'll bet it wouldn't have three things on it. I treated him good. I'm not guilty. Whatever I did, I did it in self-defense. He started killing me a long time ago. I had to get away from him. He wouldn't let me go. And look what's happened to me since. Maybe you read about it. I went to Hollywood, I got a job on the number-one network TV comedy show, I went out and found myself a whole new wonderful life. And it all happened the minute Chester wasn't there to stop me. It wasn't just a stupid dream, like he thought. It was real. It came true. I'm telling the truth, and I hope you'll believe me. Thank you very much."

She smoothed her skirt, and sat down.

The courtroom burst into applause. Even a couple of jurors joined in, the short-haired lady and one of the worthy matrons.

Bingo! I said to myself.

Judge Mead banged his gavel until he was red in the face. Meemaw dabbed at her tears.

"She's already won," Wiley said. "They can't find her guilty after that."

Farley tugged at my sleeve. "What's a diaphragm?"

36

Peejoe

Industry

Judge Mead threatened to empty the room at the very next peep out of anybody. "I will apologize to the children for my earlier remarks," he said. "They're not the ones creating these disturbances. Mr. Mackie, call your first witness."

"I'll call Sheriff John Doggett of Cotton County."

The sheriff hitched his belt, swaggered to the witness box, raised his right hand and swore the oath. He settled on the chair like a cowboy onto a saddle.

"Sheriff, I'd like you to tell us about the events of May sixth of this year. Did Mr. Bullis contact you to come to the Vinson residence in Cornelia that morning?"

"He did."

"And what did you find there?"

"Well, I didn't find it, Dove did," said Doggett. "It was Chester Vinson's body. He found it in a freezer in the basement."

"Mr. Vinson was dead?"

"He sure was," said the sheriff.

"Can you describe his condition?"

"He was frozen solid. And also his head was missing."

"What exactly do you mean by 'missing'?"

"Well, I mean it was gone. It looked like it had been cut off with something sharp."

The whole room drew in a breath.

"Sheriff, did you see any signs of how that might have happened?"

"There was a kind of toolshed on the back of that place. My deputies found a large amount of blood on the floor of that shed."

"So you think this man's head was cut off in that shed, and the body moved to the basement of the house?"

Larry Russell spoke without looking up—"Objection, counsel's drawing his own conclusion and asking for one from the witness." Like a turtle he poked his head out slowly, but snapped fast.

"Objection sustained."

"Let me cut through all this for you, Hubert," said Doggett. "Dove told me his sister killed her husband in a domestic dispute. He said she cut off his head and took it with her, and he didn't know where she was."

"Objection, that's hearsay."

"Sustained. Strike that," said the judge. "Sheriff, stick to what you saw."

The sheriff looked cocky and sure of himself—and why not? He had gotten away with murder, or something close to it, and now he didn't even have to deliver on his end of the deal. He could send Aunt Lucille up the river and never think twice.

He told how he arranged a stakeout at the train station in New Orleans, which led to the recovery of the Galaxie 500; how he followed Aunt Lucille's trail across the country to California through FBI teletypes and his network of cousins and informants; how he spotted her on "The Beverly Hillbillies" and alerted California authorities at his own expense; and how Lucille was arrested less than one week later, attempting to jump off the Golden Gate Bridge.

Mackie lifted a sheet of paper. "I move that the San Francisco Police Department report on Mrs. Vinson's arrest be entered as Exhibit A."

"Mr. Russell, do you want to object?"

"I don't think I will, your honor. I don't have any problem with a report that shows my client's state of mind on that bridge."

"So noted." The judge glanced it over before passing it to the court clerk.

The sheriff looked awfully pleased with the way things were going, which made me uneasy. I began to reconsider the surge of hope I'd felt when the audience cheered Aunt Lucille. Now that Hubert Mackie was laying out the facts, it was hard to see how the jury could get around the cold truth, which I knew better than anybody: Lucille *was* guilty.

"One more question, Sheriff," said Mackie. "Have you ever seen Mrs. Vinson wearing black before today?"

"No, Hubert, I sure haven't. She came in from California in some kind of miniskirt number. Yellow, I think it was."

"Thank you, Sheriff. Mr. Russell, your witness."

Minutes seemed to drag by while Larry Russell climbed to his feet. By the time he reached the witness stand, all eyes were focused on him. "Sheriff Doggett, had you ever seen Lucille Vinson before you took her to your jail last Friday night?"

"I'd seen pictures. Never met her before."

"So on Friday she was wearing what you call a miniskirt, and today you've seen her wearing this black, what would you call it, this black outfit. Any other clothes you remember seeing on my client?"

"Just what we give 'em in jail," he said. "It's kind of a blue-colored thing."

"So you're not really an expert on Miz Vinson's taste in clothes, are you, Sheriff?"

"No, I'm not."

"Thank you. Now when you arrived at the Vinson residence on May sixth, you saw the body of a man who had been decapitated, is that correct?"

"It is."

"And you've identified this man as Chester Vinson?"

"That's right."

"Let me ask you how you know who it was, if he didn't have a head."

Doggett looked honestly perplexed. "Well, you know, I s'pose I just took Dove's word on that."

"But Chester Vinson was a stranger to you?"

"That's right."

"So it could have been anyone. You didn't take any fingerprints, or check for identification?"

"Dove told me who it was," Doggett said.

"You consider Mr. Bullis to be a man of his word?"

Doggett glanced over to the defendant's table. "Well, he gets a mite confused now and then about whose side he's on. But I'd say he's honest, sure."

Dove answered him with a sour smile.

"All right now, you've testified you saw all this blood everywhere, did you happen to take a sample of it?"

"Somebody might have, but I didn't, no. We never thought this case would come to trial."

"You don't know whose blood that was?"

"I assumed it was Vinson's."

"Did you take any photographs of these alleged bloodstains, or the body?"

"No—come on, Larry. That's not my job."

"Just answer the question. After all this fine detective work you've told us about, you didn't even bother to take a picture of the scene of the crime, did you?"

"You know we don't work that way on a case like this."

"Sheriff, besides this alleged blood, what other evidence did you find in that shed? Did you find a weapon?"

I liked the way Larry Russell kept glancing off that word, *alledgid*, with an ironic twist in his voice.

"No," said the sheriff. "Look, except for what she did to him after she killed him, this was a domestic dispute, cut and dried. Happens all the time. We weren't dusting for fingerprints or looking for some unknown killer. We knew who did it."

"How did you know?" Russell pulled on his lip. "Did you have witnesses?"

"No. There weren't any."

"Then how did you know?"

"Dove Bullis told me."

"Did he tell you he witnessed a crime himself? Did he say 'Sheriff, I saw Lucille kill Chester Vinson with her own two hands'?"

"Not in so many words, no."

"Did he say she had confessed a crime to him?"

"Not to him. To somebody else. One of the kids."

"Which kid?"

"That one." He raised his arm to point across the room. "The one with the patch on his eye."

Three hundred eyes turned to look at me. I concentrated on meeting the sheriff's gaze without blinking.

Larry Russell went on asking questions, but for long minutes I heard only the song of blood in my ears. Of all the people Lucille must have met since that day in Meemaw's yard, I was the one who had heard her confess exactly what she did to Chester. Her children and Meemaw saw her holding that head, the police in San Francisco found the head in its Tupperware bowl, but no one else had heard Lucille tell the whole story, how Chester struggled and fought her in his dying moments, how she dragged him out to the shed rolled up in the carpet . . .

I wouldn't tell. Hubert Mackie could put me on that stand and keep me up there for forty days and forty nights and I would never tell. This was family. I had to help Aunt Lucille.

I could start by forgetting. I could play the part of a dumb kid who doesn't remember a thing.

Larry Russell led the sheriff back and forth over his story, searching for holes. Marlon and Judy grew restless, fidgeting and kicking the bench until Meemaw fixed the rest of us in place with a glance and took them out. Spectators turned with indulgent smiles to watch them go, as if those were the only children they'd ever seen.

"Now Sheriff," drawled Russell, "let me get this straight. You don't have a weapon. You don't have a witness. You don't have a confession. You don't have samples or photographs or any evidence besides an arrest report from San Francisco. You don't even know for sure whose body that was in the freezer, do you?"

"You heard the woman," said Doggett. "She told you she wanted him dead. She had his head when she was arrested. That's enough to convict her."

"That's up to the jury to decide, isn't it, Mr. Doggett?"

"Yep, it is."

"Would it be fair to say you've been so busy with civil-rights demonstrations and federal indictments and such, that you haven't had time to conduct a proper investigation of this alleged crime?"

"Objection, your honor, this witness is not on trial."

"Sustained. Mr. Russell, what's your point?"

"My point, your honor, is that Mr. Mackie and the sheriff have yet to show this jury one single shred of evidence that a crime even occurred here, beyond their own *opinion* that it did."

"The man didn't cut off his own head," Doggett snapped.

"The thing speaks for itself," murmured the judge.

Larry Russell said "Not anymore it doesn't."

"Get Dove Bullis up here," said the sheriff. "Ask him. He's the coroner. He did the autopsy."

"Mr. Doggett, didn't you assume from the beginning you could use Miz Vinson as a wedge against Mr. Bullis, and that's why you never bothered to get any evidence?"

"I heard what she said up here," he retorted, "and I can tell you I never talked to Dove Bullis about any deal."

"Did you talk to Lucille Vinson about a deal?"

The sheriff scratched his neck. "No. I never did."

That was the first flat-out lie I'd heard him tell. It even sounded like a lie when he said it.

"Are you sure?"

"I can't make deals like that. I'm not one of you lawyers, I'm just a county sheriff."

"I have no further questions," said Russell.

"In that case, this court will stand in recess until one-thirty." The judge whacked his gavel once, and stood up.

"All rise!"

We rose. The judge marched out, trailed by the jury and bailiffs. A morning's worth of suppressed noise burst forth all at once. Aunt Lucille was mobbed coming through the gate. The deputy and Dove cleared a path.

Larry Russell tried to steer her away from the reporters and cameras in the lobby, but Lucille put on her movie-star sunglasses and went for them on a beeline. Wiley and I got out there just as someone asked her why she had decided to plead not guilty.

"Because I'm not," she said. "Chester Vinson was a terrible husband. He's the one who was guilty."

"Do you think you can win?" a man shouted.

"I sure do. I think the jury will believe me."

"Mrs. Vinson—"

"It's not Mrs. Vinson anymore," she said. "I divorced him in Las Vegas."

"You divorced him? After he was dead?"

"It was something I wanted to do."

"Thanks a lot, fellows," Russell sang out, edging her on through the crowd at the steps.

The square was the scene of picnics spread on tables, on the grass, on the hot hoods of cars. Three dozen Negro demonstrators walked back and forth with signs, INTEGRATION 4-EVER and CIVIL RITES NOW. Dove met us at the foot of the steps. "Wiley, go around yonder with your grandma and all them," he said. "Peter Joseph, you need to come with me a minute."

Wiley looked jealous, but he obeyed. I followed Dove into the cool gloom of the courthouse. Many of the spectators had gotten in line as soon as the courtroom was cleared, to get the best seats for the afternoon session.

Dove spoke to the bailiff and ushered me into the empty courtroom. I heard someone say "That's the boy on *Life*" as the doors swung shut behind us.

"Where we going, Uncle Dove?"

"Just right here." He hoisted me up to the defendant's table, and eased himself down beside me. "Listen, you heard Baby Sister. She's blown off the deal. She wanted this trial. John Doggett's already got us off his case, he doesn't feel bound to his end of it anymore. I can't say I blame him.

Now she doesn't want to use a defense of insanity, which is about her only real hope, and Mackie's going for a straight conviction."

"What do you want me to do?"

"They may call you up there. Hubert has officially notified me to have you here and available. I want you to be ready, just in case."

"What should I say?"

"Tell the truth, but be careful. Don't answer anything more than he asks you. Try to remember things she said that made her sound—well, you know, crazy. It's important they understand she didn't know right from wrong."

"Do you really want me to remember? I can pretend I forget."

"No, son. As Larry put it to me, we're gonna try and confuse 'em with the truth. He's bringing in all these little doubts along the line. He's decided to put her up on the stand after all. That jury likes her, and eventually they'll have to realize she could not have been sane to do what she did. No matter what she says. It may be enough to hang 'em up. And that's what we want. Who knows? They love her so far. They might even acquit her." He patted my shoulder. "You're a good boy, Peter Joseph. Here. Here's a quarter. Think of it as a bribe."

I stuck it in my pocket.

The doors gave in to pressure from the other side. The room filled with spectators, jostling and shoving each other to get to the front.

"You better save that bench for your grandma," said Dove.

I stood at the first row until Meemaw appeared with Wiley, Sandra, and Cary. She had sent Farley and the little ones home with Milton.

Wiley sat down beside me. "What did Dove want?"

"They might call me to testify."

I could see how this ate at him—*he* was the eldest, the athlete, the winner, champeen, All-American boy; why didn't anyone ever ask him to testify? "Why you?"

"You heard the sheriff. I was there when she said what she did."

"So was I. So was Meemaw and everybody else."

"You didn't hear all of it. You ran away, remember?"

"Jesus," he muttered under his breath. "Go to hell."

"Wiley said two bad words," Cary announced.

"Shut up—"

The jurors came through the door with the bailiffs and Judge Mead. Sheriff Doggett had been replaced at the prosecutor's table by a bland young man with curly hair, a junior version of Hubert Mackie.

Mackie called Dove to the stand. Dove was nervous at first. When he produced the autopsy report for the judge I saw the tremor in his hands. "Chester Vinson died of cardiac failure," he read, "apparently brought on by an infusion of a toxic substance the lab boys have identified as roxylanoprolymol, which is the active agent in D-Con."

"D-Con," Mackie repeated.

"A commercial brand of rat poison. It's my opinion he ingested the poison some hours before his head was removed from his body."

"Do you have any idea who gave him rat poison, Mr. Bullis?"

"Well, I might have ideas, but my sister has never told me what happened."

"And you haven't asked?"

"No."

"Why not?"

"I knew I might have to testify about this."

"But you think Lucille Vinson poisoned him?"

Dove shrugged. "For all I know he poisoned himself. What I think is, my sister is having a little trouble right now sorting out what's real from what's not."

Lucille flinched and looked at her hands.

"You think she has mental problems?"

"It's not my job to make guesses about things like that," Dove went on. "I was required by the law to perform a thorough autopsy and I did, and these are the results."

"Mr. Bullis, you don't have any doubt about whose body that was in the freezer, do you?"

"No, I don't."

"And why not?"

"It was his freezer."

Mackie was practically waving his pinned-up sleeve in the jurors' faces. They followed it with their eyes, unable to look away. He kept Dove on that stand for nearly two hours.

Larry Russell made a big show of idly leafing through a lawbook. Every so often his bushy eyebrows would knit, and he'd say "Objection," and go back to turning the pages.

All the Statue of Liberty fans in the world couldn't have cooled the air in that room. To make matters worse, there were so many trucks and motorcycles blatting through the courthouse square that the bailiff slid the shrieking windows down. You could feel the people beginning to melt from inside when he did that.

Aunt Lucille held a pose of total attention, her hands folded beside the black velvet hat. She didn't look the least bit hot or bored.

At long last Mackie ran out of questions, and it was Larry Russell's turn. He began gently: "Dove, this has been a terrible time for you and your family, hasn't it?"

Dove said "Never been anything quite like it."

"And yet you're able to come up here as coroner and give an honest report. I'd like to commend you for that."

"It's my job." Dove watched Lucille.

From outside came the sound of people cheering, motors revving, a rising commotion.

Russell said "You've testified that Mrs. Vinson has difficulty telling what's real from what's not. Can you give us any examples?"

"Well, she said Chester's head was talking to her."

"Talking to her?"

"Out in California. That's why she had trouble getting rid of it, because it was talking to her."

Two reporters raced for the door.

"Can you think of anything else?"

Lucille glared.

Dove hesitated, then plunged ahead. "I would just say the whole—the whole pattern of her behavior in this thing. She's always been a good mother to her kids, a wonderful part of our family. . . . It just isn't like her to turn her back on all that and run away like that. I think she must have been disturbed to do that." Sweat trickled down his face. I knew he would rather have been anywhere else on earth.

"Dove, do you think Lucille is dangerous?"

"Objection, your honor, this witness is not a psychiatrist, or a judge."

"I'll let him answer."

"She is absolutely not dangerous," Dove said. "She's confused, maybe. But I don't think she would hurt anybody."

He stopped. He couldn't go on. He looked at Lucille, and she looked at him, and I saw the two of them piled up on that cot in the jail cell, arm in arm, brother and sister. I saw the terrible thing that was happening in this room today. Our family was dying. We had brought it out here in public so everyone could hear the death-rattle. Suddenly I felt ashamed.

"Do you think she's dangerous to herself?"

Dove coughed. "Maybe. I don't know. When all this sinks in . . ."

"Thank you, Dove. I have no further questions."

"Mr. Mackie? Redirect?"

"I'll reserve the right to call him again, your honor, thank you."

"Mr. Bullis, you may step down," said the judge.

Hubert Mackie went to his table for a drink of water. He glanced at a card in his good hand. "I'd like to call Peter Joseph Bullis to the stand."

Meemaw came out of her seat. "*What?!*"

I guess Dove hadn't warned her.

"I'll ask the spectators to refrain from comments," said the judge.

I felt myself lifting, my body suddenly light as a balloon, floating down the row through the gate across the floor up two steps and another step, to the witness box. I raised my right hand and swore.

I will never doubt the wisdom of whoever arranged the courtroom so you sit facing the audience, the judge on your right, the accused directly in front of you, the flag and the Bible and the oath. It is a setup designed to sweat the truth out of you. Hundreds of strangers watched me and only me. Aunt Lucille smiled up, her poise recovered. Meemaw was helpless to do anything about the sight of her Sweet Pea up there giving testimony. Dove held my gaze with a grave expression, followed by a positive nod: Tell the truth, nothing but the truth—but maybe not the entirely *whole* truth.

Mr. Mackie put on an ingratiating smile. "Hello, Peter, how you doing today? Are you comfortable up there?"

"Yes sir, I'm okay."

"Now Peter, I'm going to ask you some questions and I just want you to answer the best you can. How old are you, son?"

"Twelve." And I am not your son.

"What's your relationship to Mrs. Vinson?"

"She's my aunt. She's my . . . my father's sister."

"I understand your father's deceased?"

"Yeah. And our mother too." Gimp-Arm Mackie wasn't the only one who knew how to wring a little sympathy from a jury.

I had to decide what to do. If I told everything I remembered, the way she struggled with Chester before he died, the way she dragged him all over the house, looking for some place to cut him up with the carving knife, it might finish her off in the eyes of that jury.

I could clam up, withdraw, forget to remember. But this lawyer was tricky, he'd catch me if I tried to deceive him.

An old lady had a coughing fit in the back of the room. When she opened the door to step out, noise flooded in: some kind of celebration under way in the courthouse square.

"Peter, do you remember May fifth, the day your Aunt Lucille came to your grandmother's house?"

"Yes sir."

"Tell us what happened."

"She was already there when we got home . . ."

"Could you speak up, young man?" boomed the judge. "I can hardly hear you."

"I said she was already there when Wiley and me got home. She started talking about Uncle Chester. She said he drove her crazy."

"She said that exactly? 'He drove me crazy'?"

"Something like that."

"All right. And what else?"

"She said she killed him."

"Did she tell you how?"

"With D-Con."

Mackie came so close I counted the white hairs poking out of his nose. "Tell us exactly what she said, Peter."

"She gave him D-Con in his coffee."

"Did she tell you why she did it?"

"She said Uncle Chester got on her nerves."

The audience suppressed a giggle.

"He wouldn't let her go to California," I said. "He thought she was weird because she wanted to be on 'The Beverly Hillbillies.' And she made it, too. She got on there."

Lucille smiled, and winked.

"Did she tell you why she cut off his head?"

"She was afraid he might still be alive. She said a lot of—you know—crazy stuff."

Lucille's smile vanished. Now I was like Dove, calling her crazy in front of all these people. But there was also a lot I wasn't telling: how she'd schemed and planned for weeks before she killed him, staring at him every night in front of the TV, plotting out the details.

"Do you remember anything specific?"

"She said she only had one life. And she didn't want to sit around waiting for the next one. And she showed us his head. I thought that was crazy. She made us look at it."

"What else?"

"You know, just what Uncle Dove already said. She heard it talking to her."

"Think carefully, son. Did she say she gave him the poison on the spur of the moment, or had she thought about it before?"

I hesitated. "I don't remember."

"Did she say whether she'd bought the D-Con beforehand, or was it just lying around the house?"

"She didn't talk about that." There's one lie for you, Aunt Lucille, please stop looking at me that way. I remembered full well how she'd gotten Chester to bring the poison home from the hardware, she told him there was something crawling around in the house, something she wanted to kill, bring some strong poison home with you. She thought it was a rat, she told him, but she wasn't sure.

I didn't tell that.

"This is very important," Mackie said. "Did she say whether she knew it was wrong to kill him?"

The big question—the one Dove had warned me about. I thought hard before I answered.

"No. She seemed happy about it at first. But then later she started crying, and she said she didn't know what was wrong with her."

"What did she use to cut off his head?"

"An electric carving knife."

Lucille worried the edge of her hat with her fingers. The jurors sat up straighter. Dove nodded imperceptibly: *good boy.*

"What do you mean she seemed happy?"

"She just was all excited, you know, about going to Hollywood and getting on TV. She said maybe she was crazy, but she was alive, and Chester was dead. She was happy about that."

A door banged open in back, startling everyone. A bailiff marched down the aisle, through the gate, and up to the bench. "Sorry to interrupt, your honor," he said, handing up a slip of paper.

Judge Mead studied it, turned to Hubert Mackie. "Counselor, are you just about through with this witness?"

"Yes sir, just about."

"Good." He turned to the jury. "Ladies and gentlemen, I had hoped we could finish this up in one day and not inconvenience you further. I'll ask you not to discuss the details of this case with anybody, stay away from newspapers and television. I've just gotten word that the governor is paying a visit to our city, and the courthouse is closing early in honor of his coming. This court will stand in recess until Monday morning, nine o'clock." He banged his gavel, and followed the jurors through their door.

The courtroom erupted. Half the audience rushed outside to see what was up. Others swarmed through the gate to surround Aunt Lucille, asking for her autograph, complimenting her children, wishing her luck. "Tell us about Jethro!" a woman cried.

"Oh, he's adorable, looks just like Elvis." She signed her name in a memory book.

"Who else did you meet?" said a homely girl with braces.

"I met Cary Grant at a party. He kissed my hand."

They oohed and ahhed.

"And I saw Bob Hope and his wife, she looks older than him," said Lucille. She posed with a fat lady whose daughter snapped an Instamatic. "And I met Toby Clark."

The girl squealed, jumping up and down. "Toby Clark!"

"I did. I went out with him." She smiled. "He kissed me on the lips."

All the women said: "Ahhhh."

I sat forgotten in the witness box. My big moment had been upstaged by the governor of Alabama.

Wiley came up. "You didn't know anything anyway."

"I know more than I said." I climbed down from the chair. "Do you think I made her sound crazy enough?"

"You did all right." That was as big a compliment as he would ever give me.

"I can't believe I have to wait till Monday and do it again," I said.

We watched Dove and Larry Russell blocking for the deputy, trying to move Aunt Lucille through that mob of people.

37

Peejoe

Industry

There was a hard, dangerous light in that square. All the pickup-truck rednecks had come out in the heat of the wide afternoon to welcome Governor Wallace. They waved Rebel flags in the air and sang "Dixie." The Negroes melted away into the side streets.

I saw Milton hastening toward the hearse with Sandra and Cary.

A flotilla of motorcycle cops swung onto Jackson Avenue, vibrating the air with their Harley roar. There must have been forty Alabama state troopers driving their fat bikes up on the grass, scattering people, seizing command of the square.

Four of them marched up the steps. The leader flipped up his visor and said "Clear the area!" in a voice that allowed one possible answer: *yes sir.* I said it and so did Wiley. They herded us off the steps, out among the picnic tables, where we found Meemaw looking for us.

Three black Chryslers raced into the square. Men in gray suits emerged from the first car to set up a podium and a PA on the steps where we had been standing.

"This is just too much excitement," said Meemaw.

"Why's he coming today? Integration Day's not till tomorrow."

"He's smart," Wiley said. "He knows ol' King's gone to Atlanta, not supposed to come back till tomorrow morning. It's all over the papers. I bet old Georgie just figured he'd come down here and get the jump on him."

"Show some respect," said Meemaw. "He's our governor."

I remembered the pictures on her nightstand: Jesus, Grandpa Joe Wiley, and George Wallace.

He jumped from his car, a solid plug of a man in a white shirt with his sleeves rolled up. His hair gleamed with oil; he beamed his smile all around; he was wiry and quick on his feet. The crowd converged on him—"Hello George!" and "Give 'em hell, Gumner!" He handed out boisterous howdies and handshakes all the way up the steps.

He looked like a bulldog with those fierce eyes, that scrappy pug nose. Also he was shorter than everyone around him. The people loved him; he reached through the troopers to touch their hands. He swept them along in a whirlwind.

The troopers closed around him and got him up to the microphone.

People pressed forward, waving and cheering. The fever in this crowd was as high as it had been at the swimming pool when Martin Luther King got up to speak. I saw the same light in these eyes.

Meemaw stood on tiptoe, waving her Statue of Liberty fan.

"Hello, friends!" Wallace's voice buzzed the glass in the storefronts. "Good to see so many of you, hope you don't mind me droppin' by on such short notice. Move up from the back and give 'em room there, let's give everybody a chance to hear."

"Hoo-ee!" a man bellowed. "Give 'em hell, George! Yow!"

"Thank you, thank you friends. You know, when y'all elected me and sent me to Montgomery, I never dreamed I'd have to come down to Industry and help you fight off Martin Luther King and the Yankees!"

The crowd roared with laughter.

"No sir, never thought I'd see the day when the Federal Guvment would busy itself coming down here to tell you folks who you have to swim in a swimming pool with."

He waited for the applause, and it came, and he basked in it. "Now they got a federal judge up in Montgomery, name of Frank Johnson," he said, waving his hands to encourage the scattered boos. "I knew ol' Frank when he was up in Tuscaloosa, we went to law school together. And let me tell you folks, it's the same today as it was back then—everywhere I look, there's Frank Johnson's big ol' feet in my way."

They loved that. They hooted and stomped and waved their flags. A string of firecrackers went off *pap! pap! pap!*

"Now Frank has issued a court order, which is about the only thing he's good for these days. He has seen fit to declare that if you folks in Industry wanna build a pool for your chillun, you got to admit anybody, regardless of color, race, creed, religious belief, or Communist Party affiliation."

"No! Hell no!" a man cried from the back. "Niggers, go to hell!"

"Hold on now, hold on," said Wallace. "We don't want none of that. We're peaceful today. We come here every bit as peaceful and *nonvilent* as

Mister Martin Luther King himself. You folks know I have nothing against the Negro. I've said it for years, I grew up amongst 'em, like you did. Negroes have always supported me in my campaigns, and I can tell you there's a lot of 'em don't want this civil rights mess crammed down their throats any more than we do. You'd be amazed at how many friends Lurleen and I can count among the Negro voters. I never said a mean word about the Negro people, and I never will. But that doesn't mean I'm gonna let Frank Johnson tell you your chillun have to play with 'em and swim with 'em and go to school with 'em. I have come here today to stop that."

A great cheer arose in the square, and a deeper sound behind it, cannons booming in the distance.

"Last night I got word that King and his element were fixin' to get sneaky and come on in here today, and integrate this pool before I could get down here to stop 'em. And when I got wind of that, I set aside all that important state business and I said, I'm going down there and stand up for the good, honest, decent, law-abidin', hard-workin' white people of Cotton County!"

They rewarded him with another ovation. Meemaw clapped along with everyone else. I kept my hands in my pockets.

If Meemaw had a chance to hear Martin Luther King, would she still be clapping for this man? The governor spoke for the white folks, for the sheriff and his pickup-truck pals but also for regular people who were scared or just old, like Meemaw. This man was telling the whole world exactly what *they* thought, what *they* felt and wanted. He was their hero, their King.

Around the corner past Planter's Mercantile came the Industry High School Marching Rebel Band in all its red-and-white glory, marching in crisp lockstep to the cadence of drums.

Wallace greeted this interruption with a flash of annoyance, which he swiftly managed to hide. He folded his hands behind his back and stood with a polished smile as the band marched past Parker's Drug Store.

Prancing out in front, a robust and angular figure. I knew him at once. Randall Mulch, Dove's part-time cosmetologist.

He wore a tall furry hat with a red feather, his chin pulled up into three chins, whistle clenched in his teeth. He swooped his white cape and barked orders to his troops, marching them around the motorcycles, squeezing them through the crowd, re-forming them on the plaza to the governor's right.

The drums crashed to a halt. Randall's whistle went *skreet! skreet!*

skreet! and the band lit into a lively "Dixie." When the song ended, he snapped the band to attention. The crowd responded with a big hometown cheer.

"Very nice," Wallace said. "Thank you boys and girls, thank you. That's my favorite song and I'm truly grateful to you all for this warm welcome. Now friends, as I was saying, I'm here today to stand up for your rights. And I mean to do just that thing, without further ado. All I ever hear from these outside agitators is 'we gonna march here, we gonna march there,' all the time march, march, march—these are the marchin'est people in God's creation."

Everyone laughed.

"That's the honest truth," said Meemaw.

"But today I'm gonna tear a page out of their book," the governor crowed. "Today, friends, it's our turn to march."

That brought an approving shout.

"I'm gonna march down to that swimming pool, and I'm gonna stand there in the door of that poolhouse, and if anybody wants to come down there and trample over your rights, they'll have to get by me first. Do y'all want to march with me?"

The crowd shouted yes, oh yes.

"Come on, then! We can march."

Randall dashed to clear out a band-sized gap in the crowd with his baton and his whistle. The band tramped away blowing a fanfare. Wallace came down the steps in a flying wedge of state troopers.

Half the troopers set off after the band, and the enthused crowd fell in behind them. Most people assumed that the Little Fightin' Governor was somewhere in that phalanx of lawmen marching past the Dairy Dog and down the hill to the swimming pool. In fact it was a classic sneak play. I saw Wallace hunker down in the contingent that split off from the main group and headed for the line of Chryslers.

He jumped in his car and rode the long way around back streets to the pool, where he got out and hastened across the grass. The cameras recorded him striding up to that chain-link fence in the first wave of marchers. You may have seen those pictures, you may have read about George Wallace's famous march to the Industry swimming pool, but I am here to tell you: He rode.

We helped Meemaw down the grassy slope toward the pool. "Isn't he just a little banty rooster?" she said. "He's the only one who's not afraid to say what's on his mind."

"But Meemaw," I said, "he hates colored people."

"No he doesn't. You heard him. He just doesn't think they ought to be pushing us around, and I can't say he's wrong about that."

The band played "Stars Fell on Alabama." People streamed into the park. The governor stood between the stage and his car, checking his watch.

If the governor had planned to bring this crowd down here to face off against a bunch of militant Negroes, he was sorely disappointed. I searched the crowd for a single black face. The stage was only half-set for a confrontation: Wallace was here, the state troopers were here, and the worshipful crowd; Sheriff Doggett strutted up and down the fence, acting important—but where were the outside agitators? The integrators? The enemy?

Local bigwigs jostled each other to meet the governor. Their eagerness was painful to watch. Wallace greeted all the way down the line to the marching band. Randall Mulch drew up to full attention and executed a stiff-armed salute. A goofy awe-inspired grin came over his face. He reached out to shake the governor's hand.

I had to look away.

When I did, I saw a pair of dark-blue sedans bumping over the grass toward the poolhouse.

The governor saw them, too. He left Randall standing there, with his hand out and that stupid grin on his face. He lifted a finger to his troopers and moved down the fence, toward the battered gate.

The swimming pool sparkled in brilliant sunshine, its surface undisturbed by the slightest ripple or breeze. The WHITE ONLY sign had been removed by order of the federal court.

Twenty state troopers arranged themselves in two lines blocking the gate, standing at attention with visors down, rifles braced in both hands, feet apart. Wallace took up a position in front of them and slightly to one side, so the TV cameras could capture him and the troopers and the pool in one shot.

A rumble ran through the crowd. Everyone turned to witness the approach of the enemy.

The enemy was a little group led by two U.S. marshals in white helmets and green uniforms. They were unarmed, not so much as a nightstick between them. The one on the right kept glancing nervously from his partner to the muttering crowd.

There were nine in all, nine terribly outnumbered people who now proposed to walk this gauntlet for the purpose of challenging the governor of Alabama. Behind the marshals was our friend Hiram Murphy, the

Justice Department lawyer. Even in this stunning heat, he wore his three-piece suit and short-brimmed hat. Three more marshals brought up the rear, looking just as nervous.

Also there were three Negroes: Nehemiah Thomas and his sons Ben and Ramsey. Nehemiah walked with his chin in the air, unafraid. His sons looked as if they'd been drafted in the middle of dressing for something else; Ramsey's shirttail was out, and Ben had a bit of toilet paper stuck to a shaving cut near his ear.

They must have cobbled together this showdown at the last minute. How could Hiram Murphy hope to challenge all these troopers, the governor, and this large unfriendly crowd with three Negroes and five unarmed marshals?

The television cameras swiveled from the governor to the pool to the troopers to the advancing demonstrators. A reporter murmured into a microphone: ". . . and here comes Hiram Murphy, representing the Johnson administration on the scene today. Murphy's well known for prosecuting various public officials in civil rights cases across the South. . . ."

What kind of game was this, three hundred against nine? If George Wallace thought these odds were fair, he was no better than John Doggett, no more than a common bully. Look at all those state troopers fingering their rifles. Bullies, all of them.

I was sick of bullies. Sick of seeing them win. Why is it always the strong ones who win? Why is it never the ones who are good but not strong?

The jeering crowd seethed as it parted to let them through. These nine people were taking onto themselves all the sins of the people around them. I saw it plainer than any story in the Bible.

We were surrounded by people who'd been laughing and cheering the governor only a moment before. I barely recognized them. They hissed and made faces, they yelled "nigger" and "coon" and worse things. The troopers tensed up, shifting their stance.

And then I remembered Dr. King's golden sword of nonviolence. That was the weapon these people carried, that invisible sword and the U.S. flag patches on the marshals' shoulders. Let the people taunt, let them jeer and spit and twist their faces—nothing could touch these nine people. They walked alone in the midst of that hate-filled crowd. They overcame the hatred with their composure. For that moment, I thought, they were holier than anybody, Jesus included.

Wiley grabbed my hand. "Come on, Peejoe."

"Boys?" Meemaw moved to restrain us. "Boys! You come back here!"

Wiley led me by the hand. He led me away from Meemaw to join the Negroes and marshals and Hiram Murphy on their walk to the swimming pool.

I still wonder why he did it. Maybe it was pent-up envy from watching me on the witness stand, all the attention to my eye and my face on *Life*. Maybe, like me, Wiley had felt ashamed since we left Hiram Murphy dangling with thirteen suspects and no witnesses. Maybe he wanted to show Murphy we were still on his side.

Murphy's eyebrows angled up when he saw us. "What are you doing?" A man yelled, "Goddamn nigger lovers!"

"Go on, boys," Murphy said. "Go on out of here. We'll be all right."

"We're walking with you," Wiley said. And we did. We tucked ourselves in behind Ben and Ramsey and glided on through that hateful crowd, protected by King's golden sword.

"Stop right there," a man barked.

George Wallace stepped forward, one eye on the cameras and the other on the marshals, his hand upraised in a stiff gesture of rebuff. "I have come here today on behalf of the people of the great state of Alabama to stand in the way of any person who attempts to enforce this unlawful, immoral, unconstitutional, tyrannical, Communist-inspired court order," he said. "By the power vested in me, I direct you to turn around and go back where you came from."

Hiram Murphy stepped through the marshals to face off with the governor across a five-foot stretch of sidewalk. Cameras clicked in a frenzy. I know you remember that picture—the visored troopers with their rifles, Wallace's hand out like a school-crossing guard saying "stop"—and on the other side three polite silent Negroes, Hiram Murphy with his arms folded. Murphy's face held an expression of determination, mixed with a hint of amusement at this little politician blocking his way. If you look very close, behind the marshals toward the back, you can see Wiley and me, standing together.

Meemaw was out in the crowd somewhere, calling our names.

"Governor Wallace," Murphy said, "I have in my hand a legal and binding court order from Judge Johnson of the Middle District of Alabama. You know very well that despite all this grandstanding, you have no right to prevent these citizens from entering this facility. I will ask you to please stand aside."

Wallace struck another pose. "On behalf of the people of Alabama, I decline," he said. "We have our rights and we don't need anybody from Washinton Dee Cee to push us around."

"Governor, you have no legal standing whatsoever to obstruct me in this manner," said Murphy. "I will ask you once more to please stand aside peacefully and let's get on with enforcing the court order."

"I am sworn to defend the people of Alabama against this unlawful aggression," Wallace said, enjoying himself.

"And I am sworn to enforce the orders of the federal court. You have no jurisdiction in this matter."

Ben Thomas peered down at me, curious. "What are you doing here? You're Dove's boys, aren't you?"

I nodded. "We wanted to help."

Hiram Murphy said, "Governor, will you stand aside and let us pass?"

"Never." Wallace stuck out his chest. "I will never yield. The people of Alabama will never yield."

"You leave us no choice," Hiram Murphy said. As if on a signal our group turned and started back the other way—so quickly they almost stranded me and Wiley in that inhospitable crowd.

We trotted to catch up. "Where we going?" I asked Ben. "Is it over?" It seemed to me we'd stuck our noses out an awful long way just to have Hiram Murphy converse with the governor a minute and beat a retreat.

Ben said, "Don't you get it? It's a show."

"A show? What do you mean?"

"It's all the governor's show," he said. "He wasn't man enough to come tomorrow, when Dr. King will be here."

We reached the sanctuary of the shiny Fords parked around back. The crowd went the other way to watch the governor driving off in triumph.

"He called down here last night in a panic," said Murphy. "He was scared that if he came tomorrow he'd end up having his picture taken with King, and that'd be the end of his career. He begged me to do this today, so he could stand in the door."

"You mean—he was faking? The whole thing was pretend?"

"We worked out the details this morning. I didn't know what to think when I saw you two boys tagging along. If you'd said the wrong thing you could have screwed it all up."

"What happens now?" Wiley said.

"We've got more marshals on the way, and they'll be armed," said Murphy. "Wallace has guaranteed us he won't interfere, he'll get the sheriff to call off his men. In a couple of hours, soon as this crowd disperses, we'll have this pool open for everybody."

Nehemiah smiled. "And the governor will be back in Montgomery with his feet up, admiring himself on the six o'clock news."

"Boys, I think you better run along home," Murphy said. "I can't be responsible for you."

We said goodbye to the Thomases. "Be sure to extend my greetings to your uncle," said Nehemiah.

"You tell Dove something for me, too," said Hiram Murphy. "Tell him us folks from up North don't usually fold all our cards before we even start the game."

"Hold on," Nehemiah put in. "Dove Bullis is a good man."

"You're right," Murphy said. "On second thought, just tell him I said hello."

"Boys? You come here to me!" Meemaw rushed up, out of breath, in a tizzy—how dare we run away from her to get mixed up in all that? She grabbed us each by an arm and marched us off toward home. "Wiley, what in heaven's name got into you?"

"I don't know." He pulled away to walk by himself. "My feet just started moving."

38

Peejoe

Industry

The TV cameras caught us hiding behind Ben and Ramsey Thomas, advancing on the swimming-pool gate.

Dove stared at the set without speaking.

The reporter said "Governor Wallace today stood up to federal marshals and Justice Department officials in his strongest show of defiance since the Selma march."

The picture switched to the standoff between Wallace and Murphy. There I was again, peeking out behind Nehemiah, looking scared.

"I will never yield," Wallace said. "The people of Alabama will never yield."

The report ended with the governor's victorious wave as he climbed into his car. Dove's face darkened. He peered at us. He was not happy.

"Don't look at me," I protested. "It was Wiley's idea."

"Did Hiram Murphy put you up to that, Wiley?"

"No sir." He shifted on his feet. "I just—we—well, they looked so *outnumbered.*"

Meemaw said "I don't know how you've been letting them behave, Dove, but they just ran off and abandoned me."

"Mama, I can't believe you'd stand by and let them go with Nehemiah Thomas to integrate the goddamn swimming pool."

"Wait a minute, I didn't just stand by—"

"Don't get mad, Uncle Dove," I tried. "Nothing happened. We didn't get hurt."

"Peter Joseph!" he exploded. "I'm sick of hearing that from you, I don't care whether *you* got hurt or not! Don't you ever stop to think what you

351

might be doing to somebody else? Get your butt out of here. Go to your room."

I stood my ground. "No sir."

"What?"

"I said no sir. I won't go to my room." I was feeling pretty full of the spirit of nonviolent resistance, I can tell you.

He came out of his chair. "The hell you say!"

"Now, Dove, calm down," Meemaw said. "They didn't mean any harm."

"You don't know, Mama, every time I turn around they're down there digging me in a little deeper! I'm sick and tired of the whole goddamn thing."

"Dove!"

"You're just scared," I blurted. "Mr. Murphy said it, he said up North they don't fold all their cards before the game even starts."

I don't know what possessed me to talk back to him like that. He took two steps toward me. "Murphy said that to you?"

"Yeah. He did."

Wiley moved to my side. For that moment it looked as if Dove might haul off and slug me.

"Mama," he said in a strangled voice, "I want you to go home tomorrow. Take these boys with you. I've had enough." He stalked out of the room.

"Uncle Dove said a bad word," Cary said.

"Go after him, Peejoe, run and apologize," Meemaw said.

"But I'm not sorry."

"Don't you sass me. That was a terrible thing you said, good as he's been to you! You move." She raised her finger on a line for the door. Her look said I-mean-it-young-man.

I went downstairs to find Dove in his office, slumped over, his face in his hands.

I thought he was crying, but when I said "Uncle Dove, I'm sorry," he looked up at me with dry eyes.

"Have a seat." He moved a stack of casket catalogs from the chair, took his bottle from the bookshelf and poured half a glass of bourbon. "I'm sorry too, son. I don't want you boys to leave. God knows you've stood by me. My own wife didn't even do that." He took a swallow.

"I don't really think you're scared," I said. "I know you were just trying to help Aunt Lucille."

"Listen, Peter Joseph, it's easy to know what to do when you're a kid. You see everything in black and white. A lot of people think I'm already the world's biggest fool for poking my head out as far as I did. You just can't please anybody."

"Nehemiah stuck up for you," I told him. "He said you're a good man."

"Well great, I guess that makes up for everything." He took another sip. "Ahh, what the hell. At least John Doggett has discovered he can't just go around terrorizing people. And now they'll go on and integrate that pool, folks will realize it's not the end of the world."

"I don't see what the big deal is, anyway," I said. "They only want to swim in it."

"'And the children shall lead them,'" Dove said. "Go help your grandmother set the table. I'll be up."

I started for the door.

"Peejoe."

Dove had never used my nickname before. I turned, surprised.

"I was proud of you in court today. You said the right things."

"Thanks."

The phone rang. I went upstairs.

Meemaw said, "I met the nicest man today."

"Oh yeah?" Dove reached for his drink. "Who'd you meet?"

The littler Vinsons had all nodded off in a heap. Wiley, Sandra, and I watched "The Lawrence Welk Show." Six leggy blond girls dressed as daisies skipped around the TV screen singing "Where Have All the Flowers Gone."

"I don't recall his name," Meemaw said, "but he drove all the way here from California for this trial. Can you believe that? He's somebody Lucille met out there."

"Where'd you see him?"

"He came up to me in the courtroom. He was so nice, I don't know what it was. He just had a good light in his eyes. You should have seen that car he was driving, it was long as two of your hearse."

"You'll have to point him out to me," Dove said.

"I'll ask Lucille about him." She sighed. "You know that's all she ever needed, a nice man to take care of her."

"It would help if he's a psychiatrist," Dove said.

Dove shook me awake. "Get up, son," he whispered. "Be quiet. Don't wake the others."

I rubbed my good eye. "What time is it? What's wrong?"

"Come on, get up, we've got a call." I smelled a warm cloud of bourbon, but he didn't seem drunk.

"What about Wiley?"

"Let him sleep. Put your clothes on and come to the car. Hurry up." He picked his way around the pallets full of sleeping boys.

I dressed in a rush, shivering, yanked out of my warm dreams in the dead middle of the night while Wiley and the others wheezed and whistled, oblivious.

I felt my way down the stairs.

Dove waited in the white hearse with the engine running. His face still bore the creases of the pillow. In the back seat, Milton looked wide, wide awake, and frightened.

I climbed in front. "Where we going?"

Dove zoomed backwards down the drive.

Milton said, "Mist' Dove, you oughta think twice about this."

"There's nothing to think about, Milton. What am I supposed to do, leave the man where he is?"

"Uncle Dove, what happened?"

"Let somebody else take care of it," Milton said. "You've done more than your share."

"There *is* nobody else," Dove said. "Peter Joseph thinks I'm scared. I want him to see that I'm not."

I squinted at him in the dashboard glow. His voice was hoarse with sleep. Was this a bad dream, Dove dragging me out of bed to start that argument again?

"I don't want to do it," he said, almost to himself. "But there's nobody else."

"It's an awful thing," Milton said.

We lurched around a curve, squealing tires.

"I told the son of a bitch this would happen," Dove said. "He just had to push 'em a little bit more, just a little bit more every time."

"Yes suh . . ."

The headlights of three cars shone on a gaping black hole in the front wall of the Blessed Rest Funeral Home. Dove sniffed the air—"Smell that? Cordite."

"What's that?"

"Dynamite."

He drove up on the grass, bumping over shattered timbers. Half the porch had been blown away. Broken roof beams sagged into the hole.

The convergence of headlights lent a weird brilliance to the scene. One of the cars belonged to Sheriff John Doggett, who stood poking his boot in the ruins of the porch.

Dove got out. "Peter Joseph, stay here and don't move. Milton, come help me."

The sheriff held up his hand to the glare. "Dove?"

"Yeah, it's me. Where is he?"

"Inside."

Milton wheeled the clattering casket-carriage toward the house.

"You're not gonna take him to your place," the sheriff said.

"Of course I am."

"I told you, I wouldn't do that."

"The man's dead. You want to do the embalming? There's nobody else."

"I just wouldn't do that. You sign off on cause of death and let his own folks take care of it."

"They can't," Dove said, "because the bastards blew up his funeral home. Were you in the truck this time, John?"

"It wasn't a truck," the sheriff said. "Plymouth Valiant, late model, dark green. We got a good description and a license plate. We'll bring 'em in."

"Yeah, I bet you will."

"I feel bad about this one, Dove. We had our differences, but Nehemiah was all right."

A woman came to open the door, as if Dove and Milton couldn't have stepped through the yawning hole in the wall. I recognized her: Mattie Jackson.

This was a bad dream. They brought Nehemiah Thomas out on the litter, an impossibly small heap under a snow-white blanket.

I remembered the time he welcomed me to the funeral business. I had plenty of doubts about the business now.

Those men drove their Plymouth up on the lawn of the Blessed Rest and hurled their package through the front window. The blast broke every window in the house, and half the windows on that street, but it killed no one—a miracle, they were all asleep in the back.

The men trained their headlights on the door and waited. When Nehemiah came running out in his long johns, they shot him dead.

We took him home with us.

39

Peejoe

Industry

The rain started just after dawn and fell steadily all day. At nightfall Ben and Ramsey came to collect their father's body.

"He looks so peaceful," said Ramsey. "You've done a good job."

I spied on them through the peephole above the embalming room. Nehemiah lay on the steel table with a sheet pulled to his chin. His sons stood at his feet.

Dove asked where they planned to hold the visitation.

"We thought maybe the A.M.E. church," Ben said.

Dove shook his head. "That's way too small. All this rain, I'd hate for the old folks to stand outside and catch pneumonia."

"We don't know any bigger place," Ramsey said.

Dove said "You could have it here."

"No, sir, thank you, that's too big a chance for you to take." Ben coughed. "I thank you for making the offer. But you've done enough."

"If I'd done enough," Dove said, "maybe Nehemiah would still be alive. The least I can do is give him a good funeral. He would do the same for me." His gaze traveled up from the body to the ceiling, to my hiding place.

"Get away from there, Peter Joseph," he barked.

I did.

Dove opened the doors of Croaker-Moseley that gray rainy Sunday and said welcome to everybody. He crossed all the way over, as deliberately as Wiley pulling me away from Meemaw to march with the integrators.

So many colored people came straggling up the hill from Dog Junction that the line of mourners snaked halfway down the driveway in the pouring rain. Dove kept Wiley and Sandra running up and down the line, distributing cups of hot coffee as fast as Meemaw could turn it out.

Nehemiah was laid out in the front hall in a splendid bronze casket, the "Eternal Soldier," No. 1075 in the Imperial Casket Catalog, list price $2,145.00. The lack of furniture in the house was a blessing, since the first floor jammed up at once and overflowed to the second.

Nehemiah's wife had died years before; the job of grieving widow was divided among five ample women in rustling black: two sisters, two nieces, and an aunt, weeping and greeting everyone at the door. From the landing, I saw that these ladies were the cause of the traffic jam; if they'd move out of the front hall everybody could come in from the rain. Dove was nowhere around.

I slipped among the ladies and began politely urging them sideways. I got them into Parlor Two before they even realized they'd been moved.

The sheriff had phoned three times Saturday night to warn Dove off this kind of display, but on Sunday he sent four of his deputies to stand by their cars at the foot of our lawn, looking out for trouble. Dove said Doggett was so glad to see Integration Day rained out that he was acting reasonable for a change.

With the ladies-in-mourning out of the way, traffic flowed easily around the casket. I had never heard the babble of so many voices at once, fervent conversation punctuated with sobs and shouts of grief when they saw Nehemiah lying there, the quietest man in the house.

Dove's makeup skills weren't quite up to the expertise of Randall Mulch, but he had given Nehemiah's skin a lifelike sheen, unpolished mahogany. Lying with his hands folded, Nehemiah looked like a man who had stretched out for a nap in a very fine suit.

I went upstairs to help Meemaw. At once I saw the panic in her eyes: all these Negroes swarming over the house, drinking out of the cups, using the bathrooms; it would take her a week to disinfect the place; would she have to throw all these cups away and buy new?

"How you doin', Meemaw." I moved to lift a tray of coffees.

"No don't, sweetie, you'll drop it. Wait for Wiley or one of the others."

"I can do it, see?"

"Peejoe. Mind me. Go find something else to do." That flash in her eyes told me to put down the tray and get lost.

She was still upset about her morning wakeup call. A man's voice said "Is this Croaker-Moseley?"

"Yes it is," Meemaw said.

"Nigger lovers. You're gonna die."

Click.

Dove told her not to worry, it was just some redneck in a bad mood. He said the worst was over. Nehemiah's death seemed to have knocked the wind out of everyone, Negro and white. A man was dead, and people were either mad or happy or indifferent about it, but it wasn't the same as when Taylor Jackson died. The town was worn out.

Dove said Wallace and King could go back to their corners now, take their people with them and leave the people of Industry to sift through the wreckage. The TV trucks had moved up to the courthouse for Aunt Lucille's verdict, after which they would leave.

Dove said everybody, Negro and white, was going to have to learn to get along together all over again.

Meemaw was not like Earlene, she didn't raise a fuss about all those Negroes in the house, but she was snappish all day. That anonymous caller had her rattled. She banished the younger Vinsons to the third floor with orders to stay there and be quiet, or catch holy hell.

I poked my head up there to make sure they weren't destroying anything. Marilyn was lying in a dresser drawer playing the corpse in a funeral service conducted by the others. I didn't interrupt.

I threaded a path down the stairs, through the multitude. I found Dove in the mortuary hallway, leaned against the gray door talking to Ben Thomas.

Ben greeted me with a soft smile: "There's our marching man."

Dove slid an arm around my shoulder. "How's Mama holding up?"

"She looks nervous."

"Well, she's a fine lady to have us all here today," Ben said. "Pop would appreciate it, I know."

"I'm sure sorry, what happened." The words sounded useless but I said them anyway. "He was always real nice to me."

"Thank you, Peter Joseph," Ben said. "That's very kind of you."

It amazed me that a man could stand ten feet from his own dead father and be so smoothly polite—but then he was his father's apprentice, he was schooled in the technique of funeral directors: Stay out of the family's way, give them room to grieve. Speak softly. No chewing gum, no smoking, no smiling or laughing around the family.

Even when the family is yours.

Dove said "It's a new day, Ben. Look how fast John arrested those Duboce boys. I believe we'll see a conviction this time."

The sheriff had picked up three fat Duboce brothers from out in the county for the murder of Nehemiah. Firing caps and spent shotgun shells were found in the trunk of their green 1963 Plymouth. They now sat in the Cotton County jail, four cells down from Lucille.

"I don't care about a conviction," Ben said. "That won't bring him back."

"No, it won't. But it shows how he changed things."

"Pop was not an old man, you know. Sixty-three. His hair turned gray when he was still young."

"No, I didn't know that," said Dove.

Suddenly a commotion at the front door, everyone talking at once. A man in a rain-spattered ivory fedora stood with his back to us, shaking out of his raincoat as he gazed down upon Nehemiah. The mourners swarmed out of Parlor Two, surrounding him, loudly lamenting.

"Pop never said a word about civil rights until they killed my cousin David," Ben was saying. "That was what changed him. After he spoke out, he always knew he might end up like David and Taylor, but he wasn't afraid."

The ladies mobbed the stranger, backing him down the hall toward us in their enthusiasm. He turned to escape—his face brightened at his first glimpse of Ben, then a look of infinite sadness came over his eyes.

He embraced Ben. He kept one arm wrapped around Ben's neck and held out his hand to Dove. "Hello. Martin King."

"Dove Bullis." Dove shook his hand. "Welcome to my home."

"Oh, this is your home, too? Very nice. I thought it was only the Negro morticians who lived over the store."

Dove smiled. "Some of us white ones do, too."

I stood there with my eyepatch tilted up, hoping he would notice me and remember me.

"Dove's been a big help to us from the beginning, Dr. King," said Ben. "He testified against John Doggett to the grand jury."

"Oh, for a few more like you," King said. "Mr. Bullis, do you have a quiet room where I could spend a moment in prayer with Ben and his family?"

"Of course." Dove hastened down the hall. "Come on back and use my office." Here came the five wide ladies, their grief suspended at the prospect of an audience with the famous man. Ramsey went too, and Mattie Jackson, and a couple of the preacher types. They holed up in there with the door shut.

I ran upstairs to Meemaw. "You'll never guess who's down there."

"Don't bother me, sweetie, I'm busy. Sandra, those cups are dirty. Let's wash these over here."

"But Meemaw, it's Dr. King!"

"I don't know any Dr. King. Not those, honey. *These.*"

"Those aren't dirty," Sandra whined. "I just washed them."

Meemaw dropped her voice. "I said to wash them again, just do as I tell you."

"Meemaw, I'm trying to tell you, it's Martin *Luther* King! He's here, in the house!"

That stopped the conversation. Everyone stared at me a moment, then rushed for the stairs.

"Great heavenly days," Meemaw said. "I hope he doesn't stay long. Trouble just seems to follow after that man."

"Don't you want to come see him?"

"I've seen enough of him on the television."

Sandra dried her hands. "Well I want to." She made a run for it.

"You come back here!" Meemaw put her hands on her hips. "Peejoe, get over here and wash cups."

By the time I'd washed enough to suit her, Dr. King had finished his condolences and departed. Everyone on the first floor was standing around comparing what he'd said to them.

I found Dove in his office. "Where'd he go?"

"Back to Atlanta, I guess. He came all the way down just to pay his respects." He reached for a cigarette. "I must say he has perfect manners, obviously some good breeding there. Very well spoken. Lighter skin than I expected."

"It was different when he was preaching," I said. "Today he just looked like, you know, a man."

"That's all he is, Peter Joseph. Just a man. Like me. Like you're gonna be someday."

"I'm glad he came to our house, Uncle Dove."

"Yeah." He smiled. "We'll have to put up a plaque. Anyway, looks like John can relax. The Reverend is finished here. He was talking about some kind of march on Washington. Let Lyndon Johnson deal with 'em up there for a while."

The visitation went on all afternoon. The deputies stayed at the road in their ponchos, standing watch in the off-and-on rain. For the colored guests Meemaw provided hot drinks and tight smiles and several cans of stale Woolworth cookies she found in a cabinet, but for those deputies she made up plates of ham sandwiches, cole slaw, baked beans, and chess pie.

The clouds blew off to form up for a spectacular red sunset. The deputies got back in their cars and quietly drove away.

Dove and Milton closed the lid on Nehemiah. They put him in the white hearse and led a caravan off to bury him in the country at the Antioch Church, near the house where he was born.

I wanted to go, but Meemaw said I had seen enough.

She wouldn't let us have supper until we had helped her swab down all the floors, scrub the toilets, and put the coffee cups through a Clorox rinse.

"They're just people, Meemaw," I said. "They don't have a *disease.*"

"One of them might," she said. "You don't know. They're different from us, that's all."

"No they're not. Just their skin."

"You have to get older before you can see beyond yourself, Peejoe. There's a great big difference. Those people are not like us. They come from the other side of the world."

That was her last word on the subject. She fed us and put us to bed.

Monday morning was cool, the town freshly green. The bad dream of Friday night began to fade—had I really smelled the dynamite smoke, and seen Nehemiah lifted out through a smoldering hole in the wall?

Had they really killed him just for playing his part in the governor's pantomime show?

They waited until he thought he had won, then they killed him. That was the meanest part.

For the first time in weeks, the swimming pool stood abandoned in broad daylight, not a swimmer or protester anywhere in sight. The water level had gone down three feet, even after all the rain. A new sign: WILL REOPEN TUES. Dove said Mr. Peterson had quit over all the controversy.

We rode up the hill to the square. All the spectators from Friday were lined out the courthouse doors, joined by others who'd heard about Aunt Lucille from their friends.

We took our seats down front. Lucille delayed her entrance until the last possible moment. Today she wore a wine-colored linen suit, a jaunty flowered scarf, the black velvet hat. She smiled and held Dove's arm all the way down the aisle.

Larry Russell crooked a finger at me. "Hubert's not going to call you back, son, and neither am I," he said. "You did us plenty good Friday."

I tried to conceal my disappointment. I had lain awake half the night getting myself all worked up to get back on the stand.

The judge strode in wearing a sprightly yellow bowtie. He greeted everyone and called the lawyers up to the bench, where they spent the next hour hemming and hawing, sending the jury out, bringing them back.

Meemaw passed out coloring books and crayons to the younger Vinsons. Farley had stayed home with Milton; he couldn't stand to watch any more of the trial.

Hubert Mackie quizzed a string of deputy sheriffs in mind-numbing detail about what they'd seen at Lucille's house on May sixth. The blood in the toolshed, the frozen body—they went round and round over the same terrain. "I observed at that point a certain amount of a dark fluid, which I surmised to be human blood," and on like that the whole morning, after lunch and into the afternoon.

This was nowhere near as exciting as Lucille's stories of slow torture at the hands of Chester—nor did it approach the terror of my time up in that chair. I took up my Liberty National fan and doodled a string of pearls and buck teeth on the Statue of Liberty. This provoked a loud giggle from Cary; the judge frowned at us from the bench.

Meemaw reached over to pinch me. I read her lips: Behave. I closed my eye and rested my head against the bench to stop the giddy feeling.

Suddenly Hubert Mackie said, "The prosecution rests, your honor."

That was it? That was all the proof he was going to offer? Maybe I had missed something. Was Hubert Mackie giving up in defeat?

Apparently not. Larry Russell didn't look all that pleased. He scratched his head a long minute, studying his papers—so long that Judge Mead said "Mr. Russell?"

"Yes sir, Judge," he said, rising slowly as smoke from a fire.

"Mr. Mackie has rested his case."

"Yes your honor, I heard him do that," Russell said. "In that case I'd like to call Mrs. Lucille Bullis Vinson to the stand."

Lucille started for the witness box. Four ladies stood and applauded for her. These four had been in the front row on Friday; they were plain, beaten-down-looking housewives, but when they looked at Lucille their eyes gleamed with excitement and something like admiration.

The judge stared them back into their seats. "It is obvious that your behavior has not improved over the weekend," he said icily. "Now I mean for this jury to hear the defendant's testimony without interpretation from you ladies."

Lucille swore to tell the truth. She added "so help me God" at the end.

"Now tell us, Lucille," said Larry Russell, "why did you take your husband's head with you to California?"

The jurors sat up.

Lucille considered a moment. "I know it sounds crazy. You'd have to know Chester to understand."

"Please. Take your time."

"Well, I couldn't just throw him away. I mean, he was dead, but that was part of him, you know? As long as I had him with me, he was still alive somehow. All I ever wanted was to get away from him, but when it came down to it, I suppose I was afraid."

"Afraid of what?"

She hesitated. "Afraid of being alone."

There. That was the truth as Aunt Lucille saw it. It sounded plenty crazy to me. That should have done it. She should have shut up.

But she kept talking. "I'm not sorry I did it," she said. "I'm glad he's dead. He was a better man after I killed him. He told me he loved me. He never said that when he was alive. I should have done it a long time ago. He was *always* a son of a bitch."

Russell moved closer. "Chester's head talked to you?"

She folded her hands. "From time to time."

"What did he say?"

"He said he loved me." Lucille tossed her hair. "He didn't hold any grudges."

"I have no further questions," said Russell. "Mr. Mackie, she's all yours."

Hubert Mackie treated Lucille gingerly. He led her back and forth over her story. She turned his questions around to cast her marriage in the worst possible light: Chester was a mean man full of insults and petty demands; Lucille was a talented, frustrated woman, yearning to try out her wings. She kept trying to explain how wonderful her new life was, as if this should prove to anybody that her old life simply had to end—by any means available.

"Okay, now," said Mackie, "let's talk about the night of May third. You've testified you noticed a box of D-Con rat poison on the shelf above the washing machine. And you wondered how much it would take to kill somebody. Is that the first time you ever thought about killing your husband?"

"That's right."

"And what happened next?"

"I took the D-Con to the kitchen. I plugged in the percolator to make his coffee."

Mackie kept her up there a long time, circling back again and again to try and trap her, but Lucille would not admit to premeditating over Chester. She was just not that kind of person, she swore, to go around planning to kill somebody. It happened on the spur of the moment. She plugged in that coffeepot, and then a heavy gray fog lowered itself around her. She lost herself in that fog. She didn't really remember what happened after that. The next thing she knew it was two weeks later and she was in California.

She was scrambling to save herself, but I could tell those jurors didn't believe her. The more she tried to explain, the colder their faces became.

Hubert Mackie rubbed his hands together. "That's all, Miz Vinson, thank you."

The judge said "You may step down."

The lawyers made brief closing arguments. Hubert Mackie said guilty, guilty. Russell said not guilty, not guilty; one look at Lucille, he said, and anyone could see she was not in her right mind. "You won't be doing society any good to send her to prison," he said. "Find her not guilty and let us get her some help."

Lucille looked displeased, but she held her tongue.

The judge read a list of instructions to the jury, then released us to await the verdict.

We followed Dove through the jury door, through a maze of stairwells and outside to the square. He tried to convince Meemaw to take us home, but she insisted on waiting.

The reporters flocked up with questions: Had Lucille shown signs of mental illness as a child? Had she ever hurt or threatened anyone? "Mrs. Bullis, is it true you and your son hosted a private reception for Martin Luther King last night?"

"That's the most ridiculous thing I've ever heard. Now please. Go away and leave us alone."

Another man approached our table, but instead of chasing him off, Meemaw lit up. "Oh, hello! You're still here!"

"Yes ma'am, I told you, I'm here for the duration."

"All these are Lucille's—this is Sandra, that's Cary, Marlon, Judy, and this little angel is Marilyn. Oh, and Peejoe and Wiley. They belong to me."

The little man tipped his cap to reveal sparse hair combed over a shiny bald spot. "Pleasure to make your acquaintances," he said, showing a gold tooth.

"I'm so sorry," said Meemaw, "please tell me your name again."

"Norman Wirtz."

Norman Wirtz had a five o'clock shadow, cowboy boots, a white shirt bulging open at the buttons, a skinny cowboy tie. He stared at us; we stared at him.

"Tell me, Mr. Wirtz, how did you meet Lucille?"

"I had the great pleasure of driving her from Las Vegas to Los Angeles."

"She paid you to drive her?"

"That's right."

"Lord, she has gone above her raising," said Meemaw. "I still can't believe you'd come all the way here for this trial. That's thousands of miles!"

"She's the most beautiful woman I've ever seen." His eyes shone. "I just want to be near her. I won't bother you anymore." He flashed his gold tooth and went to a long, long Cadillac limousine parked in front of the Ritz Theater. He waved at us and got in.

"He talks funny," said Marlon. "Is he gonna be our new daddy?"

"No, sweetheart, I don't expect he is."

Sandra said "I think he's nice. I want to ride in that car, can we Meemaw?"

"Your Uncle Dove's car is every bit as nice as that one."

"It's not the same. Dove's is for dead people."

"It's for anybody who's lucky enough to ride in it, so there." She reached for her fan. "Lord, it's all hot again. You'd think that rain would have cooled things off."

As if a silent chime sounded, everyone in the square glanced up at the same moment. They gathered their purses and hats, and headed to the steps.

Dove came for us. "Let's go back in. It may not be too long now."

My heart leaped up. Was it possible—was Aunt Lucille going to be spared? Of course it was what I had hoped for from the very moment she scratched out of Meemaw's yard in the white Galaxie. I had cheered her every stop along her flight from justice. But now that it looked like there was a real chance she might get off, I found myself all confused. What would it mean if you could poison a man and cut off his head and have a jury find you not guilty? Was Uncle Chester's murder even a crime at all, if no one was punished for it?

The judge was still out of the room. The spectators hummed and conjectured. We took the front bench. Dove sat at the defense table, reading a newspaper.

I saw some old men pooling money for a bet.

My heart started pounding. I crossed the fingers of both hands to slow it down. I hoped my own confusion wouldn't leak into the jury room and somehow mess up Aunt Lucille's chances.

"All rise!"

Dove's eyes came up from his paper.

Everyone hustled for their places. The judge came in first, then the jury. I have never seen twelve such serious faces—they glanced first at Lucille, then at us kids, then they fixed their eyes on Judge Mead and walled themselves off from the rest of the courtroom.

Not guilty, I said to myself. Not guilty, not guilty, not guilty.

Aunt Lucille sat with her fingertips opposed, here-is-the-church, here's-the-steeple. Open the door and—here comes your destiny.

"Ladies and gentlemen of the jury," the judge said. "Have you reached a verdict?"

"We have, your honor." The foreman handed a slip of paper to the bailiff, who carried it to the judge.

He glanced at it, folded it in half. "You may proceed, Mr. Dawkins."

The foreman held up his notebook. "On the first count, citing premeditated murder, we the members of this jury find the defendant guilty."

He said it flat out with no expression, like a radio announcer reading soybean prices.

A cry of disbelief pierced the air. Reporters dashed for the phones.

"On the second count, citing willful mutilation and mayhem, we the jury find the defendant guilty."

Meemaw was crying. Sandra and the girls joined in, escalating to pitiful wails.

"On the third count, citing unlawful flight to avoid prosecution, we the jury find the defendant guilty."

Dove came through the gate to embrace Meemaw. Cary and Marlon stared at the floor. Wiley turned with tears in his eyes. "Guilty? How could they find her guilty?"

"But Wiley. She *is*." My own heart was as cold as ever.

". . . fourth count, citing unlawful use of a vehicle in the commission of a felony offense, we the jury find the defendant guilty."

Throughout this recital, Lucille stood with her hands clasped before her, wearing the same little secretive smile. It was a swell performance. She looked as if she might like to step over there and thank each juror personally, but she didn't get the chance. Three bailiffs came in around her to keep the spectators away. The jury filed out without looking at her.

Judge Mead said he would pass sentence at five-thirty the next afternoon. The bailiffs led Aunt Lucille through the jury door. She turned to throw us a big kiss, and then she was gone.

I heard an excited newsman in the lobby: ". . . has just returned a verdict of guilty on all counts, and Judge Lewis S. Mead has scheduled sentencing for tomorrow evening. Mrs. Vinson showed no reaction as the verdict was read . . ."

Meemaw and Dove got us rounded up and outside. It was just that part of twilight when the sky still held a violet hue. "Come on, Sandra, you can cry just as well at home," said Meemaw. "Marlon, grab your brother's hand."

Norman Wirtz tried to offer us a ride, but Meemaw said "I'm sorry, don't talk to us now" and brushed past.

We packed into the hearse. Dove drove us out of there.

"We tried to tell her, Mama," he said, "but she wanted the trial. She gambled and lost. Now it's up to the judge."

40

Lucille

Industry

Lucille opened the envelope with trembling hands.

Dear Carolyn Clay—

The memory of you haunts me. I smell you on my fingers. Why did you leave without saying goodbye? The party was so awkward—they always are—everyone wants a piece of me—I wanted *all* of you, then and there—I think of you now and I'm with you. But I walked away from you. I left you standing alone knowing what you knew, having done what you did—unable to tell the one man who can ever understand you all the way. The crime is all mine. I know you cannot forgive me—you are not the forgiving type, I see that in the headlines—but at least give me a chance to explain. I have tried to reach you—to tell you what is in my soul. Is it too late? Can we please go to Argentina now?

The man of your dreams,
Toby

Lucille stretched out on her cot, remembering his sweet kisses. Now, that was a man. . . .

Her reverie was shattered by a commotion down the hall.

Nowhere in the Constitution did it say she had to listen to Roy and Lester Duboce yelling at their brother Ray for getting them all arrested.

She told them to shut up. They said come down here and make us, Blondie, come make us, Miss Blondie. She hollered and banged her tin cup on the bars until the desk sergeant stomped upstairs and told the Duboces to shut the hell up or he would take away their mattresses.

Lucille re-folded the letter and went back to plucking her eyebrows. Every painful little hair she yanked out was another Duboce.

It was her last night in this jail, at least. Tomorrow night—who could say? Atmore Prison? Bryce Hospital? Anything was possible. Lucille's ability to predict the future had failed her about the time she took that stroll on the Golden Gate Bridge.

First she'd imagined she could seduce Detective Rubacky, then Sheriff Doggett. Those men were cold fish—or else Lucille's sex appeal was beginning to fade in captivity.

Then she thought she could convince that jury to acquit her. For a while she was sure she had them going, but all the time they were smiling and nodding and thinking *Guilty. Guilty as charged. Guilty as hell.*

If she had realized it was all going to come down to Judge Mead, she would have paid more attention to him from the beginning. Now it was too late. He was out there in the night somewhere, deciding her fate. She hoped he had a nice dinner and a nice rich dessert. She hoped he had pleasant dreams and awoke in a generous mood.

Lucille's big mouth convicted her. She should not have called Chester a son of a bitch. That's when the change came over the jurors' faces. The woman with the Amelia Earhart haircut glared from that moment on.

Dove couldn't see the change from where he sat. He hadn't been reading the jurors' minds all along, as Lucille had. That's how she was able to keep such a pleasant smile on her face as the foreman read down the guilty counts. She ignored the pandemonium in the courtroom. She concentrated on appearing as harmless and sensible as possible, so the judge might send her to Bryce and not Atmore.

Never mind her big talk about wanting a chance to explain. The hell with that. She had done that. Now she wanted a chance not to fry in the electric chair, thank you very much. Dove was right, Larry Russell was right, she should have taken the plea.

Ah, but her performance was sweet. The audience loved her.

Now she would be grateful for a nice padded room up in Tuscaloosa. Please sir, Judge.

She couldn't read that old man. If she thought there was any possibility, she would wear her Courrèges minidress to the sentencing and try to win him over, but he seemed starchy and prim as his bowties.

Lucille had trusted her luck once too often. She put all her money on thirteen, she spun the roulette wheel. She lost. Big time.

She still had eleven thousand dollars, after paying that bartender in New Orleans to drop the auto-theft charges against her. She would give that money to Meemaw to look after the children while she was in jail.

But eleven thousand would run out in no time, and then what would she do?

Should have thought about this when you were throwing it away on dresses and hats.

For her final court appearance she selected her most demure outfit, tailored fuzzy-pink suit and a plain silk white blouse. All day she sat on her cot, hearing the Duboces' complaints while she leafed through back issues of *Life* magazine.

At last the time came to spritz herself with Charles of the Desert and go face the lawyers, the judge, her fate.

Lucille thought the judge was a fair man, and she admired Larry Russell for doing what he could for her, but she considered Hubert Mackie a horrid little pig of a man. She wished his other hand would shrivel up. How dare he put poor Peejoe up there and make him testify against his Aunt Lucille!

She had winced hearing her own crazy words from Peejoe's mouth. It wasn't his fault, he answered the questions they put to him, bless his heart, she saw him up there struggling to decide how much to tell. In the end it wasn't Peejoe who told too much, it was Lucille.

Now they took her to the courtroom and Mackie was there and Larry and her whole family. The benches were jammed with gussied-up ladies and frowsy housewives. Lucille sensed a dark mood among them, an undercurrent of anger at yesterday's verdict. A few of them held shopping bags on their laps.

"Now listen, Lucille," Larry Russell was saying, "I want you to be prepared for any possibility. Lewis Mead is a quirky individual. Whatever it is, keep in mind: we can appeal it."

"What's the worst he can do?"

"I think you know." He cleared his throat. "Whatever happens, don't argue with him. If it's Bryce, it's a year, maybe two, we get a doctor's report, you walk out of there. If it's prison, we appeal. Don't say anything to get him riled up."

"Will they let me see my kids before they take me away?"

"Most times the sentence begins immediately. I'll see if I can talk to him."

"All rise!" The bailiff brought down the mercy of God on the proceedings, and Judge Mead bustled in, looking cheerful as ever. His bowtie of the day was dark green. Lucille couldn't figure out what kind of omen that was.

The jury box was empty. She was sorry she would never get to thank them each and every one for destroying her life.

"Afternoon, Mr. Russell," said Mead. "Do you have anything to add to your closing statement?"

Larry boosted all that legal wisdom up out of his chair. "Your honor, we're simply going to throw ourselves on the mercy of the court."

Judge Mead said "I rather expected that. Mr. Mackie?"

Mackie stood.

I'd sure like to take my carving knife to your neck, thought Lucille, with a pleasant smile.

"If it please the court, I would just remind your honor that this defendant showed very little mercy to Chester Vinson."

"Is that all?"

"Yes, your honor."

The judge glanced at his watch. "I know we're running a bit late, but I'd like to ask Mr. Russell if I might see the defendant for a moment in my chambers."

Larry Russell's eyes widened. "Your honor?"

"Only take a moment, Mr. Russell."

"Without counsel?"

"If you have no objection."

Larry considered a moment. "No sir, no objection."

The judge rose. "Mrs. Vinson? Come with me, please."

Larry whispered, "Be careful."

Lucille followed the judge to his comfortable book-lined office. He motioned her to a chair.

"I just wanted to tell you," he said, "my wife and I saw you on 'The Beverly Hillbillies,' and we both thought you were very funny."

Lucille's hopes soared. "Why thank you, your honor!"

"How'd you get a part like that in such a short time, anyway?"

She told him about Harry Hall, the audition, inside stuff about the "Hillbillies." He said he thought the show was kind of silly, but his wife was a big fan.

"I've been studying you, Lucille," he said. "You're really quite an actress. You may have noticed I'm a bit of an actor myself, in this job. I have to be a good deal more severe when we're out in front of the lawyers."

"I noticed that," Lucille said. "I had no idea you were so nice."

They chatted like old pals. It turned out the judge was a lonely man, under his robes; his wife sounded like an old nag. Lucille was aware of the clock on the wall, she knew Larry Russell must be wild with anxiety by now, but she took her time. The conversation meandered down a nice friendly path.

After a while she shook the judge's hand, and followed him back to the courtroom. Larry Russell was out of his chair, pacing.

She shot him a look: *Larry, relax.*

Judge Mead took his seat. "Mrs. Vinson, this case presents me with an interesting dilemma. And it's not for the reason these reporters have been bugging me night and day. The jury has chosen to find you guilty. After listening to the testimony, it's my opinion they were swayed by the acts which occurred after the murder itself. They failed to accept your defense—which, I must say, was a mite unconventional. I think you should have mounted an insanity defense, instead of working against your attorney's best instincts. I think the jury would have found you not guilty, and then I would have sent you up to Bryce, as you pointed out."

Atmore, here I come. Lucille fought to keep that smile on her face.

"But they didn't do that," he went on. "They found you guilty. To be honest, I don't care for this verdict. It appears to reward Mr. Mackie and the sheriff's department for one of the most incompetent performances I've ever witnessed. I'm tired of prosecutors and lawmen who think they can act as judge and jury before the case comes to trial."

Hubert Mackie frowned at the floor.

"They presented a sloppy case, and you ignored your lawyer's advice. I don't really care to reward either side."

Lucille sucked air through her teeth.

"Now, the law grants me the authority to direct this verdict myself, in other words to overturn it, but I'm not going to do that. I'm going to let it stand. The jurors are entitled to reach a verdict from the evidence that's put in front of them."

Inside Lucille the rollercoaster took a steep plunge.

"So here we are. You stand convicted of four gravely serious felonies. I can send you to Atmore, but I haven't been able to decide for the life of me what good that would do anybody. Prisons are simply not designed for people like you."

Thank you, Judge. You are right about that.

"I could send you up to Bryce, let the doctors have a crack at you. But I've thought long and hard about this, and I'll tell you, I don't think they could do anything for you either. Because frankly, Mrs. Vinson, I've seen through you. I don't think you're crazy. I think you're sneaky. You're an ambitious woman. You're an actress. And you're way too sane for Bryce. I think either you'd seduce one of those doctors, or just outsmart 'em and walk away from there." He peered over his glasses. "There's a word for what you are, but I don't think medical science has come up with it yet. I haven't seen any evidence that convinces me you're a danger to anyone except your husband, and it's too late for him. Therefore, Mrs. Vinson, I have decided to sentence you to ten years in Atmore Penitentiary."

Lucille staggered inside, but held on to her smile.

"And since it's my opinion that your children need you more than Atmore, I'm going to suspend the sentence. You are free to go. This court stands adjourned." *Bang!*

It was a miracle.

Ladies cheered. Hubert Mackie sputtered and fumed.

Lucille was engulfed by her children, Dove, Mama, and Larry, Peejoe and Wiley. She hugged them all. Over Dove's shoulder she said "Thank you, Judge."

Mead snapped his briefcase shut. "Goodbye, Mrs. Vinson. Good luck." He winked, and went out.

She followed Dove toward the door, children clamoring all around.

Norman Wirtz caught up with her in the lobby.

She'd seen him lurking in the back of the courtroom. For days she had refused the notes and flowers he tried to get past the guard at the desk.

But now he stood there with his soft eager eyes and that ridiculous string-tie, his keys in one hand. She heard people in the square, clapping and shouting for her to come out.

"Norman, what the hell are you doing here?"

"You're free!" he cheered. "It's the most fantastic news I've ever heard! I knew you were innocent! I knew it all the time. Oh, don't you see, this is our chance! Now we can have a real future together."

"Norman, go wait by your car. These people want to talk to me."

"I've gassed her up, she's ready to roll," he said. "Anywhere you want to go."

"Norman . . ."

"I knew they couldn't lock you away from me, not after all that we mean to—"

"*Norman!*"

"What?"

"If you don't leave me alone and go to your car right this instant, I swear, I—" She dropped her gaze. "I won't come with you."

His gold tooth flashed, a big grin, like a kid. "I'll be waiting. You take your time." He shot a fist in the air—victory!

"And get my things from the jail."

"You got it, beautiful." He strutted off, jingling keys.

Lucille stepped into the last heat of the day, thank God it was not hot as August yet, she would never commit another crime, thank you God.

She came to the top of the white marble steps. The four women from the back of the courtroom were waiting there, cheering her, tears streaming down their faces.

Lucille smiled. She blew them a kiss.

One of the women placed her shopping bag on the ground and brought something up from it. She held it up in both hands so everyone could see.

Tupperware.

A Tupperware lettuce keeper, translucent green, with a patented press-and-lock seal.

Applause rang through the square.

A second woman brought her Tupperware from the bag, and a third, and a fourth. Four women, four Tupperware bowls.

Lucille smiled uneasily. She supposed it was meant to honor her, to signify what she'd done. She didn't recognize the strange expression of joy in their eyes.

She started down the steps. The women stepped aside to let her through. They held out their plastic containers as an offering.

Lucille turned away from them and pressed a receipt into Mama's hand. "Give this to the county clerk. He'll give you some money."

"Lucille, where do you think you're going?"

"I'll call you, Mama."

She left them standing there and walked across the street to the limousine. "We have a stop to make first," she said.

Norman smiled, and opened the door. "Get in."

41

Lucille

Industry

Lucille lost her way in the unfamiliar darkness. She pulled a curtain aside to admit the pale light from the street.

There was Norman on the hood of his car, smoking a cigarette, watching the house. He didn't care what she was doing in here. He didn't ask questions, didn't try to rush her. He would wait out there all night, if necessary, and when she was ready he would be there to drive her away.

She found the light switch and set about repairing her tousled hair, her smeared lipstick. She ran water into the rust-stained basin and looked around for a washcloth.

This was plainly an old lady's bathroom: lace doilies, embroidered towels, pink crocheted covers for the toilet paper. No wonder the poor man was so lonesome, married to the kind of woman who would hang a picture of Herbert Hoover over the commode.

"Lucille," he called, "come on back to Daddy."

She dried her face on a corner of a fancy towel, and snapped out the light. "Ready or not, here I come!" She crept back to the musty bedroom.

"Hurry, hurry," he crooned. "She'll be home in an hour."

Lucille slid under the covers. "Where is she, anyway?"

"Garden club. A discussion of exotic camellias, I believe." He was skinny, and tiny—a sack of old bones, really—but he was warm when he wrapped her up in his arms. "You're the sweetest little gal I've ever seen."

She closed her eyes to imagine he was young as his kiss. "Come here to me, you big old judge." Wiggling her hips up to his, she lived up to her end of the bargain.

42

Peejoe

Industry

We zoomed past the swimming pool.

"I can't believe she just took off like that," Meemaw said. "She doesn't care a thing about her own children."

"Oh now Mama, you know very well—" Dove screeched to a halt at the foot of Lee Street.

He lowered the window to sniff the air. His gaze traveled up Lee Street, all the way to the top of the hill.

I sat up to crane through the windshield, and I saw what he saw.

Fire.

He slammed the pedal to the floor. The tires screamed. I grabbed the seat. Wiley tumbled the length of the hearse and smacked against the back gate.

Dove ran over the Croaker-Moseley sign, sliding sideways to a stop in the weeds.

The whole house was burning, a garden of flames blooming in every window from the first floor to the attic dormers. Dove fell to one knee getting out. His glasses reflected the blaze. He got to his feet and ran toward the fire. "Farley! Milton!" Wiley went after him.

"Oh my God," Meemaw screamed, "Farley's in there, we've got to go *help* him!" The children wailed.

I took off up the slope. The house groaned, hissing, timbers cracking and an indefinable sound, the low roar of fire sucking air. A hot ember sailed out at me from an upper window, stinging my cheek.

I stumbled around the corner to find Dove on his knees beside Farley. "What happened, son! Say something! Is Milton still in there?"

Farley shook his head. He turned away from the fire with terrible hollowed-out eyes, and pointed to the sycamore tree beside the carport.

Milton hung from that tree, a greasy rope around his neck, his hands bound behind him, a white rag around his eyes, twisting slowly in the currents of air from the fire.

Way in the distance, a siren started low and rose to a sustained scream that sang out over Industry.

The old mansion burned as if it had been built to burn. The fire consumed it eagerly, leaping up planks of heart pine, banisters, velvet curtains, flames racing in sheets up the dusty old wallpaper, devouring the silk linings of caskets. We huddled in the side yard to watch it burn.

Dove went to cut Milton down. He came back with a wad of paper from the pocket of Milton's blue workshirt.

We read the pasted-down magazine letters in the hot red light of the fire: THe NiGgeR LoveR'S NIggeR.

The roof caved in with a roar.

The fire truck arrived too late to save anything but the walls of the old house. The men turned their hose on the embers, sending up clouds of rank black steam.

"It's so useless," Dove said, almost to himself. "People are still going to die. And now who's going to take care of them?"

He got down on his knees and put his arms around Milton. That was the only time I ever saw him cry.

43

Peter Joseph

Industry

I try not to think about everything that happened. I try, but it keeps coming back. I see myself standing in the side yard as the funeral home burned, as the world came to an end.

I saw Dove on his knees with his arms around Milton. A strange tingle began at the front of my face and spread back past my ear. I stretched the elastic band over my head.

I peeled back the bandage, and closed my good eye.

I saw the light of the fire.

The vision through the bad eye was a blur, but the luminous green mist had been burned away by the hot orange firelight leaping, dancing behind wavery glass.

I saw the fire, and Dove crying for his friend, and the light came back into my eye. I will never understand it.

Had I finally seen everything I was supposed to see?

Something loomed in the blur, something large and alive. I opened both eyes. It was Wiley.

"Let's get out of here." He pulled me by the arm.

I went with him around the burning house, closing one eye then the other to make sure it was true. I was afraid to say it out loud because it might be a trick of my mind.

We walked past Meemaw clinging to the terrified children, down the hill to the foot of Lee Street, through the bushes. We came out at the swimming pool.

"Look what they're doing," Wiley said.

The chain-link fence was gone. The pool had been drained of all but three inches of water in the deep end. Two battered county dump trucks had backed to the edge of the pool to fill it with steaming asphalt. Negro workers stood beside the trucks, raking the stuff out with shovels in the light from the trucks. The blacktop hissed as it splattered into the water.

We retreated to the grassy slope below the Dairy Dog, to watch.

As soon as one truck unloaded its hot smoking cargo, another truck came to take its place.

Above, on the hill, we saw the glow of everything burning—our lives, Dove's future, the picture of Mama and Daddy. For hours we sat in the grass, watching that glow fading on the hill as the workmen filled the pool with black tar.

"I guess the law said it has to be open," Wiley said. "It didn't say nothing about there had to be water in it."

I said "It seems kind of dumb. Now nobody will get to swim."

The men tramped across the spongy asphalt with boards strapped to their shoes, packing down the black mass and laughing at how funny they looked doing it.

When they finished, only the curving aluminum ladders and diving-board supports remained to distinguish the pool from any parking lot in a field beside a concrete-block poolhouse. You can drive by today and never know there was a pool there at all.

But I know. I know the secret. There is water at the bottom of that pool. That solid-seeming mass of asphalt floats on a core of swimming-pool water, the same water that Nehemiah Thomas swam in when he opened the pool up for everybody—three inches of water as blue as Aunt Lucille's eyes, trapped under there for all time. What looks solid is not necessarily so.

"You took off your bandage," Wiley said. "Your eye looks better."

"Yeah," I said. "I can see light through it now."

He touched my hair. "You just had to let it heal."

Then Dove and Meemaw and the Vinsons drove up in the hearse, and it was time for us to go.

Peter Joseph

San Francisco, 1993

For months after the fire, Farley Vinson did not speak. He made hand-signals when he was thirsty or needed a clean shirt. One morning he said "Meemaw, I want some corn flakes," and the story came pouring out.

Four men stormed into the funeral home, waving shotguns. They found Milton and Farley listening to the White Sox. They bound Milton's hands and led them outside. They tied Farley to a tree with a rope around his middle. They beat and punched Milton for a while then strung him up from the next tree over, while Farley watched.

Milton kicked for a long time, he said. The men carried five-gallon cans from their truck through the front door. When they ran out, fire was blooming all over the house. Farley said they didn't have faces, they didn't even have heads. He said they were ghosts.

Dove tried to convince old Mr. Moseley to build a new funeral home. Old Mr. Moseley said no, Dove owed him eighty thousand dollars' worth of uninsured caskets, when he paid that off maybe they could discuss it.

The Duboce brothers served eleven months apiece for killing Nehemiah, but no one was ever arrested for killing Milton. His death got lost in the uproar over Aunt Lucille's release.

James J. Kilpatrick wrote a column charging that the Negroes' lawless demonstrating had so torn the fabric of society that perfectly sane white women were moved to kill their husbands and abandon their children—and the liberal judges were setting them free.

Lyndon Johnson was heard to remark at a state dinner that he'd asked Lady Bird to get rid of all her Tupperware, so he could get a good night's sleep.

Judge Mead retired that August. Sheriff Doggett lost his bid for re-election to Lester Willis, one of his deputies. The sheriff died in 1973 of food poisoning after he got hold of some bad barbecue.

Aunt Earlene moved to Tuscaloosa to oversee Mabel's treatment. The doctors at Bryce were doing promising work with electroshock therapy. After three or four years, they finally jump-started Mabel.

She wasn't crazy anymore, but she was never the same. I ran into her by accident once, years later, when I went to the beach. She was a thin wrung-out rag with red frizzy hair. She was glad to see me.

She had a job as a greeter at a Wal-Mart in Gulf Shores. She shared an apartment on the beach with her mother. Earlene belonged to several prominent civic organizations down there; in 1978 she was named Baldwin County's "Lady Kiwanian of the Year."

I took Mabel to the Pizza Hut. She smoked cigarettes and drank a Coke and ordered a slice of deep-dish pizza but didn't eat a bite.

She said she hadn't heard from her father in years.

After we drove out of Industry that night, Dove's only friend was his bottle of Old Grand-Dad. He stayed at Meemaw's house in Pigeon Creek for a few months, playing solitaire in the parlor, muttering. Once in a while he would stir himself to fix a leaky faucet, or to deliver some of Meemaw's ironing for her.

One day he said he was going out west to visit Lucille. He drove out of the yard in his white hearse. We never saw him again.

I think he's still out there somewhere. I imagine he got tired of driving somewhere between Alabama and California, maybe found himself a sweet homely woman who appreciated the good things about him. Maybe they settled down a thousand miles from the nearest funeral home. I hope so. I hope that woman's treating him nice. I cry sometimes when I think about how much I loved him. I wish he would call me, just once.

We got a postcard, a picture of Wes Hatfield's Empire Motel in West Hurley, Kansas. On the back it said "Gone fishing. Love—"

Meemaw said he would come back, but he never did. Neither did Lucille. She sent money, but she never came back.

Meemaw raised us up, me and Wiley and all six Vinsons. She put us through grade school and high school and sent three of us to college. She ironed her heart out for us. Before I knew it we were grown and gone, spread out all over the country, and Meemaw was rattling around in that big old house with only Marilyn, a senior in high school.

Everybody came home faithfully for two weeks in August and four days every Christmas. I know these were Meemaw's happiest times, surrounded by her grandchildren and their children.

Aunt Lucille always sent boxes of funny presents and money so Meemaw could hire a maid and not break her back cleaning house for us. On a cold December day in 1979, Meemaw was driving the maid back to town after a day's work. The maid's name was Ophelia Winston. She said Meemaw was driving along in the old Rambler station wagon when she suddenly said "Oh, excuse me," pulled the car to the side of the road, slumped over, and died.

Our family fell apart the rest of the way. I lost touch with the Vinsons one by one. I kept up with Aunt Lucille through her sporadic calls; for a long time she wouldn't give us her phone number.

For years after the trial, she couldn't get a job. Harry Hall wouldn't come near her. Everybody loved to talk about the Beverly Hillbillies killer, but nobody wanted to hire her.

Lucille cut her hair short, dyed it red, and changed her name to Sylvia Lee. Under that name she appeared in several commercials, then, as Dorothy Winters, she landed a steady job on a situation comedy called "Our Gal Sal." She played the wisecracking housekeeper in charge of a household of wacky orphans.

The show ran for six years, and is still seen on some cable channels today. The residuals allowed Aunt Lucille and Uncle Norman to buy the Holmby Hills house where Marilyn Monroe lived while she was shooting *Some Like It Hot.*

I believe they still live in that house. I'm in L.A. all the time on business, but I don't call them. Maybe I've gotten too big for my britches. I tell myself I'm able to move faster by living this streamlined life, without family or obligations.

Wiley is my only family now. We talk on the phone two or three times a week. He's a molecular physicist in Massachusetts, wife and kids, a doctoral degree involving subatomic particles called "quizzical dancers." We call ourselves the Overachieving Orphans.

Then the telephone rings, and dear God it's Lucille. All those old feelings come rushing back.

"Peejoe, how have you been?"

"I'm fine, Aunt Lucille. I've never been better. I'm working hard, you know, liking it."

"That's what I see. You're so famous these days."

"Famous, or notorious?"

"Both. Just like your Aunt Lucille. I'm reading through *Weekly Variety,* and here's your smiling face all over page three."

"I haven't seen it yet," I tell her. "How's Uncle Norman?"

"The same. He gets two fares a day at the airport, he thinks he's working too hard. And don't change the subject. What is this movie about?"

I press my thumb on the remote control. Kim Novak walks to her car. I freeze her in place. "Which one, Aunt Lucille? I've got more than one project."

"Well honey, it says right here you've just signed a high six-figure deal with Paramount for an original screenplay about a woman who kills her husband. Is that true?"

"Yeah, well actually the figure's not all that high, but they seem excited. I hope they'll make it."

"What's it about?"

"It's kind of a comedy. Hard to describe."

"Is it about me?"

"God, no. It's completely fictitious. Why would I want to write about you?"

"Well, has it got a part for me, at least?"

I press REWIND. Kim Novak backs up to the front porch, and here comes Jimmy Stewart to say goodbye in reverse.

"I don't know, there is this one part—but what am I talking about? We can't work together, Aunt Lucille, you know that. You have this reputation—wait a minute, now, you know it's true. Everybody in Hollywood says you're difficult."

"I wouldn't be difficult if you got me a part in a feature," she says. "Come on, Peejoe, this is my big break! I've never had a nephew who could swing a six-figure deal. You know you can get me that part!"

"Wait a minute—"

"Peejoe. Do you remember what happened the last time somebody said no to me?"

I should have hung up right then. I should have known that when my Aunt Lucille sets out to get something, there is no force on earth that can stop her.